MAKING
Waves

∽

Shari Cylinder

For Aunt Lenie –

you are in my heart always, and I will forever be the luckiest niece for having had you as an aunt.

Acknowledgements

*F*or as long as I can remember, I have loved the ocean. It's serenity for the soul and hope for the heart. It makes us feel big and small at the same time, and reminds us that so many horizons are ours for the taking, if only we reach out for them like the sea does for the sky. And as I learned while working on this book, we all have our own tiny drop in the ocean. Except that no one's drop really is that small, after all, not if we believe in it enough and find the courage to make the most of it. Only then can we see just how far those ripples will reach.

Just as the drops of the ocean join together to form something beautiful, so do we. I am infinitely grateful for the people in my life who have helped me make a splash.

To my family, for the unconditional support, understanding, and love you've always given me. You are there to cheer me on, to listen, to advise, and to share a smile when it's needed most. I love you, and I'm thankful every day to have you in my corner. Cita, you have always been my staunchest and most encouraging champion in everything I do, and I so appreciate you being one of the first readers (and editors!) for Making Waves. Dad, you've encouraged me to go for my dreams, because that in itself is a homerun, and I am very thankful for that and for your humor. Marissa, you are a sister, but also a friend and confidante. Thank you so much for being one of the first readers and editors of this book, as well!

To Jasper Jellybean, for being my best little buddy! You are my bunshine, and I adore you. You are always there to brighten every day with your sweet twitchy nose, your flops on my feet, and your "hoppy hour" binky performances. Adopting you is the best decision I ever made. Thank you for changing my life for good in more ways than I can count.

To Stacy, for your unwavering dedication and guidance over the past several years. You have shown me how to navigate through choppy waters and taught me that we all have the strength to choose the currents along which we sail. Thank you for reminding me how much mental health matters, and that when we "do it afraid," we can grow through what we go through and make some waves of our own. I am grateful beyond words.

To Annette, for all your hard work in literally turning this dream of mine into a reality. From the beautiful cover, to all the formatting, to your generosity in sharing your knowledge throughout the publishing process, I couldn't have done this without you. Thank you for indulging my many, many emails, and for all your enthusiasm along the way.

To my friends who have become family and the family who are my friends, for being so interested and invested in not only the stories I've written, but the ones I've lived. I'm so lucky to know you.

To Mrs. P., Mrs. Ruckel, and all the teachers who have left a handprint on my heart, for your wisdom, and faith, and encouragement. The lessons you taught go so far beyond the walls of a classroom and their heart and soul stay with me always.

And to anyone who reads this book and goes on a journey alongside the characters – thank you for choosing to embrace them! I hope you enjoy reading about them as much as I enjoyed writing about them. And most importantly, I hope their journeys inspire your own – may you always remember that we are the authors of our own stories and that we can all make some waves, if only we believe in ourselves enough.

Table of Contents

～ 1 ～

Grace

I still remember the exact moment when I learned that magic is real. It was a damp day in early March, that time of year in Atlanta when spring is starting to bloom, but winter refuses to give up its grasp just yet. A mist hung in the air, playing hide-and-seek with the skyscrapers and curling my hair into wispy blonde tendrils around my face. It was my eighth birthday. I was hurrying along the city sidewalk with my Gram, her skin whisper-soft as she held my hand and told me there was a surprise waiting when we reached our destination.

"What is it?" I asked, jumping into a puddle with both feet and laughing out loud as she did the same. My Gram was the best. She did all the things other grandmothers did – knitting scarves and making chicken soup and playing Go Fish with me until we'd each won at least one game – but then she also did things like taking ballroom dance classes with my grandfather, scurrying my sisters and me away for impromptu trips to the amusement park, and, like on that dreary day, leaping forward without giving a second thought to where she landed.

"All in good time, my dear," she said, as we shook the water droplets off our shoes. "I can't give away the secret before we get there."

"Get where?"

She winked at me. "You'll see."

And I did.

Ten minutes later, when we rounded the corner onto Peachtree Street, I saw exactly what she'd meant. A small bouquet of balloons bobbed from the entryway of a store two doors down, the wind catching their strings and sending them flying forward like a welcoming committee. One yellow, one turquoise, one purple. My three favorite colors, and a pop of vibrancy against the gray skies. As we got closer to the balloons, my mouth curved into a smile. Because it wasn't just any store they were spiraling out from – it was The Book Boutique, my grandparents' place. They'd dreamed of owning a bookstore for so long and had saved their money for years, setting aside part of each paycheck from their day jobs until they managed to gather enough together to rent a retail space which previously belonged to a children's toy shop. It had been six months since they signed the lease and started to transform the empty area into one full of life.

My sisters and I loved to help out on the weekends. Abigail, Josie, and I would wake up early to eat whatever cereal our mom had set out on the table for us before leaving for work, and then we'd hurry to the window in the living room and wait eagerly for Gram's white car to pull up by the curb. It'd been two weeks since we were last inside the store, though. The weekend before had been our time with our father for the month. He had moved out to Tybee Island after a divorce splintered our family the December before. Although it felt strange, just getting to see him in smaller spurts, it also seemed like a special treat. It was the only thing that could tear me away from our weekends at the bookstore. On that cool March day, as Gram and I slowed to a stop in front of its door, I glanced up at her in surprise.

"Did you and Pop-Pop finish getting the place ready while we were away?" I asked.

There was a glint in her eyes. "Why don't you go inside and check it out?"

I pulled open the door and walked into another world.

That was it, the freeze-frame in time when magic sprinkled its pixie dust over reality.

The bookshelves were fully stocked, lined with rows upon

rows of colorful spines, and the mural on the back wall was finished. The electric fireplace glowed bright and warm, and the stained glass skylight bathed the store in jewel-tone hues. It was truly perfect. It was also filled with people. My parents were sitting in the armchairs by the fireplace. Both of them, in the same place, for the first time in months. My granddad was there, too, along with my sisters and the kids I was friendly with from my class at school. It was my party, I realized. I got to celebrate turning eight in the place that had instantly become my very favorite.

Twenty-five years later, The Book Boutique is *still* my very favorite.

Even when it's breaking my heart.

I stare down at the paper in my hand, the sharp blank ink printed on the crisp white paper. It's so cut and dry. Of course it is. What else would I expect from the landlord who has been raising the store's rent for the past two years? This area of the city is prime real estate. I get that he wants to capitalize on that. Midtown's the epicenter of Atlanta's music and arts scene, brimming with culture and intrigue. My grandparents chose an excellent location for their shop. I just hope my sisters and I don't destroy it now.

"Again?" Abigail asks, as I pass her the paper.

"Again," I confirm.

She raises an eyebrow in her quintessential big sister look. "You realize this is ridiculous, right?" she asks. "At this point, we actually may start to lose money on this place. Sales are down this year, and it's already mid-October. We might not break even by December, let alone make a profit. How much longer can we pretend it's a smart idea to keep the store open?"

Before I can answer, the little bell on the front door jingles as Josie walks inside. As always, she is late. She doesn't even bother to address it, and neither do we. It's simply become expected. "So what's going on?" she asks, flopping into the chair next to Abigail. She drops her messenger bag on the hardwood floor and listens as we fill her in on the letter from our landlord. "Honestly," she says,

"I agree with Abigail. I think it might be good to shut the doors. It isn't like bookstores are popular anymore, at least not in the way they were when we were kids. Everybody shops online now." She begins twirling one of her long, ginger curls around her finger. "Gram and Pop-Pop gave it their all, but we're in charge now, and we've gotta be real about the fact that the store's holding us back and weighing us down."

"It's becoming too unpredictable," Abigail adds, "and a risk we can't afford."

I can't believe what I'm hearing.

How can they say something so awful? This store is none of those things. It's a gift. I know they aren't as invested in this place as I am, but I thought they'd at least want to fulfill our grandparents' wishes. When Gram and Pop-Pop passed away four years ago, both within months of one another, they left The Book Boutique to the three of us. We decided from the start that I'd be the one to run it. Abigail was already working long days in the enrollment office of a local college and Josie was on the audition circuit in multiple cities up and down the east coast as she tried to carve out her role on stage. Neither of them had time to take on a job this all-encompassing. I did. It was perfect for me, actually. After a stint at an advertising firm that had left me never wanting to work in that field ever again, I had just finished going back to school for a masters in library science. I wanted to spend my days surrounded by books and the worlds authors create when they open a vein and let their heart bleed onto the page. The choice was obvious: I'd continue to build up the catalogue and community that Gram and Pop-Pop had created. Though the shop would belong to all of us, it'd be my labor of love.

"Look," I say, "I didn't ask you to meet me here so we could give up on the store. Let's not make any rash decisions."

"It wouldn't really be rash, though," Abigail points out. "This has been going on for a long time." She shakes her head, making the ends of her brown bob brush against her chin. She looks so much like our mom. She and Josie both do – or, well, Josie did until she turned herself into a redhead and pierced her nose with a tiny diamond stud. She's always doing things like that, finding new ways to announce her presence and declare her perspective.

Maybe that's what I need to do, too.

Being the middle sibling isn't easy. I often feel like I get lost between my sisters' larger-than-life personalities. They're so determined, the two of them, so sure of what they want. It's hard to keep up. Tonight, though, as we open the pizza box I got from the restaurant down the street, I realize I'll have to do more than keep up. If I want our grandparents' work of heart to continue beating, I have to take the lead.

"We can't close the store," I say.

"Why not?" Abigail asks. "We could find a buyer. You know that. We could probably find quite a few."

"Who? Another restaurant owner? Someone who will sell phones, or computers, or tablets?" I take a slice of pizza from my third of the pie – plain cheese for me, broccoli and spinach for Abigail, and red peppers for Josie – and drop it onto the paper plate as it burns my hand. Scorched. That is how I feel. "That's the opposite of what we need," I say. "Yet another place that puts technology at our fingertips." I wave my arms around, gesturing at the bookshelves towering above our heads as we sit at a table in the café I added to the store after taking over. "What happened to having *words* at our fingertips? What happened to flipping through the pages of a book, and dog-earing a corner, and highlighting a paragraph because it speaks to you?"

"The twenty-first century?" Josie offers.

Abigail sighs. "She's right. Bookstores are going the way of newspapers and becoming obsolete. It's better we get out now, before we lose everything."

A furious flush creeps up my neck. Why can't they see that selling the store is exactly *how* we'd lose everything? Everything our grandparents worked so hard for, everything we found solace in as children, everything we turned to when our mom couldn't be there for us. The Book Boutique is our family's legacy. The thought of letting it die is unbearable.

"You don't know what you're talking about," I tell my sisters. "You're not the ones who are here every day. You don't see the customers' faces light up when they find the book they're looking for, or hear the excitement in their voices when they thank me for recommending a new author." I feel something swell in my chest as I stand up, march over to the closest bookshelf, and pull a paperback from between its neighbors. "You don't feel the pages brush against your hand," I say. "The paper of a book, it's different. It's special. Here, see for yourself." I open the cover and fan the pages for them.

And that's when something falls out.

A newspaper clipping flutters to my feet, and as I bend to pick it up, I notice that it's yellowed around the edges. There's a second paper stapled to it, this one covered with large, loopy letters that look like they spilled from the tip of a pen with a frenzied urgency. The blue ink is faded now, a shadow of what it once was. How old is it? I check the letter for a date, but find nothing, so I try the newspaper next.

Holy cow.

"You have to see this," I tell my sisters.

They gather around me, Abigail to my left and Josie to my right, and I hold out the clipping so we can all read it together. It's from more than sixty years ago, dated July, 1955. A tiny piece of history, right here in my hand. The clipping seems to be from an ocean liner, a daily newspaper of sorts that announces all the on-board activities and competitions. Ping-pong. Shuffleboard. Bridge. It strikes me how different things were then as compared to cruise ships today. My friend Sofie just sailed to Bermuda with her family earlier this year, and her photos painted a picture that looked so energetic and colorful. This, though ... it appears to be more reserved. Elegant, even. Then there's the letter that's attached. I flip back to it, and the three of us lose ourselves in the words.

To my beautiful North Star –

What a surprise these five days have been! When I boarded this ship back in Manhattan, I never could have guessed what was waiting for me. I imagined it would be my time to relax: to sleep late, read a good book, and enjoy nightly music from the band. A solo oasis on the seas sounded grand to me, especially since I must dive into my work once we dock in Europe. Then I met you, with your eyes that glitter in the sunlight and your laugh that reminds me of the wind chimes my mother hung up in the kitchen window. Perhaps it was fate that brought us together, or maybe it was simply that we're two souls who were seeking one another out. How wild is that? Of all the people on this planet, we still found each other.

I do not want to lose that ... or you. I know you are angry with me, but I am begging: please give me a chance to explain everything. Even if you cannot forgive me, at least make that decision based on the entire story. Our love deserves it. I do love you, that is a promise, and if you give me a second chance, I think we could go on an extraordinary adventure.

Stay with me in Europe. We can go on this journey together.
I will be waiting for you when the ship docks in the morning.
Love,
Henry

Wow. I just stare at the letter for a moment after reading its last line. I have no idea who Henry is, or what he did to upset this woman, but I immediately want to find out. One of the things I love about meeting a story for the first time is the way it can draw me in right from the beginning. I feel that pull with this, almost desperately.

"This is incredible," I whisper, tracing my finger over the faded writing.

"I have so many questions," Abigail says. "Did she forgive him? Did they end up together? Why is the note inside ... " She peers at the cover of the book I'm still holding, Anne Morrow Lindbergh's *Gift from the Sea*. "Alright, I suppose that part's obvious, since this is a couple who met on an ocean liner."

There's so much more to that book than just the sea part, but I don't get a chance to delve into it, because Josie lets out a low whistle. "This is like something straight out of a romance novel," she says. "How did we get this, though?" She jabs her thumb in the direction of the book. "Doesn't our inventory come straight from the publishers?"

"I hold a used book buyback sale twice a year," I say. "January and July. You've probably never been around for one, since you're usually out of town, but people can donate the books or sell them to the store for a reduced price. Someone must've brought it in then."

"Do you think the person knew the note was inside?" she asks. Her blue eyes sparkle curiously. We all have those blue eyes, same as our father, but I'm the only one who inherited his blonde hair. It falls in front of my face now, as I drop my gaze to reread the letter. Was Henry the one to tuck his note between the pages? Or the mystery woman? Or was it someone else? And why? Why would anyone want to hide that away?

Because it was overwhelming, maybe.

I think of my boyfriend Jonathan. I love him, but no question it would've scared me off if he had sent me a letter so intense after just five days. Henry's longing is palpable in each word. If his North Star didn't feel the same way, I can certainly understand how a note like this could be too much for her to process.

Abigail's voice cuts into my thoughts. "I want answers," she says.

"Me, too," Josie says with a nod. She strides back over to the café area, drops cross-legged into her chair, and pulls another slice of pizza from the box. It's no longer scorching – no longer even hot – but she takes a bite anyway, catching the string of gooey cheese before it can drop onto the sleeve of her green suede jacket. "You have records, right?" she asks me. "You're, like, the most organized person ever when it comes to this place. Can't we look up the info and get in touch with the person who gave us the book?"

"If it's one I paid for, yes. Hang on." I pass everything off to Abigail, then go over to my office in the back of the store. It still looks the same as when my grandparents used it all those years ago. I couldn't bring myself to change anything. The floor-to-ceiling bookcase, the blue and white curtains on the small window, the framed picture of my sisters and me that sits on the desk, it's all still there, just as Gram and Pop-Pop left it. I like to think that they peek down from the heavens sometimes to check in on us and that it brings a grin to their faces, seeing how hard I'm always trying to keep their memory alive.

What would they think of my discovery?

They'd probably light up with joy. They loved love, and they lived it, and I think they would want to pursue this as much as I do. I grab my laptop from its place atop the cherry wood desk and hurry back out to join my sisters. Abigail's sitting next to Josie at the table now, holding her cell phone as she talks to her kids.

"Mommy won't be home before bedtime," she says, "but I promise to come in and kiss you both goodnight ... yes, I'll give you a hug, too. And hugs for your stuffed animal friends. I've got it. Pinky swear." She smiles at me as I sit down, and I smile back. There's been a lot of tension between the three of us lately, as the bookstore flounders on its foundation, but I realize we are all just trying our best.

I don't know if that will be enough.

I don't know whether The Book Boutique will be granted a To-Be-Continued, or if it's headed for The End.

I don't know if it's wise for us to stop talking about the present in favor of investigating the past.

And yet, I do know.

Somehow, deep in my bones, I know we have to do this.

"Okay," I say, as Abigail ends her call. "Let's find Henry."

∽ 2 ∾

Rose

It was a beautiful day. The sunshine warmed my face as I stepped out of my apartment building, the birds were singing a song that seemed as though it was meant only for me, and the sugary scent of lilies hung in the air as I approached the flower stand at the end of my block. I paused in front of it to breathe in the splendor. There were violets and roses – my mother's very favorite flowers and the ones my twin sister and I were named for – along with daisies, dahlias, and more. Their velvety petals were a rainbow of colors that stretched toward the sun, and I never could resist marveling at them. It was the absolute best part of my daily walk to the law firm up the street, where I worked as a secretary. Goodness knew there was not much vibrancy in that monochromatic office. It was gray and beige and tan. Sometimes I would stop at the flower stand for longer than normal, mulling over the choices before purchasing a bouquet to brighten my desk.

Today, I decided, I would pick out the flowers on my way home from work instead. My parents had invited Violet and me over for dinner before we went to see the new stage production of *Damn Yankees*. It had been a month since the curtain went up on the show, and though tickets were hard to get, my father had a bandleader friend who had been able to secure some for us. It was going to be a birthday celebration for Violet and me, as we were turning thirty the next day. I could not wait. The thought of the evening's festivities would get me through yet another tedious day of answering phones, setting up meetings, and composing legal documents on the typewriter that malfunctioned more than it actually worked.

My job paid the bills. It gave me a way to afford an apartment on my own, and even to enjoy an occasional splurge at a dress shop or a dinner out in Manhattan. My girlfriends Lucy and Alice often joined me for those. They were secretaries, too – Lucy at a doctor's office and Alice at a publishing house – and we loved to kick up our heels after being stuck at our desks all day. Our dinners were a time to daydream, to imagine what our lives might look like if we could do anything we wished, and to envision a world far beyond what 1955 had to offer. Alice wanted to be an author. Lucy wanted to be a politician. I did not know what I wanted. All I knew was that it was not what I currently had: a boss who greeted me with a list of ten things to accomplish the minute I walked through the door, a typewriter that needed its ribbon changed after I had written just one page, and, on this particular day, a lady who snapped at me when I called to reschedule her meeting with my boss.

"That is unacceptable," she said, and gave a little huff. "You tell Mr. Jones that it's of the utmost importance for me to speak to him in short order. I'm paying him to do his job, and I expect him to be prompt about following through."

"Yes, ma'am," I said. "I'll pass along the message, and let me assure you that he values you as a client very much. A hearing for another client was pushed up by an entire week, that's all. As soon as it's straightened out – "

"No," she interrupted. "He can find some way to fit me in to his schedule today, or he can lose my business. There are plenty of attorneys in New York. In fact," she said, her voice rising, "you can go ahead and tell him that his services are no longer required. I'll find somebody who will be able to give me the attention I need."

She hung up on me before I could even respond.

I shook my head and stood up from my desk. I would have to tell my boss what had happened, and I knew he was not going to be pleased about it. I took a deep breath before knocking quietly on his door.

though, bounced around with no say as to where I was going. If I was being honest, I did not want to work as a secretary anymore, either. I was tired of spending my days tethered to a desk by an invisible rope. How many times had I hoped for a break from the monotony, for a chance to go outside and let the sun warm up my soul? Being a secretary was suffocating.

Perhaps this was my time to breathe.

Working at the law firm had been a job, not a career, not a purpose, and certainly not a passion. Could it be that getting fired was a blessing in disguise? Now maybe I could figure out what I craved, what I truly and urgently wanted, in the deepest crevices of my heart.

I smiled. "Thank you for the offer," I told Mr. Jones, "but I think I'm going to be just fine."

* * *

The sweet scent of the flowers – a pretty mix of irises and tulips – wafted up toward my face as I shifted the bouquet from one arm to the other and pressed the doorbell to my parents' townhome. They lived near Central Park, my favorite place in all the city, and as I waited for them to answer the door, I thought of the memories we had made in that lush green oasis. We had spent every Sunday morning there, the skyscrapers surrounding us like glass stems that had sprouted from the ground. When Violet and I were young, our parents would take us to the playgrounds and zoo, and when we got older, we would go for walks around the reservoir and have picnics on the Great Lawn. I did not get to Central Park as often anymore, not after working long days and having to cook my dinner and straighten up the apartment after getting home, but I liked knowing it was there, ready and waiting for me to visit.

The same was true of my parents. We did not agree about much, especially my refusal to settle for a marriage that did not make my heart skip a beat, but I still loved them a lot and found comfort in knowing they were only a taxi ride away. Violet, too. How odd it had felt at first, when we went our separate ways. Everything had seemed off-kilter without her. For as irksome as it was when our parents would compare us, two identical halves of a whole which did not quite match up, the reality of life without my twin by my side was jarring.

People frequently asked me if it felt bizarre, seeing my own reflection on Violet's face, but it was the opposite. I genuinely loved being part of a pair. My sister and I shared a bond that was so much more than skin deep. It had felt empty without her, after our lives diverged and we were no longer headed in the same direction. Violet had followed a traditional path: a big wedding to a cardiologist who worked at Mount Sinai Hospital, a divine apartment on the Upper East Side, and a never-ending cycle of housewife duties. I positively could not understand how she enjoyed it. She had called me the day before, chatting animatedly because she had tested a new recipe and could not wait for her husband Thomas to try it when he got home. It was, as she described it, "the highlight of the day." How? Why? Her life was so different from mine that it might as well have been on a different plane entirely. The thing about being a twin, though, was that you could intrinsically encourage something even if your mind did not do the best job of wrapping around it. I always supported Violet, and she supported me as I navigated my way along a much curvier path.

We were each other's failsafe.

She was already sitting in our parents' living room when I walked inside, gesturing animatedly as she regaled our mother with a story about the knitting class she was taking. "It was a total disaster at first," she said. "We were supposed to make a scarf, but it took three tries before I came up with something any person would ever want to wear." She glanced up as I came in, with our father close behind.

"Look who I found on the front step," he said, grinning widely.

My mother smiled, too. "Hello, sweetheart," she said, standing up to give me a hug. "How are you?"

"Good," I said, and I meant it. Despite what had happened earlier, I really was feeling optimistic. I had spent the walk home from work pondering what would come next, what I could do with my life once the last honeysuckle sweet days of spring seeped into the summer's heat, and I was a little bit delighted to find that I had no idea. Uncertainty meant possibility. "It has been quite an interesting day," I said. "I'll tell you all about it over dinner." I held out the flowers. "These are for you."

Her eyes sparkled. "They're beautiful," she said. "Thank you."

"My pleasure."

"Remember when we'd make our own bouquets?" Violet asked me, as our mother went to put the flowers in a vase. She was talking about the blossoms we used to pick from the small garden our mother had created out on the balcony. There was no front yard to plant anything, so she made do with what she had. Violet and I had loved to watch the green stems poke out from the soil. We had spent many afternoons outside, watering the flowers and carefully snipping them.

"There was something so soothing about it," I said.

"You should try knitting," Violet suggested. "It has that same calming effect." She giggled. "At least, it does once you've figured out how to not get the yarn twisted around the needle every time you make a stitch."

I scrunched up my nose. "I think I'll leave that to you."

"You never know," she said, "you just might like it."

I considered her words as we sat down to dinner around the table our mother had set so nicely. Violet was right. I might like knitting, or dancing, or bicycling, or painting. There were many things I could do once I stopped going to the office in two weeks. I would need to get a new job, obviously, but this time it did not have to be one that faded my soul around its edges. I would find something that let me live in technicolor instead of a palette of pastels.

"I have news," I said, once we had all helped ourselves to salad. Everyone turned to look at me, and for a split second, nerves swayed in my stomach. I knew they were not going to see this as the same golden opportunity I did. Perhaps it would be wise to wait before telling them, so we could all enjoy dinner and the show.

"Rose?" Violet shot me a quizzical glance. "Are you alright?"

She always could tell when something was up with me.

She could also always tell when I was hiding the truth, and not only because I was a terrible liar who was incapable of spinning a web of deception without getting tangled up inside. Violet just got me, and I got her. As I looked back at her, the same hazel eyes, porcelain skin, and auburn hair that was cut into a shorter style than mine, I knew there was no point in delaying. Violet would realize in a heartbeat that I was not telling the whole story, so it would be better to come right out with it and deal with the consequences.

"I'm fine," I said, and then I let the explanation tumble from my mouth. "I was let go from work today. My last day will be in two weeks. My boss is merging his firm with a bigger practice uptown, and since they already have their own secretaries, my position will be superfluous." I braced myself for the reaction from my parents. There would be indignation, quite possibly, and maybe a touch of smugness from my mother, who had never wanted me to take the job. A woman's place was in the home, she had insisted, and it would serve me better to do as Violet had.

That was the only difficult thing about being a twin. It was sometimes a challenge for people to see us for who we were individually, not who the two of us were together. That was especially true of my parents, and my mother's response showed it. Instead of being dismayed, she exhaled a puff of air and clapped her hands together.

"Oh, that's marvelous!" she exclaimed.

Marvelous? I was thrown by that. She was celebrating the fact that I had been fired?

"I'm sorry," she said, and it looked as though she was forcing herself not to smile. "I understand that you must be upset about this, but Rose, honey, it's a second chance. You'll be able to focus on more important matters now. It's not too late to find a husband. There are plenty of fish still in the sea."

I loathed that expression. She used it all the time. I knew she meant well and that all she really wanted was for me to be happy, but I could just never seem to make her realize that my sense of joy did not revolve around what society thought was right. It made no difference to me that I was not a doting housewife who spent her time vacuuming the rugs, ironing her husband's shirts, and making sure dinner was piping hot when he got home. It was not who I was, or what I thought love should be. To me, it was the chance to give your heart wings, not lock it in place. It would happen when it was supposed to, not when I tried to manipulate it.

"Can we please not have this discussion again?" I asked.

My mother could not seem to derail her own train from its tracks, though. "Look at your sister," she said, and Violet shrunk in her chair, like she was trying to hide from the role our parents thought she played in this. "Think of how nice it'd be to have the kind of liberty she does," our mother said. "She doesn't need to worry about paying bills. She has a husband for that. All she has to do is make certain their checkbook is balanced. Don't you want that? Wouldn't you like to cook dinner for two, and to have somebody to make your apartment shine for? You should want a partner to share your life with every day."

"Yes," I said. "I want the *right* partner, not somebody I marry just because people think time is speeding by and leaving me behind. For now, I'm perfectly content to make my apartment shine for myself. I'm worth that all on my own, and believe it or not, I don't mind eating by myself. The quiet can be very peaceful. You don't have to keep pushing me on this. I don't need or want you to play matchmaker." She and my father were always doing that, trying to convince me to go out on dates with the single sons of their friends.

"We're only looking out for you," my father said. "We want you to have the same happiness as your sister."

"Please stop," Violet said. "Let her be. Just because marriage is right for me – "

"Marriage should be right for all women your age," our mother interrupted. "Turning thirty and being unattached is practically unheard of these days."

I sighed. The air was deflating from my lungs, a balloon that had lost its ability to float.

I should have realized they would react this way.

"Why don't we all agree to table this for now?" Violet said. "This is supposed to be an enjoyable evening. Let's finish dinner, go to the theater, and have a good time."

"I'll try," our mother said, "but for the record, I love you both very much and I'll never apologize for trying to do right by you."

"Even if your right is my wrong?" I asked.

Now it was her turn to sigh. "Your sister's correct," she said. "It's probably best to set this aside for now."

For now.

I knew the reprieve I had been granted was only temporary, but I had no plan to back down. For as much as I respected my parents and cared deeply about what they thought, I refused to let them dictate my life. It was the eve of my thirtieth birthday, a milestone I was determined to embrace. It would be a wonderful year.

No matter what my parents said or did, I would make sure of that.

∾ 3 ∾

Grace

"**W**ell?" Josie looks at me expectantly. "Is the book listed in your database? Is there a name of the person who dropped it off? Email address? Phone number?" She taps her nails on the tabletop and their bright orange polish catches the overhead lights. "C'mon, don't leave us hanging here. Is there a verdict?"

Abigail smiles wryly. "You're never going to know, unless you stop asking questions long enough for Grace to answer them. You sound like my kids. They do the same thing."

"Are you comparing me to a five-year-old and a three-year-old?" Josie asks. For a split second, I think that she's actually annoyed and this is going to kick off an argument. We have been having far too many of those lately. How to deal with the rising rent. Bumping up prices for our books versus charging extra in the café. Continuing to hold children's classes every Saturday or scrapping them in favor of more profitable events. None of us agree on practically anything, but as I prepare myself to be the moderator of yet another fight, I realize that Josie's smirk is a light-hearted one.

"Ben and Macy *are* the best kids ever," I tell her. "So at least you're in great company?" We all laugh a bit, and I breathe a sigh of relief at the avoidance of any more tension. "And yes," I say, "to answer your questions, I did find something. Take a look." I turn my laptop around to face her and point at a line near the middle of the spreadsheet I've opened. Next to the title of the book and the price I paid for it, there's a name listed: Ivy Elizabeth Wethersby.

"Ivy?" Josie asks. "Who's that? What happened to Henry?"

"Maybe it's the woman he was writing to," Abigail suggests. "She could have met him like he'd asked and forgiven him for whatever he did to hurt her. Maybe he bought her the book as a gift and she tucked the note inside as a reminder of what happened overseas. She could've forgotten about that when she sold the book to Grace. It's been more than sixty years. She'd have to be pretty well up there in age."

"Even so ... " Josie gestures at the letter. "How do you forget about something like that? It's a once in a lifetime thing. If you have an experience like this, you remember every last detail of it." A flush colors her cheeks. "At least, I damn well imagine you would. It's not like I'd know personally, since I can't seem to find a guy who wants a commitment lasting more than a month. Henry wasn't like that," she declares.

"How do we know?" I ask. I think about my initial reaction to the note, the immediate desire to go on a journey with these characters. But that's the thing: they aren't characters. They don't have to travel along a set story arc or fall in place with the plotlines we often see in literature. Sure, they could've lived happily-ever-after, and I really hope they did, but it's just as real a possibility that they didn't. "Henry may have broken their relationship beyond repair with whatever he did," I say. "For all we know, Ivy could be somebody he met years later. There's a chance she has nothing to do with it."

"It's worth considering," Abigail allows. She nods at my computer. "Let's look her up and see if we can find anything."

I swivel the laptop back around, double click the icon for the Internet, and type in Ivy's name to the search bar. Anticipation seems to surround us all as we wait to see what materializes. I scan the links that pop up. "Sorry," I say, shaking my head. "There are hits for Ivy, Elizabeth, and Wethersby separately, but nothing together. We'll have to try something else." I pick up the clipping from the ship's newspaper. "Let's see," I say, as I skim it. "We know they set sail in July of 1955, and that the boat left from New York City and docked in Europe somewhere. Ah, here we go," I add, as I come to a crucial detail. "The ship was named the *SS Harmony*."

I do another Internet search, and this time the links are plentiful.

I click on the first one. "The *SS Harmony* was a commercial ocean liner that was commissioned in 1950," I read aloud. "It set sail from Manhattan and made stops in port cities such as Genoa and Gibraltar. The transatlantic voyage took less than a week, during which time ship-goers could enjoy a variety of on-board activities, ranging from shuffleboard tournaments to nightly shows by popular bandleaders. Known for its chic accommodations and elegant grandeur, the *SS Harmony* was one of the leading ocean liners of its time. It sailed the seas for thirty-seven years until it was retired in the late 1980s."

"Cool," Josie says. "But still no help for us."

"No," I say. "I guess not."

"We may as well just forget it," Abigail says. "We're not getting anywhere, and this isn't why we were supposed to meet tonight. Our focus has to be on the store and what we're going to do about it." She stands up and strides over to the display windows up front, heels clicking on the hardwood floor with each step. "Look at it out there," she says, peering at the sidewalk. "It's the typical Friday night crowd. The restaurant across the street has a waiting line, the ice cream place is packed with customers, and the music shop essentially has a revolving door. Then there's us. Do you see people expressing interest in coming in to The Book Boutique?"

"Maybe that's because the 'closed' sign is on the door?" Josie quips caustically.

Abigail's back is to us, but I just know she's rolling her eyes. "We obviously aren't drawing in the crowd we need," she says, ignoring Josie's comment. "Our regular customers are great, and I know you appreciate their loyalty, Grace, but if we want to thrive – even if we want to survive – that's not going to cut it. We have to either find a way to drive new business into this place, or cut our losses and sell." She turns to look at us. "Gram and Pop-Pop didn't want us to go bankrupt trying to keep the store afloat. They'd be the first ones to tell us to jump ship, pardon the pun."

"I don't think so," I say. "When did they ever advise us to give up?"

"She's got a point," Josie says. "They were always the first ones to tell us to keep going. Gram's catchphrase was 'If you think you can, you will.' Remember?" Nostalgia sweeps over her face at the memory. Mine, too. Our mom wasn't around too much when my sisters and I were growing up – it was hard for her to make ends meet after the divorce and she had to pick up an extra job to support us – so it was our grandparents who'd help us with our homework, take us shopping for clothes, and treat us to cookies from the bakery. They'd bring us to The Book Boutique often, too. I have many recollections of sprawling on the carpeted area to solve equations for my math class, write journals for my English class, and study rock formations for my science class. It was fun to do my schoolwork at the bookstore. Between the stacks, I felt at home.

I still do.

Gram and Pop-Pop adored this place. It was second only to their family as the love of their lives.

I refuse to ignore that, or all the memories we've made here.

Josie putting on endless puppet shows in the kids' section. Abigail spraining her ankle when she was helping shelve books in the floor-to-ceiling case along the wall and missed a step on the ladder on the way down. Me reading to the elderly customers whose eyesight had betrayed them, which is something I enjoyed so much I turned it into an intergenerational reading program after I inherited the store. It's not only rewarding to see the children reading to those who once read to them, but it reminds me of my own time here as a kid. My sisters and I grew up in this store. I cannot, will not, dishonor that, no matter what they say.

"If you think you can, you will." I repeat our Gram's mantra as Abigail walks back over to join us. "And if we think we can't, we won't. So which one is it?" I ask. "Are we going to give this our all, or are we going to bail out just because the water's choppy?"

I stare at them.

They stare back.

Silence.

* * *

It's late by the time I get home, the silvery half-moon shining bright in the inky night sky. I look up at it as I walk across the parking lot of my condominium complex. I don't often get to see stars in Atlanta, not with all the lights from the city casting their own glow, but in the suburbs I'm treated to the whole celestial tapestry. It's part of the reason why I chose not to move into Midtown after the bookstore fell into my hands. It would've been easier, sure. I could have avoided the insane traffic that characterizes the city's highways. I did tour a couple apartments, including one in the building where my friend Sofie used to live. She and I met when I joined the advertising firm she worked at, and we've stayed close, despite the fact that neither of us is an account executive there anymore. I know Sofie enjoyed living in the city, but it isn't for me. The hustle and bustle, the electricity pulsing in the air ... it's fine in small doses, but I like to have a quiet place to come back to at the end of the day.

Marietta is perfect for me.

It's a charming town near Acworth, where I grew up and my mother still lives, and I love that it's close enough to the city to provide fast access, but also far enough to be a respite from the constant thrum of Atlanta's rhythm. Marietta is filled with many parks and a gorgeous historic area which is home to the town square, with its quaint stores, pretty fountain, and a gazebo where couples pose for their wedding pictures. My grandparents were one of those couples. They renewed their vows there on their fiftieth anniversary. It was the sweetest thing. Warmth covers me like a blanket each time I think about it. Tonight, though, as I walk up the steps to my second floor condo, it's another couple I can't get off my mind.

Henry and ... whom? Ivy, or someone else?

I reach into my shoulder bag and pull out the newspaper clipping. I know I should be focused on the stalemate I'm in with my sisters when it comes to the store, but my thoughts keep returning to the mystery behind Henry's letter. I'm inexorably drawn to it. Are Abigail and Josie still thinking of it, too? Probably not. Abigail left The Book Boutique early, irritated when I refused to – yet again – raise the prices on our new releases in order to generate more money. She is probably home now, peeking in on her children and then settling onto the couch with her husband Scott to share a glass of wine and watch HGTV, and Josie said she was going out with some friends to see a band perform. I offered her a key for afterward – one thing my little sister is not good at is finding a place to stay in town in advance of when she's here – but she said she didn't want to wake me up and would "crash with a friend" instead.

That means it's me, myself, and I tonight.

And Henry.

I slip my key into its lock as I reach my door, twisting it swiftly and stepping inside my condo. It's quiet, save for the ticking of the antique clock that hangs in the entryway, and I stifle a yawn as I set down my bag on the paisley-printed ottoman. Coffee. I could use a cup. I head into the kitchen, flip the light switch that instantly brightens the room, and set about making myself some espresso with a dash of cinnamon. That was my Gram's favorite drink. Maybe it sounds absurd, but having it now makes me feel like she's wrapping me in a hug. My sisters and I discuss that frequently, how certain smells, tastes, and noises remind us of our grandparents. I like to think of it as their way of letting us know they'll always be here in spirit.

"What do you think, Gram? What should we do about that letter? And the store?" I murmur, as I carry my mug into the living room and settle myself at the small desk beneath the window. It's the most peaceful place in my condo. I love looking at the world outside. The flowers blossoming in the spring, the pool water sparkling like diamonds during the summer, the leaves changing to a canopy of fiery reds and golden yellows each fall, the occasional whispery snowflake swirling through the air in the winter ... it's like having a front row seat to Mother Nature's performance. Tonight, I crack the window open slightly, letting the cool air trickle past the gauzy curtains and into the room.

"Okay," I say, turning on my computer. "Let's do this."

Two hours later, as the clock hits midnight and one day fades into the next, I'm still no closer to figuring anything out. I slide Henry's letter into my desk drawer, power off the computer, and rinse out my mug. Then I shuffle down the hallway to my bedroom. It's just as I left it that morning, with the blankets all ruffled and a book folded face-down on the pillow, waiting for me to dive in again. I always read before bed. Tonight, though, I don't get even halfway through a chapter before I reach up to turn off the lamp on my nightstand and fall into a deep sleep that holds me in its grasp until an especially persistent wake-up call from my alarm the next morning. When I pick up my cell phone to silence it, I see that I have a text waiting from my boyfriend.

Are you busy today? I'm finished work at 1:30. Can I steal you away for a bit afterward?

Sounds good, I type back. *I have to run to the store for a couple hours this morning, but that's it. Want to meet for lunch?*

Jonathan's response pops up almost immediately. *I actually have something else in mind – and don't bother asking what it is, because I'm not telling you. Just be ready for an adventure.*

An adventure?

I don't do adventure, not unless it's one that unfolds between the pages of a book. Jonathan is well aware of this. In fact, the entire Tuesday morning office staff at his veterinary practice is, after I came rushing in one day with what I thought was a very ill puppy on my hands. I'd been dog-sitting for Abigail last year while she and Scott took the kids on vacation, and had woken up to their totally adorable, totally mischievous little guy sitting on my couch with a dazed look on his face and stuffing – both from the cream-colored sofa and the pastel throw pillows – spilling out of his mouth.

"Oh my God!" I screeched. "Freckles, what did you do?"

He'd tilted his head at me, barked, and then slumped down on top of the mess.

I panicked.

I didn't know what to do. It was my first time having a dog in my care, and I was terrified that I'd end up costing Freckles his life. I dashed through my condo, throwing on a t-shirt and shorts before grabbing my car keys in one hand and scooping up the whining puppy with the other. His leash got tangled around my arm as I darted downstairs, but I didn't stop. I just loaded him into my Prius and drove to the closest vet's office. If I had paused to think, I would've realized that I should have taken him to the vet Abigail used, but I was so gripped with fear that I acted purely on instinct. Jonathan's practice is only a couple blocks from my condo, and when I rushed through the door in a frenzy, the entire waiting area fell silent.

"Please," I said, "you have to help me. I'm dog-sitting for my sister. She and her family got this guy from a rescue at the beginning of the summer. He was five months old then, I think. Maybe six. I have the paperwork." I tried to reach into my purse for the papers Abigail had left with me, but it was impossible with Freckles squirming in my arms. "Anyway," I said, half out of breath, "they're on vacation in South Carolina, so I'm watching him for the week. I didn't realize he was such a chewer. My sofa and the pillows ... they've seen better days. I'm not sure how much he ingested, but he just ... he doesn't look so great. See?" A tear slipped out of my eye as I held Freckles up for the woman behind the front desk to appraise. I felt so helpless.

And then the receptionist paged Jonathan, who walked right out.

"Hi there," he said, extending his hand. "I'm Dr. Miller. Try not to worry. We'll get him fixed up right away. Come with me." He motioned for me to follow him back to an exam room, then closed the door behind us and offered me a tissue from the box on the counter. "We see this sort of thing much more often than you'd think," he said. "Sometimes the dog is fine on its own and sometimes we give medicine to help with the upset stomach. Either way, he should be okay."

"Are you certain?" I bit my lip nervously.

He gave a little wink. "Well, I *did* study veterinary medicine for years."

A blush crept into the curves of my cheeks. "I'm sorry," I said. "That was rude of me. This was just so unexpected and stressful. Definitely not the kind of adventure I was planning on today, and I guess it has me out of sorts. I promise, I don't mean to sound like a jerk."

"You don't."

His smile reached all the way to his gray eyes.

It was a wonderful smile, a heart-fluttering one, and it instantly put me at ease.

Fourteen months later, it still does.

But an adventure?

What is he talking about? Where is he taking me?

∽ 4 ∾

Rose

*C*awoke the next morning to the sound of rain tap dancing against my bedroom window. It was the sort of steady, lulling noise that made me wish I could cocoon myself under the covers and sleep for a little while longer. Alas, that was not a possibility. I still had a job for another two weeks, and honestly, I likely would not have been able to drift off again anyway. I was usually up with the birds, wide awake and ready to greet the day with arms wide open.

I would do that despite the rain, I decided. So what if it looked like New York needed a gigantic umbrella to shelter the city? It was my birthday, the start of a year that felt as though it could be my most important yet. I remembered something one of my grammar school teachers once said: "Each year is like a new book. It's up to us to choose how we fill the pages." As I got out of bed, I thought about how that could apply to my situation. Thankfully, my parents had taken a step back the night before, setting aside their commentary as requested, but I knew it was only a matter of time before their judgment crept around again. What would I say when that happened? When they asked what my plan was, how would I answer?

I had no idea.

On one level that terrified me, but on a greater one, it added a pep to my step. There might not have been enough opportunities out there for women like me, but perhaps that just meant I had to create them. This could be my chance to reinvent myself. Rose the secretary would be gone, and I would not miss her. "Not one bit," I said aloud, as I paused on my way to the kitchen to retrieve the newspaper the paper boy had dropped off. I always enjoyed reading it while I ate breakfast. I liked to keep up with current events, to learn about the world and all its intricacies. My soul was curious. I wanted to know as much as I could about as many things as I could.

I set the newspaper on the counter in the kitchen, poured myself a glass of juice, and got started on breakfast. The scrambled eggs were steaming hot when I sat down to eat – and, I quickly realized as I took a forkful, more than a bit overdone. That was another way Violet and I were different. Her meals were so delicious they could have been served in a restaurant. Mine were not. Violet always offered to help me out, to share her tips and tricks, but I simply did not have the patience to work in the kitchen for hours. Who wanted to be cooped up in an apartment instead of going for a walk on the city sidewalks or buying flowers to plant in a makeshift garden? That was actually one tradition of our mother's I had kept up with over the years. There was something so peaceful about working with the flowers, feeling the smooth stems and silky petals in my hands, and I loved to watch as they grew taller, stronger, and brighter.

The analogy was not lost on me: now it was my chance to do the same.

I considered that as I paged through the morning's newspaper. My thoughts were drifting back and forth, meandering everywhere as I tried to envision what my life might look like in a month or a year ... until I flipped to the travel section of the paper. That is when I saw it, staring up at me in all its glory.

The *SS Harmony*.

Even in black and white, it was beautiful.

Everything else faded away as I read the article about the ocean liner, which was celebrating its five year anniversary that month. It had made more than two hundred voyages in that time, taking passengers between America and Europe. It was amazing to think about: this luxurious ship crossing the grand, vast waters of the Atlantic in only five nights. The opposite shore of the ocean seemed so very far off, but it was not, really. It was only a boat ride away, and a boat that set sail from virtually my own backyard, no less.

It occurred to me then, that this ocean liner could be what came next for me.

I had always wanted to tour Europe, and what better way than this? Alice and her husband had taken a ship to England for their honeymoon, and it had sounded so exciting when she told Lucy and me about it. They had spent their mornings relaxing by the swimming pool, their afternoons playing deck tennis, and their nights dancing until their feet hurt. I could do that, too. This was the perfect time. There would be no job tying me to New York, and no great love to convince me that it was the most romantic place on earth – because, if you were with your soulmate, the glass skyscrapers and the bright lights of Broadway probably did seem like they were created from Cupid's arrow. To the rest of us, though, they were mesmerizing, but perhaps not enough to hold us in one place. If I took this chance, I could experience something entirely new and different. Why not do it? I could sublet my apartment for a couple months, board that ocean liner, and see what was waiting for me on the other side.

Just the thought of it made adrenaline zip through my bloodstream. For so long, I had followed the map laid out for me. I had gotten straight As all through school, joined the Fine Arts League and the Women's League, and worked first as a salesgirl at a clothing boutique and then as a secretary. I had tried to find love, and failed miserably, and then tried again and failed again. I had done a lot of living in my thirty years, but I had never felt truly alive.

Perhaps this was how I achieved that.

It would be an expensive endeavor, but I had been good about saving the money that did not go toward my bills. If I withdrew it from the bank, and combined it with the rent I got by subletting the apartment, I thought it might be feasible. I would just have to be thrifty, or maybe I could find a job overseas. I could work as a waitress at an outdoor café in Rome, or as a clerk in a chic shop in Paris, or as a nanny in Madrid. The possibilities seemed endless.

The world was so big, so overflowing with things to discover, and I wanted to see it all. I wanted to know what was beyond the walls of Manhattan, which was the only place I had ever lived. For as larger-than-life as the city was, sometimes it still felt too small for the many people crowded into it. It would be fascinating to step outside its bounds. Magic was everywhere, after all, hiding inside the tiniest nooks and blanketing the widest expanses. I pictured myself stepping off of the *SS Harmony* and walking into a whole other world. There would be no plans, and no rules, and no people looking over my shoulder and saying I was foolish to live on my own terms. Instead of letting society anchor me in place, I could go with the waves and see where they took me. Maybe I would even be able to create some waves of my own.

First, though, I needed to discuss the idea with the one person I talked to about everything: my sister. Our mother was always saying that Violet and I began to communicate with each other even before we knew how to speak, and I believed that, because it often seemed like we were connected on an intrinsic level. The time she fell down the steps at school and sprained her ankle, I was sitting in history class and could suddenly sense that something was wrong, even though I was all the way on the other side of the building. Violet had an almost identical experience on the day when I took a train up to Connecticut to visit a girlfriend and it broke down right in the middle of the tracks. When I was finally able to call home four hours later, she answered on the first ring and instantly asked if I was okay. Intuition, a sixth sense … whatever people wanted to call it, Violet and I surely shared it, and ever since we were young girls, we had confided in one another.

This was no exception.

I wanted to run my idea by her. She would tell me if I was being short-sighted, because that was another thing about sharing life with a twin: words were never minced, opinions never hidden. We were honest with each other, even if it hurt. So, after leaving work later that day, I headed uptown on the subway instead of walking home. It was nearly five-thirty by the time I got to the apartment Violet and Thomas had moved into the day they returned from their honeymoon, and I bit my lip as I knocked on the door, hoping I would not be interrupting dinner. Thomas had such an unpredictable schedule at the hospital that it was an impossible feat to know when he would actually be home. He had been supposed to join our family for dinner and *Damn Yankees* the night before, but had gotten delayed by a surgery that ran longer than expected. I wondered if the same was true this evening. I liked Thomas very much, particularly the way he made Violet smile, but this was one talk I preferred to have exclusively with her, just the two of us.

Just the two of us.

Violet had spoken those exact words to me on her wedding day. I was her maid of honor, and as I helped button her into her lacy gown, she had whispered a promise: "Thomas will be my husband, but you'll always and forever be my best friend. Just the two of us, right?" She had met my gaze in the mirror, and we both grew misty-eyed as I wrapped my arms around her in a hug.

"Right," I said.

Today, as she opened her front door, she was the one to reach in for a hug first. "Hi," she said, with a smile. "Happy Birthday."

"Happy Birthday to you, too." I gave her the gift I was holding. "For you."

"You shouldn't have. Actually," she said, amusement dancing in her eyes, "I take that back. You definitely should have." Her laughter filled the air between us as she motioned for me to come in. I followed her into the living room, with its floral couch and polished piano and picture windows that looked out onto the river. Violet's apartment could have been right out of the pages of *Ladies Home Journal*, it was so pretty.

"Is Thomas here?" I asked.

"Not yet," she said. "He wants to take me out for dinner tonight, but one of his patients spiked a fever, so he has to stay awhile longer to monitor her." She bustled into the kitchen, returning with a bottle of red wine and a plate of chocolate-covered pastries. "This is all I have to offer, I'm afraid. I didn't cook anything since we're going out."

"Oh goodness, this is fine," I said, as we sat down on the sofa. "Actually, it's better than fine. It covers my – "

"Favorite food group." She laughed again. "Chocolate. Same here." She uncorked the bottle of wine and poured a small amount into two glasses. "To celebrate our birthday," she said, clinking her glass to mine in a toast. "Here's to a swell year ahead."

"One in which all our wishes come true," I added. I took a sip of the wine, but it wasn't the crisp liquid that turned my cheeks rosy. It was the thought of all this year could have in store, if only I was brave enough to let it. "Before we open our gifts to each other," I said to Violet, "I have something to ask you."

Her eyebrows rose into two perfectly shaped arches, the way they always did when her curiosity was piqued. "Alright," she said. "Is this about Mother and Father?" Her mouth tipped downward in a frown. "They simply don't quit sometimes. I loathe how they compare us. You'd think they would have realized by now that we're not the same person."

"Oh, they have realized it. That's the problem. I'm not you."

"I'm sorry," she said, twisting her fingers around the stem of her glass.

"Don't be. It's not your fault," I told her. "You're you, and I'm me. Whether they accept that or not is on them and no one else. Besides, it may have been a good thing: losing my job, arguing with them, all of it. I think sometimes it takes those drastic moments for us to be able to reevaluate life. That's what I wanted to talk to you about, actually."

"I'm listening."

I took a long breath. "I look around your apartment, and I see a place that's home to you," I told her. "When I look around mine, I feel like … " An image of my small apartment floated through my mind. There was the candy dish on the table in the living room, filled with chocolate in crinkly paper wrappers, and the pictures hanging on the wall over the mantel. There was the potted plant next to the desk, its leaves vibrant but also fake, and the furniture our parents bought for me when I moved in, its floral pattern similar to the sofa at Violet's. My apartment was perfectly framed, but what did that matter, when the photo inside was getting dusty, its edges curling in on themselves? "I feel like it's too much," I said. "It's overwhelming, like I'm playing dress-up in a life that doesn't fit. I think I know how to change that, though." I opened my purse and removed the article I had cut out of the newspaper. "Take a look at this."

"An ocean liner?" She glanced at me, her hazel eyes ringed with confusion. "I don't understand. What does that have to do with anything?"

"I want to book a ticket on one," I told her. "I could go to England, France, Italy, Switzerland." I turned my hands face-up. "Wherever the inspiration takes me." Just thinking about it made a smile blossom on my lips. "Imagine how thrilling it would be. I could ski in the Alps, ride a bicycle all along the Riviera, wait outside of Buckingham Palace and catch a glimpse of the Queen … the options are infinite. Doesn't it sound marvelous?"

"It does," she agreed, "but Rose, it also sounds impossible. How could you afford it, and would it even be safe to travel alone in foreign countries? How would you communicate with people if you don't speak their language?"

"I still remember some of the Spanish we learned in high school. I can brush up on that, and buy one of those little translation books to help with people who don't speak English. I'll make it work." I told her about my idea to sublet my apartment.

"I don't know," she said. "This is quite risky."

"And what's life without risk?" I stood up and started to pace around her living room. It always helped me to think, moving around. People spent far too much time staying still, and what was the point? We could not go forward if we refused to take the first step. "Look," I said, "I see how happy you are. You found all you ever wanted in Thomas, and that's wonderful. For me, though, I suppose I'm searching for something I don't even know I want."

"If you don't know you want it, how will you realize when you've found it?"

It was a good question.

I paused for a moment and stared out the window. It was still raining, and the glass was so wet that it seemed as though I was seeing the world as a watercolor. "I think ... I'll just know," I told my sister. "Much the same way as you did with Thomas." I turned away from the window to face her. "You were over the moon after your first date with him. Remember how you rang my doorbell ten times in a row?"

She chuckled. "When you finally heard it and got out of the shower, I talked your ear off for an hour straight, all while you were sitting there in a robe because I was too giddy to wait until you got dressed. Yes, I remember well. I knew right away he was the man I'd marry. There was something about how I felt when I was with him. He made me see things differently."

"That's exactly what I'm looking for," I told her. "A different perspective. It's like ... we all live in these little boxes these days. There are four walls, a top and a bottom, maybe a window to look out of every now and then. I'm tired of looking out. I want to be on the outside looking in." I sat down next to her on the sofa. "I was content with my life, but never truly satisfied, and after I lost my job, it occurred to me: why do the same thing over again? If the path I'm on isn't fulfilling, it's up to me to seek out a different direction. Nothing will change unless I do that."

Violet was silent for a long while, fiddling with her bracelet as she stared at the paintings on the wall, and for the first time in forever, I could not tell what she was thinking. Normally we were great at knowing what one another would say and hearing what the other did not say. Now, though, I was at a loss. My sister's expression was entirely unreadable.

Finally, she smiled. "You should go," she said.

❦ 5 ❦

Grace

By the time Jonathan knocks on my door, I already have my jacket on and my bag slung over my shoulder. To say I'm eager to find out what's going on is an understatement. Jonathan and I usually spend a good portion of the weekend together, so his invitation didn't come as a surprise, but all of his secrecy and spontaneity did. He figured out pretty early on in our relationship that I'm the kind of person who craves structure. I think it comes from being a middle sister. Bookended by Abigail's take-charge meticulousness and Josie's over-the-top flexibility, I have always felt like I needed to be the mediator. The common ground. The even-keeled one who navigates life in the safe and steady lane. The irony of that hits me now, as I go to open the door. Saying goodbye to The Book Boutique would be the safe choice, for sure, and yet I am the one fighting against it. But I don't want to think about that today, not when Jonathan greets me with a kiss that immediately makes me feel all fuzzy around the edges.

"Wow," I murmur. "That is quite the hello."

"Good," he says. "That's what I was aiming for." He kisses me again, fast and familiar this time, like we've been doing it forever. "Are you ready?"

"Ready for ... what?" I smile as enticingly as I can. "Can I at least have a hint? You know I'm not a fan of surprises."

"I think you'll like this one." He offers me his hand. "Come on. Don't you trust me?"

I do. I trust him more than I've ever trusted any man, and so I make a deliberate decision to let go and let loose – or to try to, anyway. I thread my fingers between his, enjoying the softness of his skin against mine as we head downstairs and out into the crisp air. It's a perfect autumn day: chilly enough to make me glad I tied a scarf around my neck, but still warm enough in the sun to give the illusion that Georgia is ensconced in a golden glow. This is one of my very favorite times of the year down South. It isn't too hot or too cold. It's just right.

Jonathan lowers the windows in his car, inviting in the breeze as we pull out of the lot. "So how did it go with your sisters last night?" he asks.

A sigh escapes my mouth. "Apparently they think the store is becoming too much of a burden," I say. "They're tossing around the idea of shutting its doors for good." My chest tightens as I recall the way we left things last night, so unsettled and uncertain. "I don't know what I'd do without that place," I tell Jonathan. "So much of it is wrapped up inside me. So much of *me* is wrapped up inside it."

"Which is why you should get the final say on its fate, not them." He shakes his head. "Abigail's too busy to stop in more than once or twice a month, and Josie's hardly ever in the city these days, let alone the store. It isn't their place to decide. I don't see them interacting with the customers for eight hours every day." He keeps on talking, about the local author nights I host and the book clubs I invite to hold meetings in the shop, and it's funny ... I know he's right, that it's basically what I told Abigail and Josie the night before, yet I still feel the need to speak up on their behalf. It's one thing for me to point out their flaws. It's another for someone else to do it.

"To be fair," I say, "they were adamant from the beginning about not wanting to be involved in the day-to-day business. Abigail even floated around the idea of selling it then." I think back to the day after our Pop-Pop passed away, when we were sitting in the kitchen of our grandparents' home and our mom presented us with an envelope that had our names written on it.

Inside had been the rental paperwork for the store, along with a note explaining their choice to leave The Book Boutique to us. Tears had instantly flooded my eyes as I read it. Our grandparents were giving us their most prized possession.

How could my sisters even consider turning their backs on such a priceless gift?

"Don't worry," I say to Jonathan, "I'm not going to let it happen." As he takes the ramp onto the highway, I suddenly feel a desperate need to change the subject. "Hey, guess what I found in a book yesterday?" I ask. "There was a newspaper clipping from a 1950s ocean liner and a love letter from one passenger to another." I fill him in on the details of Henry's note and my efforts to uncover the story behind it.

"Whoa," he says. "That's awesome. It sounds like Henry was totally fascinated by that mystery woman. I know how that goes." He flashes a wide, almost boyish smile, and my cheeks flush a rosy pink. He's always saying sweet things like that. I didn't really believe him at first, not after the way my previous two relationships had crumbled seemingly out of the clear blue, but somewhere along the line he'd managed to slip past the walls I thought I'd constructed around my heart. Jonathan is not Will, who broke up with me on the eve of our second anniversary because his college girlfriend had moved back to town and asked him for another chance. He's also not Drew, who was offered a wonderful job that would take him across the globe – and away from me. Will chose someone else. Drew chose something else.

Jonathan chooses me.

We are good to each other. Good *for* each other.

He sends flowers to the bookstore, for no reason other than to let me know I'm on his mind, and I stop by his vet clinic to bring him lunch because he often gets so involved with his patients that he forgets to take a break. He goes to Josie's shows with me and volunteers to tag along when I babysit Ben and Macy for Abigail, and I always look forward to joining him and his parents for their monthly bowling night. And my favorite things – Jonathan will say anything, just to make me laugh, and even after a year of officially being together, he still smiles whenever we kiss. So do I. When I feel his lips brush mine, his thumb rubbing circles on my wrist or grazing the side of my cheek, my mouth curves up almost involuntarily.

Will and Drew made me wonder if love actually existed, or if it was nothing more than a cleverly crafted mirage. They were a reminder, much like my parents' divorce was, that promises were often shattered and words could be fleeting. But they can also be powerful, and so, as Jonathan pulls into the parking lot for Stone Mountain Park forty-five minutes later, I am immediately reminded of the beautiful moment we created here. It was last April when we visited for the first time together. We took the train ride around the grounds and watched the laser show on the side of the mountain, but it was what happened on top of the mountain that left the greatest handprint on my heart. With an unbelievable view below us, Jonathan took my hand, tracing his finger along the lines in my palm as he said he loved me for the first time.

Those words didn't tarnish. They gleamed.

They were bright, and shiny, and new.

"I love you, too," I told him. "You came into my life when I least expected it, you know that? I'd all but given up on having a relationship. Decided it wasn't worth the heartache." I shook my head a bit. "And then you showed me that real love, the kind you don't only feel in the big moments, but also the small ones, is always worth it."

He grinned. "So what you're saying is that I'm like a white knight in a romance novel."

My laughter had floated through the air, which somehow seemed clearer up there, closer to the sky and the clouds and the stars that were just waiting for the chance to sparkle again that evening. "Yes," I said. "I suppose so."

Stone Mountain became our place that day. No matter how

our story unfolded from then on, it would always be a turning point in the pages we were writing together. Being back again now feels like the most refreshing escape.

"Okay," I concede, "you were right. This *is* the type of surprise I enjoy."

"So is this a good time to say I told you so?" He winks at me, a move that'd seem corny coming from somebody else, but is just endearing when he does it. "I thought it'd be nice this time of year," he says. "Everything is decorated for the season."

As we make our way into the park, I see what he means. There are fall-themed displays in more than one location, towering hay bales that are surrounded by scarecrows, cornucopias, and so many pumpkins. A brightly painted sign announces the entrance to a corn maze, and a group of kids dart by us as they run over to the Azalea Stage for a pie-eating contest. It is a treasure trove of autumn's glory.

"What do you think?" Jonathan asks, handing over the pamphlet he picked up at the front gate. "We could check out the scarecrows, go for a hike around the lake, take the Skyride up to the top of the mountain." He smiles a bit at this, but leaves the decision up to me.

"All of the above." I stick the brochure into my messenger bag. "Let's start with the scarecrows. Did I ever tell you I won a decorating contest when I was a kid? It was at an orchard near my mom's house, and you should've seen the look on Abigail's face when she lost the blue ribbon to me. Let's face it," I say. "If I can out-decorate her, I can out-decorate anyone."

"Including me?"

He can barely get the words out with a straight face, because he has the artistic talent of ... well, honestly, Ben and Macy could do a better job at it than him. In fact, they *have* done a better job on more than one occasion when we're babysitting. The image of him sitting at their little table comes to mind, his fingers smeary with magic marker as the kids giggled about how his drawing looked like the opposite of what he'd intended. He was such a good sport about it. It's one of the things I love most about him, how he's willing to laugh at himself and find joy in everything. Fitting, since he has helped me to do the same.

"Including you, Mr. Miller," I tell him.

"That sounds like a challenge, Ms. Anderson," he retorts. He pauses for a moment after saying my name, and I glance at him in curiosity, but whatever flicked into his thoughts seems to disappear just as quickly. It's strange, and I notice it happening time and again as we immerse ourselves in the park's activities. When we snap pictures of the scarecrows, when we go for a walk around the lake, when we buy caramel apples and hot cider from the concession stand ... I keep catching him looking my way as though he's seeing something for the first time. Finally, as we wait in line for the Summit Skyride, which will lift us over eight hundred feet and drop us off atop the mountain, I decide I have to ask him about it.

"Is everything okay with you?" I say.

He runs a hand through his dark hair. "Sure. Yes. Of course. Why do you ask?"

"Because you keep staring at me," I say. "But not like usual. Like ... I don't know, sort of like you discovered some sort of secret and it's making you second-guess everything you thought you knew." I take a step forward, following the people in front of us as they move closer to the cable car. "You know you can talk to me. If something's bothering you – "

"No." He throws out the word before I can even finish my sentence. "Nothing is bothering me." He slides his hands into the pockets of his jacket. "Honest. I'm fine. I'm better than fine," he adds, and leans over to kiss my cheek.

I don't necessarily believe him, but the ride starts to board then and we're ushered inside along with dozens of other people. Definitely not the place for a personal conversation. We stand quietly, listening to the chatter of the adults around us and the high-pitched exclamations from the kids who can't wait to "stand on top of the whole wide world," as the girl in front of us describes it. The cable car climbs higher and higher, and by the time it drops us off at the peak, the sun is just beginning to sink lower in the sky. It makes my breath catch in my throat: the ribbons of pink and yellow spiraling around the cotton ball clouds above, and the tapestry of blazing orange and yellow leaves reflecting on the lake water way down below. It's like living inside a postcard. Atlanta's city skyline stands tall and proud in the distance, and when I spin around in the other direction the Appalachian Mountains greet me with their majesty.

"Oh, Jonathan," I say. "Look at it. Have you ever seen anything so magnificent?"

"Yes."

His voice sounds different. Rocky, almost. Nervous.

"Are you *sure* you're alright?" I ask. "Because – " As I turn to look at him, whatever I had been about to say completely fades from my brain. Everything freezes. Time. Space. The very beating of my heart. Because Jonathan is down on one knee. He's down on one knee, and he has a velvet box in his hand, and he's smiling at me like no one and nothing exists in this universe besides us. It's like a scene straight out of a fairy tale, except this isn't a world brought to life by a writer's imagination. This is *my* world. *My* life.

I think back to what Jonathan said earlier.

Just be ready for an adventure.

Holy crap.

"Jonathan?" I whisper.

He looks at me with his warm gray eyes. "I love you, Grace," he says. "Fully. Boldly. Fearlessly. You make everything bigger, in a way. Brighter. You're the person I want to talk to when I've had a bad day, and also the one I want to talk to when I've had a great day. That morning you came into my office ... " He smiles. "Let's just say I'm forever indebted to Abigail's dog for getting into all that mischief. He did me a huge favor. I knew being a vet would be rewarding, but I never imagined that it'd introduce me to my soulmate."

His soulmate.

My heart expands about three sizes.

"I want to build a future with you," Jonathan says. "A family. I've always wanted a big one, you know. Kids running around, toys strewn all over, dogs barking like crazy. I want the chaos, and the laughter, and the life that feels too big to contain within the walls of a house. I never had that when I was younger, and I always felt like I was missing out, but now I see it was the opposite. Growing up as an only child just made me more certain about what I want as an adult. Love means never being lonely again, never being alone again. That's what you've given me. And now, I have something to give you."

I should say something.

Do something.

But I am rooted in place, so shell-shocked that I can barely process what's happening, much less respond to it. All I can do is watch, goosebumps blanketing my arms, as Jonathan stands up. We're eye-to-eye, the windows to his soul trying to uncover what lays inside mine, as he opens the jewelry box. Nestled inside is the most exquisite engagement ring I have ever seen. The center diamond is blue, square cut and set into two glittering bands that catch the brilliant rays of the setting sun. For a moment, all I can do is stare. I am mesmerized by this ring and by this one-in-a-million man who's actually asking me to spend forever with him.

"Grace Katherine Anderson," Jonathan says, his voice thick with emotion. "Will you marry me?"

I knew those words were coming, but they still take my breath away.

It feels like I'm dreaming with my eyes open.

"I ... I don't know what to say," I whisper.

"'Yes' would be a great place to start." He smiles at me again, and it's so sweet, so full of hope, that it makes tears form below my lashes. This ... this is why he's been stealing glances at me all day, why he sounded so nervous on the ride up to the mountain. All along, he's been planning to ask me to marry him in the very same spot where we exchanged those precious first I love yous. Without a shadow of a doubt, it's the most amazing, romantic thing that anybody has ever done for me. For all the times Abigail's talked about her love for Scott, how he makes her feel weightless in a reality that she insists on staying grounded in, I never really understood what she meant. I get it now. Because, standing here with Jonathan, I feel as though I'm defying gravity, too. It's like what that girl said on the way up: we're on top of the whole wide world.

I wish we could stay here, inside this moment when everything hangs in the balance.

When promise and possibility ring clearly.

When life is ours to cradle in the palms of our hands.

When a story arc is just waiting to start anew and take us to places we can't even imagine.

This moment, it is rare, and delicate, and perfect in so many ways.

I don't want to let it out of my grasp.

Because the truth is, I *do* know what I'm going to say to Jonathan.

I know what my answer is.

∾ 6 ∾

Rose

I knew my parents would never be as supportive about my choice as Violet was, so I delayed for as long as possible when it came to telling them and concentrated on other details instead: finishing my final two weeks at the office, making lists of what I had to pack and where I wanted to visit once the ship docked, and finding someone to live in my apartment while I was off seeking the answers to so many questions. The latter proved the most difficult, not because there was a lack of inquiries in response to the ads I placed, but because I wanted the right subletter to come along. I did not fancy the thought of turning over my keys to just anyone. It took six tries before I finally met Mr. and Mrs. Smithson, a couple who had moved to New York to be closer to their grandchildren.

"We always assumed we would live our golden years in the country," Mrs. Smithson said, as she sat on my couch. "The city was not in the cards." A web of laugh lines appeared around her mouth as she smiled. "I suppose when it comes to the people we love, though, all our plans simply become weightless as a feather. Ours carried us here. We just want to be sure it's a good match before we invest in a permanent place."

"We're excited to be close to our family," her husband added. He took out his wallet, removed a worn photograph from inside, and showed it to me, beaming with pride as he pointed out all of his grandchildren and told me a little about each one.

These people, they lived and loved for something.

They were the ones, and not simply because I knew they

would take care of the apartment like it was their own. It was also because I knew, right in that sweet spot where my heart met my head and intuition was born, that I could learn something from this couple. I adored what Mrs. Smithson said about plans growing weightless when it came to the people we loved. Perhaps I would find that overseas. I was giving myself permission to try, to spread my wings and fly.

I could not wait to see where I would land.

However, before I could take flight, I needed, finally, to tell my parents. I invited them over for dinner the day after I walked out of the law office for the last time, and I spent the whole afternoon in the kitchen as I prepared our meal. I decided on a main course of rice stuffed chicken and roasted peppers, along with fresh baked bread and vanilla pudding for dessert. It took forever to make, but by the time I finished setting the table and wiping the puffs of flour from my cheeks and apron, I was fairly proud of what I had cooked. It would not be as flawless a meal as Violet set out whenever we visited her and Thomas, but nothing was charred. In fact, the food actually looked good. Hopefully that would be a point in my favor.

As it turned out, it was the opposite.

"You see, dear, you *can* be a fantastic cook when you put your mind to it," my mother said. She sipped the coffee I had brewed to serve with dessert. "If I didn't know any differently, I would have thought this was one of Violet's dinners."

A flicker of irritation ignited inside my chest, but I worked hard to extinguish it. This was exactly why Violet had told me she felt it was best for her to stay home that night. "Perhaps if I'm not there it will be easier for Mother and Father to see things from your perspective," she said. "Instead of it being a contest between which one of us is living the life they imagined for us, it will be a chance for them to open their minds to another possibility."

I had faltered when she said that, teetering on the line between wanting her there and knowing that, even though we would always and forever stand at each other's side, it was also time for Violet and me to stand alone. It would make us stronger in the end. In that moment, though, I did not feel very strong.

"Please stop," I said, as my mother started in again with her usual remarks. "Just because it was a decent meal does not mean I have a desire to repeat it on a daily basis." I shook my head and my hair swished over my shoulders, the curls I had carefully crafted falling neatly back into place. "I did this because I love you," I said, "and because I hoped it would be a peace offering." I summoned up all my courage. "There's something I have to tell you."

My father cleared his throat. "The last time you had something to tell us, you dropped quite the bombshell," he said.

"Speaking of which," my mother added, "we still need to discuss that further, especially since it is July now and your time at the law office is finished." Her smile was pleasant on the surface, but, I could tell, riddled with tension underneath. Over the past two weeks, she had tried to lead me into this conversation more than once, but I had sidestepped every effort.

Now I had to jump in with both feet.

"Yes, it is finished," I said, "and I know what comes next." I stood up from the table and walked over to my desk, where I took the article on the *SS Harmony* from the top drawer. Nerves twisted in my stomach as I handed the newspaper to my parents, then sat back down and watched them read it. I could see the confusion etch itself across their faces as they tried to draw a connection between the article and their seemingly wayward daughter. "I'm buying a ticket for the ship," I explained. "I would love to explore Europe now that I have the time. I'll start in England and go on from there." I could feel the bubble of excitement rising in me again – it seemed to do that whenever I so much as thought about my upcoming trip, let alone talked about it – and I clasped my hands together with an almost involuntary grin. "France and Italy are definitely on my itinerary, and perhaps also Spain and Sweden. It'll be a one-way ticket for now. I'm going to leave things open-ended."

There was complete silence from my parents. All I could hear was the ticking of the clock on my mantel. *Tick, tock, tick, tock, tick, tock.* It was counting down until the explosion, or so I thought. It was eerie, the way my parents were so quiet. My father was staring at me, his fingertips white as he gripped the table, and my mother was looking anywhere *but* at me, her gaze so icy it very well could have frozen lava.

Finally, she spoke. "That," she said sharply, "is the most irresponsible thing I have ever heard. I cannot believe any child of mine would do something quite that impulsive and impudent." I opened my mouth to explain further, to tell her how desperately I was craving something I could not find in New York, but she steamrolled right over me. "You are not a teenager anymore, Rose. The time for foolishness has long since passed. When I was your age, your father and I had been married for nine years, and I was already expecting. Don't you want that? Don't you want to experience the delight of falling in love and becoming a parent?"

"Mary – " my father said, reaching out a gentle hand to my mother. "Calm down."

"No." Her eyes morphed from ice to fire. "I can't."

"And *I* can't, either," I said. "I can't talk about a husband and a baby who don't exist."

"Perhaps they don't exist because you don't want them to," my mother said. "You simply refuse to open your eyes to the world around you. You act as though we're living in the Stone Age, not the 1950s. That makes me very disappointed. You're going to miss out on so much."

"Don't you see?" I asked. "That's exactly why I have to get on that ship. Sailing to Europe is my way of not missing out. Life here isn't filling me up inside. I think ... there's a hole somewhere, and I don't quite understand how to close it yet."

"You mentioned a one-way ticket," my father said. "How long are you planning to stay away? A month? A year?"

"Honestly, I don't know," I told him. "Until I find whatever I'm looking for ... whatever I need." I let my gaze travel between my parents. "I realize this isn't what you want for me," I said, "and I do respect your opinion, but I have to follow my heart."

"This is a mistake," my mother said, and she no longer sounded angry, just sad.

Her words made my eyes fill up with tears. I had so badly wanted my parents to support, if not my choice itself, then at least my right to decide my own destiny. Perhaps it was too much to hope for, but perhaps, also, it was a lesson learned: that although I had no control over the current which surrounded me, I could instead focus on the direction I sailed. This time, I was opting to go into the wind.

Maybe one day my parents would understand that, or maybe they never would.

It did not matter.

I was still going, and no one could change my mind.

I purchased my ticket the very next day and set about the not-so-easy task of packing up all my belongings. Everything I needed for my trip went into two suitcases, and the rest of it I boxed up to take to Lucy's apartment. She lived in the same building as me and graciously offered up her spare bedroom to store my overflow until I returned. Alice joined us as we transferred the boxes. "Thank you so much," I said, after we had finished transporting the last of it and were sprawled on the sofa to catch our breath. "You're the bee's knees ... truly the best friends a girl could ask for."

"We're happy to help," Lucy said. "I still can't believe you are doing this. All the times we went out to dinner and talked about the things we'd love to accomplish one day ... you're making good on it. I admire that. I admire you."

Alice nodded her agreement. "It takes a brave person to embrace uncertainty."

"Oh, I'm not brave," I said. "Just restless."

"You're doing something about it, though," Alice said. "Look at Lucy and me. Being secretaries is not exactly our idea of fun, either, and yet we still put on our pearls and high heels every morning. We still spend our days sitting at a desk and following instructions. Soon you will be spending yours looking at the ocean."

Hearing her say it aloud made the entire thing seem so very real.

In three short days, I would board that ship and sail away from everything I had ever known. It probably should have scared me, or at least made a curtain of intimidation fall around my shoulders, but it was the opposite. Each time I envisioned it, little frissons of excitement ran down my spine. I wondered what treasures were out there, just waiting for me to find them.

First, though, I wanted to soak up the gifts I had at home, including the friendships I would never be able to duplicate, no matter how far I traveled. Lucy and Alice were more than my girlfriends. In a way, they were my family, too. I treated them both to milkshakes at the corner drugstore to thank them for helping me, and as we sat at the counter, giggling over everything and also over nothing, it occurred to me that I was in the middle of a memory. Too frequently, it seemed, the full value of an experience did not reveal itself until after the present became the past. People so often took all the little things for granted until we realized they were, actually, the big things.

Standing on the cusp of this new journey, I vowed not to do that anymore. On the SS Harmony, in Europe, even after I came back to New York City, I would live inside every moment. I would enjoy them for what they were, instead of what they could be, and I would shed the cloak that kept me in line with what I was told to believe.

I would challenge that. I would challenge myself.

I would be free.

That sense of freedom rose higher and higher to the surface as I enjoyed my last days in the city. Alice and Lucy threw me a going away party the following night, Lucy's apartment filled with friends from the Women's League, and the next morning, I walked to the flower stand one more time. The blooms seemed especially vivid that day: ranunculus, lilies, marigolds, and more. I breathed in their sweetness, breathed it all in, before carefully creating a hand-chosen bouquet that combined all my favorites.

Flowers were happiness, they were promise and potential, and I was excited to see what kinds I would find overseas. For now, though, I walked back to my apartment, placed the bouquet in a vase I had left unpacked, and put it on the coffee table for the Smithsons. Manhattan was still a maze of metal and concrete to them, and I thought it might make the transition more welcoming. I added a short note the following morning – *May your time in this apartment be as sweet as the aroma of the flowers* – and set it next to the vase. Then I sat on the couch and looked around at the place I called home. I did not necessarily think I would miss it, but I wanted to remember its nuances just in case. There were memories to be found around every corner, some I remembered with clarity and others I did not even realize I had made. It was funny how they could stitch themselves into the very fabric of your life without your permission or even your awareness.

I would take them with me, wherever I went.

It was time to go.

Violet had insisted on seeing me off, and as she drove Thomas's car to the pier where the ocean liner was docked, I tried not to think about the fact that this was the last time we would be together for the foreseeable future. It had been hard enough living thirty-five blocks from her. Now I would be thirty-five hundred miles away.

"I'm going to miss you," I said, as she parked the car.

"I'll miss you, too. I'm so proud of you, though. I get to be, since I'm the older sister."

"By two minutes."

We both laughed. It was our customary exchange, one we had

spoken more times than I could count. Violet always joked about being the older, wiser sister, and although I knew she was teasing, I secretly thought there was a nugget of truth to it. Violet had her life all wrapped together and tied up with a neat bow. I did not know if I would ever have that. Quite honestly, I did not even know if I wanted it.

Hopefully this trip would help me find out.

I took my suitcases from the backseat and walked toward the ship. It was a humid day, the heat from the summer sun blazing down and scorching the city below, but the closer we got to the water, the more of a breeze there was. It seemed to curl around me, calling my name. The whisper of the sea was majestic and transcendent, especially juxtaposed against the hustle and bustle of New York. People were scurrying this way and that, passengers with their suitcases in hand and their passports ready to go, families and friends who hugged them tightly and made them promise to keep in touch once the boat docked.

"That goes for you, too," Violet told me. "Send a postcard, okay, and call once in awhile, even if you have to do it collect?"

"Yes," I said. "Of course."

We were quiet for a long minute.

"You know," Violet said finally, "I think Mother and Father will come around."

I did not.

They had spoken to me only once since I told them about my plans, and that was just to remind me that I could always "cut my foolish idea short if I came to my senses." They would be glad to pay for a plane ticket home, they said, because money was no object when it came to ensuring the well-being of their daughter. I had been tempted to explain, yet again, that the SS Harmony was exactly what their daughter's well-being yearned for, but then I opted to go the route of least resistance. It was clear that my parents were listening without being ready to truly hear me.

"It's fine," I said to Violet, adjusting the scarf I had tied around my long hair. "Even if they don't come around, I have your support. That's what matters most."

She reached over and squeezed my hand. "Be safe," she said. "Have fun. Find your passion and let your passion find you."

I looked at the ocean liner. It was bigger than I had imagined, its smokestacks standing tall and its exterior painted a shiny white with red and blue accents. Rows of small windows lined the lower decks, and the gangplank was already down, inviting people on board. My heart pumped a bit faster as I regarded this regal ship. It was awe-inspiring in person, grand and sleek, but still so elegant and welcoming. Suddenly I could not wait a second longer to join its ranks.

"Find my passion," I repeated. "I intend to." I hugged Violet and kissed her cheek. "I love you," I said, and then I headed for the boat. My heels clicked against the wood of the gangplank, crisp and precise, and I turned around at the top to wave to Violet.

It was time to board, time to sail, time to make those waves.

∾ 7 ∾

Grace

"I'm so sorry," I whisper, and Jonathan's smile instantly collapses. It kills me to see it. Crumbles my heart into dust. It's quite possibly the worst feeling ever to know you're responsible for stealing another person's happiness. It's almost more than I can take, staring into his eyes that look back at me with such bewilderment.

"But ... I don't ... this isn't ... we've been so good ... " he stammers. He can't seem to form a full thought.

Neither can I.

They all rush around my mind, these fragmented beginnings and endings, frenzied in their silent desperation to find somewhere to stick. But they don't. They can't. I don't know that I can, either. Explaining to Jonathan why I can't accept his proposal feels impossible. And yet, as I wrap my hand around his and lead him over to a quiet area where we can talk free from interruption, I know there is no other choice. Jonathan is a good man. A kind, compassionate, generous man who lights up my life. I can't let him think I don't love him enough to make the future forever ours. Love might be the problem, but not in the way it seems.

"Thank you," I say softly, as we sit down. "For wanting to be my husband, for wanting me to be your wife. I can't even begin to tell you how overwhelmed and touched I am."

"But not touched enough to say yes?"

He sounds so sad, I could cry. After all the effort he put into making this moment special for me, here I am repaying him with what must feel like the deepest kind of betrayal. It's not fair. "I wish I could say yes," I tell him. "Please believe that. Believe *me* when I promise that if there was any man who could make me consider marriage, it'd be you. The thing is ... " I cover his hand with mine. "A commitment like that scares me. You know what happened to my parents. It was a hideous divorce and an even uglier path leading up to it. Every good thing about their relationship was ruined. They ended up despising each other. You know my father has basically nothing to do with my sisters and me, and even less to do with my mother. To this day, they barely speak."

My chest tightens as I think about it.

All this time later, I still can't get over how my father has acted.

"We're not your parents, though," Jonathan points out.

"No," I say. "I realize that." I stare down at the rock we're sitting on, at its dips and curves, the gradient of colors fading into one another. "My parents practically ran straight to the altar. I mean, who gets married after only a month? Sometimes I wonder what would've happened if they'd held off." I turn to look at Jonathan, but he keeps his gaze focused somewhere on the distance. "If they had taken things at a slower pace instead of jumping into a marriage they weren't ready for, maybe they would've been able to handle it better. Acting on passion is all well and good in books, but my parents ... they barely even knew one another on their wedding day. There was no foundation, you know?"

"But didn't they build one?" he asks. "It's not like they got divorced in five months or anything. They were together a long time. And we already have so much they didn't. We've been dating for a year, Grace. You know me better than anybody else does, and I'd like to think I know you that well, too. I'm not saying we don't have more to learn about each other, but the thing about marriage is – it gives us time to make those discoveries." Finally, he shifts his attention in my direction. "I'm not sure why you never told me you wouldn't be willing to take our relationship any further. I deserved that."

At this, I *do* start to cry. The tears break through the floodgates and tumble freeform down my cheeks. Because Jonathan's right: he *did* deserve that, and I would have told him, if only I'd known. "I didn't realize how I felt until you got down on one knee," I explain. "What you just said to me was everything I could've dreamed of, and more ... and that terrifies me. It feels too big, with too much potential for heartbreak down the line, and I don't know how to be okay with it. That is why I can't agree to marry you. Not yet."

"Yet?" Something lifts in his voice. "Does that mean there's still a chance?"

God, I hope so.

I'm not ready to let Jonathan put that ring on my finger, but I'm also not ready to let him go.

I don't think I ever will be.

"Here's what I know," I say. "I love you more than I ever thought possible. You make my world a better place, and you challenge me to be the best version of myself. Falling asleep next to you and waking up with your arms around me, it's like everything is perfectly lined up. But things felt steady with Will and Drew, too. Until they weren't any longer. You're not them, I understand that, and I'm not the same person I was when I dated them. They did leave, though. They walked away without looking back."

"I'd never do that."

"Even if our marriage were to fall apart?"

"It wouldn't," he says. "But even if it did, I couldn't just erase you from my life. I know you have a lot of experience with that. Your father, Will, Drew ... I can't speak for them, but I can promise you that I'm different. Your heart is safe with me."

Safe.

He *is* my safe place. It's why I've allowed myself to sink into the comfort of being with him. He's got to be more than that, though. He has to be the one who can convince me that safety is a crutch. That sometimes it's okay to embrace a plot twist, or better yet, to create my own.

We aren't there yet.

I'm not there yet.

I'd like to be, though. I'd like that very much.

"I remember something my Gram said once," I tell Jonathan, "about how life's most meaningful moments transcend words. I thought she was crazy." My laughter echoes, up here on the mountain where paradise seems just a bit closer to our reach. "You know me. Words are my everything. But I see now what Gram meant, because I will never be able to fully describe how it felt when you asked me to marry you." I lean into him, resting my head on his shoulder. "I'm not saying yes, but I'm not saying no, either. Can you give me some time? Hang on to that ring, and hopefully one day I will ask you to put it where it belongs."

"Where it belongs," he echoes. "I won't lie, I'm disappointed today didn't go how I'd imagined. But you ... you're all I *ever* could've imagined, so of course I'll wait for you. I'm not going anywhere, and neither is this." He slips the ring box back into his pocket. Then he links his hand with mine. It's more than I could've hoped for, and I hold on tight.

"Thank you," I say.

He kisses my forehead. "You're worth it," he says. "I'm okay with keeping things as they are for as long as you need. Just promise to be open with me about how you feel?"

"You've got it."

It occurs to me, as Jonathan keeps his hand wrapped around mine, how lucky I am. Being here with him, our eyes to the sky as the last rays of sun brighten the landscape before bowing to all the twinkling stars ... it is remarkable. I told Jonathan what was in my heart, stripped the layers off and left myself more vulnerable than I've ever been, and he didn't leave, even though he certainly would have been justified in doing so.

Part of me is still worried, though.

Sure, good things come to those who wait, but at the same time, no one can wait forever.

I steal a peek at the man who wants to be my fiancé.

How long will I have to figure this out before I lose him?

* * *

I'm up before the sun the next morning, my eyes bleary and my brain fuzzy from a night spent in the iron-clad grasp of so many wicked dreams. Each one was worse than the last. My wedding day, complete with gray skies that poured rain on the outdoor ceremony. My honeymoon, when a huge wave pulled Jonathan into the turquoise water and carried him away. My divorce, filled with bitter tears and toddlers who clung to me while I sobbed. They were the most horrific nightmares, and as I throw back the covers and head for the kitchen to make myself some coffee, my legs wobble with the task of keeping me upright.

"Stop," I command myself out loud. "They were just nightmares. There's nothing to them."

Logically, I know that.

But sometimes logic takes a backseat. Sometimes, despite our very best efforts, we can only live inside our fears rather than outside of our expectations. That's why, after choking down a breakfast I can barely even taste, I'm out of my condo and on the road to Smyrna, where Sofie lives. Normally my sisters would be the first ones I'd go to for advice, but I can't even think about confiding in them right now. Abigail would tell me to accept the proposal before I could even finish explaining why I'm tentative.

"Marriage is the next step," she'd tell me. "That's how it's supposed to go. Put that ring on and start planning the future." Plans and schedules and boxes to check off. That's how she approaches life, and it works perfectly for her. She and Scott are a model couple, and their family is the kind you would see on the inserts that come inside of picture frames at a store. She wouldn't understand my hesitation, and with so much strain already swirling around us as of late, we would just dissolve into an argument I don't have the energy for today.

The same would happen with Josie. "C'mon," she would urge. "Live a little. Sometimes you've gotta risk it all to find it all." That's what she would do. Josie is the kind of person who acts first and thinks later. Sometimes it serves her quite well, and other times Abigail and I are left to pick up the pieces.

I will not let my relationship be one of those pieces, so Sofie it is.

She's playing outside with one of her kids when I arrive, a sea of toys strewn across the yard and wraparound front porch. Her little girl comes dashing over the moment I step out of the car. "Miss Grace!" she exclaims, her red pigtails swinging as she bounces on the balls of her feet. "I got super-duper excited when Mommy said you were coming. Wanna play dolls?" When she smiles, it makes it look like her freckles are dancing across her cheeks.

"I would love to," I say, and bend down to give her a hug. Addilyn is the middle of Sofie's three children, and she's at that sweet age when all the world is her playground. "I need to talk with your mom for a little while," I tell her, "but after that, I'm all yours. Deal?"

She nods and scampers back to the porch. I follow. Sofie gives me a hug when I reach her, then leans down to tickle Addilyn's cheeks with her pigtails. "Why don't you go play with Ellie and Jordan while I talk to Grace?" she suggests. "They're out back on the swing-set with Daddy." Addilyn gives her a double thumbs-up, and we both watch as she runs around the house.

Sofie's family is another one that looks like it's right out of a TV show, but as is so often the case, there's more to it than the eye can see. What isn't visible on the surface is the terrible struggle they went through when Sofie had a miscarriage six years ago. The pain of losing a child nearly shredded her heart beyond repair, and then, only a couple months before they were set to adopt a baby, Sofie discovered that she was quite unexpectedly pregnant again. I remember listening with my heart in my throat as she told me how afraid she was that she wouldn't be able to carry to term again. Add to that the concern of Addilyn's birth mother changing her mind about the adoption, since Sofie was already pregnant, and she'd been a mess. She'd sat on my couch, clutching one of the throw pillows and crying until her eyes were red and her face raw.

That day is in the past now, but it'll always be a part of Sofie's story, folded around the crevices of her heart as a reminder that things are rarely what they seem. Looking at Sofie today, you don't see how deep she had to dig to find her strength when it felt like none was left. Instead, you see an incredibly grateful woman who doesn't ever take her family for granted. And perhaps that *is* where you can catch a glimpse into what once was. There is, despite it all, an appreciation in my friend for the miracles she never thought she'd have. It makes me wonder: how would I react if I were in the situation she'd been in? Sofie and her husband Brandon banded together instead of letting life pull them apart. My parents hadn't been able to manage that. How about me? If Jonathan and I do get married, will we be solid enough to stay an unbreakable force, or will our foundation crumble under the pressure?

Much as I want to believe we can make it, I just don't know.

If anyone can help me figure it out, it's Sofie.

"So what's up?" she asks, after we're settled on her living room couch, right under the patch of sunlight angling in through the bay window. "You sounded really anxious when you called earlier. Is everything okay?"

"No. It should be, but it's not."

"Elaborate?"

I sigh. "How did you know Brandon was the one?" I ask.

Her smile is instantaneous. "It's simple," she says. "I didn't want to imagine my life without him in it. People always say they can't picture a world without the person they love, but it was different for me. I could clearly envision being away from him, but I just didn't want to." She glances down at her golden wedding band. "He made me feel like I could do anything, be anything. Like the universe would expand for us. Loving him was like coming home again. It still is." She touches me lightly on the arm. "Why do you ask?"

Here we go. Deep breath.

"Jonathan proposed yesterday." I wince as I see her smile start to grow, then freeze in place as she realizes there's no engagement ring on my hand. "I wasn't expecting it," I say. "You know how some people have an intuition about that sort of thing? I am clearly not one of them. He flipped my entire sense of ... of everything, honestly ... when he asked me to marry him."

"And you said no?"

There is a softness in the way she asks, a warmth that's full of curiosity, but free from judgment.

This is why I came here.

It's why I tell her everything, starting with the way I turned around to see Jonathan holding that exquisite ring and ending with how we had stayed on Stone Mountain until it was the last call to go back down before the park closed. Sofie listens intently, but her expression is unreadable. "What do you think I should do?" I ask her.

"Oh, Grace." She puts an arm around my shoulder and hugs me. "You know I can't answer that. This has to be your choice. I do think you should give yourself time, though. Don't feel pressured to decide right now. It should be organic. Intrinsic. At some point, you'll just know. But I will say this: I see the way he looks at you, like there's nobody else in the room. You might not realize it, but you look at him the same way."

"Is that enough, though? There are still so many things that could go wrong."

"And so many that could go right."

"I do *want* to say yes," I confess. "I want to build a life with him."

"That's a good first step."

"But what about the rest of the steps? I don't know where they lead."

"Maybe you don't have to."

I consider that.

I've never much believed in destiny or fate. I read about them in books and love to follow along with the characters, but when it comes to my own life, I have always thought it better not to let my daydreams float into the clouds. If ever there was a time to let my hope rise, it's now. If ever there was a person who could inspire me to take that chance, it's Jonathan.

I shake my head a little. "I'm so confused," I tell Sofie.

"And that's okay. You'll be confused, until suddenly you won't be anymore. One day, it'll all be crystal clear." She snaps her fingers. "Just like that." She leans forward a bit. "Hey, what did Josie and Abigail say? I bet they were a great sounding board. Your sisters are really good at sharing their opinions."

"Maybe a little too good," I say. "Which is why I actually haven't told them yet."

Her eyebrows go up. "Seriously?" she asks. "I know there's been some tension between you all lately, but I would've thought they'd still be the first ones you'd tell. After Brandon proposed, I was on the phone with my sister for a good fifteen minutes before she calmed down enough to put our parents on the line. I bet Abigail and Josie would be just as excited for you, and also just as willing to talk things through with you as I am."

I open my mouth to answer her, but am stopped by my cell phone pinging.

Once.

Twice.

Three times.

I pull it out from my purse to see a message from Josie in all capital letters.

OMG.

YOU HAVE TO CALL ME ASAP.

I HAVE A LEAD ON HENRY.

～8～

Rose

The *SS Harmony* was unlike anything I had ever seen. It was grandeur personified, this queen of the seas that reigned with complete confidence that she alone could take her passengers wherever they wanted to go. The deck was crowded as I walked on board, and I eased my way through all the people. I hoped to get back in time to watch the ocean liner slip out from the pier, to see the skyline of New York shrink as the vastness of water surrounding us grew, but first I wanted to take a look at my stateroom. I imagined it would be quite sophisticated.

Indeed, it was. There was a couch, the shade of blue that matched the water we would soon be sailing upon, and an array of paintings hanging on the wall above it. A square table sat in the middle of the room, a lovely vase of silk flowers in its center, and on the far wall were two portholes which doubled as windows. I walked over to unhook their latches. Air swept in from outside, so fresh and pure, and I just stood there for a minute to breathe it in.

I was here.

I was actually here.

It felt like I was living in a daydream as I left the portholes cracked open and went to explore the bedroom area, but then again, being on the ship also made everything incredibly tangible. The Rose I had been so desperate to leave behind in New York already seemed to be fading away. Aboard the *SS Harmony*, I had the opportunity to be anyone and do anything.

It was an intoxicating thrill.

This was the beginning of something. I did not know what

that something was, but as I shut the door to my room and started back toward the outer deck, I was both excited and relieved to realize that I did not have to figure it out right then. There was time, and I had nobody to answer to except myself, and perhaps the ship. It had such an imperial feel, almost as though it was challenging all its passengers to make the most of this journey and allow it to make the most of us.

"Impressive, isn't it?" asked a woman as I squeezed in next to her at the railing. She looked like she was around my mother's age, and as she reached up to fix her hat, I noticed the shiny diamond rings on her left hand. They paired perfectly with the black and white dress, the high heels, and the red nails that did not have a single chip in their cherry coat. This lady was the kind of person the SS Harmony typically saw on its decks. The tall man standing on her other side, who I assumed was her husband, oozed the same wealth and propriety.

I nodded pleasantly at them both. "Yes," I agreed. "Very impressive."

"We're here for our second honeymoon," the woman said, patting the man's arm. "Forty years of marriage, and we love each other more today than when we said our vows. I could barely believe it when he surprised me with this trip as an anniversary gift. Every woman should be so lucky as to find a life partner like my Joseph. He's the best."

I was not sure what to say. Listening to a stranger talk about her husband was a bit awkward. I knew that going on an ocean liner meant a chance to interact with many new people – that was part of its intrigue – but this was not exactly how I had imagined starting off. Perhaps that was the point, though. This trip was supposed to be the antithesis of what was expected, and I decided to embrace it. "Congratulations," I said. "What a marvelous way to celebrate an anniversary."

"I couldn't agree more. It's the – "

She was cut short by the captain's voice blaring over the

loudspeaker. "All ashore who are going ashore," he declared, and I felt a chill skate down my spine. This was it. In mere minutes, I would be off on what I hoped would be the greatest adventure of my life.

All around me, people were waving to their families and friends down below. It was so exciting that I thought my heart might beat out of my chest. The breeze kissing my face, the horn sending its signal up to the sky, the passengers cheering and clapping ... it was the closest to untouchable I had ever felt.

I had thought about this moment so often, wondering how I would react when the ship's engine sprang to life and we began to move. Closing my eyes to it, shutting out the rest of the universe and concentrating on the magnitude of what was happening, seemed like the natural choice. Now that it was a reality, though, I kept my eyes open. I wanted to see everything, hear everything, smell and touch and taste my very first minute of true freedom. It was an unbelievable rush, and it even made me emotional enough to pull a handkerchief from my pocketbook and dab at the tears beading atop my eyelashes.

This was beyond anything I could have imagined.

I kept my gaze focused on the cityscape as it slowly disappeared into the distance. Smaller and smaller it became, until eventually we were our own island in a sea of blue. Even then, after the rest of my fellow passengers started to disperse, I stayed on the deck. I was not ready to go inside yet. I thought of Violet, who had given me a diary to record all the starbursts of magic I uncovered, of Lucy and Alice, who had made me swear to write with updates about my travels, and of my parents, who had never even managed to say goodbye. I would miss them all, but I was pleased to find that I did not feel like an outcast on the ship. I was alone, something most people were not, but there was no loneliness. In fact, I realized, as I considered my life in Manhattan, perhaps the loneliest place to be was actually one where you were constantly in the midst of a crowd.

"Hits you right in the heart, doesn't it?"

The voice that startled me out of my thoughts was deep, but with a lilt which practically made it sound musical. I jumped a bit as I registered whom it belonged to, a man who was now standing at my side. He was taller than I was, his close-cropped curls a dark blonde and his eyes the color of rich cocoa. I noticed them immediately as I met his gaze. Where had he come from? Had I been so lost in my own reflections that I never even heard him approach?

"Henry," he said, extending his hand.

As soon as my fingers touched his, something tingled at the base of my neck. His grip was firm, but his skin was soft, and I lingered for a beat longer than I should have before pulling back. "Rose," I introduced myself.

When he smiled, two dimples created tiny half-moons in his cheeks. "Nice to meet you, Rose," he said. "I didn't mean to intrude. I just saw that you dropped this." He held out the handkerchief I had used to dry my tears.

"Thank you." I smiled, too, as I took back the handkerchief and tucked it away. "I suppose I was so mesmerized that I didn't even realize it had fallen. This is my first time on an ocean liner," I said, "and I simply cannot believe how extraordinary it is."

"I'll second that." He tossed me a look I could only describe as dazzling. This man might as well have been a film star. He was positively dreamy. "I travel often for work," he told me, "but usually by train or airplane. This is my first time on an ocean liner, too, and I can tell I'm going to enjoy it. If only all my work engagements were overseas." He curved his hands around the railing, and I could not help noticing how tanned his skin was, like he had been out in the golden sunshine for precisely the right amount of time. "And you?" he asked. "What brings you to the *SS Harmony*?"

How to answer that?

"Nothing in particular," I said, "and also everything that is important."

"Cryptic."

I laughed. "But true."

"That's a tall order to live up to," he said. "Everything that's important. I surely hope it doesn't disappoint." He glanced at the silver watch around his wrist. "I should get going, I'm afraid. I have a prior commitment. Perhaps I'll see you around, though?"

There he went again, with those dimples.

Something fluttered inside my chest. "Yes," I said softly. "I would like that."

I watched as he walked off, the soles of his shoes clicking smartly against the wooden boards of the deck. I hoped I would run into him again and have the chance to talk with him for longer. That was one of the things I wanted to get out of this journey: the opportunity to meet all types of people whose paths I would never normally cross, people who stepped outside their own shadows, who not only dreamed, but also took action to make those dreams come true. Maybe Henry was like that, or maybe not. I knew nothing about him, beside the fact that I wanted to know more. In the course of a single conversation, that man had captured my curiosity. It was a bit unsettling.

Not that it mattered. On a boat that carried so many, the odds of me actually finding him again were slim, like two ships passing in the night. I was certain that our interaction would be limited to this solitary encounter, which saddened me more than it should have. What was it about that man? Why had he made such an impression?

By the time I returned to my room, I had convinced myself that it was nothing more than the sea air making me feel so heady. The SS Harmony was sailing from the Hudson River into the welcoming embrace of the Atlantic, and, after all, there was not anything quite so romantic as the ocean. It was Mother Nature's greatest gift to us, this never-ending swath of blue that had the ability to make us feel big and small at the same time. I remembered the vacation my family had taken to the beach at Coney Island the year Violet and I turned eighteen. Standing at the water's edge, I had watched the sailboats glide gently by. It had made me feel as though I could do anything, the whole world sitting in the palm of my hand, but it had also been an important reminder: that even if I *did* do something, so, too, could all the billions of other people on the planet. Each of us was only one: one drop in the sea, one force to be reckoned with, one hope of making a difference.

I wanted my drop to count. I wanted it to make a splash.

I pondered that as I sat down on the sofa. I was tired. The night before had been sleepless, my mind too filled with anticipation to nestle itself into the cradle of quiet, and I knew it would be wise to take a nap before the ship's festivities got underway. There was a formal dinner that night, and a band playing in the lounge until long after the moon would become a light bulb in the sky. I planned to stay until the very last note. If I was going to do this whole living-out-loud thing, I was going to do it a hundred and ten percent.

I would sleep now so I could be well-rested later.

I closed my eyes, let the energy drain from my body, and waited for my thoughts to turn fuzzy. I waited, and waited, and waited some more. Finally, after it became obvious that sleep was elusive, I opened my eyes back up, reached for the suitcase closest to me, and took out the diary from Violet. Balancing it atop my legs, I turned to the first page and let my pen do the talking.

Sunday, July 10th, 1955

Well, we are off! The ship set sail with all the fanfare I expected. We are cruising on the Atlantic now, and I cannot wait to sit out on the deck and watch it. Speaking of the deck, I met an interesting man there earlier. His name is Henry, and it's bizarre: even though he was a complete stranger, I felt at ease with him instantly. He mentioned that he hoped to see me around, and I am hoping for that, too.

I paused for a second, fingers still wrapped around the pen.

Had I really just written that about a man?

This diary was supposed to be a record of the discoveries I

made, the experiences I created, the purpose I found. It was *not* meant to be a place where I babbled about a man who, even if I did see him again on the ship, would still be nothing but a brief blip on my radar. The boat would dock, and we would go our separate ways, never to find each other again. That would happen a lot while I was away. People would come into my orbit and spiral off just as quickly.

What else was to be expected?

Why was I so swept up in this one encounter?

I set the diary on the table and stood up to change for dinner. I had brought two fancy dresses, one a vibrant purple and the other an emerald that made my eyes look an entire shade deeper than usual. I opted for that one, accentuating it with pearl earrings and a matching necklace, and pulled my hair back on the sides with a set of pretty combs. Then I slipped my feet back into my heels and spun toward the door.

It was show time.

The dining room was big, an open and airy spaced filled with dozens of tables. Some were large and round, others set into booths that lined the walls. Music was drifting down from the speakers in the ceiling, and as I walked inside, a waiter passed by carrying a tray lined with wine glasses. It was an electric atmosphere: glitz and glamour, excitement and energy, light and luster. My eyes flicked to the left and the right, back and forth across the expansive, high-ceilinged, chandelier-lit room that was filled with happy people. There were white-haired couples, their wrinkles creating roadmaps on their faces, middle-aged couples like the one I had met earlier, and young couples, their faces bright with smiles as they held hands and stole kisses.

Everyone was paired up – everyone, it seemed, except me.

That is when I felt a gentle hand on my shoulder.

"Excuse me," said a voice from behind. "Can I interest you in sharing a table?"

Henry.

I knew it was him before I even turned around, and sure enough, when I did, his handsome face was only inches from mine. There was a gleam in his eyes as he gave a little half-bow. "So we meet again," he said, straightening back up. His cologne drifted toward me, musky like driftwood that had been left on the beach for a bit too long.

I raised an eyebrow. "What a coincidence," I said.

He winked. "I might have been keeping an eye out for you."

"Even so, how did you find me in this crowd?" I gestured around us.

"Easy," he said. "We can find anything we want to, if we only look hard enough."

It was a fascinating perspective. He was a fascinating person.

I caught his gaze and held it for a long moment. "Okay," I said. "I would be pleased to join you for dinner." A hostess motioned for us to follow her to a corner table, and when we arrived, Henry paused to pull out my chair. It was the type of thing I normally hated, a man automatically assuming I could not fend for myself. Both Violet and my mother always dismissed my complaint, assuring me it was just the polite thing for gentlemen to do, but it still made something bristle in my bones. I did not need someone who opened doors, or held my coat, or offered me his arm when crossing a busy street. I was capable of doing those things myself. With Henry, though, I did not feel the usual burn of indignation. I just felt happy. It was bizarre and unfamiliar ... but in a way that left me delightfully off-balance.

I was not ready to steady myself quite yet.

"So," I said, once he was seated across from me. "What shall we talk about?"

"Whatever you like. Anything. Everything."

That is exactly what we did. As the clock ticked on, its minute hand making one revolution after another, Henry and I breezed through many topics. "What's your favorite color?" I asked. "Favorite sport?"

"Green," he said, "because it reminds me of a baseball field. That should answer both questions at once." He grinned. "Have you ever been to Ebbets Field or Yankee Stadium? They are probably my two favorite places in the city."

"I haven't been," I said, "but perhaps someday. So you're from New York, then?"

"Maine, originally," he told me, and our conversation spun off in yet another direction. I learned that he had moved from the coast of Maine down to Manhattan fifteen years ago to attend college, that he had never used his history degree and chose to work as a jewelry salesman instead, and that one of his favorite things about his job was "seeing the beauty even inside the broken." I learned all that and more, and I reciprocated by elaborating on the real reasons I was on the *SS Harmony*. I did not think twice about telling him how suffocated and stifled I felt at home, how I had taken a chance on this trip in the hope of finding answers to the questions I was not even certain how to ask. I had never planned to speak those truths so quickly, but Henry was like a magnet who drew the honesty out of me without even trying.

"Wow," he said, letting out a low whistle. "You are one strong-willed woman."

I smiled. "Most people don't like that quality in a woman."

His dimples came out to play. "It's a good thing I'm not most people, then."

Slowly, he inched his hand across the tablecloth, and I found myself holding my breath until his fingers teased mine, delicately, tenderly, just the slightest caress, before retreating. It was part of a cat-and-mouse game that we played the whole night long. When the waiter brought dinner, Henry nudged his chair a little closer to mine. When we finished eating and the band began to turn up the noise, I grabbed Henry's hand and pulled him up to dance. When we went outside to the deck, after twirling until our hearts were tapping a two-step, I not only allowed Henry to slide his jacket around my shoulders, I also took a step closer to him as we stood by the railing and looked out at the gentle ocean.

The moon was shining brightly, casting a glow that made it look as though someone had turned on a light underneath the surface of the water. There was no horizon now, just a dark night sky that reached down to greet the waves. It was the sort of beautiful that made me immeasurably grateful to be on this earth to witness it ... the sort of beautiful I had dreamed of when I decided to take this journey in the first place. Maybe that's why I was feeling so daring, or maybe it had more to do with the wine warming my veins and the man warming the spot next to me. Either way, I could not seem to help myself. Every inhibition faded away. I turned to face Henry, rested my hand on the nape of his neck, and leaned into him, into the air between us that suddenly seemed like it held an electrical charge.

Then I kissed him.

∾ 9 ∾

Grace

By the time I leave Sofie's house an hour later, Josie has sent another four texts asking me to call her. It doesn't matter that I answered her initial one, questioning what was going on and telling her I'd be in touch as soon as I could. My sister has the patience of a child on Christmas morning. With her, it's like time becomes stuck in its hourglass and she wants to overturn the whole thing to get it out.

"Seriously," she huffs when I call. "Could you have possibly waited any longer? I *told* you it was too important to discuss through texting."

"Sorry," I say. "I was in the middle of something important, and – "

"Never mind. Come to Mom's, okay?"

She hangs up before I can ask what she's doing at our mother's house, let alone what that could have to do with Henry. I can't tell if she's annoyed or simply eager to share her breakthrough, and it makes me sad. Once upon a time, I could read my sisters like they were my favorite book. Now it's more of a challenge to see between the lines. And so I don't know what to expect when I pull up to my mother's split-level home. Josie's car, with its *All the World's a Stage* bumper sticker, is already there, and she has Mom's front door open before I can even place my key into the lock.

"You drive too slowly," she says, as she ushers me inside.

"No, I don't. I just happen to believe in obeying traffic laws."

She rolls her eyes. "Better watch it, or you'll turn into Abigail."

I can't help laughing. Abigail is the most careful, aware driver on the face of the earth. Her kids can be throwing a tantrum in the backseat and she still manages to never go a tick above the speed limit. She used to take me to practice driving when I was preparing to get my license, then we both went with Josie. I still remember the way Abigail gasped in horror the first time that Josie slammed the brakes to avoid sailing through a stop sign. From that moment on, whenever Josie approached an intersection, Abigail's foot would start pumping an imaginary brake. I'd found it hilarious. Josie, not so much.

"Speaking of Abigail," I say to her now, "is she joining us?"

Josie shrugs. "She's at one of Ben's soccer games. She said not to wait for her, because she had no idea how long it'd go, and then apparently the parents take the kids for pizza afterward. I guess even the health food queen lets her children have the good stuff every now and then." She shakes her head a bit. "It's probably better that she isn't here, because you know how she is. She'd never want to go along with the plan."

"What plan?"

A gleam appears in Josie's eyes. "Follow me," she says, and heads for the kitchen.

Our mom is fixing lunch at the counter. "Hi honey," she says, glancing up from the tomato she's dicing to smile at me. "Josie's been telling me about your mystery man."

"And she had a fab idea," Josie says. "Old school, but super smart." She waves her hand toward the table, where there's an open phone book. "All the times we teased her about tossing these and joining the rest of humanity in using the computer instead, and now it turns out this may be the key that unlocks our next clue. Check it out."

I take a seat at the table and lean forward to examine the long list of names printed on the page. "You couldn't have found Henry," I say. "We don't even know his last name."

"Nope. Not Henry, and not Ivy, either, but look at this." She grabs a pen and circles three of the names: Delia Wethersby, Jacob Wethersby, and Kendall Wethersby. "Obviously it's not a sure bet," she says. "But there's at least a chance that one of them is related to Ivy. Maybe they can point us in her direction." She flashes a grin so bright it reminds me of when she plays a character on stage. "Go on," she says. "You can thank me now."

"Thank you," I say dutifully. "I didn't realize you were still thinking about this."

"Yeah, well, occasionally I surprise people."

"Like your visit today," Mom says. "I was so happy to see you when I opened the door. Hey, do you girls have some time for lunch before you step into private investigator mode? I would love the company." She carries over three plates and a salad bowl.

I glance at Josie, and she nods. "Sure," she says.

I breathe a sigh of relief, because honestly, I was half expecting her to turn Mom down. It's rare for her to be in Georgia anymore, period, let alone here in the house we moved to after the divorce. She says it's because she has to go wherever the auditions take her, and I know that's part of it, but I think her breezing in and out of town also has a lot to do with not wanting to revisit the past. It has taken a lot of time and effort, but Abigail and I have been able to rebuild a closeness with Mom that was yanked away from us when she had to work so much after our father left. Josie isn't all the way there yet. She still hides behind that distance sometimes.

I get it. Mom worked fifteen hours a day to support our family after the divorce. She sacrificed a whole lot of herself so my sisters and I could have a good life. Even at a young age – my mom and dad split when Abigail was eleven, I was seven, and Josie was only four – I had realized it was Mom's way of dealing with things. She and Dad had broken each other's trust. There had been accusations of cheating and lying – and even though they'd been unfounded in the end, the chasm created had been too deep to claw their way out of, and really, I don't think they cared much to try at that point. When it came to my sisters and me, though,

I know Mom felt guilty about the lack of a father figure in our lives. As our monthly visits with him became something we could count on less and less, she tried to compensate by ensuring we wanted for nothing else. What she didn't realize was that we'd much rather have had her around. As painful as it was for Mom to be in the house where we'd once been a happy family, it was equally as scarring for us. Even when we moved to a new home, things were still tough.

It's strange: out of the three of us, Josie is the one who has the least memories of what life was like before our parents' marriage crumbled. And yet she's the one who resents it most. I swear it's why she can never seem to find a relationship that lasts longer than the run of one of her shows and why she often doesn't even tell our mom when she is floating through town on the way to her next destination. But not today. Today, she seems glad to be here. She tells us all about her most recent auditions as we have lunch, and is in the middle of a story about a play that required her to speak in a British accent, when there's a knock on the door.

A few seconds later, Abigail's voice drifts through the house. "It's only me," she calls. "I thought I might startle you if I came right in." She walks into the kitchen, clad in jeans and a purple cardigan. "Scott took Ben to the pizza lunch," she says. "He just brought Macy along. That way I can be here for ... " She looks at Josie. "What, exactly? You said you had news about Henry?"

We bring her up to speed.

"I can make the phone calls," I offer. "Since I'm the one who found the letter."

"Phone calls?" Josie scrunches her nose. "That's boring. Why don't we check it out in person?"

"You just want to go to their houses?" Abigail asks.

"Why not?" she says. "It's a hell of a lot easier to hang up on people than it is to shut a door on them."

She does make a good point. Plus, it will take more time to drive around and find these people than it will to pick up a phone and see if they answer. Usually I'm all for efficiency, but today I really have no desire to go home. Once I do, I'll spiral right back into thinking about Jonathan's proposal. For now, I'd rather keep it tucked into its own compartment in my mind, where I can pull it out from whenever I'm ready.

I look at Josie.

Abigail.

Our mother.

I could tell them about it. All it'd take is one quick release to let them in. Maybe I shouldn't be worried about my sisters' responses. How many times, after all, have we confided in one another? When we were younger, there were so many pinky swears in the bedroom and whispers in the dark, long after we were supposed to be asleep. We had always been the fiercest keepers of each other's secrets.

I want it to be like that again, but at the same time, I'm not sure it can be.

We're too different now. Life just insists on coming between us.

My mom would be supportive, I know, but at the same time, how can I possibly tell her that the divorce is one of the main things preventing me from giving Jonathan an answer? It seems unfair to place that burden on her, especially when we've been having such a nice lunch. And so, when Josie asks what we're thinking, all I say is "Okay. Let's do it."

We turn to look at Abigail, who purses her lips for what feels like forever. Then she sighs. "Fine, but for the record, I think it's a mistake. I wouldn't get my hopes up if I were you."

I know she's right, so as we climb into her minivan, with its seats that are somehow totally free from the toys and crumbs and other assorted paraphernalia that usually go along with having young children, I try to temper my anticipation and focus on something else. "How'd the soccer game go?" I ask Abigail, as she checks in both directions – and then does it again – before backing out of Mom's driveway.

"Let me guess," Josie says. "Ben's the star of the team."

"Well ... " Abigail laughs. "I don't know about that. He does run toward the ball now, instead of away, so I'd say he's at least making some progress. You should come to one of his games sometime when you're home. I know he'd love that. He and Macy are always asking for you. I'm fairly certain they think their aunt is actually Princess Jasmine."

Of all Josie's roles, that one, her most recent, has been her biggest. It was her first time playing one of the leads rather than being an ensemble member. The stage version of Aladdin had been put on by a theater company in Nashville, and we'd piled into Abigail's minivan to go see Josie perform. Ben and Macy were enthralled, and so was I, in a way – watching my sister shine on the stage made my heart burst with pride. Josie is exasperating sometimes, the way she lives on whims and wishes, but when she's in front of an audience, so alive and in the moment, it's really an incredible thing to behold.

I wish I could get her and Abigail to understand that The Book Boutique makes me feel the same way. "You know," I say, as Abigail turns out of our mom's neighborhood, "I have some fairy tales at the bookstore the kids might love, if they're into Aladdin. You should bring them by sometime and I'll show them how exciting it is in the store."

"Is it, really?" Josie says. "Seriously, I'm not asking this to start a fight. I sincerely want to know. What is it about The Book Boutique that makes it exciting? Why would someone want to shop there instead of going to one of the bigger stores or just buying online? Because the way I see it, the only thing we have to offer them is a higher price."

Immediately, irritation flares up inside my chest. Here we go again.

"That's the way you see it," I say quietly, evenly, forcing myself to keep my annoyance in check, "because you never stick around long enough to experience the rest of it. Neither of you do. You're right, we can't offer prices as low as other places. We don't always get the new releases on the day they come out, and our selection isn't as extensive as it could be if the store were bigger. But we do have customers we've known for decades. They've seen us go from the girls who would help shelve books to the women who have made lives for ourselves. And we get to watch their lives unfold, too. There's the couple who actually got married in the store, because it's where they met during a story time twenty years ago. There's the family with three kids who always have their birthday parties in the store, and the man who used to visit every day after his wife walked out on him just two weeks after their wedding. He found comfort in our books, and he isn't alone. People don't only come to the Book Boutique to shop. They come to learn, and grieve, and hope, and dream. It's important to them. It's important to me."

I pause for a breath.

"Geez," Josie says. "That was quite a speech. And you're supposed to be the quiet sister."

I *am* the quiet one, wedged between two presences that often overshadow mine. Normally I'm cool with that. I've found that people end up hearing you better when you speak softly rather than shout. Right now, though, all I can think about is defending the store that is so much more than just a business to me. "Listen," I say, "I know you both want out. But can you please give it until March? That'll be the store's twenty-sixth anniversary. If we can't turn things around by then, I won't stand in your way."

It's a risky statement to make.

Four and a half months might seem like an eternity to Abigail and Josie, but I know they'll fly by. Four and a half months to pull our sales numbers back up to what they were in the shop's heyday, to convince people that sometimes experience can be better than convenience, to invent new ways to compete in a marketplace that's ever-expanding. Truthfully, I don't know that it can be done. Gram and Pop-Pop would've tried, though. If they were alive today, they would've stopped at nothing to give The Book Boutique a fighting chance.

I remind my sisters of that. "Our grandparents poured everything into that place," I say. "Their hearts and souls, their money, their time. Over twenty years of their lives were dedicated to turning the store into a home away from home for its customers. The least we can do is give it until March. And hey, you don't even have to be involved. I'm not asking you to drop everything and come work with me. We'll keep it the same as always."

"No."

Abigail's swift answer makes me bristle. After that impassioned plea, she can't even give me the respect to consider it for more than ten seconds?

But then she surprises me.

"It's not fair to keep things as they are," she says. "Not if we're expecting a different outcome. I'll agree to wait it out until March, but I'd also like to be more hands-on." She pauses for a second to listen to the GPS as it directs her to turn onto a street in nearby Kennesaw. "I don't have time to help with the daily running of the store," she says, after putting on her blinker, "but I'll make myself available to work on finding solutions."

A rush of gratitude washes over me. This is the Abigail I used to know, the one who was always there to bolster up her sisters when we needed it. So much of that has been lost lately, fading into the disagreements and the different points-of-view, but maybe, just maybe, it's on its way to being found again.

Maybe we're all on our way to that.

God, I hope so.

"Josie?" I ask. "Are you in?"

There's a long silence, too long, and my hopes dip back down. I assume she's trying to think of a way to say no. Finally, though, she twists around to look at me from the passenger seat. "Alright," she says, the diamond stud in her nose glittering as it catches the sunlight. "I really still think this is a sinking ship, but if it's that important to you, what's another few months?"

Something warm curves around my heart.

Maybe I've been underestimating my sisters. Maybe we've been shortchanging each other. We always used to band together when the going got tough. For the first time in awhile, I have faith we can do it again.

"Thank you," I say. "Truly. You have no idea how much this means to me."

I think they do, though.

I think it's why they went against their better judgment and agreed.

Four and a half months.

We will plug the holes in that ship. I am determined. We will make it happen. First, though, it's time to make something else happen. Abigail is creeping down the street, peering at the addresses as we look for a house belonging to the first Wethersby on our list: Delia. We finally get to it at the end of the block. It's a cute place with blue shutters, a bird house hanging from a tree out front, and a vegetable garden planted by the side.

"Here goes nothing," Abigail says, as we get out of the car.

"Or everything," Josie contends. "Maybe it's everything."

We head up the walkway, and it occurs to me: maybe Henry is right here, inside this very house. It's unlikely, but who knows, real life is indeed often stranger than fiction. The thought of it makes a bolt of energy zip through my veins. How awesome would it be, to meet the man who penned such a touching letter? I'd like to return it to him. Words that precious belong with their author.

But he isn't at this house.

"I'm sorry," Delia says, after we've rung the bell and explained the story to her. "I don't know a Henry or an Ivy. Wethersby is my married name, and all of my husband's relatives live in California. We only moved here for his job."

Abigail, Josie, and I have no luck at Jacob's house, either –

or what was once his house. The man who refuses to open the door and only calls out to us says his name is Paul and he bought the place six months ago. That's the problem with phone books: they're so obsolete now that even my mom's most recent edition is two years old. Things have changed since then, clearly.

On to the next – and final – possibility.

It's a cheerful looking house in Sandy Springs, with a rainbow of fall flowers blooming out front and a welcome mat by the door. The windows are open and classical music drifts out. It sounds like someone playing a violin. I hate to interrupt, but when I look at my sisters, they both motion for me to ring the bell. The music stops abruptly, and I can hear footsteps growing louder before the door swings open. Standing before us is a young woman, perhaps in her early twenties or so, her auburn hair twisted into a messy topknot and her brown eyes curious.

"Can I help you?" she asks.

"I hope so." I give her my most friendly smile. "My name's Grace, and these are my sisters Josie and Abigail. We're trying to track someone down, and our search led us here. Do you know anyone by the name of Kendall Wethersby?" I ask. "Or Ivy?"

She narrows her eyes, like she isn't sure whether she should trust me, so I explain all about the letter and the book I found it in. When I mention that it was dropped off in July, by someone named Ivy, her face relaxes.

"Indeed I do know her," she says. "She's my mother."

～10～

Rose

*I*t was like being a heroine in a romance picture.

I saw Henry's eyebrows lift in surprise as I grazed my mouth against his, but he did not pull back. Instead, he circled his arm around my waist, his fingers resting ever-so-lightly atop my hip bone, and used his other hand to tuck my hair behind my ear as the sea breeze ruffled it against his cheek. His kiss was sunshine on my skin and inside my soul, spilling over everything, everywhere. I wanted it to never end.

"Wow," I whispered, when we finally broke apart.

Henry trailed his fingers down my arm, and it made tiny goosebumps rise to the surface. "That was most definitely a wow," he said, staring at me so intensely it felt as though the air was catching in my windpipe. Kissing this man had literally left me breathless. There were other people outside, perhaps like us, not wanting the night to slip away just yet, but they faded when I met Henry's gaze. For me, there was no one except us.

"I'm sorry," I said. "I'm not usually that forward."

A smile flickered on his face. "Well, I am most glad you decided to change that."

A laugh escaped me and spiraled toward the stars. There were so many glittering up above that night, and I swore, the longer we were outside, the more of them appeared. "Have you ever wished on a star?" I asked Henry. "When I was a child, my twin sister and I would look out the window and try so hard to spot them. It never happened, since we were in the city, but we always talked about what we'd wish for if we ever got the chance."

"And what did you choose?"

I lifted my gaze to the sky. The stars reminded me of dozens of tiny diamonds resting against a deep, dark velvet backdrop. "Oh, lots of things," I said. "A puppy, a backyard where we could have a swing-set and enough space to really turn my mother's flower garden into something terrific, a car so my father could drive us around." I smiled at the memories. "Of course, there were also wishes like new hair bows and bicycles with streamers tucked into the handlebars. Our parents must have heard us talking about that one, because they surprised us with them the Christmas we were eight. Mine was pink and Violet's was purple."

"Pink for Rose," Henry said. "And purple for Violet."

I nodded. "Exactly."

"How about now?" he asked. "If you were to make a wish tonight, what would it be?"

I considered it.

The list of things I hoped to get from my trip seemed never-ending, and yet, none of it alone was what I would ask the universe for, if I only had one chance. "Joy," I said finally. "The kind of joy that wraps itself around you so you know it will always be there, even if you lose sight of it. The kind that makes you feel at peace. The kind that convinces you miracles are real. What about you?" I asked. "What would your wish be?"

He tilted his head to the side, thinking. "As a child," he said, "it would have been something like a horse, or a scooter, or one of those kits to make a toy airplane ... anything involving motion, really. I was always on the go, especially after my brother James was born. Our parents used to joke about not being able to keep us in one place for longer than a minute."

"Why your college degree in history, then?" I asked. "It surprises me. Not that it's all textbooks and research, of course, but I imagine a good portion is. That sounds like the polar opposite of what you would want." The second the words were out of my mouth, I regretted them. How absurd was it for me to make an assumption about what he would want? I barely knew him.

Thankfully, Henry did not seem bothered by my comment. "Sometimes plans change," he said, cupping his hands around the ship's railing and staring into the night. "Sometimes people change." There was something in his voice that stopped me from asking more, a sadness I wanted to bar from what had been a lovely night. Henry must have been on the same wavelength, because he swiveled around to face me and his impish grin returned. "If I were to make a wish now," he said, "it'd be to kiss you again."

Warmth flooded my cheeks.

Oh, how this man made me swoon.

This was not how I was supposed to be spending my time away. I had hoped to find myself, not a man. I thought of the way I stood in Violet's apartment, explaining why I so desperately needed to put New York both out of sight and out of mind. Life had felt fuzzy, undefined, and I was confident it would come into focus on this trip. I wanted that. So what was I doing with Henry? I was proud of my independence. I wore it as a badge of honor, not one of shame like other people saw it as, and I simply refused to let anyone steal that away, even this incredibly dreamy man who made me feel as though all the world was aglow.

Yet, I simply could not help myself.

When Henry brushed his hand against my cheek, I did not step away.

When he asked if it was okay, I nodded.

When he skated his lips over mine, all I could do was kiss him back.

I could not shake the tingly feeling he gave me. Even after he walked me back to my room and I invited him in to play a game of cards – which turned into multiple games as we talked long into the night – the feeling persisted. It was like butterflies. That was how Violet described the way Thomas made her feel, and I had never truly understood what she meant until that moment. The men I had dated before never affected me in that manner. Henry made me feel more strongly in one day than those other men had over the course of weeks, even months in some cases.

I climbed into bed after he left, reached for the diary on my nightstand, and flipped open to the next blank page.

Monday, July 11th, 1955, 2:00AM

I should be asleep now.

After hardly getting any rest last night and failing at taking a nap in the afternoon, I have no idea how my eyes can possibly be open at this point. I suppose my mind is racing too quickly to grant me any quiet just yet. It was a simply marvelous evening with Henry, and I should be happy about that – I am happy about it – but I am also so confused. When I stepped onto this ocean liner, I was ready to jump at full-force into something bigger than myself. It was supposed to be about my self-discovery. Why, then, can I not get Henry out of my thoughts?

I cannot fight my attraction to him, and I do not necessarily want to, anyway. The chemistry we share is unlike anything I have felt. It is scary, terrifying even, to imagine that everything I thought I knew could be flipped upside down in the space of one day. It is like something opened up inside me, a compartment in my heart I never realized was there. Henry makes me feel ... more. I wonder if I do the same for him.

I set the pen down, my eyelids heavy now that my thoughts had tumbled onto the page. That is how I fell asleep: the diary spread open on the bed beside me and the ocean lulling me into dreams that were filled with hazy images of stars and gardens and wishes come true. It was not until there was a knock on my stateroom door the next morning that those dreams faded around their edges. I yawned as I sat up in bed, blinking the grogginess from my eyes before walking out to the main area and over to the door. "Who's there?" I asked.

"Room service," a voice called merrily. "I come bearing breakfast and your daily newspaper."

Henry.

It made me smile, just hearing him.

"Room service, hmm?" I asked. "Do they even have that on ocean liners? Either way, I'm afraid I didn't order anything. You must have the wrong passenger."

"Let's see: fun-loving woman with hazel eyes and auburn hair. The prettiest dame on the whole ship. Fantastic dancer and an even better kisser." This made my face flush. I could not believe that he actually said those words out loud. People simply did not do that. It was refreshing, though, and exhilarating. Henry seemed to march to the beat of his own drum, and I liked the rhythm it created. "So what do you think?" he asked, and I could hear the amusement in his voice. "Do I still have the wrong passenger, or did I get it right?"

"One minute," I said, "and then you'll find out."

I hurried over to my suitcase and quickly exchanged my nightgown for a dress and a flowy scarf I had bought from my favorite clothing shop in Manhattan. There was no time to re-curl my hair, so I just ran my brush through it and dabbed on a touch of make-up before making my way back over to the door. Henry was still standing there when I opened it. He had my copy of the ship's newsletter tucked under his arm, a fresh muffin in one hand, and a flower in the other.

"A rose for Rose," he said, giving it to me. "I would have loved to buy you a real flower, but this silk one from the vase in my room is the best I can do today."

"This is pretty, too," I said, holding the door open so he could come inside. "Thank you. Its color reminds me of the ones my mother grows. She has a beautiful little garden outside on the balcony of the townhome where I grew up. Violet and I used to help her tend to it when we were children. I always enjoyed it so much. It's what inspired my own love of flowers."

He sat down on the couch, and placed the newspaper and muffin on the table. "What are your favorites?" he asked.

"Oh goodness, it's impossible to choose. Sunflowers, perhaps, because there's something truly cheerful about them, or baby's breath, since it's so delicate." I sat down next to him. "I also have a special fondness for ivy. It's probably one of the most unique varieties there is. Do you know it can actually produce flowers? Sometimes it takes ten years. Isn't that wild?"

"Pretty neat," he agreed.

"Really, though," I told him, "I love all flowers. I have so many wonderful memories of our times on the balcony. Sometimes, when we were working out there, Violet would tell our mother that we had rainbows in our hands. I can still hear my mother saying we should cradle those rainbows close, and then set them free."

"But not anymore?" Henry asked. "You said you felt stifled at home, especially by your parents and their opinions. When did that change?"

I shook my head a little. "It's bizarre," I said. "She was so adamant about wanting us to hold all our possibilities, to cultivate them like she did with her flowers, yet when I did that, she balked even at the mention of it. I guess she only wanted her preferred seeds to grow roots." It occurred to me then: it was like the sad, but inevitable truth of planting too many flowers too close together. They would not all bloom. The ones that lost the competition for sunlight and water would never make it to their fullest potential. I wished my mother, who was always so very particular about situating her seedlings so that did not happen, could have realized she was trying to inflict the same thing on me. "Do you ever feel like you're playing catch-up?" I asked Henry. "Like life is dashing off and you have to run to keep up?" I turned to look at him. "Or perhaps it's different for men. Do people give you grief for still being single at your age?

His gaze flicked to the ring finger on his left hand. "I do think it's a very different expectation for men," he agreed. "Not that there is no pressure, it's just ... I hate to say it, but people seem to think it's more of a necessity for a woman. I happen to find that ridiculous, by the way. We should all get to dictate our own lives."

Even if I had not already been falling for him, his feelings on that subject would have earned my admiration.

"Thank you," I said, "for being one of the few people to see it that way."

He smiled. "My mother always taught me that everyone should be treated equally." Something shifted in his eyes for a beat, a cloud that lingered momentarily before drifting off. As soon as it did, he cleared his throat and picked up the newsletter from the table. "What's on today's agenda?" he asked.

It was an abrupt change of subject, but I went with it. Curious as I was about what had caused a shift in his mood, I did not want to push. We had already delved into some pretty deep subjects for having met less than twenty-four hours earlier. Perhaps it would be good to lighten it up. "There's a ping-pong tournament beginning at noon," I said, reading over his shoulder. "Shuffleboard at two o'clock ... bridge at four ... the band is playing by the pool in the afternoon ... " I glanced at him. "Do you want to be partners for a tournament? Are you good at any of the activities?"

"All of them." He winked. "Stick with me, Rose, and you can't lose."

That was, I came to realize as the day went on, a complete lie.

Henry was quite possibly the worst ping-pong player I had ever seen. He missed hitting the ball at least three-quarters of the time, and when he did manage to make contact, it either crashed into the net or went careening off in the distance. One particularly wild shot whizzed by our opponents' heads and smacked straight into the wall behind them. We were paired against a husband and wife who might as well have been the same person, that is how in tune they were. I returned the ball as they sent it flying over, and for awhile Henry just watched, his mouth slightly agape as we went back and forth. Then, right when it seemed as though the other couple's arms might be getting tired, the husband hit the ball directly toward Henry. "I got it!" he called, and for the first time, he hit the ball over the net and onto our opponents' side of the table. It would have been a perfect move ... if not for the fact that Henry's paddle flew from his hand and arced through the air before clattering to the ground.

I could not help it. I burst into giggles.

He planted his hands on his hips. "Are you laughing at me?"

"No," I managed to spit out, but he just raised his eyebrows and made me giggle harder. "Okay, yes. I am. I'm sorry, it's just that ... did you *see* the way that paddle tore across the room?" This set me off again. It was a deep laughter, the kind that burst from my soul, and by the time we gave up and forfeited to our opponents, I had tears streaming down my face.

I could not even remember the last time I had laughed like that.

"You lied to me," I said, playfully swatting Henry's arm. "Ping-pong is not your forte."

"No," he conceded. "I just wanted to impress you. But you had fun, right?"

I looked at him for a minute, really looked at him, and I wondered – was my fascination with him my way of overcompensating? I had been so resolute about not needing a man in my life, but what if my mother's comments had impacted me more than I realized? Was this – well, whatever it was – with Henry a reaction to that? I searched his face, those warm brown eyes and the smile that held a touch of mystery in its curve.

No, I did not think so at all.

I was my own woman, and the connection I felt with Henry was only because of him, because of us. Nothing else factored into it. I enjoyed being with Henry because he made me feel lighter, freer, as though my feet did not quite touch the ground. It was like

I was floating above the expectations that the Earth, and everyone on it, had to offer.

"Yes," I said reaching for Henry's hand, "I had a lot of fun."

He made a move to take my hand, too, but before his fingers could close around mine, a man in a white uniform strode over to join us. "I'm sorry to interrupt," he said, "but you're Henry Jackson, correct? I need you to come with me."

∾ 11 ∾

Grace

*J*vy's daughter.

A smile stretches across my face. After striking out at the first two houses, I'd been beginning to think this entire endeavor was a lost cause. Now, though, as Ivy's daughter gestures for us to have a seat on the porch swing to our right, my commitment to finding Henry redoubles. I notice, as we sit down, that the swing's blue cushion is accented with pillows featuring outlines of what seems to be the New York City skyline. My curiosity is piqued. Porch swings are such a quintessentially Southern thing. Where does New York fit in?

"This is Manhattan, right?" I ask, motioning to the pillows.

She nods as she settles, cross-legged, into one of the wicker chairs by the swing. "Sure is," she says. "My family is from New York. My parents still live there, actually." She gestures at the house. "This is my older brother Kendall's place. I'm just housesitting this weekend while he's out of town. Oh, I'm Lily. Don't think I mentioned that."

"It's nice to meet you," Abigail says. "Thanks for agreeing to talk with us."

"We're safe," Josie adds, holding up her hands in a show of innocence. "I swear."

Lily laughs. "Yeah, I figured." She turns to me. "I've been to The Book Boutique a few times, so once you made that connection, I realized you look familiar. I love the place, by the way. It was one of the first stores I discovered after I moved here for college six years ago." She grins. "Well, after I followed my brother here six years ago. He moved down to Atlanta for work and I loved it so much I wouldn't consider going to college anywhere else. I'm even staying for grad school now. Anyway," she says, "my mom was here in July to bring us some stuff from our grandmother's house. She just moved into a retirement community and had to get rid of a lot because there wasn't any room for it. When I saw the big carton of books, I told my mom about your store. I had no idea about the letter, and I'm sure she didn't, either."

"I'll get it back to you," I promise. "It's in my desk at home for safekeeping. In the meantime – " I scroll through the photos on my phone until I get to the one I snapped of Henry's letter. "Here you go." I turn the phone around to show Lily. "Is your grandmom the person he was writing to?" I ask. "Did she forgive him? Were they able to travel Europe together?"

Abigail leans forward a little. "You'll have to forgive Grace," she says, shooting me a look. "She doesn't mean to pepper you with questions."

A blush creeps into my cheeks. "No," I say. "I don't. I'm sorry if that's how it came across."

Lily flits her hand in the air. "No worries. I get it. And to answer your question, yes, Henry was definitely writing to my grandmother. Her name is Rose, and they met out on the deck of the ocean liner. Henry Jackson, with dimples that made her melt and strength that won her heart. That's how she describes him, even to this day. They had a whirlwind of a romance, that larger-than-life, drunk-on-each-other kind of connection. They couldn't get enough of it, as you probably figured out from that letter. But I think a love like that is hard to maintain. The flame that burns brightest will often extinguish itself first, you know?"

"So they didn't stay together?" Josie asks. She sounds disappointed.

I am, too. If Henry and Rose didn't make it, if a love like theirs, so big and bold, couldn't survive, then how can I expect Jonathan and I to beat the odds? Maybe I should have turned him down right away. It's not fair to leave him hanging if I'm only going to cut the thread and send our relationship into a free-fall.

But then Lily says something completely surprising. "Honestly, I'm not sure what happened with my grandmother and Henry," she tells us. "She'll talk for hours about her time on the *SS Harmony*, but it's like she shuts down when she gets to a specific point. She says the day they docked over in England was one of the toughest of her life, but if you ask for details, she just says some stories are better left in the heart, where they're safe and protected. We never feel right pushing."

"Aren't you curious, though?" Josie asks.

"Of course," Lily says. "But I don't want to upset her. If she prefers to leave Henry in the past, I respect that." She leans forward, resting her elbows on her knees. "I hoped she'd finally open up to us when we were packing her house for the move. Kendall and I flew up to help, and it seemed like whatever we put into a box had a memory attached. It took forever," she says, "because she'd want to tell us about every single thing. I think it was difficult for her, saying goodbye to her house, even though she was moving right next door to her sister at the retirement community. My grandmom is a twin," she tells us. "And they are super close. My Great Aunt Violet is probably the only one who knows about what went down with Henry, but she isn't talking, either."

"It must be great to have a twin," I say. "Someone you can always rely on."

"Grandmom says it's like having a built-in forever friend."

A built-in forever friend.

That sounds nice.

I glance to the left at my sisters and am met with their gazes staring back.

None of us says anything. None of us needs to.

We do talk to Lily for awhile longer, though, and we learn a little more about her grandmother. She tells us that Rose is a vibrant woman, with a laugh that'll make everyone else join in and a talent in bridge that is unmatched by anyone who tries to challenge her. Even at ninety-one-years-old, she still likes to go for long walks and volunteer with a local charity that beautifies area parks by planting flowers. Her favorite thing is to sit near the water at the lake house Lily's parents own, and she even joins them out on their boat every now and then. The more Lily talks about her, the more I can tell how much she adores her grandmother.

I can see why. Rose seems terrific. She reminds me of my own Gram, actually, particularly with the volunteer work. When my sisters and I were younger, Gram insisted we choose a cause and get involved. Helping others was what life was meant for, she told us, and it stuck. Even now, the three of us all have a charity near and dear to our heart. Abigail dedicates time every month to a women's shelter, Josie volunteers with theater groups for underprivileged kids, and ever since I met Jonathan, I have discovered a passion for animal rescue. I wonder why Rose picked the charity she did. Does she have a special interest in flowers? She must, since her daughter and granddaughter have floral names. Does that also have something to do with Henry, or did he only factor in to one tiny slice of her life?

I guess we'll never know.

Not if you ask Josie, though.

"Okay," she says, taking out her phone the moment we're back in Abigail's car. "Henry Jackson. Let's see what we can dig up on you, Sir." She begins tapping at the screen, but before she can pull anything up, Abigail reaches out and snatches the phone. The look on Josie's face is comical – with the wide-as-saucer eyes and the o-shaped mouth, she seems like a cartoon version of herself. "Uh, what do you think you're doing?" she says to Abigail.

"What do you think *you're* doing?" Abigail retorts.

"Looking up information on Henry. Obviously."

"Did you not hear a word Lily said?"

Josie grabs the phone back. "Of course I did. What does that have to do with anything?"

"She made it pretty clear that Rose doesn't want to talk about what happened with him," Abigail says.

"Which is why we aren't asking Rose."

Abigail glances at me in the rearview mirror. "Want to help me out here?"

I'm torn. On the one hand, I'm all for doing some research on Henry now that we know his last name. On the other hand, I am not too comfortable with the idea of going against Rose's wishes. If she doesn't even want her own family to hear the truth, then what gives a trio of strangers the right to pry? I think of the fights my parents used to have before the divorce. I know they'd both cringe if people were clued into the horrible things they said to each other. What goes on in a relationship is supposed to be private. It's not right to crack the window open and let others peek inside. And yet ... it isn't like we are going to type in Henry's name and gain access to the intimate moments he and Rose shared. The most we are likely to find is some cursory information.

"I'm not going to be the one to do the actual searching," I say. "But I also won't steal the phone if Josie wants to try."

Abigail gives a little harrumph. I imagine it must be the way she responds to her children if they do something after they're expressly asked not to. She doesn't make a play for Josie's phone again, though. "Fine," she says. "If you want to invade their privacy, that's on you, but don't tell me what you find."

"Spoilsport," Josie says, and starts typing on her phone again. We all fade into silence as Abigail drives. It's too quiet. I guess Abigail thinks so too, because she presses the button for the CD player. Seconds later, a high-pitched, overly enthusiastic voice pumps out of the speaker, followed by three more. There's a twangy guitar in the background and a loud horn section, providing a soundtrack to a song about brushing teeth, fastening buttons, and tying shoes. It's enough to make even Josie pop out of her annoyance and crack a smile.

"Sorry," Abigail says. "This is Macy's new favorite song. She insists I play it on repeat. It's called 'Dress Yourself, 1-2-3,' by the Giggly Wigglies. Clearly, it has a Grammy Award in its future."

"How do you not want to tear your hair out, listening to this stuff?" Josie asks.

"Oh, I do." Abigail swiftly turns the dial to switch from the CD to the radio. "But sometimes it's just easier to let the kids have their way. I've learned to pick my battles. Giving in a little often gets me a lot."

"A lot of headaches, maybe," Josie quips.

"Wait until you have children," Abigail says. "You'll understand."

"Honestly," Josie says, "I don't even know if I want children … not that it matters, seeing as how I'm not exactly doing a bang-up job finding a man who has a prayer of being father material. Always the fling, never the relationship." A sliver of frustration curls around her voice. "Whatever. It'd be boring if everyone were the same. I'm cool with my life the way it is."

"Are you, really?" I ask. "Because if not, you know you have the power to change it, right? Any man would be lucky to have you in his life. Maybe you just need to start looking for the ones who'll recognize that."

"Eh." She shrugs. "I'm not sure there are any."

"There absolutely are," I say. "Remember when Will left me to go back to his college girlfriend? I was convinced that all men were scum. You two came over, and I think we went through an entire carton of Rocky Road ice cream. I was miserable, and it was the same thing after Drew took that job in Singapore. But look at me now. Being with Jonathan has made me realize that sometimes we've got to date the wrong men so we'll know when we've found the right one." The words tumble from my mouth without hesitation. I pause for a second, caught off-guard by their truth. Jonathan *is* the man for me. He's my one-in-a-million, my partner and my friend, my chance at lasting love, if only I can convince myself to grab on and never let go.

I look at Abigail and Josie.

They could persuade me to do that – or they would try their hardest, anyway.

Maybe that's what I need.

Instead of shrinking away from my sisters' responses to the proposal, perhaps I should embrace it and let them give me the courage I can't seem to find on my own. I think of what Sofie said earlier in the day: "Don't feel pressured to decide right now. It should be organic. Intrinsic." Can it still be those things if I allow my sisters' opinions to play a role, or will it instead turn into a ball which rolls away from me with increasing speed? This is *my* future here. Do I want it to be influenced by other people, even if they're my sisters?

All my life, I've heard "This is what Abigail would do," and "Josie would handle things this way." I know my method is a little less direct, filled with a confusing web of paths instead of a singular one, but I don't think that makes it any less valid.

Tell them.

Don't tell them.

Which should it be?

Abigail is talking now, relaying the often-told story of how she was already thirty by the time she met Scott in the produce section of the grocery store. It would be easy for me to interrupt, but this conversation is supposed to be about helping Josie. I decide it's best to hold off on all the proposal discussion. Instead, I listen as Abigail goes on and on about love being an algorithm – how the other parts of our lives have to add up before that makes it into the equation.

"I don't know," Josie says.

"I do," Abigail counters. "It makes complete sense. We have to be sure of ourselves before we can be sure of someone else."

Hmm. She makes a good point.

"I *am* sure of myself," Josie declares.

"True," I chime in. "In fact, I don't think there's anyone more confident than Josie."

"Thank you." She turns around to smile at me. "I knew you were my favorite sister."

"Ha, ha," Abigail says. "That's incredibly funny."

"I thought so. But enough about it. I'm supposed to be concentrating on Rose and Henry's epic romance, not my lack thereof." She returns her focus to her phone, and not even five minutes later, she pumps her fist in triumph. "Who's the queen of the Internet? That'd be yours truly, thank you very much."

"You found something?" I ask her.

"Check it out," she says, passing me the phone. "You know, since Abigail wants no part of it."

From the driver's seat, Abigail shakes her head but says nothing.

She is so stubborn.

I take Josie's phone. She's pulled up what seems to be a program for a fundraising event held by a horticultural society in New York. There's a list of all the donors, along with the amount of money they contributed. Right at the top?

Henry Jackson.

"There's obviously a chance it isn't him," Josie says. "It's a pretty common name. But it *is* from New York – "

"And it has to do with flowers," I add. "Which makes it seem like more than just a coincidence, don't you think?"

"Look at the date of the event, though," she says.

I do.

July 2005.

Even if this is a real lead, it's more than eleven years old.

I slide my finger along the screen of Josie's phone, scrolling through the website. There goes my vow not to do any searching. Now that we're on the brink of something, the clue literally right here at my fingertips, just waiting to be uncovered, it feels absolutely impossible to ignore. We're so very close.

And then I see it.

"Oh!" A little gasp falls from my mouth. "You're not going to believe this!"

∾ 12 ∾

Rose

I shot a quizzical glance in Henry's direction, expecting him to look as puzzled as I felt, but to my surprise he simply nodded at the man who I quickly came to realize was the captain of the ship. His uniform was smart and crisp, starched to perfection with a row of buttons down the front, and from beneath the bottom of his cap a bit of salt-and-pepper hair poked through. "I'm Captain Collins," he introduced himself, holding out his hand. "I hope you are enjoying your time on this beauty. I think the *SS Harmony* is the finest ocean liner to ever sail the seas."

"It is a fantastic ship," I said, shaking the captain's hand. "I couldn't be more impressed."

"That's what I like to hear." He gave me a friendly smile before turning to Henry. "I need some additional information on the matter you discussed with my colleague yesterday," he told him. "It'll only take a minute. I promise to have you back to your wife before she can miss you."

His wife?

It took a second to realize the captain was talking about me.

I waited for Henry to correct him, but instead he gave me a conspiratorial wink. "How about if I meet you by the pool when I'm finished?" he asked.

"I ... we aren't ... yes, of course, certainly," I sputtered, bemused by the entire thing. "That'd be swell." Henry nodded, the captain gave a little salute, and the two of them started toward the front of the room. I watched them go, wondering why the captain had requested a private audience with Henry. It was odd.

I thought back to the day before. Henry had said something about having a prior commitment, when we were out on the deck and talking for the first time. Could that be what the captain meant when he mentioned Henry having a discussion with one of his colleagues, and what exactly was that conversation about, anyway? Henry had not breathed a word about it to me.

It was all so intriguing.

"Henry Jackson," I whispered. "What are you up to?"

I must have turned around a dozen possibilities in my head as I walked to the upper deck, where the pool was located, and sat on one of the available chaises. A handful of children were playing in the water, and it made me grin to see their enthusiasm as they swam. I had always wanted to learn to swim, too. How thrilling it would be, gliding through the water and feeling it rush against me with its gentle grace.

"You're not going to take a dip?" asked the man on the chaise next to mine. He was dressed in a Hawaiian print shirt, the brim of his hat pulled low over his forehead and an old, weathered book in his hand. He must have been in his sixties or so, and as I shook my head, explaining that I could not swim, he sat up a bit straighter. "You shouldn't let that stop you," he said. "It's like I always told my children when they were young: never let your limits prevent you from becoming limitless."

It was good advice. It was great advice, actually.

I closed my eyes and considered it.

Perhaps it was the hazy sunshine, or the lack of sleep lately, or a combination of both, but I must have dozed off, because the next thing I knew, the end of my chaise dipped down with the pressure of someone sitting on it. I opened my eyes, squinting into the light because I had left my sunglasses in my room, and saw Henry. He was wearing a different shirt, this one more casual with its sleeves rolled up to reveal his muscular arms, and he had a bottle of suntan oil in his hand.

"Hello there, sleepyhead," he teased.

"I really did not mean to do that," I said, stifling a yawn as I sat up and smoothed a wrinkle from my polka-dotted skirt. "I see you came prepared," I added, motioning to the suntan oil and the pile of towels he had placed on the chaise.

"I always do." He smiled. "Although you are far too overdressed for the swimming pool, pretty lady." He reached over, tracing his finger along the pearls in my bracelet, and something hot rushed into my cheeks. All it took was an accidental – or accidentally on purpose – graze of his skin against mine to set my world ablaze.

"I suppose I can't say the same about you," I murmured. "You look perfect."

Oh, how I wanted to kiss him at that moment, but it did not feel right, outside where everybody could see us, so I opted to lay back against the chaise instead, shielding my eyes from the sun as my gaze focused on Henry. He was saying something about how he had stopped off at his stateroom to change clothes, and I tried to listen, I truly did, but it was so distracting, the way his eyes caught the light and seemed to sparkle at me.

"It's a beautiful afternoon, isn't it?" he asked.

"Gorgeous," I agreed. "Your wife is very glad to share it with you." I let a touch of coyness slide into my voice and was rewarded with another dazzling smile.

"I figured it would be easier to play along," he said. "I think most of the couples on this ship are married, so it was a natural assumption on his part. This way he didn't have to be embarrassed, and we didn't have to explain that we're ... " He paused. "What are we, exactly?"

"We're ... " I hesitated, too, wanting to give a good answer. The truth was, I did not know what we were. Being with Henry felt like more than simply flirting with adventure, and yet it was still too hard to define in more specific terms. "We are belief," I finally settled on. "You know that period of time when you are waiting for a magician to finish the trick? It's all anticipation and excitement, and in that moment, it's like magic is real, even though the audience knows full well that there's a logical explanation. They're still willing to believe, or at least to suspend disbelief. That is what you are to me, Henry. You're my moment to believe."

He said nothing.

He simply stared at me for what seemed like an eternity, and anxiety began to crawl through my stomach. Was that too much? Did I scare him off? Perhaps I had misread the situation and this was nothing more than a brief interlude for him – and if I was being honest with myself, was that not all it was for me, as well? When the *SS Harmony* docked, I would have to say goodbye to Henry. Much as I wished this voyage to England could last longer, that I could call a time-out on life and hide away in this little part of it, that was impossible. That meant I needed to savor every second of this before it was too late.

Henry appeared to agree. "Well then," he finally said, "let's see how we can make our moment last."

"How about by filling me in on your meeting with the captain?" The words fell out of my mouth before I could stop them. I had planned to follow Henry's lead and let him bring up the subject, but he did not seem to be in a hurry to share, and I was oh-so-curious. "How did it go?" I asked, careful to keep my tone light. The last thing I wanted was for Henry to think I was a busybody. Violet and I had a friend like that when we were teenagers, this girl who made it her mission to find out as much as possible about as many people as possible. Her talent for interrogation was unmatched. I did not want to be that way, especially with Henry. If he thought I was trying to pry, then he might ... what? I did not have the faintest idea.

There was still so much about him that was a mystery to me.

"My meeting was no big deal," he said, popping open the cap of the suntan oil and squeezing a bit onto his palm. "It was just business." He rubbed the oil on his face, then offered me the bottle. "Want some? And what do you think about swimming? I wouldn't say no to seeing you in a bathing suit."

It was a completely transparent attempt to change the subject.

I could have refused to let it drop, but I had learned from personal experience that sometimes if you pushed people, they pushed back even harder. How many times, after all, had my parents tried to thrust their opinions on me and ended up creating a larger gap between us, rather than a smaller one? When people told me what to do, it only made me dig my heels in even more firmly. I saw no point in going a similar route with Henry. His meeting had nothing to do with me, and if my pressing him on it would cause us to dissolve into an argument ... well, I had no interest in it. The sand in our hourglass was slipping away with every minute, and I wanted to enjoy the rest of our time together for what it was, instead of turning it into something that neither of us wanted it to be.

He was looking at me expectantly, awaiting an answer, so I explained that I did not know how to swim, that I had always wanted to learn but had never had occasion to, and he suggested we just sit at the edge of the pool instead. As we dangled our feet in the cool water and he told me about life growing up in Maine, the band set up their instruments on the deck and began to play songs by the Four Aces, Frank Sinatra, and Bing Crosby. "My mother used to love music like this," Henry told me, and I turned to look at him.

"Used to?" I asked softly.

He dropped his gaze, staring down at the water as our feet made little swirls below the surface. "Yes," he said, so quietly I had to strain to hear him above the sound of the band. "She passed away when I was sixteen. She came down with pneumonia, and it was awful, she was so sick ... but we all assumed she'd get better. I would have never ... you just don't think of ... it was horrible. Numbing. By far, the very worst day of my life." His posture seemed to deflate. "It was fifteen years ago that it happened, but sometimes it feels like yesterday." He sounded as though his words were tripping on unshed tears, and my heart broke for him.

"I can't even imagine how painful it was," I said, "and how painful it must still be."

"Like a raw wound," he said. "No matter how many times it gets stitched up, it's never entirely closed." I reached out to rest my hand on his as he continued. "My brother was ten," he told me. "I tried to protect him from the worst of it – he was only a child, you know? – but that wasn't possible, not really. Our father was so beaten down by grief that he basically shut himself up inside the house every day, and of course James noticed that. It was mostly the two of us from that point on." Henry stole a glance in my direction. "You asked why I studied history in college, why I went for something more stable. James is why. I had to look out for him, give him a good life. I would've done anything for him, even if he didn't want me to. Even if he still doesn't want me to." Henry returned his focus to the water, but not before I caught a glimpse of the agony in his eyes.

I wanted to say something to take that anguish away, but what was there, really?

Nothing.

Nothing could make it better.

"I'm sorry," I whispered. "I am so, so sorry." I inched a little closer to him. Sometimes being by someone's side was the most important thing you could do. "James is very lucky to have you," I said to Henry. "Certainly he must know that."

"Sometimes." He gently kicked at the water. "Let's not talk about it anymore. We're supposed to be having a good time."

It felt odd to simply set the conversation aside, especially since Henry was the one who had first brought it up, but if that was what he wanted, it was what we would do. Perhaps he needed a break from the emotions that had been stirred up by confiding in me. I could give him that.

"A good time," I echoed. "Absolutely."

It *was* a good time. We stayed by the pool for hours, and

later, we danced the evening away for the second night in a row, outlasting nearly all of the other people on the dance floor. I had always been more of an early bird than a night owl, but things were different on the ocean liner. My wings stretched in directions I had never considered, and that allowed me to take flight in ways I had never imagined. As Henry walked me back to my stateroom, I almost felt like I needed to pinch myself to make sure it was not a dream.

"Breakfast tomorrow morning?" Henry asked, as we slowed to a stop in front of my door.

I smiled. "I would love that."

"Then it's a date, doll. Until then, I guess it's time to say goodnight."

He took a step closer, tipping my chin up with his index finger and bringing his lips to mine. As I wound my arm around his neck, drawing him to me, my purse slipped out of my hand and tumbled to the floor. It was wrong, that public of a display which would make the other passengers cringe if they happened upon it, and yet it felt so right. That kind of passion, that clouded my ability to think straight and made my mind turn all misty, was electrifying. It made my heart pick up several paces and my knees go weak. They still felt a bit like jelly after Henry stepped back and stooped to pick up my purse.

"Here you go," he said, handing it to me. His fingers brushed against mine ever-so-gently, and it sent a tingle careening down my spine. "Until tomorrow," he said.

"Until tomorrow," I echoed.

I all but floated into my room. What a day it had been. The rose Henry had given me earlier was still sitting on the table, and I took a second to tuck it into the vase with the others before kicking off my heels and heading for the bedroom. Tonight, my eyes closed the instant I sank into the pillows. There were no dreams like the ones that wove their beauty through the night not even twenty-four hours before, but I slept soundly and woke up feeling ready to greet the new day. It was early, that brief slice of time between dark and light, between night and day, when all of the world was so quiet and pristine that it seemed too perfect to be real.

I wanted to get outside to see it.

People frequently talked about the magnificence of sunsets, how the sky became a canvas for all of the brightest colors Mother Nature had on her palette, but I thought sunrises were even prettier. There was nothing like watching the dawn of a new day. Sometimes I did that back in Manhattan. I would make a cup of tea and perch on the window seat in my living room. The view was always the same – the park straight ahead, adjacent apartment buildings to my right and left – but the picture it framed changed daily. Sometimes the sky simply lightened, the black of night fading into the gray of dawn and finally to the blue of morning. Other times there were streaks of color, pinks and yellows and oranges that reminded me of the crayons Violet and I had used as children. There were also the days when clouds won out and rain dripped from the heavens. I even liked those.

On the morning of my third day aboard the *SS Harmony*, there were no clouds. As I slipped out of my stateroom, my diary in one hand and the camera my friends had chipped in to give me at my going away party in the other, there was nothing but a clear sky. I stood at the ship's railing, my hair ruffling in the salty sea air, and watched as the sun peeked its crescent face over the horizon. It was a pale pink at first, but then it brightened into the most vibrant hue I had ever seen in my life. It was almost neon, and the higher it rose in the sky, the more colors mixed in: marigold, tangerine, even a touch of lilac. It was like the sky was on fire, and the sea, too, as it reflected the spotlight of the sun in the middle of its blue blanket.

It was positively out of this world, far beyond anything I could have imagined.

I wanted to take pictures, to somehow document that

breathtaking beauty, and yet I knew that no camera could ever capture the pure majesty of it. I would become so invested in preserving the moment that I would lose out on experiencing it. That was the exact opposite of what this trip was supposed to be, and so I did not even try. The camera remained in my hand until after the sun had finished its ascent and assumed its rightful place, casting a glow on the ocean that was so blinding I could not look at it without my sunglasses. I slid them on, settled onto a chaise lounge, opened my diary, and began to write.

∾ 13 ∾

Grace

"What?" Josie and Abigail ask in unison.

I glance up from the phone. "What happened, big sister?" I tease. "You made it clear that you wanted no part of this. Having a change of heart?"

"Shush," she says, but I can hear the smile unfold in her voice.

"You so shouldn't tell her," Josie says. "Just give me the phone and it'll be our little secret."

"She wouldn't," Abigail says.

"She totally would," Josie retorts.

"Excuse me." I raise my hand in the air. "Right here. I can speak for myself. And I think you get a pass this time, Abigail, because this is awesome and I want you both to hear. There's a dedication page later on in the program," I say. "I suppose so the donors can explain why they chose this place. Listen to what Henry wrote." I begin to read. "'It was fifty years ago this week when I met a woman who changed my life. She taught me about flowers, the different varieties and what they symbolize, but more than that, she taught me what love means. I can think of no better way to mark the date and celebrate Rose than to support an organization that helps flowers to spring up around the city. Like Rose told me on the night we declared our love: there is beauty everywhere, when we're willing to see it.'"

"Wow," Abigail says. "That's so sweet."

"But kinda sad," Josie says. "Clearly this guy's been carrying a torch for her for decades. Do you think she just couldn't forgive whatever he was alluding to in that letter? Or what if they did run off together and something broke them up while they were in Europe? Though I guess that wouldn't fit with the idea that the day the ship docked was one of the hardest in Rose's life. Hmm." She gnaws on her bottom lip, deep in thought.

"Well, either way, we have proof now," I say. "This is definitely the right Henry."

"Except it really doesn't help all too much," Abigail says. "Henry could've sent a donation from anywhere. He may even still live overseas. There's another possibility: one of them wanted to stay in Europe and the other wanted to come home." She sighs. "I think it's time to give up on this now. The trail we're following is practically non-existent. A few bread crumbs here and there won't lead us anywhere, and all this time we're nosing our way into other people's business could be spent on The Book Boutique instead. March is it," she reminds me. "Don't you think that is where we need our attention to be?"

Reluctant as I am to let this go, I know she's right.

"Okay," I say, and pass Josie's phone back to her. "The bookstore it is."

Except it isn't, at least not for my sisters. Josie leaves for California three days later, headed to a round of auditions for various stage shows and even for a bit role in a TV pilot, and although Abigail only lives fifteen minutes from me, she may as well be as far away as Josie. As the weeks go by and the calendar flips from October to November, I find myself growing increasingly frustrated with her. Half the time she doesn't even return my phone calls until the following day. I know she's busy with work and her family, and I totally understand, but then why offer to be part of this in the first place? I don't get it.

"I wish she'd just have been honest," I tell Jonathan one evening, as he's helping me carry boxes of art supplies to my car after a Make-Your-Own-Origami class at the store. "If she doesn't have the time to dedicate to this, fine. But then why say she wanted to be involved? She was adamant about stopping the search for Henry in favor of doing this, and then ... " I shake my head, thinking, not for the first time, that maybe I was too quick to give up on that search. I took the letter and newspaper clipping to Lily, so she could get them back to her grandmother, and I vowed to put the whole thing out of my mind. I haven't, though. Even as I've been spending my days in the bookstore, planning a slew of new events, and my evenings with Jonathan, trying to figure out what exactly it is that I need before I can ask him to put that ring on my finger, I find my thoughts drifting backward to the 1950s. I just can't shake the feeling that it's important.

"You could jump back into it," Jonathan suggests. "Looking for Henry, I mean."

"I'm tempted," I say. "I can't seem to let it go."

"Do you think maybe it's because it sounds like the plot of a book?" he asks. "You're used to an emotional payoff at the end of a story, you know?" It is an insightful observation, and one I'd never have thought to make about myself.

I consider it as we head across the parking lot behind the store. "I guess when you're a lifelong reader, you do kind of hope that reality will play out in a similar fashion," I muse, sliding a box onto the roof of my Prius so I have a free hand to take out my keys. "Or maybe it's just that I can't stand not knowing how a story ends. Either way, there's not much I can do, short of contacting hundreds of Henry Jacksons to see who's the right one – and let's be honest, there's certainly a possibility that he isn't alive anymore." I pop open the trunk and push aside a pile of posters from the kids' section of the store to make room for the boxes. "Thanks for doing this," I say to Jonathan, as he sets them inside.

"Of course," he says. "I'm glad to help out. I want this place to be successful as much as you do. It seems like you're off to a good start." He reaches up to get the box I'd set on top of the car. "You had a pretty packed house tonight."

"Who knew so many people like origami?" I smile. "I guess that's what happens when the class is being taught by an artist who just published his second book on the subject. You know," I say, "it never ceases to amaze me how diverse this industry is. Last night we hosted a discussion on a novel set during the Civil War, today is an art class, and tomorrow will be a classic movie night." That one was Josie's idea. She texted from Los Angeles, saying she was inspired by Hollywood and thought I should show films based on famous novels.

Because not everyone is a bookworm, she wrote. *But who can resist a good movie?*

I won't lie, it rubbed me the wrong way at first. The Book Boutique is about losing yourself in a labyrinth of words, not making popcorn and staring at a screen. I can't afford to be picky, though. If it gets people inside the store, I'm willing to try it.

"I don't know how you do it," Jonathan says. "An event every night this week. You've got to be tired." As he straightens back up and shuts the trunk, the glow of the streetlight surrounds him and elongates his shadow. I step backward a little so the same happens with mine. Two silhouettes, so close and yet still not touching.

"I am tired," I admit. "It's worth it, though, if it helps us stay open."

"Do you think it's working?" He takes my hand as we walk back across the parking lot.

"It's hard to tell just yet. I'll know better at the end of the month, when I tally all the numbers. I will say that I've seen a lot of new faces lately, but that won't matter if they're not buying anything. Half of our events are free – which Abigail and I actually had an argument about yesterday, because she doesn't understand why we aren't charging book clubs to use our space – and the fees from the other half won't cut it on their own." I push the door of the store open and the bell chimes merrily into the quiet.

"So why don't you do what Abigail suggested?" Jonathan asks.

"And charge people? I can't." My ponytail whips back and forth as I shake my head. "Some of these book clubs have been meeting here since before my sisters and I even owned the place.

It's a tradition. I wouldn't feel right turning it into a fundraiser. We need something unique. Compelling. Something that'll convince people The Book Boutique is different from everything else and that it's worth saving. I've been brainstorming, but ... I don't know. I'm basically just going around in circles. I think sometimes, if you're too focused on solving a problem, it becomes impossible to see outside of it."

"I get it." He joins me as I head for the café to wipe up the tables. "It's like when I see an animal whose symptoms don't fall in line with a typical diagnosis. We can do ultrasounds, x-rays, and blood work, but there's nothing of concern, even though the animal is obviously having an issue. It's really frustrating when all the tests come back normal and the pet's owners are doing everything right, yet there's no solution. I go back to my research with cases like that, but sometimes it seems the more studies I read, the less I know." He grabs an extra towel to help me clean. "I became a vet because I wanted to help animals. Because my childhood pets were all the company I had sometimes, with no brothers or sisters. The bond between people and their pets is special. I hate feeling like I'm letting them down if I can't fix things right away."

I stop what I'm doing to look at him. "You should never feel that way," I say firmly. "You're the most wonderful vet. You care about those animals like they're your own."

"Which is why I think it's tough for me to take a step back sometimes," he says. "But when I do, and I clear my head, that's when I find myself coming up with answers I might never have thought of otherwise. Maybe that's what you need now. You've been working so hard. If you let yourself take a break, even for just a weekend ... " He comes up behind me, circling an arm around my waist, and I lean back into him. "Why don't we plan a getaway for later this month?" he offers. "My practice is closed Thanksgiving weekend. We could go then, maybe up to the mountains or down to the beach. You need to recharge, and it'd be nice for us to have some time just with each other."

Because we're never really alone anymore.

Anytime we're together, Jonathan's proposal is in the room with us.

He doesn't say it, but he doesn't have to. I feel it, too.

No matter what we're doing – cooking dinner at his place, watching television at mine, going to the aquarium or Centennial Park on one of the rare Saturdays when we both have the day off – the proposal is right there, too, an omnipresent reminder that I must make what could very well be the biggest decision of my life. Maybe if we get out of town for a little bit, we can leave that behind. I'd like that so much.

"So what do you say?" Jonathan asks me, dropping a kiss onto my cheek. "Want to be my travel companion?"

Travel companion.

Somewhere in the depths of my brain, a light bulb illuminates.

How did I not think of this before?

"Oh!" I exclaim, turning around to face him. "I think that might be it." He gives me a funny look, because of course it is a complete non-answer to his question, so I grab his hand and lead him over to the children's section. It is one of my favorite areas of the store, with its colorful covers and bean bag chairs and the same puppet theater Josie used to commandeer when our grandparents owned the place. There's a cheerfulness to it, and, I hope, the same magic that used to surround me when I spent countless hours here as a kid. I think that's my greatest wish for The Book Boutique: that it'll instill the same sense of enchantment in others as it did within me. I want everyone, especially each child, to feel the wonder that comes from opening a book and jumping into its adventures. And now – thanks to Jonathan – I think I might've found a new way to do that and to generate interest in the store at the same time.

I bend down to select a book from the third shelf.

"Jasper Jellybean Jumps for Joy," Jonathan reads, as I hand it to him. "Cute title."

"It's one of my favorite children's books," I say. "The basic premise is that a bunny escapes from his carrier while on the way to a shelter. At the beginning, he's alone, and scared, and lost, but then he starts to make friends with other animals. They travel all over and bring awareness to the plight of abandoned animals, and then at the end, Jasper's adopted into a home of his very own and finally gets to jump for joy."

"Sounds like a book I should have at the office," Jonathan says.

"You can take this copy," I offer. "I'm going to have to order new ones anyway."

"Why?"

"Because you," I say, giving him a kiss, "are a genius."

He grins. "I mean, I'm not gonna argue with that, but what exactly did I do?"

"What you said before, about being a travel companion, it made me think of something. People are always taking books with them everywhere, right? On an airplane, at the beach, in a hotel lobby ... you can find somebody reading just about anyplace, because a book is like a portable friend. But suppose the book did the traveling all on its own?"

"Like a mobile advertisement for the store?" he asks.

"Kind of," I say. "Here's what I'm thinking. I buy, say, two dozen copies of this book. We charge an entrance fee for people who want to take part in the contest, which will involve passing the book on to as many different readers as possible within a set amount of time. Each person will sign inside the front cover before sending it on to the next reader. The books will have to be back at the store by a certain date, and the person with the most signatures wins a prize. Not only will it raise money with the entrance fee, it will also show what an impact a book can have, and all the people its words can reach. Maybe we can even get the author on board," I say, growing more excited by the second.

"She could do a signing at the store. We can really promote it all on social media, so people are able to follow along with where the books are. And hey, we could even get some animal shelters to help out." A smile takes hold of my face. This alone won't be enough to save the store, but it could help make a name for us and also aid some animals.

"Wow," Jonathan says, and the corners of his eyes crinkle up as he smiles, too. "I *am* a genius. Who knew?"

I laugh out loud, then kiss him again, for longer this time.

"That's a yes, by the way," I say. "I would love to be your travel companion. Just let me get the ball rolling on this, and then I promise I'm all yours. Do you have a preference between the beach or mountains?"

"The mountains could be pretty," he says. "I think the leaves hang on a bit longer up there. We might get to see some spectacular colors. What do you think? A lakeside cabin, hikes on the trails, a cozy fire ... could be fun."

"Let's do it," I say. "I'm looking forward to it already."

"Me, too."

Happiness floods over me as I finish up at the store and lock its door for the night. Things are up in the air still, of course, but I feel much more optimistic now. Having a plan for The Book Boutique and the promise of an escape with Jonathan makes me hopeful that maybe, just maybe, everything will work out after all.

Where there's a will, there's a way.

Gram used to remind us of that all the time.

Whenever we were facing something that seemed far beyond our reach, she would tell us, in a gentle voice and with her arm wrapped around our shoulders, that we could do anything we set our minds to, but only if we believed in it fully and if we put in the hard work. "It isn't enough to simply want something," she said. "You have to want it enough to *make* it happen."

It was wonderful advice.

Wise advice.

If I close my eyes, I can still practically hear her say it, can feel the comfort of her hug as she held me tight. Sometimes, even four years later, it shocks me to think that she and Pop-Pop are gone. I suppose it just never felt like a possibility. Grandparents were invincible. They were the foundation of support, the chicken soup and the checkers game, the constant that was never meant to fade. At least, that's what my Gram and Pop-Pop were. It's what they still are. Because the people who we cherish most, they never fully go away. They just live in our hearts instead of by our sides.

Where there's a will, there's a way.

But not if you ask Abigail.

I call her the minute I walk into my condo, so excited about the new idea for the bookstore that I can't wait a moment longer to share it. She picks up after four rings, right before the phone goes to voicemail, and I immediately hear screaming in the background. Ben? Macy? Perhaps both of them at once.

"Can I interest you in taking my children for the night?" Abigail asks wryly.

"Problems in paradise?"

"That depends," she says, "on whether you consider a lack of red jellybeans to be the end of the world. They went to a friend's birthday party tonight and the jellybeans were part of the favor, but they only got purple, green, and yellow in their bags. You'd think it was a national emergency. They should be happy I'm even letting them eat that junk."

"Sounds fun," I quip. "Alright, well obviously you need to go take care of that, but call me when you're finished. I have a great idea for the bookstore."

It takes a full hour for my phone to ring, but when I answer it, there is no longer any bellowing in my ear. In fact, it's so quiet that it sounds as though Abigail is all alone in her house. "In case you're wondering," she says, "sherbet cures all. Who needs crappy candy when you can have that instead? The kids are in the playroom with Scott, running off all that energy before bedtime, so that means I might actually have an entire twenty minutes or so to myself. So, what's up? What's this great idea of yours?"

I tell her about it, the words practically stumbling all over themselves in my enthusiasm. "Well?" I ask, when I've finished. "What do you think?"

My hopes soar sky-high.

Then they crash back down to Earth.

"No," Abigail says. "No way."

❧ 14 ❧

Rose

*F*or a long time, I was alone out on the deck. The solitude felt quite odd on this ocean liner that was always bursting with life, but it was also lovely. Things had been moving so fast since I first set foot on the ship. Getting to take a breath, to be still and quiet and notice all the detail of everything around me, was exactly what I needed. There was the cloud shaped like a seagull, the red and white life preserver that hung from a rope against the outer wall, and the green silk handkerchief that laid in a jumble by the railing, left behind by somebody who probably did not even realize it was gone. I had missed out on seeing things like this so far, and it made me wonder: how often had it happened back in New York? How many times had I been so ensnared in the complexities of the everyday that I was basically oblivious to the simplicities of every day?

Not anymore, I vowed, as I turned my attention to what I had written in my diary.

Tuesday, July 12th, 1955

When Violet and I were younger, we used to disagree about whether it was better to go to sleep late or wake up early. I would cocoon myself beneath the covers and let my dreams carry me off – or I would try to, anyway, because it was difficult to fall asleep when Violet was in the bed next to mine, using a flashlight to help her read in the dark. I have no idea how late she would stay up, getting lost in the pages, but it was generally impossible to jog her awake in the morning. Instead, I would sneak out quietly from our bedroom, then creep through the house and crack open the door to the balcony to check on Mother's seedlings. I loved watching them grow taller with each day. Now, life aboard the SS Harmony reminds me of that. Seeing the dawn begin again, the sun reaching down to caress the surface of the ocean the same way it did the petals of the flowers, shows me once more how glad I am to be the early riser. Imagine everything I never would have seen otherwise.

Violet no longer sleeps through the ring of an alarm clock. These days, she gets up when Thomas does so she can prepare his breakfast before he goes off to the hospital. I hope she takes advantage of the beautiful mornings now, that they bring her as much fulfillment as today's sunrise brought me. She deserves that kind of peace and joy. I love my sister more than anyone on this planet. I want her to be happy always.

How had an entry meant to be about the sunrise turned into one on Violet?

I supposed because of Henry – or, more accurately, James.

It was obvious that the brothers had a contentious relationship, and even though I did not know any specifics of what happened, it made me sad for them. There was nothing like having a sibling to go through life with, to share moments and create memories with, to celebrate the good times and help make the bad ones a bit less difficult. The idea of Violet and me not being there for each other was positively unimaginable. How had that become a reality for Henry? It sounded like he had been selfless in trying to help James. That made me like him even more. Beyond the handsome face and all the charm that went along with it, there was a man with a good heart, and wasn't that the most important quality?

Henry's drop in the ocean counted.

Even if it was not appreciated the way it should have been, he still made a difference.

I wanted to do that, too.

Whatever was waiting for me on the other side of this trip, I decided right then and there that it would be something to help others. I wanted to leave people's lives – or even just their days – a bit brighter than I had found them. How could I achieve that? I sat outside on the deck for a long time, watching the water that was so strikingly calm out in the middle of the Atlantic, but nothing came to me. I was actually okay with that. The answers would show up when I was ready to see them.

For now, it was time to head inside and meet Henry for breakfast.

The deck was starting to get more crowded, the other passengers awakening to the third day of our shared journey, and as I stood up from my chaise and swiveled around to take one more glance at the ocean, I nearly crashed into a woman who was hurrying by at a clip so speedy she seemed to have come out of nowhere. She jumped backwards to avoid a collision as I let out a yell of surprise. "I'm sorry," I said. "I didn't see you."

"No, no," she rushed to say. "It was my fault. I clearly wasn't paying attention." She held up a bottle of ginger ale and a sleeve of crackers. "I am just on my way back from the dining room," she explained. "This is my son's first time on a ship, and unfortunately he's seasick. I was in such a rush to get this to him that I wasn't watching where I was going. I apologize."

"It's alright," I said. "I understand. I hope he feels better soon."

Did I understand, though? Would I ever know what it was like to feel a fierce love for someone who had grown beneath the curve of my heart? More importantly, did I even want to? Violet spoke often of her desire to be a mother, and I knew she would make an excellent one. She would dote on her children and give them the moon, if they wanted it. When I fast-forwarded my own life, though, I could never quite sense if the pitter-patter of tiny feet reverberated through it. Perhaps someday or perhaps not at all, it was yet another question I was unsure of – but one thing I did know was that if I ever became a mother, I wanted to have more than one child. No son or daughter of mine would ever grow up alone, without a sibling.

For the rest of the day, I was not alone, either.

As Henry and I sampled practically everything the breakfast buffet had to offer, as we relaxed in the lounge and pushed our luck all the way to the final round of the shuffleboard tournament before losing to a newlywed couple, I found myself reaching for his hand time and again. It was almost like I needed to convince myself that he was real. Sometimes he seemed too good to be true.

That was even the case when he was being delightfully mysterious.

It was approaching twelve o'clock that night when there was a knock on my door. I was still up, writing letters to Violet, Lucy, and Alice that I would mail once we docked. I set down my pen on the table and walked to the door, a little confused because I had already said goodnight to Henry half an hour before. I had not been expecting to see him again until the morning, but sure enough, he was standing there when I opened the door.

He twinkled at me. "Ready for some fun?" he asked.

"Now? It's almost midnight."

"Which is the best time for an adventure," he said. "Everybody's either asleep or dancing in the lounge. No one will ever know what we're doing."

I raised my eyebrows. "What exactly do you have in mind?"

"Do you trust me?" he asked.

"You're dodging the question."

"I know," he said, "but humor me anyway."

I paused for a second, looking into those rich brown eyes that were windows to a soul I wanted to know so much better. They were the only answer I needed. "Yes," I told him. "I trust you. Don't make me regret that, please."

"Never." The way he said it, I truly believed him.

Then he stepped into my room and handed me a large shopping bag. When I peeked inside it, I discovered it was filled with pool towels and goggles. "Wait," I said, as it dawned on me, "you're not thinking of going – "

He grinned. "You said you wanted to learn how to swim, right? Well, it just so happens that I'm an expert. I used to be on the swim team in school. I can teach you. It's the perfect time," he said. "The pool is closed, so we won't have to worry about anyone getting in our way."

I stared at him. "If the pool is closed, how can we use it?"

A hint of impishness crept into his face. "Creativity, my sweet Rose. Creativity and stealth." He took a step toward me. "Think about it: the water, the moonlight, you and me. Only the two of us, like the whole ship is ours." He was close enough now that I could smell the last hint of his cologne. "You know," he whispered, taking a final step into my personal space, "I've always found the water to be romantic. Something about it makes you feel invincible. That could be us. Invincible. All you have to do is say yes."

I knew it was a risk, that we could get caught and find ourselves in a world of trouble.

I also knew, as Henry held my gaze, not speaking, not moving, just letting the charge between us do the talking, that I wanted to do it. This man, he inspired me to take chances, to reach up toward the highest ceilings. For so long, too long, my life had been shaded inside of the lines somebody else had drawn. Now it was time to break out of those boundaries.

"Yes," I said. "You can count me in."

Fifteen minutes later, we were walking down the hall, trying to seem as nonchalant as possible. With our swimsuits hidden under our clothes, we looked just like every other couple who was taking a late night stroll. It was exhilarating, knowing we were the keepers of our own little secret, and so was the thought of learning how to swim. Plus, I could not lie: I would take any excuse to be close to Henry. The ship was farther from the New York coastline now than it was near it, so it felt important to spend as much time together as possible, even if that meant sneaking around.

"Alright," Henry said, as we reached the upper deck. "Here

we are."

It was bizarre to be there at night, all the noise from the daytime quieted to silence, and I could feel my heartbeat pick up a little as Henry boosted me over the locked gate before scaling it himself. "Do we have a plan?" I whispered, as we tiptoed across the deck and went straight by the sign that clearly said the pool was closed. "We should probably decide how exactly we'll get out of here, just in case."

"You worry too much." He dropped a kiss onto my nose. "Some rules are meant to be broken. But if it'll put you at ease ... " He glanced around, then gestured to the far end of the deck, where all the chairs were stacked for the night. "How about that way? We can duck behind the chairs if need be, then hop over the gate to make our escape down the back corridor."

I eyed the area for a minute. "Fine with me," I agreed. "That sounds good."

He flashed me a thumbs-up. "Then let's do this," he said.

We shed our clothes, moving softly as shadows against the night, and I slipped on a bathing cap. With no sun to illuminate the pool water, it looked like a dark teal, and it rippled against my legs as I climbed down the ladder into its cool embrace. Goosebumps blanketed my skin. It was a lot colder than I had imagined it would be.

"Are you okay?" Henry asked, as I gave a little shiver.

There was genuine concern in his eyes, and it warmed my heart. "I'm fine," I said. "A bit chilly, but that's nothing some exercise won't fix. I'm ready for my lesson now. Teach me everything you know."

The water lapped against me as he waded over to my side. "Let's start with the basics," he said. "The most common stroke is the front crawl. It propels you forward, sort of with a cutting motion. I think it might work best if I show you first, and then break it down into smaller movements. Okay?" I nodded, and he pushed off the pool wall, gliding beneath the water before breaking the surface. I watched as his arms and legs moved steadily, splashing into the water as he made his way down to the deep end and back. The sheer strength of his motion sent waves from his body, and by the time he slowed to a stop, I was mesmerized. "And that," he said, "is how you do it."

"No," I countered, "that is how *you* do it."

"Have a little faith in yourself," he said. "It will go a long way."

"Either that, or it'll make me overconfident and you will have to save me from drowning."

"Not happening," he said. "The drowning part, not the saving. I would always save you."

There they were again, those butterflies.

They always seemed to know when Henry was around.

"Okay," he said, moving behind me and placing his arms over top of mine. "With this stroke, it is not so much about finesse as it is force. You want to get momentum going from the beginning, and then you kind of chop through the water while you're kicking. It's not the most graceful stroke, but it is the easiest to learn." He bent his arms at the elbow and I did the same, mimicking the motions as best I could. "You'll want to take a breath on alternating arm movements," Henry told me. "Left, right, breath. Right, left, breath. Oh, and you want to turn your face to the side when you breathe, so that you don't swallow water."

"This is an awful lot to absorb," I said.

"I know, but you'll get it. Start off small. See what it's like to put your head under the water or to do the arm movements. Want to try those on your own now, or should I practice with you some more?"

He was holding me so close I could feel the tap of his heart pulsing against my back, his wet skin pressed to mine in a way that made my legs feel as though they might buckle at any second. I could not concentrate on breathing while swimming, because I was finding it a challenge simply to breathe while standing in such close proximity to him. He had been right. There was something so romantic about this.

"That depends," I said, and twisted around to smile at him. "If I opt for the latter, will you hold me some more?"

The smile he gave me in return was brighter than all the stars dotting the sky. "I could hold you forever," he said.

That time, my goosebumps had absolutely nothing to do with the water. For a brief moment, an idea crossed my mind that I was barely willing to even recognize, let alone consider: that maybe this did not have to be it for Henry and me. Maybe there was a way to build something real and lasting, something that would not have to end when the cruise did. What would Henry say if I told him that right now? Was he thinking along the same lines, or was he simply being his flirtatious self? It was obvious that he got a kick out of making me swoon, so perhaps that was all it was.

"Forever," I said quietly, "sounds divine."

As soon as the words were out of my mouth, I was embarrassed, wondering if he thought I was turning our connection into something it was not. I slipped out of his arms, took the longest breath I could manage, and pushed my feet back against the tiled pool wall before propelling myself forward as best I could. It was an odd sensation, the feel of the water underneath my body as I glided on top of it. I moved with all the polish of a six-year-old, but I did manage to get a few feet before I had to stop.

"Well, well, well," Henry said, beaming. "Look who's an overachiever. That was fantastic."

"It was an unbelievable rush," I told him. "But also, it wasn't really that fantastic. You are just a sweet talker."

"Honest," he said. "It was great. Now, the next time you try, it'll help – " He broke off abruptly as a clicking sound came from the side of the pool deck where we had snuck in. It was quiet at first, but then it grew increasingly louder and sharper, clearly the call of somebody's rapidly approaching footsteps.

Oh no.

Oh no, oh no, oh no.

"Henry," I whispered. "Someone's headed this way. We'll get caught." Terror jabbed at me. If a crew member found us here, I could not even imagine the depth of the trouble we would be in. It would be impossible to kick us off the ship at this point, but what about when we docked overseas? Could they press charges for trespassing? My heart raced a good five beats ahead of itself. "Henry," I said again, more urgently this time. "We have to get out of here."

His eyes darted in the direction of the noise, which could not have been more than twenty feet off. "Yes," he said. "We probably should."

He grabbed me by the hand and we scurried up the ladder, stopping only to grab our clothes as we darted for the spot Henry had marked as our escape earlier. I could hear the footsteps closing in on us, louder, louder, louder, and I was already trying to concoct some kind of story we could use in case we were spotted when Henry vaulted over the gate and helped me over behind him. Then we were off, racing down the hallways, our feet slipping and sliding because we had not even taken the time to put on our shoes. The quicker we ran, the hotter my cheeks grew, and I was just starting to think we may be in the clear when Henry spun around to look at me and tripped over a loose board in the floor. He threw his arms out to the sides in an attempt to regain his balance, and I just could not help it – I knew I had to be quiet, I knew everything was riding on how fast we could get away – but I broke into giggles anyway. He looked so comical.

"Sshh!" he whispered, putting a finger to his lips, but that only made me laugh harder, and soon he was joining in. It was, I learned that night, one of the hardest things ever, to keep yourself under the radar when the laughter was overtaking not only your body, but also your soul. Tears streamed down my face from the effort, and Henry's shoulders were shaking with amusement as he pulled me behind a door to hide when one of the ship's crewmen walked by. "Don't move," he said.

"Sshh!" I mimicked him, and it set us off all over again.

Henry's lips twitched. "We are not very good at this," he said.

"We are the worst," I agreed, clamping a hand over my mouth.

In that moment, though, I realized that the worst could also be the very best.

We waited after the man disappeared, for one minute, two minutes, and then a third. "What do you think?" I whispered. "Are we safe?"

It was quiet out there, or so it seemed, at least.

"Maybe," Henry said, and yet we still made a run for it. Henry's room was closer than mine, and by the time we got to it, my heart felt like it might beat right out of my chest. I was drained and still a little on edge, but, my goodness, I had never felt more alive.

Henry pulled out his room key and gave me his most charming grin. "Do you want to come in?" he asked.

∾15∾

Grace

"No way?" I repeat. "What? Why not?"

Abigail exhales a puff of air. "It'll never work," she says. "We'll end up losing money in the long run, and that is the last thing we need. Don't get me wrong, it's a good idea in theory, but ... Grace, did you really think this through? Suppose only a handful of people participate? Then we'll bring in next to nothing, and we'll still have to put out the cash for a prize. And what is to stop people from cheating? Do you know how easy it would be to forge a list of names without ever sending the book anywhere?"

"Our customers wouldn't do that," I retort. "They're good people. Honest people. You'd know that if you ever came in and actually spoke to them instead of making judgments from afar." A pop of anger bursts inside me. Why does she always have to be so negative? First with the whole Henry thing, and now this. "Besides," I add, "that's the point of social media. For each signature, there will have to be a photo to document it."

"Even so, what's to stop someone from simply taking the book to their office and asking a bunch of coworkers to sign it? I know you're envisioning this as an ongoing thing, where it moves from one place to another," she says, "and I agree, it could be great publicity for the store if it were to unfold that way – "

"Yet you still refuse to give it a try." I jump up from the couch and start pacing around my living room in circles. The window, the wall of built-in shelves, the end table that once belonged to Gram and Pop-Pop, the needlepoint of a beach scene that my mom made in the months after the divorce, when she needed something to keep her mind busy late at night. I pause by each of these and then keep going, fueled by the frustration I have been feeling toward Abigail ever since she went back on her word. "What happened to making yourself available to work on this?" I ask. "You swore it'd be different this time, but here you are, dissecting things until nothing is left. You always do that."

"I do not."

"You do, too. You have ever since we were kids. Remember the time I wanted to set up a candy stand by the sidewalk so we could raise money to buy Mother's Day gifts? You said the candy would melt out in the sun, and no one would want it. Then there was the time I decided to surprise Dad by showing up at his house for his birthday. I had it totally worked out, bus routes and all if Mom didn't want to take us, and you told me we'd only be disappointed because he would be busy with his new family and wouldn't want to see us. And what about the time, just last year, when I wanted to start a Book of the Month club at the store and you said it'd be too expensive to order in all those copies with no guarantee of anyone buying them? Need I go on?"

"No," Abigail says briskly. "Because the truth is that I was right every one of those times, even if you don't want to admit it. It was really warm that May, so the candy *would* have melted. Plus, you know as well as I do that Dad stopped putting any effort into maintaining a connection with us once he got remarried, not to mention the fact that there really *was* no guarantee on the books and then we'd have lost a lot of money we could have spent elsewhere. You might not like the way I dismiss things, but that doesn't mean I'm wrong. I'm realistic. I think, deep down, you know that."

At this moment, all I know is that I'd like to hang up on her.

Instead, I sit down at my desk and look out the window at the darkened silhouette of the leaves rustling on the trees. "Okay," I say. "Then what do you think we should do? I was telling Jonathan it needs to be something big, to capture the attention of people outside the usual store community. I happen to think this book hop is a good option, but if you're so set on shooting that down, what do you suggest we do instead? Because for someone who promised she wanted to be more involved ... well, let's just say I've still been doing most of this on my own. Which is fine," I hurry to add. "I am happy to do it. But don't tell me you'd like to help, and then make your only contribution a veto of my plans."

There is a silence.

A long one.

When Abigail finally speaks, she sounds sad. "I'm sorry," she says, and it catches me off-guard, because they're not words that often come out of her mouth. If Abigail is apologizing, she genuinely means it. "I honestly had the best of intentions," she continues. "I thought I'd have more time that I could dedicate to this. It's just that work has been even busier than normal lately, and then when I get home, all I want to do is spend time with the kids before they go to bed. You're right, though. It isn't fair for me to veto anything. At the end of the day, you're the one managing the store, so you get the final say, but I do really think a more traditional fundraiser is the way to go. Maybe a dinner or a run? I know Scott's company sponsors a lot of 5Ks. I can ask him what it would take to set that up."

"I'm all for that," I say. "I just don't understand why it has to be one way or the other. We need a steadier income than a single event can provide, so why not explore all our options? How can that hurt?"

"If it takes up too much of our resources, then ... " She stops, mid-sentence. "Let me ask you a question," she says. "Is it worth it to go through all this if it still won't be enough in the end?"

I think about it. All my life, I've opted for the quieter routes, the ones that would get me where I needed to go with the least amount of fanfare. Abigail has always been the practical sister. Josie is the free spirit. And me, I was the one who kept her imagination between the pages and her dreams inside her heart. It's why I quit my job at the advertising firm only a few months after Sofie did. The electricity of a career like that, with all the clients and presentations and the ever-growing pressure to always think bigger and glitzier, was the exact opposite of what I wanted. It had sounded exciting in theory, an opportunity to shed my introverted shell, but in practice, it used to fill me with anxiety every time I walked through the office door. When I enrolled in the library science program for grad school, I relished the thought of spending my days traveling along the whimsy and whisper of stories big and small. I wanted to live an unassuming life. But when The Book Boutique fell into my hands, it changed everything. Interacting with the customers each day, seeing how different books shaped and inspired them ... it inspired me, too. I don't want to lose that.

Even if it means putting up a fight for what I believe in.

Even if it means I have to shout to make myself heard.

"Yes," I tell Abigail. "It's worth it. We won't know unless we try."

"Okay," she says. "Fine. I know you won't forgive yourself if you don't do everything possible to save the store, so if you really have your heart set on this contest, I'll stop trying to talk you out of it. Let's research it first, though, and make sure we've ironed out all the wrinkles. Hang on a second." I hear some shuffling and clicking as she types away on her phone. "Alright," she says. "Let me see ... I can probably leave work by four-thirty tomorrow, if I hustle all morning. How about I meet you at the store and we bring Josie in via video chat? We can fill her in on the plan and draw up a blueprint for what we want to do going forward. It'll also give me the chance to ... how'd you phrase it? Stop making judgments from afar."

I wince. "Sorry about that," I say.

"No, don't be," she tells me. "You were right."

I know it's taking a lot for her to say that. She never likes to concede that her carefully thought-out opinions might actually have a hole or two in them. If she can extend the olive branch, the least I can do is take it.

"You made good points, too," I say. "The idea needs some fleshing out before it's feasible."

"So ... tomorrow?" she asks. "Does that work?"

"Perfectly."

I smile.

Maybe I don't have to shout, after all.

Maybe, this whole time, I only had to speak up.

* * *

Gray skies and a light, rolling fog greet me as I walk outside the next morning, a few stray drops of rain spritzing down from the clouds and dotting the shoulders of my denim jacket. It's the sort of day that reminds me of the one when Gram led me into the finished bookstore for the first time and changed my world without even knowing it. Hopefully that's a sign that things will go well with Josie and Abigail later. This could be a turning point for us, I think, but only if we let it be. I am willing to do my part. I even stop at Abigail's favorite health food café on the way to work and buy a box of all the muffins she likes: banana cranberry, strawberry kiwi, and apple walnut. I grab a gingerbread tea for myself, too – normally I'm more of a coffee person, but on this soggy morning there's something about the sweet tea that sounds good. I sip it as I park in the back lot at the bookstore and make my way to the sidewalk, dodging the tiny leftover pools of rainwater.

When did that happen?

When did I stop being the kind of person who jumps in puddles?

I miss that person sometimes.

And so I do something about it. As I join the people navigating the morning rush on Peachtree's crowded sidewalks, I slosh right through the water, creating little geysers with my feet. It leaves my boots wet, but my heart warm. It's what Gram would have done.

As I approach The Book Boutique, I reach up and feel beneath the folds of my scarf for the heart-shaped locket I always wear. It was a present from Pop-Pop to Gram for their twentieth wedding anniversary. She wore it all the time, an omnipresent homage to their love, and I cried the biggest crocodile tears when I found out she'd left it to me after she passed away. Out of all "her girls," as Gram would call Abigail, Josie, and me, I was the one who adored that necklace most. It means the world that she entrusted it to me. It isn't the same as her being here, as hearing her voice on the other end of the phone or seeing the grin on her face whenever I stopped by the house just to say hello, but it helps to have this piece of her with me as I go about my days.

I pause for a moment as I reach the front door of the bookstore.

I have this piece of her, too. I have this piece of them both.

If I lose it, if I'm forced to give it up ... I honestly don't know what I'll do.

Not now. Not yet. I refuse to even consider it.

I pull my keys out of my pocket, unlock the door, and step inside for what has become my most favorite part of every work day. There's something special about the moment I walk into the silence of the bookstore, its shelves bathed in darkness, the whole place just waiting to come to life as I flip on the lights. It's weird: after so long, I pretty much have every nuance of the shop memorized, and yet sometimes I still happen upon something different. Today, it's a new creak in the hardwoods as I head back to my office and drop off the muffins for safekeeping. It's like even the floor has a story to tell in this place.

The best stories, though, are up front. They're inside the covers and inside the people.

I'm reminded of that every day, and this is no exception.

First up is Mrs. Barker, the elderly woman who stops in each week for a bagel from the café and a new book from the mystery section. "Maybe this one will stump me," she says, as she checks out at the register. It's the same thing she tells me every time, and then when she returns, she laughs in this deep, knowing way, and says that once again, she was able to figure it out before the characters did. "Maybe I should become an author myself," she says. "It's never too late, right? As long as we are breathing, there's still a chance to try something new."

"Absolutely," I agree. "And I happen to think you'd make a wonderful author. I would definitely buy your novels for the store. Just promise you'll hold a signing here once you're famous?"

She chuckles. "Of course. I'll always remember where I got my start." She takes the bag I hand her and gives a little wave as she turns toward the door. "Have a good day, Grace. I'll see you next week."

"See you next week," I echo, watching as she heads out and a young man with shaggy blond hair walks in. He heads straight for the biography section, which admittedly could use some fattening up once I can afford to do so, and though my first instinct is to go over and ask if he needs help, I hang back instead. Good customer service is important, of course, but I hate when it takes away from the overall experience. To me, there's nothing like being left alone to wander the aisles of a bookstore. Sometimes it's nice to just slip through the folds of time. To return to those days when bookstores *were* the place to go when you wanted something new to read. To see the colorful spines waiting in neat rows, to hear the rustle of pages, to carry a tower of books to one of the tables and sift through the choices, deciding what to buy. Expedient as it might be to approach my customers from the get-go, it wouldn't be nearly as fun for them.

As it turns out, though, the guy does need some help, after all. He comes up to the register with a half dozen books in tow, fanning them out on the counter so I can see. "Hey," he says. "I've gotta do a paper on a president for one of my government classes in grad school. I was originally planning to write about someone well-known, like Kennedy or FDR, but I found these biographies on some of the ones we don't hear about as much. I was wondering if you have other books on them? It has to be a thirty-page paper, so I'll need more than a single source as research."

"Hmm," I say, scanning the titles. Each is about a different president: Coolidge, Madison, Hayes, Buchanan, Polk, and Taft. They are older books – honestly, I think they've probably been here since my grandparents were running the place – but I click away in the online database anyway, searching for companion sources. A short list of titles comes up. "We don't have any in the store currently," I explain, "but I'm glad to order them for you." I swivel the monitor around to show him the choices. "There's another one on Coolidge, Polk, and Hayes, and another two about Madison." I glance up at him. "Is it a possibility for you to write the paper on a grouping of presidents? Or does it have to be just one? Because we also have a great book on the legacy of presidents in the Reconstruction Era." I hold up my index finger, gesturing for him to wait, then disappear into the stacks to grab the book I mentioned.

"Wow," he says, as I slip back behind the register and slide the hardcover over to him to peruse. "Do you know where every book in the whole store is? You didn't even have to look it up. You went straight to it."

I smile. "This store has been a second home to me for a long time," I tell him. "I know it pretty well."

"Impressive." He starts to page through the book. "You know," he says, "I'm not sure about the answer to your question. Our assignment is to write about a single president, but my professor does constantly encourage us to think outside the box. I kinda like the idea of doing something different. I'll email him to check if it's okay." He stacks all the books into a neat pile on the counter. "Can you hold these for me?"

"Absolutely." I take a slip of paper from the shelf. "Your name?"

"Blake Johansson."

I write his name on the paper, then rubber band it to the books. "Okay, great. I can hold these for a week. Just give us a call once you hear from your professor."

"Thank you," he says. "I appreciate it. This might shape up to be a really cool assignment, after all."

This is one of my favorite things about owning a bookstore, getting to be there when something new and exciting grabs hold of a customer's thoughts for the first time. I remember my grandfather saying something similar one day. I was thirteen at the time, and spending the afternoon helping at the store after Pop-Pop picked me up from a newspaper club meeting at school. We were shelving new books while Gram worked up front, and as I arranged a handful of paperbacks, I looked at Pop-Pop and asked what he liked best about the store.

Behind his wire-rimmed glasses, his eyes twinkled. "No question about it," he said. "Seeing the customers discover something about themselves. That is the wonderful thing about reading, Gracie Girl." He always called me that. I adored it so. "Books are special for lots of reasons," he said, as he handed over a fresh stack of novels. "Especially when they act like a mirror. They let readers in and help them find their own reflections."

I considered that. "Cool," I said. "I hope they like what they see."

I am still fascinated by that thought, all this time later, and it always makes me look at The Book Boutique's customers with gratitude. What a joy it is to get these glimpses, however small, into the subjects that fill them up with passion. Politics for this man; science fiction, fantasy, and cinema for the group of teenagers who come in after school with backpacks in tow; and both photography and music business for the couple who walk in with a blonde curly-haired little girl and a baby boy who is the spitting image of his mom. She tells me she and her husband are visiting from Nashville and that she's a songwriter who loves to find inspiration everywhere, especially in unexpected places like

The Book Boutique. She and her family stay for quite awhile, picking out picture books for the children, and they're just leaving the store when Abigail comes in.

I glance at the clock. Four-thirty on the dot.

"See?" she says, heels tapping on the floor as she joins me. "I keep my word sometimes. I even made a stop first." She sets a small bag on the counter. "For you. I hope you're hungry."

I open the bag and find a box of Snowcaps – my favorite candy ever since the first time I went to the movie theater as a kid. Pop-Pop took Abigail and me to see 101 *Dalmatians*, while Gram stayed with Josie because she was too young. I remember pressing my nose to the glass of the concession stand when Pop-Pop told us we could each pick out a snack for the movie. Abigail chose soft pretzel nuggets and I went for the Snowcaps. It makes me smile, knowing she remembers that, too. "Great minds think alike," I tell her, then pop back to my office to get the muffins.

She laughs a little when she sees them. "The key to compromise is obviously dessert," she says.

"It's a good thing Josie isn't here. You know she'd steal all of it."

"And then give us that wide-eyed innocent look. She's an expert at that."

"Youngest child syndrome," I quip, and Abigail laughs again. It's nice to hear, nice to share such a light-hearted moment together. I fear it'll fade fast once we get down to business, but still, I wave my hand at the chairs by the fireplace and suggest we work over there. "That way I'm still available if a customer needs me," I explain.

"I wish we could hire some more employees to help," she says.

"Me, too. Instead, I had to let all but two go this year because I couldn't afford to keep up with their salaries." Just like that, my mood drops. I don't mind being the sole person who takes care of the store during the week – Anna and Mark, my two employees, only come in on weekends – but it does weigh heavily on me that the store's finances have sunk so low as to require that. "Maybe that will change soon," I say, summoning up all the hope I have as Abigail and I settle into the chairs and she starts a video chat with Josie on the phone.

"Maybe," she says, but I hear the doubt in her voice.

Abigail is doing this for me, not because she thinks it will save The Book Boutique.

I'll prove her wrong. I have to.

"Alright," I say, once Josie's connected, the ocean behind her as she joins us from what looks to be some kind of beach bar out in California. "Let's begin."

～16～

Rose

I held Henry's gaze for a moment, trying to determine the weight behind his words. Was he just asking me to come inside as a way to ensure we were out of eyeshot, or was there something more to it? I could not tell, but either way, there was no denying that I wanted the night to stretch on for as long as possible. Henry was like a gravitational pull to me. I simply could not help being drawn to him.

"Yes," I said. "I would love to come in."

He grinned, and opened the door to his room. It was similar to the one I was staying in, with the couch and the table and the portholes, but the paintings were different. There was also, I noticed, a large briefcase on the table, along with a bunch of papers spread out next to it.

"My apologies for the mess," Henry said, hurrying to straighten it up. He shoved the papers into the briefcase without even glancing at them, then set it on the bottom shelf of the smaller end table by the wall.

"Were you getting a head start on work?" I asked. "I would imagine you have to prepare quite a presentation for each time you meet with people interested in purchasing your jewelry." I looked at Henry, suddenly curious. He had not talked much about his job or what it entailed, other than being a liaison between his company and their buyers. Again, I found myself wondering what it had to do with the *SS Harmony* and why exactly he had been so tight-lipped about his secret meeting with the captain.

"It's not as exciting as you might assume," Henry said.

"People hear about gold and gemstones and automatically think it's a glamorous career, but honestly, it's just like everything else. The goal is to impress our potential clients and get them to place as large an order as possible. Sometimes it takes a little wheeling and dealing, but more often it's a matter of explaining the high quality of our pieces and the extensive care that goes into creating them. Believe it or not, face-to-face meetings are actually my least favorite part of the job. I'd rather be at our headquarters, helping out with the sieving process."

"The sieving process?" I asked. "What's that?"

"It's how we filter the stones," he explained, his voice playing hide-and-seek around the walls as he went into the bedroom of his suite. When he returned, he was holding a pile of towels. "All the gems must be examined before they're used in jewelry," he said, wrapping one of the towels around my shoulders. "The finished products have to be flawless, so if the stones have any imperfections in them, they can't be used."

"What happens to them, then?"

Henry took a towel for himself and set the rest down on the table. "It depends on the extent of the issue," he said, drying off his hair that had curled even more in the pool. "If it's something major – a crack or significant discoloration, for example - the stone is a total loss. If the problem is minor, like a chip, we can try to cut that part off and salvage the rest."

"Is that what you meant when you said you love to find beauty even inside the broken?" I asked him.

"Something like that." He fell quiet for a moment, but quickly bounced back into conversation. "Would you like to see some of our new collection?" he asked. "It's top secret, until the designs are in stores, but I'll make an exception for you."

I loved that.

I loved being his exception.

"Of course," I said, and he pressed a soft kiss to my cheek before disappearing into the bedroom again. When he returned, he had changed from his swimsuit into the green shirt and black pants he was wearing earlier. There was a briefcase in his hand, and by the time I reemerged after changing back into my own clothes in the bathroom, it was unlatched and waiting on the table. "Okay," I said, as I joined Henry. "That's much better. Now you won't have to worry about me getting your room all wet."

"I wouldn't have minded." That time, when he smiled, there was almost a dare inside it. "If I'm being honest," he said, "I am quite fond of seeing you in less clothing, rather than more." He traced his finger along my jawline, and I let my eyes flutter closed, enjoying the chill he created at my nerve endings.

"You are awfully forward, do you know that?" I murmured, as I opened my eyes again. "You're always saying things that most people would only think to themselves."

He chuckled. "Guilty as charged."

"You don't even *try* to deny it."

"Why bother?" His shoulders popped up, then down, in a shrug. "What's the point of living life as somebody other than our true selves? We only get one chance at it, right? We might as well take full advantage."

I thought of my life back in New York, all the beiges and grays and tans I had been so desperate to leave behind and all the hints of color I had tried to infuse with the flowers I bought. Henry was a hundred percent correct. There was no sense in hiding who we were and what we wanted. I was so tired of dimming my own light. "You may be onto something," I told Henry.

"I do see how it could be difficult," he said. "Sometimes it feels like there is so much pressure to conform. If you don't check off all of the boxes, or even if you do, but in a different order than what others suggest ... " He sighed. "After my mother died, there were people who tried to tell my family what to do, how to feel. They thought my father was mourning for too long and that he let his grief swallow him whole. They weren't wrong, but I think that's when I learned that there is no single or common path to take in life. Sometimes the universe throws us a curveball and we have to adjust. I think it just takes some of us longer than others."

"Like your brother?" I asked.

"Yes." Henry lowered his gaze, suddenly intent on unzipping the various pouches nestled inside the briefcase. "It nearly broke him, losing our mother at such a young age. It nearly broke me, too, but I had to be strong. This might sound strange, but it was actually easier in the beginning. We all muddled through the best we could and relied on each other for support. When my father couldn't snap out of his misery, though ... when he holed himself up inside the house and it fell to me to take care of everything ... James had a really hard time dealing with that. If he couldn't have our mother there, he didn't want anyone else. He certainly didn't want me."

I rested my hand on Henry's arm. "What did he do?" I asked.

"He would act out all the time," Henry said. "He constantly got into trouble at school, he found a new group of friends who were a terrible influence, and after I moved to Manhattan for college ... it didn't go well. I got a job as a waiter so I could send checks home, but James didn't use them the way I'd intended. I think maybe he felt like I had abandoned him. He'd already lost our mother, and now, in a way, he was losing me, too. I sent him letters, but it wasn't the same." He shook his head. "Sometimes I feel guilty for not choosing a college in Maine, but after everything that'd happened, I just felt like I needed to get some distance and find a new perspective. James must have resented it, even though part of the reason I did it was so I could build a good life and help him. Instead, things got pretty bad between us."

"And now?" I asked softly.

"And now ... " He met my eyes. "Now, I dazzle you with my jewelry."

It was exactly like the conversation we had had by the pool.

Henry was willing to talk about James until, suddenly, he was not. I could respect that, though.

"I'm prepared to be dazzled," I said, "but just so you know, I am also always glad to listen. If you ever need to talk, I'm your girl."

"My girl." He reached over and grazed the outside of his fingers against my cheek. "I could get used to hearing that."

"I could get used to saying it."

I could get used to living it.

As we sat there on the floor, Henry opening the various jewelry pouches and wowing me with all the glittery stones that rested inside, I realized just how much I did not want this to end. Being with Henry felt right, like the most beautiful serendipity, and the thought of having to leave him in only a couple of days hurt my heart. I wanted more swim lessons, more stolen kisses, more chances to talk to him long into the night.

I wanted more time, and it seemed as though Henry did, too.

"Would you like to stay?" he asked, after we finished looking through his inventory. I had one of the pieces around my wrist, a gorgeous bracelet with a rainbow of stones in every color imaginable, and I fiddled with it as I considered the invitation. How easy it would have been for me to accept it, to let myself be close to Henry in the way I yearned for so very, very much. I knew, though, that was precisely why I had to turn him down. Being with Henry would simply make me want to be with him again in the future – a future we were far from promised. I just could not set myself up to hurt like that.

"I'm sorry," I said, "but I think I should go."

The next night was a different story. Instead of our usual evening routine of dinner and dancing, we opted for a walk around the *SS Harmony* instead. With only two nights left, I suppose both of us were feeling an urgency to spend time just with each other instead of all our fellow passengers. The pizzazz and glamour that had called to me so loudly at the beginning now paled in comparison to the peaceful sense of contentment I felt with Henry. I adored the adventure he brought into my life, the way

I felt a starburst explode inside my chest whenever he was near, but there was more to it than that. As we were walking hand-in-hand, I realized it did not have to be all or nothing. I could crave the discovery and the escapades, but also the serenity in between.

"It's so beautiful tonight," I said, as we paused by the railing. The moon was full, a circle of light that bathed the ocean in a silver glow. It made the water look like a mirror.

"It is beautiful," Henry agreed. He was not looking at the vastness of the sea, though, but rather at me.

My heart skipped a beat. This was exactly what I had told my parents, over and over, when they asked why I often declined to go on a second date with the men they had suggested I see. The spark was not there, I explained. It was a connection whose ends did not quite touch. I did not care that I had reached the point where I was supposed to settle down. Settling down should not have meant just plain settling. I wanted to build a life only with somebody whose soul clicked with mine, and all that time, I had been waiting for my heart to tell me who was right. Standing next to Henry, his suit jacket draped around my shoulders as the breeze sent ribbons of salty air in our direction, I heard it loud and clear.

"If tonight were a flower," I said, "it would be a forget-me-not. I want to remember this – all of this – forever. I wish it didn't have to end."

"Why does it have to?" Henry rested his hand atop mine. "All I know about flowers is what you have told me," he said. "But I would have to describe this, and us, as a rose."

Something fluttered in my chest. "You know what roses symbolize, right?" I asked.

"I do." He waited until I turned to look at him, then cradled my face with his hand and brushed his thumb against my cheek. "Love."

I had known he was going to say that. The truth was that roses actually sheltered a great many meanings within their petals, but to most people, they were the flower of romance. Maybe I should have been prepared, then, to hear Henry say it, but what I realized in that shining moment, that felt-like-a-dream, feet-not-touching-the-ground kind of moment, was that it was impossible to really be prepared for a declaration like that. It took everything I thought I knew, and turned it upside-down in the best way.

"Love?" I breathed.

When Henry smiled at me, it was different than usual, more delicate. "It seems crazy," he said, "to feel so strongly about someone this quickly, but honestly, Rose, I think it was love at first sight. I knew you were special as soon as I saw you."

I gazed at him for a long while. I wanted to memorize absolutely everything about this snapshot in time: the feel of his hand creating a shell around mine; the musky smell of his cologne as it mixed with the ocean air; the sight of how intensely he was looking at me; the sound of the waves lapping lightly against the ship; and, finally, the taste of Henry's mouth as his lips teased mine. It was, truly, everything I had never known I wanted.

"If you don't know you want it, how will you realize when you've found it?"

Violet's words drifted through my mind. She had asked me that when I first told her about going on this trip. There would be more to it, I knew, in the months ahead – a purpose I was still seeking, a significance I was yet to discover – and still, this felt like a vital part. Henry was one of the reasons I was meant to go on this journey.

"I love you, too," I told him. A tear escaped my eye and rolled down my cheek. "You're right. It *is* absolutely crazy, but I think life's best things sometimes are. When I told my parents I was doing this, leaving everything behind to go to Europe, they said I was being irresponsible and impulsive. I was so angry at them, so hurt ... but now ... perhaps you and I are proof that being impulsive is really a good thing. Look what we've found. I guess there's beauty everywhere, when we're willing to see it."

Henry pulled me into his arms. "Come back with me tonight,"

he whispered in my ear.

That time, I did not even hesitate.

"There's nowhere I would rather be," I whispered back.

He kissed me, long and light and lingering, then took me by the hand and led me across the ship to his room. "Tonight," he murmured, shutting the door behind us, leaning me back against it, "will definitely be a forget-me-not." He was deliciously close, his mouth on my neck and his hands resting on my hips, and I tried to memorize that, too, to imprint every single detail on my mind, but I could not seem to think straight. I could only act and react. Being with this man was a whirl of sensations and a firestorm of feeling.

I looped an arm around his neck, my fingers playing with his curls as he lifted me up and carried me into the bedroom. His hands teased the pearl buttons on my dress, making slow work of them, one by one, as he kept stopping to kiss me. I was not sure how much longer I could stand it. "Your turn," I said, my voice about two octaves lower than normal as I unknotted his tie and let its smooth fabric slip through my fingers to the floor. I laid my hand on his chest, and it almost brought tears to my eyes again as I felt his heart pounding in double time.

It was beating like that because of me. Mine was beating the same way because of him.

It felt like I was living in a fantasy world of the very best kind.

As he lowered me onto the bed, capturing my mouth with his as I let my fingertips dance on his back, I wanted nothing more than to explore each inch of him and to have him explore every inch of me. "Tonight isn't just a forget-me-not," I whispered, as his touch created electrical currents under my skin. "It is also a yellow iris."

He pulled back to look at me. "What does that stand for?"

I smiled.

"Passion," I said.

He rested his forehead against mine. "Passion," he echoed.

It was more than passion, though. It was excitement and anticipation, newness and desire, faith and hope. It was love. As Henry and I got to know each other in the most intimate of ways, as I fell asleep in his arms, lulled into my dreams by the tapping of his heart against my back, I knew that he was what I had been waiting for all along.

For the first time since I had stepped onto the *SS Harmony*, there was no journal entry that day. It was not necessary.

Some things were better lived than recorded.

Some memories would never fade.

When I woke up the next morning, the sheet ruffled around me and my hair splayed over one of the pillows, it all came flooding back. I felt giddy inside, like I wanted to laugh and squeal, but when I rolled over to share that with Henry, I noticed that the covers were thrown back and his side of the bed was empty.

Where was he?

He had not mentioned having to go anywhere.

I was growing more and more confused, when I heard his voice coming from the outer room of the suite. He was talking quietly enough that I could not hear what he was saying. I got out of bed, wondering what was going on, but then something stopped me clear in my tracks: his voice was not the only one filtering into the bedroom. He was speaking with somebody else ... a distinctly female somebody else.

Who was that?

∽ 17 ∾

Grace

I lay out my plan for the contest again, trying my best to convince Josie of its merits. I'd like for at least one of my sisters to be excited about it. "I figure we can call it a book hop," I say. "And the goal is to have it be a pretty large-scale thing." I add this second part because I know Josie jumps at the chance to be involved with anything that'll make a splash. Abigail doesn't even have to relay her ideas about a fundraising dinner and a 'Book It for Books' charity run for us both to realize that Josie would say they're too commonplace. I think I can get her on board for the contest, though.

"Just how large a scale are you thinking?" she asks. "Like, what if we added a rule saying that in order to win, the book has to have a signature from every single state. That could be hard to prove, but ... "

"It'd be impossible to prove," Abigail contends. "Unless we require people to take photos of the book with state landmarks, and then we're making it overly difficult. There's a fine line. We want it to be unique enough to really grab people's attention, but not so over the top that they won't want to give it a try. Plus, we're talking shipping fees if the books are being sent state-to-state, and then there are logistics to consider. Suppose it gets down to three states left and no one knows anybody who lives in them? Wouldn't the whole thing be pointless, then? We'll end up with a lot of irritated customers."

"But what if it doesn't come down to that?" Josie counters. "What if the books get to each state and introduce The Book

Boutique to a ton of people in the process? This could bring us a lot of new business. I know you're mostly focused on the in-person stuff, Grace, but the online aspect is every bit as important. This could give that a boost."

She makes a good point.

I've been doing everything I can recently to grow our online presence. I hired Jonathan's friend, who works in web design, to overhaul the store's website and make it more user-friendly. I spend at least an hour every day posting pictures and hosting giveaways on social media, and I offer a special online-only discount each week. It's helped, but we still have a long way to go, and I think Josie is on to something here. Gram and Pop-Pop always insisted on keeping the bookstore a local institution. It didn't even *have* a website until my sisters and I took over. That means we have a lot of ground to cover.

"What if we compromise?" I suggest. "The fifty state part doesn't have to be mandatory, but we can offer some sort of bonus if people do it. Like, hmm ... " I gaze at one of the bookshelves, trying to come up with an idea. Much the same as when I sit at my desk at home and look out the window for inspiration, I often find myself staring at the books here. If all of those writers can dream up the worlds and words that make their stories come alive, then surely I can let my imagination take flight, too.

I can't just be the reader anymore.

I have to be the author of my own destiny.

"Maybe we can have different prize levels," I muse. "I think the winner needs to be the person who collects the most signatures, but there can be incentives for anyone whose book gets around to multiple places. Ten states wins them the book of their choice, twenty wins them a gift basket with our newest releases, things like that."

"Sounds good to me." Josie's smile beams at us from the phone.

"To me, too," Abigail says, not even a little begrudgingly.

"Plus, if our customers know that their participation is helping save the store – "

"Wait," I say. "You want to tell them about that?"

She raises an eyebrow. "You don't?"

"No. Definitely not." I drop my voice as the door opens and a family with four kids walks inside. "They don't need to know yet," I say, watching the children make a beeline for the shelves with their parents following behind. "I'd rather people just enjoy the store instead of worrying about it closing down. That'll put a stigma on the place, and all its quirks and magic will fade away. I only think we should tell people if we absolutely have to."

"Josie?" Abigail asks. "What's your opinion on this?"

She reaches up to fix her hair as the California breeze sends it flying in front of her eyes. "Tough call," she says. "I mean, I totally get what Grace is saying. It'd be a bummer if people couldn't come in to the store without being concerned about it shutting down. But on the other hand, I really think the customers would want to help out. Hey," she says, squinting at us through the sunlight, "maybe that's another option. We could set up one of those crowdsourcing pages and ask people to donate. I bet they'd be happy to preserve The Book Boutique's legacy."

The thought of that makes something squeeze inside my chest.

I hate the idea of having to ask our customers to save us.

We're supposed to be giving them something, not taking it from them.

"Why don't we use that as a last resort?" I say quickly, hoping we won't actually have to use it at all. "Let's hold off on saying anything at least until after the new year. The holiday season is always the busiest time for us, and maybe that combined with the book hop will be enough to steady us on our feet. If not … " I trail off, and to my surprise, Abigail reaches over and squeezes my hand. It's a flashback to our childhood, when she took her role as big sister very seriously. She was always there for Josie and me, whether it was to play dress-up, or teach us how to ride a bike, or offer her words of wisdom before first dates and final exams. The fact that she's here now, supporting me even as *I* support the business that's wedged itself between us, reminds me that some links don't ever break completely. Josie, Abigail, and I may disagree about a lot, but when it counts, we'll still stand up for one another.

Forever sisters.

It's time I honor that.

And so, after the family with the children selects their books and Abigail offers to ring them up, even asking the kids why they picked out those particular stories, I shut the front door behind them and flip the sign to 'closed' temporarily. Business can wait. Family can't ... or, at least, it shouldn't. Abigail stares at me in confusion as I walk back, but I just smile and take her phone so I can see Josie. She's sipping a neon blue drink now, her face bright as she tells us about a callback she got and how positive she is that it'll be her break.

"It's a shame you never dream big," Abigail says, and Josie laughs.

"You've gotta dream big to achieve big," she says. "Successful people don't climb to the top by refusing to take risks."

Her words are the perfect opening for the secret I should've confided in them a long time ago.

I clear my throat.

"Speaking of taking risks," I say. "Jonathan proposed."

Abigail's eyes go wide, and a high-pitched shriek blasts from the phone. "Holy crap!" Josie yells. "Grace! That's freakin' awesome. Seriously, though, you've been holding out on us? Where's your ring? I want to see it. He better have picked a gorgeous one."

"Well, the thing is ... " I say, and out of the corner of my eye, I notice Abigail steal a surreptitious glance at my hand. No ring. Her mouth flattens into a straight line as she registers this, and I hurry to speak before she can bombard me with a billion questions. "I don't have a ring just yet," I explain to them. "There is one, and it's beautiful. Blue diamond, square cut, double band. It's so exquisite, and I love it – "

"Then why the hell aren't you wearing it?" Josie demands.

Abigail says nothing, just watches me intently as she and Josie wait for my answer.

"Because I haven't said yes yet," I tell them.

Silence.

It's rare for either one of them to be left speechless, let alone both. It's almost funny: the mild-mannered sister shocking the two bold and confident ones into quiet stillness. That doesn't last for long, though. Soon they're interrogating me with such a rapid-fire intensity I can barely keep up, let alone answer.

"Why not?" Josie asks. "Don't you love him?"

Abigail piggybacks off her question. "How could you not love him?" she asks. "He's terrific. He has a good heart, a steady job – helping animals, no less – and he'd do anything to make you happy. He *does* make you happy, doesn't he?"

"Definitely a whole lot happier than Will and Drew, right?" Josie pushes.

"Oh wait, is that it?" Abigail narrows her eyes. "You're worried he'll leave you like they did?"

I finally manage to get a word in. "It's not that," I say. "At least, not entirely."

"Then what?" Josie asks. "Does he only do laundry one time a month? Talk in his sleep? Prefer movie adaptations over the books themselves? Something has to be causing you to make such a big mistake." She leans in close to her phone and lowers her voice to a stage whisper. "Is he horrible in bed? Because, okay, if that's the case, I'll give you a pass for refusing to put the ring on your finger, no matter how pretty it is."

"Josie!" Abigail exclaims.

"What?" she says.

"That is absolutely none of your business."

"She's my sister. Of course it's my business. Yours, too."

This is exactly why I waited so long to tell them – and, I realize now, exactly why I shouldn't have done so. Josie's right. When you grow up with sisters, what happens to one of you happens to all of you. It's rough sometimes, having your business be theirs and vice versa, but it can also be fantastic. Even though Abigail and Josie may be my toughest critics, they're my most ardent cheerleaders, too. They challenge me because they care. How can I be angry about that?

"For the record," I tell them, "Jonathan and I have no problems in that department. We have no problems in *any* department, and yes, I'm well aware that he isn't Will or Drew. He and I have had a lengthy conversation about it already. Also, I haven't turned down the proposal, so you don't have to worry that I've made a huge mistake. I just told him I need more time to figure things out. I really do want to say yes."

"Good." Abigail smiles. "That's a start."

"So what is it, then?" Josie asks. "What's keeping you from becoming his wife?"

"Mom and Dad."

"Ah." Recognition flashes in Abigail's eyes. "That makes sense."

"It does?" I ask. "Because it surely didn't keep you from getting married."

Her fingers go to her infinity necklace that has two gemstones set into its curve, one for Macy's birth month and one for Ben's. "No," she agrees. "It didn't, and I am so grateful for that every day, because Scott and the kids are the light of my life. I get it, though. Our parents' divorce was so ugly, and the way Dad practically forgot about us after he remarried ... that cut deep."

"It sucked," Josie says flatly. "Still does. But Grace, you and Jonathan aren't Mom and Dad."

"Far from it," Abigail chimes in.

"I know," I say. "When Jonathan tells me that he'd never walk away from our life together like it meant nothing, he's speaking from the heart and he believes it a hundred percent. I do, too, but the thing is, so did our parents at the beginning. We've all seen the pictures of their wedding day. They were glowing, and proud, and happy ... and look what happened."

"You know, thinking back, it's remarkable that they lasted as long as they did," Abigail says. "For a couple who got married after only a month, staying together for all those years is actually quite an amazing feat. And yes, it got horrible at the end, but they did have good times with each other, too. I bet if you ask Mom if she regrets it, she'll tell you no."

"So you're saying I shouldn't worry about the future, only the present?" I ask.

"What she's saying," Josie tells me, "is that the divorce screwed with us all in different ways. It made me shy away from any commitment, even though it's what I want, it made Abigail search for a relationship steadier than our parents ever could've dreamed of having, and it's made you afraid to put your faith in a marriage because you know firsthand how it can crumble." She shakes her head. "I think what you have to see, what all of us have to, is that our lives are not defined by Mom's and Dad's. Their choices are theirs. Ours belong to us."

"It's just ... " I give a helpless little shrug. "Jonathan makes me feel at home. Everything seems different when I'm with him, like I'm safe from the world. I guess it's because I love him, but what if it's also because of how comfortable we are together? Do you think that's a bad thing?"

"Comfort is never a bad thing," Abigail says. "Neither is wanting a solid foundation."

"Even if it could disintegrate?"

"Even then."

"Let me ask you something," Josie says. "If you and Jonathan were in a similar position to Rose and Henry, if you could either run off with him or risk never seeing him again, what would you do?"

I surprise even myself with how fast I answer. "I'd go with him."

A triumphant smile paints itself across Josie's face. "See? Maybe you aren't quite as unsure as you thought. Take some time and mull that over, but not for too long. As awesome as Jonathan is, you can't expect him to wait forever. But you should only say yes if you're certain."

"I agree," Abigail says.

Whoa.

I was not expecting that from her.

"You mean you're not going to tell me that being in a relationship for over a year should logically lead to a permanent commitment?" I ask her. "That the next steps should be to get married, buy a house, and have kids?" I say it teasingly, but I'm not joking. Abigail's reaction is not at all what I had imagined.

"Look, would I love to see you go down that path?" she says. "Clearly. I think it is the best one to follow, and I'll make no secret of that. You have to do what *you* think is best, though. Josie and I will support whatever that is."

"Damn straight," Josie says. "Sisters stick together."

It makes me feel incredibly guilty. I should have trusted in that before. I should have trusted in them. Instead, I let our differences and disagreements overshadow the bond that's supposed to tie us together, even when life tries to yank us apart. So what if we've been up in arms over the store? I should've realized that we still had a safe place in each other – even if that safe place was also *from* each other.

"I love you both," I say. "And I'm so sorry I didn't tell you sooner."

"Sooner?" Abigail shoots me a quizzical glance. "Wait ... when exactly did he propose?"

◈ 18 ◈

Rose

*T*he woman looked like a model straight off the cover of *Vogue*
or *Harper's Bazaar*. She was tall, practically at eye-level with
Henry as they stood together by the sofa, and her dark hair fell
in waves against her lilac dress. As I peered around the door,
attempting to figure out what was taking place, Henry murmured
something that made her break into a glittering smile. Something
painful pinched my stomach. I had no idea who this woman was,
but already, I disliked her. What was she doing in Henry's room?

I gripped onto the door so tightly my fingertips turned white,
watching as he gestured for her to sit down. He perched next to
her and opened his hand to reveal something, but I could not tell
what it was from my vantage point, only that it was tiny enough to
fit in her palm as he passed it over. He did not linger with her as he
did with me, and yet I could not shake this terrible sense of dread
that something was going on between them. What, though? I was
not so certain I wanted an answer to that question.

Still, I knew I would have to ask. It would needle me if I did
not, doubt poking and prodding into every crevice of my thoughts.
Perhaps, I rationalized, as the woman examined whatever Henry
had given her, there would be a reasonable explanation. If that
was the case, it would be better to know so I could put my worries
at ease. The night before had been spectacular. I did not want
something to cast a shadow over it, and if I stayed quiet about
what I had seen, that was what would happen. I would confront
Henry instead, I decided, and get it out into the open. As I watched
the two of them stand up from the sofa and shake hands, I ducked

away from the door and tiptoed back to the bed. I surely did not want to get caught eavesdropping. Henry's footsteps grew louder as I tucked myself back under the covers, and no more than a minute after I heard the cabin door shut, he strolled into the bedroom.

"Oh," he said, with a grin. "You're awake. Good morning, doll."

"Good morning to you, too," I said.

I waited to see if he would offer any explanation on his own, but he just walked over, sat on the edge of the bed, and leaned down to kiss me. "I quite enjoy this," he said. "Beginning my day with you."

"I wish mine could've started the same way," I said, propping myself up on my elbow and gazing at him. "You were already gone when I woke up. Where were you?" Perhaps it was wrong, testing him to see if he would be honest, and yet it felt like something I needed to do. The reality was that so much of Henry was still a mystery to me. I only knew the parts of him he wanted me to know. It would take more time for us to weave ourselves through the complexities of each other's life. That was why I wanted our relationship to keep blossoming. For that to happen, though, it needed water and sunlight, trust and truth.

"I was just out in the front room," Henry said. "I was up early, so I figured I would do some work while I was waiting. You looked so peaceful, sleeping with a sweet smile on your face. I didn't want to wake you."

"I was having a dream," I said. "I remember it vividly. We were in Europe together – visiting the Eiffel Tower in Paris, throwing coins into Trevi Fountain in Rome, and touring the National Gallery in London. We bought flowers in each city we traveled to, and by the time we boarded the ship to go back home, I had pressed them all into the pages of a scrapbook."

"That sounds great."

"It was." I stole a glance at him, waiting for him to say

something else, but he only reached over and tucked my hair behind my ear. My curls from the night before had started to straighten, and as his hand grazed their silky strands, I could not help thinking about that other woman's runway-ready appearance. Henry had told me he was the lone employee from his company headed to do business in Europe, so where did that leave her? I could not figure out what role she could have played in the work he was supposedly doing while I slept. My mind bounced back and forth: was it better to push the issue further, as I had originally intended, or to let it drop?

"Rose?" Henry's voice drew me out of my ruminations. "Are you alright?"

Water and sunlight, trust and truth.

I wanted to trust Henry. I wanted to think that he had a perfectly good reason for not telling me about her. Most of all, I wanted to believe that the flame we had sparked together was not already on the verge of fizzling out – and so I did. I chose to hold that belief close, to grip it to my chest and refuse to let go. Even if it only served to get me burned in the end, I just was not ready at that point to extinguish the blaze we had created.

"Yes," I said. "I'm fine."

I really *was* fine for the remainder of the day. Henry and I spent it soaking up the sunshine and competing in the last tournament before the ship docked the next morning. Deck tennis proved to be our best attempt yet. We made it to the final round, just as we had in shuffleboard, but this time I scored the winning point, earning us a shiny gold trophy.

"Victory is ours," Henry declared. "We make an amazing team."

We did indeed, and as we tried to draw out every last drop of our final full day aboard the ship, I managed to set aside how it had started. When Henry convinced me to join him for a second lesson in swimming, when we shared a piece of chocolate cake for dessert that evening and I reached over to wipe the frosting from the corner of his mouth, when we ducked out of the lounge and danced by ourselves to the sound of the band playing inside and the waves lapping against the boat outside ... it was as though the morning had never happened. Henry had an uncanny ability to make me focus all my attention on whatever moment we were living inside of.

"I would very much like to spend the night with you again," he said, as we swayed to the rhythm of the music that drifted out to meet us. It was a warm night, despite the sea breeze, and the air felt sticky, as though it was closing in, as though something was creeping ever nearer. I shut my eyes to it, resting my head on Henry's shoulder. Dancing with him was like flying. My feet seemed to float above the ground, my heart above the clouds.

"I would like that, too," I murmured.

"Good." His breath was warm as he whispered in my ear. "Meet me at my room in a half hour. I have a surprise for you."

A surprise? My curiosity was instantly piqued, and by the time I arrived at his door, I was full of the butterflies that just refused to leave me alone where he was concerned. I did not mind, though. I actually quite liked having them around. I took a deep breath, straightened the hem of my pleated skirt, and raised my hand to knock. When there was no answer, I tried for a second time. "Henry?" I called quietly. Still, there was silence, so I reached for the doorknob and found that it twisted easily in my hand. That was odd. Why would he leave the door unlocked? I pushed it open, took one step inside, and froze.

Henry was not alone.

That woman was back again.

They were standing by the portholes, facing away from me, and this time his arms were around her. She was saying something to him, but I could not seem to hear any of it. Everything felt muted. All I could do was stare. I was suddenly cold, so cold, like all of my outer layers had been ripped off. Was it possible for heartache to cause physical pain? That is what it felt like as I stood, motionless. A hammer to the chest would have hurt less.

I let out some kind of strangled cry, and Henry whirled around so quickly that he practically lost his balance. A panicked expression seized his face when his gaze fell on me. The color drained from his cheeks, his arms dropping limply to his sides as he came to realize that I had just walked in on his ... what? His girlfriend? His other seaside fling? Horror smashed into me as yet another possibility came to mind. Could this woman be his wife? Perhaps he had been lying the entire time. It would have explained why the captain of the ship assumed that he and I were married.

It was all too awful to even consider.

My thoughts dashed ahead of me in a tangled mess.

I felt positively ill.

"Rose," Henry implored, crossing the room to me in two seconds flat. "I swear, this isn't what it looks like."

"Now there is a clichéd line if I ever heard one."

Henry flinched. "Please," he said. "You have to believe me. Marjorie and I haven't ... we barely even ... she's just here because ... " Try as he might, he could not get the words out in anything even remotely resembling a coherent sentence. He tried to reach for my hand, but I took a step back and folded my arms squarely over my chest.

"What about this morning?" I asked, and my voice was cooler than I had ever heard it before. "I know she was here then, too. I was willing to set it aside, even when you deliberately opted to keep the truth from me, but this ... I can't ignore this. Twice in one day is not a coincidence. Please don't insult me by insinuating otherwise."

"You have it all wrong, Rose," Marjorie said. Her saccharine sweet voice only served to infuriate me further. How could she sound so innocent when she was stealing Henry from me? That's when a light bulb went off in my head: if any of my earlier suspicions were right, I could have been the one stealing him from her. The thought was enough to turn my skin clammy. Never in a thousand years would I have wanted to be in that position. The room shook violently around me, and I had to pinch my eyes closed to force the dizziness into the dark. Marjorie was still talking, going on and on about a necklace and some sort of rare gemstone, but her words just drifted by with nothing to adhere to in their quest to be heard.

I inhaled sharply and let the breath out gradually.

I counted to ten.

I counted to ten again.

Then I opened my eyes slowly, pausing to see if the room had stopped spinning. At least for the moment, up was up again and down was down. I waited to be certain it would stay that way before leveling my gaze on Henry. "You said you loved me," I told him. "Maybe I was a fool to believe that ... maybe I only thought it was love because I wanted it to be, or because I had never experienced it before and had nothing to go by ... but I don't think so." I struggled to keep my voice from shaking. "When we were together, the connection was real. I let you hold my heart in your hands. Perhaps that was my mistake, perhaps I should've been more cautious, but that was one of the things which set you apart from the other men I've tried to date: you made me want to throw away my restraint. If you are going to lie to me, though ... " The words stuck in my throat as hot tears pricked my eyes. "You told me you were the only one from your company going overseas," I choked out, "so what she is saying about a necklace ... there's obviously more to the story."

The tears spilled out of my eyes then, running down my cheeks in rivers.

It was mortifying. Never before had I cried over a man.

"Please, just give me a chance to explain," Henry pleaded.

"Careful," Marjorie cautioned him. "Think about what you're doing."

Henry hesitated for a moment, and it made my insides clench. Even so, when he made another play for my hands, I let his fingers encase mine. My vision blurred with yet more tears as I looked at him, praying for the words that would somehow make everything okay.

"Rose," he said softly. "I *do* love you. Meeting you has changed my life. Things haven't always gone according to plan for me, and it's been hard sometimes, knowing I can't do anything to fix that, but when I met you ... these past five days have shown me that life's best things don't have to come from our plans. You filled up a hole inside me I didn't know was there. I think you're like my North Star, meant to guide me to something wonderful. I don't want to lose that, and I don't want to lose you."

My heart was beating so fast it felt as though it would burst right through my chest.

"Why didn't you tell me about her?" I asked.

"Because I couldn't."

"You *couldn't?*"

"No." He gave my hands a gentle squeeze. "And I really shouldn't be now. But think about it: if I was seeing Marjorie, if I was dating the two of you at the same time, or whatever it is you imagine I am doing, then what on earth would've possessed me to ask you here tonight? Why would I be with her when I knew you would be coming over?"

"Maybe she knocked on your door and you just couldn't turn her away."

"Oh, for goodness sake," Marjorie said. "That's absurd."

"Is it?" I narrowed my eyes at her, which was actually quite hard to do when I still had all those unfortunate tears refusing to let up. If this was what love meant, these feelings so strong it felt like they were controlling me instead of the other way around, then maybe I had actually been better off without it. Life might not have been exciting then, but it also had not been excruciating. This was a pain that cut straight into my soul.

"Perhaps you should go," Henry told Marjorie. "Let me talk to her alone. I'll be in touch."

He would be in touch?

After everything, that is what he chose to tell her with me standing right there?

It was too much. It was all too much.

"No," I said, dropping my hands from Henry's. "You stay, Marjorie. I'm the one who has to go." I fixed a penetrating stare on Henry. "I thought you seemed too good to be true," I told him. "That should have been my first clue. We've had a great time together, but I think we need to leave it be. I let myself fall for you in a way I couldn't possibly have imagined, and that was obviously a grievous mistake."

"No," he beseeched. A wild desperation shot into his eyes. "It was not a mistake. You are just afraid, and that's okay, because it means what you feel for me is real. It's making you overreact to a situation you know nothing about yet. You aren't thinking straight or basing anything on facts. Such as: we've been practically inseparable. When could I have found time to be with her? Please don't jump to conclusions. Give me a chance to tell you what's been happening."

I shook my head. "I can't," I whispered. "I cannot risk it. This hurts too much." I raised myself up on my tiptoes and pressed a kiss to his cheek. "Goodbye, Henry." Then, without looking back at him – because I knew that was all it would take for me to change my mind – I spun around and fled. I could hear Henry calling after me, begging me to reconsider, but I kept on going, lowering my head to avoid the inquisitive gazes of the other passengers who were still out and about, enjoying the last evening on the ship. It was not until I reached my own room that I slowed down, my breath raspy as I shoved my key into the lock and the door sprung backward more forcefully than I had intended. I let it slam behind me and headed right for the bed, flinging myself onto my pillows and sobbing until my face felt raw and it seemed like I had nothing left to give. Perhaps there *was* a logical reason for why Henry had been in an embrace with Marjorie. Maybe she was not his girlfriend or his wife, but even so, this had to be the end for us. I never again wanted to feel the way I had tonight, not ever.

Love was beautiful.

It was also overwhelming, and intimidating, and heartbreaking.

I had dipped my toes into its waters, and now it was time to retreat back to shore.

When my tears finally dried, I sat up in bed and looked around. My diary was on the nightstand, its pages waiting to be filled with more stories from this trip I had been looking forward to so much, but I could not even bring myself to open its cover. All I wanted was to go to sleep in the hope that it would dull the ache throbbing around my heart.

There was no such luck.

I was exhausted when I woke up in the morning, drained from a night spent tossing and turning. Still, I had to get out of bed. There were only a few hours left until the *SS Harmony* would dock, and I needed to finish packing. An insuppressible yawn tugged at my mouth, my eyes bleary and stinging from all the tears that had assaulted them the evening before. Gone were the rose-colored glasses, that was for sure. I walked over to the coffee table to gather up the magazines I had left there, but as I was reaching for them, something else caught my eye: the flower from Henry, nestled among all the others. My fingers tingled as I traced its petals, and somewhere behind my eyelids, so did the emotion I thought had drained out of me during the night.

"No," I whispered firmly. "Stop. Please stop."

I let go of the flower, pivoted on my heel, and that is when I noticed it: a sheet of paper sticking out from beneath the door to my room. It was white, and it looked like it was covered with writing. What was it?

I bent down, picked it up, and began to read.

∽19∾

Grace

I could lie.

I could bend fact into fiction, twist the truth in a way that would be less likely to hurt my sisters' feelings. I know how horrible it's going to sound if I tell them it's been over a month since Jonathan got down on one knee. Sisters don't keep something so major from one another, especially not for that length of time. And yet, the thought of being anything but honest makes my stomach flip-flop. If we're trying to patch up the holes in our relationship, the last thing I should be doing is slicing any new tears into the fabric.

So I don't. "A little more than a month ago," I say, mentally steeling myself for the fallout.

It's immediate.

"Excuse me?" Abigail asks.

"You can't possibly be serious," Josie says.

I don't know which one of them sounds more incredulous. I get it, I really do. If there was a role reversal, I'd feel the same way. Surprised. Confused. Maybe even a bit betrayed. That's why I have to make them understand my reasoning. "Don't be angry," I implore. "At least not until I explain. I know we've always gone to each other for advice, and I did consider it. It's just … I knew how you'd react, or I thought I knew, anyway. You both love Jonathan like a brother, and I assumed you'd tell me to marry him. You always act first and save your questions for later," I say to Josie. "And you," I tell Abigail, "are about as transparent as can be when it comes to your feelings on having a life plan. I figured you'd be talking about babies and white picket fences before I could even go into detail on why I was unsure about walking down the aisle. But I was wrong, clearly."

"Insultingly wrong," Abigail says.

"Yeah," Josie agrees. "How uncool. You didn't even give us a chance."

"Have you told anyone?" Abigail asks. "What about Mom?"

I shake my head. "I wasn't ready to talk about it with her yet. I was afraid she'd feel guilty once she found out that the divorce is one of the main things keeping me from saying yes. She has always tried so hard to compensate for the way Dad treated us after he got remarried. I didn't want her to think I was blaming her for any of this. I just couldn't hurt her like that, you know? The only person I confided in was Sofie."

"So you told your friend before your sisters." Josie leans back in her chair. "I know things have been strained between us lately, but geez. How could you have not realized we would support you? It's pathetic how we've let a dusty old store create a wedge between us. Gram and Pop-Pop would be really pissed about that. They'd be the first ones to tell us to cut it out."

"It's not a dusty old store," I say, although I know that isn't what I should focus on here. I can't help it, though. My instinct is always to defend The Book Boutique. "But you're right," I add. "They would be upset. I have been, too, but I'd like to think we're working our way through it. That's why I decided to tell you about Jonathan." I raise my left hand. "This is me, solemnly swearing to try my hardest to make things better."

For a moment, neither of them reacts.

Then Abigail raises her hand, too. "Count me in," she says.

Josie holds up her glass. "I'll drink to that."

"Thank you," I say. "For listening to me, and especially for understanding why it took me so long to tell you. If it helps, Sofie's been saying all along that I should bring both of you into the loop."

"Smart woman," Josie says.

She is.

When we meet for coffee the following week and I fill her in on my sisters' reactions, Sofie nods and gives a little smile. "Told you so," she says. "There's a loyalty with siblings that's hard to ignore. I'm always saying that to my kids. They get into the most ridiculous fights sometimes, over who ate the last goldfish cracker or who gets to use the blue Play-Doh, and I tell them to calm down and talk it out, because at the end of the day they're so lucky to have one another. Know what the best part is?" She sips her white chocolate mocha. "When I see they've realized how true it is. There are so many rewarding things about being a parent, but that tops the list. No matter what else is going on, watching my kids together is good for the soul."

I wonder: was it like that for my mother, too?

In her bleakest moments, when she was screaming at my dad and he was hurling insults back as though he had no regard for how they sliced into her, did she find any comfort in my sisters and me? When my dad stormed out, the door slamming so hard it rattled the picture frames on the wall, and she shut herself inside their bedroom, crying the tears she tricked herself into believing no one else could hear, did it help to know that she had three girls who still loved and depended on her? I hope it was a pinprick of light in a life that had grown to be so much darkness for her. Mom doesn't really like to talk about the divorce, and Abigail, Josie, and I respect that, but just this once I would like to get inside her head. Maybe it'd help me make up my own mind.

"How much of our lives," I say to Sofie, "do you think are influenced by our parents' decisions?"

"That depends," she says, "on if we allow them to be."

"What about you?" I ask. I lean forward and rest my elbows on the table. "When you made the choice to tell Addilyn she was adopted as soon as she was old enough to understand it ... would you have done that regardless, or was it because your parents hid the truth about your own adoption? If they had been open with you instead of keeping it a secret until you discovered those papers in a drawer, do you think you would have done things differently? How much was your decision actually swayed because of theirs?"

Sofie wraps her hands around her coffee cup and sighs. "I was crushed when I realized what an enormous secret my parents had kept," she says. "There were a lot of wrong choices made for the right reasons, and sure, it definitely factored in when Brandon and I were discussing how we should tell Addilyn she was adopted. I refused to do to her what my mom and dad did to me, however well meaning they were."

I consider this. Sofie's adoption has clearly left an indelible mark on her life, just as my parents' divorce has on mine. The difference, though, is that she's used it to push herself forward instead of allowing it to hold her back. I so admire that. Not only was she able to talk things through with her family, she's even forged a relationship with her biological parents. She took a difficult situation and made it work. Why can't I seem to do the same?

"Do you ever regret your choice?" I ask, picking up the wrapper from my banana chocolate chip muffin and folding its crinkles into smooth lines.

"No," Sofie says. "I don't regret it. It was the right decision for Addilyn and the right one for me. That is what your answer to Jonathan has to be, too," she adds. "Right for you. Forget your parents, your sisters … you even have to forget about Jonathan. If his feelings weren't part of the equation, if you knew he could still live his best life even if you turned him down, what would you do?"

It's a good question.

But, unlike the one Josie asked me about Henry and Rose, this time the answer eludes me.

"I don't know," I say.

A future without Jonathan in it feels unfathomable, but one

in which he and I don't have to sign our names on a marriage certificate ... I'm not convinced it'd be such a bad thing. We would still be able to keep all the best parts of our relationship without having to worry that a formal commitment would steal them away. Sure, marriage can elevate the happiness and promise and hope. I've seen it firsthand with my grandparents, who grew up next door to each other and were best friends for so many years before they fell in love after graduating from high school. They had just celebrated their sixty-seventh anniversary when my grandmom passed away.

And so I know it's possible. I know devoting your life to the person you love doesn't have to end in shattered dishes and accusations of cheating and wedding rings that are thrown across the room. But those things do happen, too. Happily-ever-after can turn into the stuff nightmares, not dreams, are made of, and I think it's the pressure of marriage that often delivers the final blow. Who would sign up for that? Usually people say yes to a proposal because of love, but I kind of feel like I should say no for the same reason. My grandparents had the great love story and my parents are the book that was shelved. What's written on the page, and in the stars, for Jonathan and me? What do I tell him when he asks why I still haven't given him an answer?

Ugh.

I do? Or I don't?

As the days pass by, each one longer than the last as I stay at the bookstore increasingly late to finalize plans for the book hop slated to start in December, I find myself returning to those questions whenever I have a spare moment. "What would *you* do?" I murmur, pulling a book off the shelf. It's a romance novel set in the nineteen-forties about a woman who writes a letter to her husband each day after he's drafted to fight in the war, only to receive them back, along with the tragic news that he has been killed in battle. But still, she keeps the letters, hanging on to the life she thinks she will never again live – until, a year later, there's a knock on the door and she opens it to see her husband standing there. He tells her he was able to escape enemy fire by camouflaging himself in the nearby brush and then doubling back to stage his own death. Risky as it was, it meant he got to come home to her.

I know what those characters would do in my situation.

I know what hundreds of other characters would do, too.

I could pick up any book I have read, flip through its pages, and understand how its protagonists would act. Some would fall in line with what readers would expect from a certain genre, but others wouldn't. The beautiful thing about writing is that the author has the freedom to craft fantastically nuanced characters who don't have to follow every predetermined stereotype. Sometimes they can surprise you.

I would really like to be able to surprise myself.

I just can't figure out if I have it in me.

How sad is that? It's absurd that I can get inside a fictional character's head better than I can my own.

Books were my escape as a child. They were my friends, my place to hide when the security of a happy family crumbled into something much scarier. When our parents first began to fight, Abigail would bring Josie and me into her room, turn the music up high on her stereo, and try to drown out the bitterness raging below us. Josie was too young to understand what was going on, but not me. "Thanks for saving us from the bad stuff," I remember telling Abigail once, and she pulled me into a hug.

"That's what big sisters are for," she said.

The longer the arguments went on, though, the more hostile they grew, locking ourselves away wasn't enough. That's when I fell into the comfort of books. I was a pretty advanced reader for my age, and each week, I'd borrow a new *Boxcar Children* story from the school library. When my mom and dad started in on each other, I would go to my room, settle onto my bed, and join the siblings as they solved mysteries. It was the first time I realized how much books could change a life.

They were my safe place.

They still are.

I know it, and Jonathan does, too.

He has never once said anything negative about all the late hours I'm working. He just comes to visit me at the bookstore at the end of his own workday. "So the forecast seems good," he says one evening. It's the Friday before Thanksgiving, and he's waiting patiently for me to finish shelving the books that came in earlier so we can head out to grab dinner. "A bit on the chilly side," he tells me, "but we should be fine. You might want to pack an extra sweater, though, and a pair of warm boots for the hikes."

I hear him talking, but as I heft out a stack of hardcovers, I'll admit that my attention is split. It's been a long day filled with one customer who wanted to return books that had clearly been marked up, another who spilled coffee all over the new display I had created for the kids' section, and a third who kept asking me to order a book that was self-published and only available online. Add another letter from the landlord, a 'friendly reminder about the rent increase,' as he phrased it, and I cannot seem to keep my attention from wandering tonight.

"Hmm?" I ask Jonathan, as I slip the books neatly into their places.

He glances up from his phone. "Our trip next week. Remember? You, me, the mountains?"

Oh, God.

It's not that I forgot, exactly, because I've actually been looking forward to the getaway, it's just that time has been whizzing by so fast. Thanksgiving still seemed far away when we decided on that weekend to go out of town. But now it's almost here, and I'm not sure I can afford the time away. I have two author events scheduled for next week – a signing with a local author whose debut novel released last month, and a question and answer session with Remi Parker, the writer who's made it onto all sorts of bestseller lists with her book *All that Glitters is not Gold*. It is the real-life story of a woman named Charlotte Carter, who set aside her chance at the

Olympics in order to run away with the man she loved. The pair of them went on to become coaches who led many swimmers to glory on the world stage. Charlotte and her husband are in their upper seventies now, but they still own a training gym, and I've been emailing with them, trying to convince them to join Remi on Wednesday for the event. I'm pretty sure they're going to do it, especially because Remi is five months pregnant and Charlotte says it'll be a perfect excuse to shower her with baby gifts. I need to be here for that. I need to give it my full attention.

And then there's Black Friday.

I could ask my two employees to work, and Abigail swore she'd help out too, but I don't know if that'll be enough. Christmas Eve is normally our busiest day, but Black Friday is the most hectic. I'm not so sure I should be away in the mountains.

I leave the cardboard box with the remaining books on the floor and go over to join Jonathan in the café. "I hate to say this," I start, then stop when I see his eyes flicker away from me. He knows exactly what I'm going to tell him before I even get the words out. "Hey," I try again, taking the seat next to him. "I love you. You know that, right?"

He nods, but says nothing.

"I can't wait to go away with you. But ... this isn't ... maybe we could ... " No matter how I try to explain myself, it sounds all wrong. "This isn't a good time for me to leave the store," I finally settle on. "It's the kickoff to our most profitable month of the year, and with the contest beginning in less than two weeks ... could we postpone for the week between Christmas and New Year's?"

He's quiet for a long time. Too long.

Even when he finally speaks, he refuses to meet my gaze. "I have appointments scheduled that week," he says. "You're not the only one with a busy job, Grace. That week is a jam-packed one for vets. People are off from work, so that's when they bring their pets in." He drags his hand through his hair, making it stand up at the ends, and I have to resist the urge to smooth it down. Something tells me this is not the time for the little affectionate gestures Jonathan and I normally appreciate so much. He's annoyed, more than I have ever seen him. "I already booked us a cabin," he says. "The one we discussed, remember? With the front porch overlooking the lake? You were excited about it. Or I thought you were, at least."

"I was. I am."

"Then why are you backing out?"

"I just told you why. This is a really terrible time for me to leave. And I'm sorry, because it was unfair of me to assume you could go in December without asking you first." I reach for his hand and breathe a sigh of relief when he doesn't pull away. "I know it seems like I'm putting the store before us," I tell him, "but that isn't it, I promise. Things are just especially crucial right now, and I need to see them through."

He tilts his head to the side. "Is that all it is?" he asks. "Or are you using it as an excuse because you're worried about spending four entire days together? Maybe you think I'll pressure you into an answer about the proposal ... or maybe," he continues, "you're worried you'll have such a good time that you'll want to say yes."

"I *do* want to say yes," I tell him. "But it's complicated."

Even to my own ears, that sounds evasive.

"Do you really want that?" Jonathan challenges. "Because it's been practically two months, and you refuse to barely address it with me, let alone discuss it." He sighs. "Look, I said I was willing to wait, and I am, but if this is all it's ever going to be, me wondering what you're thinking while you try to avoid actually talking about it, then maybe we should save ourselves the agony."

"And what?" My voice pitches up. "What are you saying? Are we over?"

"I don't know," Jonathan says. He meets my eyes in an unblinking stare. "You tell me."

ᗡ 20 ᗡ

Rose

I had to read the letter twice before the magnitude of its words truly registered.

To my beautiful North Star –

What a surprise these five days have been! When I boarded this ship back in Manhattan, I never could have guessed what was waiting for me. I imagined it would be my time to relax: to sleep late, read a good book, and enjoy nightly music from the band. A solo oasis on the seas sounded grand to me, especially since I must dive into my work once we dock in Europe. Then I met you, with your eyes that glitter in the sunlight and your laugh that reminds me of the wind chimes my mother hung up in the kitchen window. Perhaps it was fate that brought us together, or maybe it was simply that we're two souls who were seeking one another out. How wild is that? Of all the people on this planet, we still found each other.

I do not want to lose that ... or you. I know you are angry with me, but I am begging: please give me a chance to explain everything. Even if you cannot forgive me, at least make that decision based on the entire story. Our love deserves it. I do love you, that is a promise, and if you give me a second chance, I think we could go on an extraordinary adventure.

Stay with me in Europe. We can go on this journey together.

I will be waiting for you when the ship docks in the morning.

Love,

Henry

Oh, goodness. He wanted me to travel Europe with him?

It was just like I had dreamed the other night, except this was not my subconscious delighting in the things I was too hesitant to consider when the sun was shining rather than the moon. This was reality. I tried to imagine what it would be like, getting to explore all the countries with Henry. Not even twelve hours earlier, I would have been elated at the prospect, and although that sense of joy was crushed after what had happened, I still wanted to say yes. Even after the night before, I could not help being tempted to take his hand and hold on tightly – which was precisely why I also wanted to say no.

If he could make me feel so strongly in mere days, what would transpire in weeks? Months? It scared me. Before Henry barreled into my life, I had been able to experience my emotions without letting them get the better of me. The previous night, though, had been an unwelcome onslaught. I thought of the way my heart had pounded as I stood there in his room, the pulse in my wrist beating in double time as my ears seemed to ring with anguish. For all the times Henry had made me feel so wonderfully giddy, there was also this. There was also this one time his love lurched me into a free-fall.

I had no idea what to do.

Oh, how I wished I could talk to Violet.

Our entire lives, we had shared stories and secrets, smiles and tears, hopes and fears, questions and answers. She was the one I always turned to for advice. When I was debating whether or not I should apply for the secretary job at the law firm, Violet was the first person whose opinion I asked. When I could not bear to go on even one additional date with Fred, a friend of Alice's husband and a man I simply was not compatible with, Violet offered to call him so I would not have to be the one to break it off with him. There were hundreds of other instances, too. Violet was consistently the first person I opened up to, and so I felt lost, having to make such a monumental decision without talking to her. It seemed wrong. I knew I had been the one to say Violet and I needed to stand on our own, but that did not change how homesick I felt for her. I would have given anything to pick up a phone and hear her voice at the other end. It would be possible once the ship was docked, but that would be too late. Henry needed an answer before then.

I traced my fingers over the words he had written.

His letter was like something out of a picture at the theater. Grand gestures such as that – bold, sweeping, dramatic gestures – simply did not happen in real life. They did not happen in *my* life, at least. Love had always been an abstract notion. It was something I listened to my sister and friends discuss, something my parents tried to push on me, something I watched on television. Henry made it more than that, though. He made it tangible.

I was deeply touched. I was deeply terrified. I was deeply torn.

I was also running out of time to make a decision.

The clock on the wall ticked steadily, counting down to the moment I knew would shape my life forever, no matter what I chose. Even as I settled everything back into my suitcase, and as I opened the porthole windows to breathe in every last drop of the salty air, I could hear the rhythmic sound taunting me. Tick-tock, ticktock, ticktockticktockticktock. I had to get away from it, so I gathered up my room key and my diary, and hurried out the door, hoping to leave the countdown to my destiny behind.

It partially worked.

Although the ticking sound disappeared as I made my way through the ship and out to the deck with the chaises facing the sea, the weight of my decision remained. There were two options – sink or swim. Which choice would lead to which outcome? It was so ironic, how confident I had been in that dream of mine. In it, Henry and I had explored all of the excitement and history Europe had to offer, and I had been secure in the knowledge that it was where we were supposed to be. Now that I was faced with the actual opportunity, though, my mind filled with questions I could not even start to answer.

It was funny: for someone who loved to watch the sunrise,

I realized, as I sat down and opened my diary, that the sun could also be intimidating, because it illuminated so many truths. Maybe that was why the nighttime created such boldness: because we could only see a few steps in front of us. We had nothing to rely on but our intuition and the hope that if we stumbled, we could get back up again. It was different in the daytime. The entirety of the path was clear, with all its holes and traps and trails winding in opposite directions.

I thought maybe it might help me to reflect on them, so I let my pen take over.

Friday, July 15th, 1955

I caught Henry with another woman yesterday. Marjorie is her name. I have no idea who she is or what they were doing together, and I will admit I was not the most rational about letting them explain. How ridiculous is that? I certainly have no claim to Henry. I just thought we had something special. He must agree, though, because he asked me to stay with him as he travels through Europe. I am curious: was it hearing about my dream that sparked the idea? Would he have asked anyway, even if I had not walked in on him and Marjorie? I cannot tell if it was an action or a reaction on his part.

Would that even matter?

I am not sure.

What I do know is that I refuse to let the purpose of my own journey get overshadowed. Even if Henry is a part of what I am meant for, he is not the only part. Will running off with him negate the rest? How can I discover my truest self if my focus is being pulled in multiple directions? Here is the thing: if Henry had asked me this before the situation with Marjorie last night, I would have said yes in a heartbeat. I would have believed it was serendipity. Now I am simply confused.

As my pen came to a stop, I gazed out at the water, its waves stronger now that we were getting closer to shore. I wanted to just stay and watch it, but that would not be an option for much longer. The ship would be docking soon, Henry would be waiting, and the decision needed to be made: day, or night?

* * *

It was bittersweet, shutting the door to my stateroom for the last time. For all of the activities I had packed into the cruise, it still felt like I had just set foot on the *SS Harmony*. The days had been long, but the trip short. I took a photo of the door, complete with its room number, then tucked my camera away and set off. I would miss the ship – the lounge, with its velvet drapes and dim lighting; the dining room, with its chandeliers and delicious food; the pool, with its cool water and the scent of suntan oil hanging in the air. I would miss the glamour, the serenity, and the continual inspiration it seemed to offer up. That ship had refilled my own well, and I was endlessly appreciative, but I was also excited for the next step.

Europe awaited.

It seemed that my fellow passengers were eager, too. The outer deck of the ship was filled with people, much like when we set sail, but this time hardly anyone was standing still. They were ready to move on. The *SS Harmony* had connected us for a week, and now we would go our own separate ways, just like that. I thought of the people I had met and the conversations I had shared. Some of them had already slipped from my mind, but others, such as the one with the mother hurrying back to her seasick son and the one with the elderly couple staying in the next cabin, who had invited me to join them for lunch, would linger. Perhaps they would stay with me for awhile, perhaps forever. That was the humbling thing about life: you never knew how far a moment could reach, how lasting an impact it might have, until it turned into a memory. I was lucky to be leaving the ocean liner with so many memories.

As I walked down to the docks, a surprisingly cool breeze ruffling the scarf tied around my neck, I knew there was still one more to come. Henry was waiting, as he said he would be, and his mouth curved into a smile the second he saw me. "Rose," he said quietly, as I slowed to a stop beside him. "You came."

"I did."

We were both silent for a minute, ensconced in our own snow globe as life pulsated around us. People were everywhere, retrieving luggage and waiting to show their passports, and though I could see them, it was like they were a mirage. I only had eyes for Henry. He looked especially handsome that morning, dressed in gray slacks and a blue shirt, his face so filled with faith and promise. "So," he said finally, taking a step closer to me but stopping short of grazing his hand against mine, "does this mean you are willing to hear me out?"

I nodded. "I owe you that. I owe *us* that."

He heaved a sigh of relief. "Thank you," he said. He gestured to a nearby bench and I followed him to it, locking my gaze with his as we sat down. My friend Lucy was always saying you could tell a lot about people by their eyes. If they were hiding something, their eyes would give it away. I paid careful attention to Henry's eyes now, as he fidgeted with his watch, spinning it around on his wrist.

"Go on," I said gently.

He cleared his throat. "First of all," he said, "I want to apologize. I should have handled it better last night. I really had no idea that Marjorie would be coming by. We'd finished our discussion that morning, or so I thought. When she knocked on my door, I just assumed it was you. Obviously that wasn't the case, and I was so flustered by seeing her when I knew you were on your way that I guess I forgot to lock the door behind her. You see," he told me, "Marjorie actually works on the ship. She deals with sales and marketing."

Of all the scenarios I had played out in my mind, that was not one of them, not even close. "So that day with the captain," I said, as something occurred to me, "when he referred to a colleague of his you had spoken to, was that her?"

"It was," Henry confirmed. "Technically, she's employed by the ship's parent company, but right now she's mainly working on the *SS Harmony*. Ocean liners are starting to fade a bit in popularity," he explained. "Airlines are taking over in international travel, so the company which owns this ship and the *SS Majesty* is trying to come up with new ways to attract people. My boss's cousin works in the cruise industry and told him about it, so we decided to arrange a meeting to discuss the idea of opening a jewelry store on board. A shopping area could help ocean liners make a profit. Marjorie was intrigued by the idea," he said, "as was the captain."

I tilted my head slightly, appraising him. "Why didn't you tell me this from the start?" I asked. "I personally think it's a swell plan. Why did you feel like you couldn't trust me with information about it?"

"No, no, it wasn't that," he rushed to say. "I trust you completely, but it wasn't my call to make. I was explicitly cautioned by the ship's personnel not to discuss it while negotiations were ongoing, especially because ... " He sighed, averting his gaze from mine and looking at the ship as people kept disembarking.

"Because what?" I prompted.

He faced me again. "Because not all the stones I have with me are owned by my company."

What? I stared at him, perplexed.

"What are you talking about?" I asked.

"Remember the night I showed you some of my inventory? And you asked what happens to the stones with flaws? I said the worst ones become a total loss, and while that is true in the eyes of my boss, I've always disagreed. It's no secret that the perfect stones sell for the most money, but I have always been drawn to the others." He gave a dimpled half-grin. "The misfit ones, so to speak. They remind me of my family, broken apart and full of cracks. I had a thought one day that it would be so interesting to save the stones and turn them into something greater than they were originally meant to be." Here, he chuckled. "As you can imagine, my boss hated the plan, so ... I'm not very proud to admit this, but I started keeping the stones I was supposed to discard. I've been experimenting with them, trying to find the best way to show off their unique kind of beauty."

It felt like my eyes were nearly popping out of my head at that point. "Is that even legal?"

"I hope so," he said. "They never would've been used for anything, anyway, and I have actually been paying my boss for them without him knowing it. I just add in extra money to the cash I bring back from the sales I make. I know it could cause an uproar, though, if people find out. So yes, part of the reason I couldn't tell you what was going on is because I was obligated to keep quiet until the contract was signed, but it was also because I didn't think it was fair to ask you to keep my secret. I couldn't do that to you."

"And Marjorie?" I said. "You left out an important detail from your explanation. Why were you standing with your arms around her when I walked in last night?"

That question is what finally prompted him to take a chance and reach for my hand. "I'm aware of how terrible that looked," he said, "but you have my word, Rose, that it was absolutely nothing. I was putting a necklace on her because she was having trouble with the clasp. It got caught up in her hair and she couldn't see to untangle it. She came by to try on a couple more pieces of jewelry," he added, "before making her final decision about partnering both with my company and myself. I just could not turn her away, not when the deal was close to being finalized. I didn't think it'd take long, and it wouldn't have, if not for the problem with the necklace. She should've been gone before you ever arrived." He traced his finger along the lines of my palm. "There it is," he told me. "The entire story."

He stopped speaking then, but I heard the words he did not say.

Is it enough?

Do you believe me?

Do you forgive me?

It was enough. I did believe him, and I did forgive him.

"Thank you for being honest," I said. "It means so much to me."

"Thank *you* for listening," he said. "It killed me last night, knowing I was the one who caused all that pain. Hurting you is the last thing I want to do." He paused for a second as he linked his fingers with mine. "Does this mean you'll come with me?" he asked, and his voice was so full of optimism, overflowing with the kind of unfettered hope that makes you think the whole world is yours for the taking, that it brought tears to my eyes.

I had made my decision.

The truth was, I had made it before we even sat down on that bench.

"I'm so sorry," I said, and it came out as a whisper, my heart fighting my brain, trying to stifle the words. "I love you, Henry, and I want to say yes, I want us to go out into the unknown together, but I just can't."

My heart splintered as his face fell. Now I was the one causing the pain, and it felt dreadful ... so horribly, pathetically, unbearably dreadful. I knew that no matter what came next for me, wherever the remainder of my travels led, I would never forget the sorrow of that moment. For the rest of my life, I would carry around the image of the despair filling Henry's eyes.

"Why not?" he asked, and his voice cracked.

I took a shaky breath.

"Because my love for you scares me," I said. "This journey was supposed to be about finding my own way, and I got completely wrapped up in you instead. If I fell that fast, I cannot imagine what it would be like if we spent every day together for the foreseeable future. Last night, when I thought something romantic was going on between you and Marjorie ... it was like I didn't recognize myself. I got entirely lost in my emotions."

"That isn't necessarily a bad thing," he pointed out. "It means you're invested."

He was looking right at me, right into me, right through me, like he could see the deepest parts of my soul without even trying. It made me want to take the whole thing back, take *him* back, but at the same time, it also made me realize why I had to do the opposite. I let my eyes flutter closed for a second, and when I opened them again, I looked right back at him. The hope was gone now. Only disappointment remained.

"I am invested," I said. "More so than I was ever supposed to be, and I can't let that happen." I inched closer to him, until our legs were touching and I could feel the warmth from his body so near to mine. "There is a lot I have to learn about myself before I can even think of taking a leap like that again." I raised a hand to his cheek, his skin cool to the touch beneath a sky that had turned cloudy. "Please understand," I said. "This is about me, not you."

His arm trembled as he reached up to cover my hand with his. "I do understand," he said. "The timing isn't right. But God, do I wish it was."

I wished it was, too.

I also almost wished he would fight me on my decision, but I knew he would let it stand. Henry would never get in the way of me finding what I needed. He was far too good a man for that, and it made it even harder to tear myself away. Tears streamed from my eyes as I leaned close to him, so very close, and pressed my mouth to his for the last time. "I love you," I said. "I don't know if I will ever stop."

"Same here." He kissed me again, sweet and sad, and then, right as I was about to stand up, he took out a box from his pocket. "This is for you," he said. "It was the surprise I'd hoped to give you last night." My hand instantly curled around it, desperate to hold onto this piece of him, whatever it was, and I was going to thank him, I was going to say I would remember him for the rest of eternity, but he did not give me the chance. He simply brushed his lips to my forehead and stood up from the bench. "Goodbye, my Rose," he said.

∾ 21 ∽

Grace

*T*here are so many things I want to tell Jonathan. That he is the best man I've ever known. That I feel like the heroine from a novel each time he kisses me. That I love the way he hums beneath his breath when he's fixing a meal. That it shocked me at first, when I saw the paw print tattoo peeking out from his shirt cuff, but that now it's one of my favorite things about him. That, if we really were to go our separate ways, I'd miss biking with him in Piedmont Park, and volunteering together at the animal shelters, and attending shows at the Fox. I would miss the times when he makes me laugh so hard it hurts, and the ones when he gets choked up as he tells me about an animal who survived its risky surgery, and the ones when we're sitting on the sofa, doing nothing but still enjoying it because we're doing nothing together. The big moments are great, but as I look at Jonathan, I realize it's the small ones that'd be the largest loss. If I had to go the rest of my life without them, a light would go out inside me.

Maybe *that* is what I should tell him.

Instead, I stand up and offer him my hand. "Come with me," I say. I lead him to the side of the store, to the current events section, then sit down cross-legged on the floor. Jonathan looks at me, puzzled, but takes a spot at my side as I point out the artwork drawn onto the bottom of the nearby bookshelf. It's a big puffy heart, the letters ILTBB written inside and the whole thing surrounded by squiggly lines. The marker is faded now, many shades lighter thanks to the decades of sunshine that have streamed through the shop windows, but the memory of how it got there is as vibrant as ever. "You probably wouldn't peg me for a graffiti artist," I say to Jonathan, and the tiniest of smiles plays on his mouth, "but this is my handiwork."

"You? Defacing property?" he asks. "In a bookstore, no less?"

I chuckle. "I was ten," I say. "And my dad's new wife had just given birth to their second baby in as many years. It was amazing, how he suddenly remembered my sisters and me at times like that. He wanted us to meet our half-brother, he said, which was pretty absurd, since he basically shunned any contact with us otherwise. Anyway, my mom said she couldn't be the one to take us, not after how things ended between them, so my Gram did. That made it a bit easier. For all of her strength, she also had a sense for when we needed her to wrap her arms around us and hold tight. She knew exactly how to make it better for us, having to sit there and see our dad with his perfect new family that basically made it seem like ours had never existed. He was happy with Sharon and their kids in a way that just hurt. A lot."

Jonathan rests his hand on my knee. "I'm sorry," he says. "That must've been impossibly hard."

"It was. Abigail cried half the drive home."

"And you?"

I gesture to the bookcase. "I did this," I say. "The letters stand for 'I Love The Book Boutique.' I still remember how the store was my sanctuary that day. Gram had to work after we got back, and I went with her. I can't even tell you how many books I flipped through, trying to find one that would erase the pain, and then after I did ... I don't know, I guess I wanted to express my gratitude." I lean forward, running my fingers over the light oak bookcase. "Gram wasn't too pleased, but I think she appreciated the sentiment, if not the actual result."

"Is that why she kept it there?" he asks.

"I asked her that once. She said she'd considered trying to clean it off, but in the end decided to leave it as a love letter of sorts. She told me that we can never go wrong by expressing our feelings for how much something means to us." I turn to him. "And I think that is where I have been lacking. Maybe I need to be more vocal about the feelings I have. I don't want us to break up. Not now, not ever." I take a deep breath, let it out, and tell him every single thing I was thinking of earlier. "I love you with all my heart," I say. "I'm just so scared that marriage will end up destroying what we have already built."

"Let me ask you something," he says. "Is every book within a certain genre the same?"

"No. Of course not."

"But some people assume that's the case, don't they? They pigeonhole books according to the shelves they're on, without even taking the time to open the covers and read what's inside. If they would, they'd see that although there may be similarities, there's also something unique about each one."

"Exactly."

"Well," he says, "maybe it's the same with marriage. I get why you are making a generalization. It's the natural thing to do after what happened in your family. I can't, and I won't, pretend to know how it feels, having everything ripped apart. I may have grown up as an only child, but I realize how lucky I am to have parents who'd go to the ends of the earth for one another. A lot of people don't. But I think it's like the book thing. Every marriage is different. We can't judge the potential for one by the pain of another." He circles his arm around my shoulders. "Look, I'm not saying we wouldn't have bumps in the road. All couples do. Our marriage wouldn't be your parents' marriage, though. It'd be ours."

I think about his analogy.

It's a good one.

An inspired one.

"I really do want to go away with you," I say softly. "If you're set on next week, I'll make it work. Josie's flying in for Thanksgiving, so maybe I can twist her arm to come in and help. The bookstore is a priority, but so are you. I want you to know that."

"Thank you," he says. "It would be selfish to take you away from Atlanta now, though. Forcing you to set aside something important isn't what love is. We'll find a time that works for both of us."

I smile at him hopefully. "So does this mean we're not over?"

"I don't want us to be."

The rush of relief that floods over me feels palpable. "Me either," I say. "Thank you for sticking with me. I know I don't always make it easy." I press a kiss to his cheek. "You're the absolute best, just for the record."

"You give me too much credit," he says.

I think it's the opposite. As we sit here in the store, only the two of us tucked away amongst all the shelves, I realize that I haven't been giving him enough credit. I've allowed my past to spread its dark ink over the blank page that could be my future. What happened to writing my own story? It's up to me to do that, not my sisters or my parents or even Jonathan. And maybe I do know my own mindset better than I thought. Maybe, in the tiniest, most hidden away part of my heart, I am fully aware of what it'll take to decide how to answer Jonathan's proposal, once and for all. I just have to find the nerve to do it.

I reach up and rest a hand on my Gram's locket.

"I believe in you, my girl." She used to tell me that all the time.

God, how I wish she was still here. I miss her and Pop-Pop always, but every now and then I feel the absence more acutely. This is one of those times. It's like the grief, which has calmed down into a steady hum over the years, has suddenly roared back as something louder. I know how to quiet it. I know how *they* would want me to quiet it: by gathering up all the courage which seems so elusive. That is how I can honor them and their fierce belief in me.

So it's exactly what I do the next day.

Every Saturday morning, no matter if it's sunny and hot or

cloudy and cold, my mom leaves her house at nine o'clock sharp and heads to Centennial Park. Sometimes she'll eat breakfast and read a magazine, sometimes she'll go for a walk, and sometimes she'll sit by the reflecting pool and people watch. She first began doing it after the divorce, and in those days she'd bring Abigail, Josie, and me along. It'll be nice to join her for it again. I'm at her house bright and early, sneakers on my feet and a grin on my face. Because this is how I'm going to do it. This is how I'm going to find that courage … or, at least, how I'm going to create it. I will drag it to the surface, kicking and screaming, if I have to.

"Grace!" My mom's face registers surprise when she walks outside to find me getting out of my car. "What are you doing here?"

"I thought you might like some company this morning. I even come bearing bagels and coffee," I tell her.

"That sounds delicious," she says. "And yes, of course I would enjoy your company. I always do. Come on." She motions toward her car, and I spend the half hour drive into the city simultaneously making small talk with her and also trying to figure out the best way to broach a subject I know she would rather not discuss. Finally, as we get out into the chilly November air, it occurs to me: there's never going to be a good way. Sometimes there isn't in life. Sometimes the first step just has to be onto rocky terrain.

"Hey, can I ask you something?" I say to Mom, as we walk into the park.

"Always," she says.

I fall into place beside her as she heads in the direction of the garden pavilions. It's a sunny day, the light strong enough that I need sunglasses, but there's no doubt that autumn has finally gotten a firm grip on the city. I tug the zipper on my fleece jacket a little higher as I gaze across the park and out at the buildings towering beyond its limits. I want to do that, too. I want to grow far beyond my limits.

"Do you ever regret getting married?" I push the words out

quickly, before I can lose my nerve. I've been wondering about it ever since Abigail brought it up the other week. She seemed confident that our mom would say no, but I'm not so sure.

"I hate that you have to ask that," Mom says, and her grip tightens around her coffee cup. "For as awful as the divorce was for your father and me, the worst part was how it affected you and your sisters. That killed me. It still does." She sighs. "I regret a great deal about that time in my life. All the fighting, and accusing, and jumping to conclusions ... I look back on all that and am so ashamed. Regardless of how your dad and I felt about one another, we could've done better by our daughters. We should have done better. I regret *that*," she says. "The way it impacted you three, and the fact that I became so wrapped up in my anger and hurt. But no." She turns to me. "I could never regret getting married, because that gave me you, Abigail, and Josie. You all make everything worth it."

Something struggles to break free inside my chest, but I don't let it.

Not yet.

"But what if we weren't a factor?" I persist. "Then would you wish you had never said yes when he proposed?"

"I can't answer that," she says, "because bringing our three wonderful daughters into the world is the best thing your dad and I ever did. To exclude that from our history isn't right. What I can tell you is this ... the good in our marriage got destroyed by the bad, but now that I've had enough time and distance to be able to look back on things with a cooler head, it's easier to remember that your father and I did love each other. Things were great for a long time."

"Until they weren't."

"Yes," she says. "Until we both made a lot of mistakes." She regards me curiously as we get to the pavilion and sit down at one of the benches to eat our breakfast. "What made you bring this up today?" she asks. "Is everything okay?"

I take a deep breath. "Jonathan proposed – "

"Oh!" she exclaims, and her eyes go wide as saucers. "That's the most fabulous – "

"At the beginning of last month."

"What?" Now her eyes narrow. "Why am I only hearing about it today?"

"I'm so sorry," I say. "I wasn't ready to talk about it before. He caught me completely off-guard, and I wanted to say yes, but all I could think of was how afraid I was. How desperately I didn't want to risk our relationship getting swept into a downward spiral. And I just couldn't put that on you. I didn't want to hurt you."

"Because of the divorce." She immediately understands what I mean. "You're worried that the two of you will end up like your father and me." She reaches over, creating a shell around my hand with hers. "Honey, please don't. Don't let fear keep you from joy. I see the way you light up when you're around Jonathan. He makes you happy. Don't ignore that, and don't throw it away. No one can predict what the future will hold, but what I do know is this: even if something were to happen that pulled you and Jonathan apart, you'd handle it with so much more grace than your father and I did." She smiles. "If you ask me, though, I honestly believe the two of you are right for each other. If you take a chance on him, and on yourself, you just might find that it's the best thing you've ever done."

"Thank you," I tell her. "I love you."

"I love you, too." She leans over to hug me, and in that moment, I feel like perhaps it is possible to finally leave history in the past. But first there's another person I have to talk to, even though the mere thought is enough to make a jumble of nerves twist their way through my stomach.

My father.

He's still living on Tybee Island these days. It's a four-and-a-half hour drive, one I haven't made since the last time I saw him two years ago for his sixtieth birthday, and so I make certain to leave as soon as the sun rises the next day. I have to be back for work on Monday, which means I'll be in the car for nine hours in one day. As unappealing as that seems, I know this is something I have to do in person. I have to be able to see what truths his eyes hold as he answers my questions.

Why was it so easy for him to all but abandon the family he once proclaimed to love?

Does *he* regret the marriage to my mother?

It wouldn't surprise me if his answer is very different than hers.

After the divorce, Dad headed south on I-75 and built himself a new life. It was exciting at first, almost like a vacation from real life when my sisters and I would get to spend time with him there. I used to pack up my duffel bag for the weekend, always choosing a new book to bring along for Dad to read to me. Abigail, Josie, and I had to share a bedroom there, and I still remember the way they would gather around when our dad was reading, even though Abigail was really too old for the story and Josie too young. We enjoyed it, though. It was special. And then our dad met Sharon in a surf shop by the beach. It was a quick engagement for them, too, although not as brief as the one to my mother. Even so, Mom nearly went through the roof when he called to invite my sisters and me to be flower girls in the beachside ceremony.

"Are you out of your mind?" she snapped. It'd been too soon. The betrayal had cut too deep. I wonder, sometimes, what would've happened if she'd made a different choice that day. If she'd let us go, would we have ended up having a more permanent place in our father's life? And, even more importantly – knowing how he's treated us, would I even *want* that place?

The thoughts swirl through my mind as I pull up in front of his house. It's a small cottage type of home, its siding painted the hue of the ocean and its shutters the color of sand. A bicycle is leaning against the garage door, and my father's car is parked in the driveway. I can feel my heartbeat pick up as I walk by it. I don't want to do this. For as much as it was a treat to come visit my father after the divorce – he'd take us onto the beach, building sandcastles, buying ice cream, and letting us stay out until the moon crept into the sky – it is the opposite now. Everything changed after he married Sharon. He had a new wife, and soon enough new children, and we grew to expect the phone call in which he'd ask us not to visit for our scheduled weekend because something had come up.

Something always came up.

Josie's called him out on it more than once.

Abigail prefers to, as she says, "deliberately ignore him like he ignored us."

And I've always stayed quiet.

Until today.

As difficult as it is, as painful and gnawing and emotional, I need to know. I breathe in as I reach the front door, the salt air buoying my resolve and stirring up feelings I thought I'd buried long ago. Oddly enough, their reemergence somehow serves to embolden me. I can do this. I can speak out. I raise my hand and knock on the door.

It's jolting when it opens. There he is, standing in front of me.

His hair is lighter than the last time I saw him, gray creeping in around his temples, and behind his glasses, his eyes train on me with the steadiest focus. He just stares for a few moments, like he's unsure whether I'm actually there on his front step or if he's only imagining things. "Grace?" he says finally.

I nod. "May I come in?"

"Yes. Yes, of course." He holds the door open and motions me inside. "Is everything okay?"

"Grace." Sharon's voice echoes in the entryway as she comes over from the kitchen. "It's good to see you." She turns to my father. "Grace emailed last night," she tells him. "She wanted to make sure you'd be home today."

"Thanks for getting back to me, and for keeping it between us," I say, and offer her a smile that I hope reflects my gratitude.

In another life, I would have liked Sharon. She's a high school English teacher with a personality so bubbly it's infectious. Her laughter is the kind that makes you want to join in, and when she asks questions you get the sense that she's actually interested in the answers. But for my sisters and me, it was decided early on that we could never warm up to her. In our young eyes, she took our daddy away from us. Now I realize that was never the case. Dad took himself away, and that is on no one but him.

"What's going on?" he asks me.

"I need to talk to you," I say.

"Okay." He sounds cautious. "Shall we go out back?"

He leads the way onto the porch. It overlooks the beach and ocean, a peaceful spot that seems discordant with the person I know him to be. Not only was there the detachment from us, but there was also the hostility he threw around in the days before the divorce. I know that isn't a particularly fair assessment, that it took two tempers to blow up my parents' marriage, but Mom stuck around. He didn't. I don't know that I can ever forgive him for that, but still, I would like to hear what he has to say.

"I have to ask you something," I tell him. "And please, don't sugarcoat your answer. Just be as honest as possible."

His fingers curl around the arm of his chair. "Alright," he says tensely.

He almost seems nervous.

I am, too, but I dive in anyway. "Do you regret marrying Mom?" I ask him, and his reply almost knocks me out of my chair.

It is immediate, resolute. "No," he says, like he can't fathom how I could think so. "She was, at the time, the love of my life. We may not have lasted, but while we were happy ... I'd never change that. However, I *would* change the way I treated you and your sisters." He looks first at the waves, then at a passing boat, then down at the slats of the porch. Anywhere but at me. "It was terrible to shut you out like that," he says quietly.

"Yes." I twist my hands together. "It was."

"I've thought about calling to apologize," he tells me. "More than once, especially over the past couple of years. But so much time has gone by. The three of you have lives I know next to nothing about, and there is nobody to blame for that but me. I suppose I feel like I haven't earned the right to reach out."

Wow.

I don't know what I expected him to say, but it wasn't that.

"So you just decided not to try?" I ask.

"Yes," he admits. "But does it help to know I never meant to hurt you?"

I raise my eyebrows. "What did you think would happen when you never wanted to see us?"

He finally meets my eyes.

"I *did* want to see you," he tells me. "Always. I can't tell you how often I wanted to pick up the phone and call when you were all younger. But when I did it, and I heard your excited voices telling me about school, or soccer practice, or piano lessons, it reminded me that I wasn't there to be a part of it. And I know it was my choice to move here, to not be close by and only see my daughters once a month, but ... " He pauses, taking off his glasses and rubbing the bridge of his nose. "It was tough to be near you, because you were a reminder that everything I'd imagined for myself hadn't come to pass. When I saw you all, I saw the implosion of my marriage. You were a living, breathing reminder of how I had failed. It was too painful. So I left, and focused on my new life here. It was easier that way."

"But easier isn't always better," I say. "At least it wasn't for us."

"I know," he says. "And for that, I apologize."

I shift my gaze to the beach, watching as a little boy makes his way along the shoreline, stopping to pick up seashells and slide them into the pocket of his sweatshirt. A man follows closely behind – his father, I assume, judging by the way the boy beams up at him – and out of the corner of my eye, I see my dad regarding them steadily. "You know," I say softly, "we could've had times like that, too. Abigail, Josie, and I loved it here, until you gave us a reason not to."

He closes his eyes briefly, and when he opens them again, they are glossy with unshed tears. "I was wrong," he says. "And I'm sincerely sorry."

I'm surprised to find I actually believe him, and it makes me wish I'd done this sooner. Maybe it would have changed things. At least I know the truth now. It should be enough for me, hearing his explanation and understanding, finally, that in his heart of hearts, he truly did care. It's just that his love for us got caught up in his own insecurities. I'm still not sure I can forgive that, but I can make sense of it.

And yet that isn't enough.

There is still one more person I want to talk to.

I'm exhausted by the time I get home that night, but first thing in the morning, I sit myself down at the desk in my living room before I leave for work, double click on the Internet browser, and type in a name.

Henry Jackson.

∿22∿

Rose

ondon was magnificent.

I gazed out of the taxi's windows for the entire drive to my hotel, completely spellbound by it all. Set against a sky that was white with thick clouds, the colors of the city seemed to pop. Everything competed for my attention – the cobblestone streets, and the phone booths, and the double decker buses which looked larger in person than I had pictured them to be from the photographs I had seen in books. It was interesting: for as excited as I had been to get out of Manhattan, to step beyond the boundaries of the place so many people considered limitless, I was just as eager to immerse myself in this new city. I wanted to listen to its heartbeat and feel it thrum through me.

"Pardon me," I said to the taxi driver, as he navigated the streets. "This is my first time visiting, and I was wondering if you could give me some information on the best places to go. I already have the well-known ones on my list – Buckingham Palace, Piccadilly Circus, the Palladium, the things any good tourist should see – but I was also hoping to explore some areas that are more tucked away. Is there anywhere you'd recommend?"

"Isabella Plantation," he said in a thick British accent. "It's in the south part of the city. It's not as popular as Hyde Park or St. James's, but the gardens there are absolutely fantastic. I proposed to my wife there," he added, "so it'll always be special to us."

I loved that. It was exactly the kind of response I had been hoping for.

The real magic of a place, I was starting to understand, had nothing to do with how it looked on the outside, but rather the stories it held on the inside. The SS *Harmony* was meaningful to me not because of the fancy staterooms, or the delicious food, or the sparkling swimming pool. For all of its grandeur, that ocean liner had etched itself into my heart because of the special memories it led me to create. That is what I wanted to find in England, too. I wanted to see the country through other people's eyes, in the hope that it would open my own to things I could not imagine as of yet.

"Thank you," I said to the taxi driver. "I'll make certain to visit there."

"I hope you enjoy it," he said, as he slowed the car to a stop in front of my hotel. "And your stay here, as well. London is a great city. It's full of hidden gems." He opened his door and stepped out to help me with my luggage. That was a good thing, but it led to quite the conundrum: I had no idea how to determine his tip. I had researched the conversion rate between the dollar and the different forms of money used overseas, but I could not seem to remember all I had learned. Henry was still taking up so much room in my thoughts that there was a limited amount of space for anything else. I simply had to guess what a pound was worth and hope that I was at least marginally close. I must have been, because the man tipped his hat at me before driving off. I watched the car retreat, then picked up a suitcase in each hand and walked into the hotel.

It was time to begin the next part of my trip.

First, though, I had a phone call to make. After I was settled into my room, which was decorated in shades of green and gray and had a lovely view of a park across the street, I picked up the receiver and dialed Violet's number. It would have to be a short conversation since long distance calls were expensive, but even still, I needed to hear her voice. So much had happened since the last time we spoke.

"Violet!" Her name bubbled out of my mouth as soon as she answered.

"Rose!" she exclaimed. "Oh, I'm so glad to hear from you. I have been thinking about you every day. I didn't know what to do with myself, not being able to call you whenever I wanted. It felt very strange."

"I agree. There's been so much I wanted to tell you about, too." I launched into the story about Henry, knowing that Violet would listen without judgment. She and I had always been an objective sounding board for each other, a safe place to share and contemplate and wonder.

"Wow," she said, when I finished talking. "That's a lot to process."

"I know." I wound the phone cord around my finger and then let go, watching as it sprang back into place. Could I do that? Could I spring back to the way I was before Henry? I looked over at the table, where I had set the velvety box he had given me. As desperately curious as I was to see what was inside, I had not yet opened it. I was too afraid it would make me want to go back to him, which was no longer a possibility. I did not know where he was staying, or even how long he planned to be in England. "Walking away was the right decision, wasn't it?" I asked Violet. "Henry's a real dream, but if I stayed, I would have been risking myself."

I was praying she would back me up.

She knew that, and as always, she came through. "Love is tricky," she said. "It grabs a hold of us when we least expect it. That can be a beautiful thing, but it can also be frightening. I think perhaps it's magnified for you, because this is your first real experience with it. What you and Henry shared ... sure, it might have grown into the sort of love that comes around once in a lifetime, or maybe you are right and it would have stopped you from getting to the place you needed to be. Only you know that, and I think it is so important that you listen to your own heart."

"Suppose my heart doesn't know what it's saying?"

"Oh, it does," she told me. "It always does."

"It doesn't feel like it," I confessed. "I know I made the choice I had to, but I miss him already."

"Of course you do," she said. "You can't just turn off your feelings for somebody." She paused. "You know I'd love it if you could find the same kind of happiness Thomas and I have, but when you first talked to me about this trip, you were focused on discovering your own path. If Henry would've derailed that, then yes, I think you made the right decision."

It was exactly what I needed to hear.

Violet believed in love and marriage, and I was positive she would have been over-the-moon if I told her I had found my soulmate in Henry. She wanted that for me. She wanted my life to be full in as many ways as possible. This was proof, though, that she only cared about that because she cared about me. Whatever I wanted was ultimately what she wanted for me.

"You're the best," I told her. "Thank you. I think we should change the subject, though. Tell me about you. Has anything exciting happened since I left?"

She started to talk about her week, about the new dress she had bought for a charity fundraiser for Thomas' hospital and the different recipes she was testing out for a baking contest. It was being sponsored by a magazine, and the winner would receive both a cash prize and the opportunity to be featured in its glossy pages. I zeroed in on every detail Violet relayed about it, grateful for a chance to concentrate on her life instead of mine.

The reprieve was, truly, a breath of fresh air.

Even so, I was acutely aware of the jewelry box still sitting on the table. It was as though it was daring me to open it. I stayed strong, steady, unwavering ... until I was forced to hang up the phone for fear of spending too much money on my first day off the ship. The call had already gone longer than I had planned. Without Violet for company, the room was filled with nothing but the ticking of yet another clock, and all of my resolve disappeared. I reached over, picked up the box, and opened it.

Oh, goodness.

It was remarkable.

Nestled inside was the loveliest necklace I had ever seen. It was a rose gold infinity symbol, and the gemstone that was settled into one of its curves was the color of the ocean at sunrise. Was that why he had selected it, or had he opted for this particular piece because it was rose gold, instead of yellow or white? Maybe it was neither of those things, but rather the infinity sign. What had Henry hoped to tell me with this? What would he have said when he presented it to me, if I had given him a chance to explain? Now I would never know.

I lifted the necklace from the box and fastened it around my neck. How long I must have stood in front of the mirror, looking at it, marveling at it, wishing I could thank him for such an exquisite – and, more importantly, exquisitely meaningful – gift. I wondered, not for the first time, if he missed me, too. Was he thinking of me as I thought of him, or was he too busy? Perhaps he was already in meetings with his clients, or he could have been out on the town to visit one of the many parks or to take in a show.

It did not matter – or it should not have mattered, anyway, not anymore.

I took one final look in the mirror, then whirled around and grabbed my purse. I was tired, but I suddenly felt like I needed to get out of my room. I had not come all the way here just to stay inside a hotel. I would wander around for a little and see where the streets took me. Camera in one hand and the pile of postcards to Violet, Lucy, and Alice in the other, I set out to explore. I had no plan or route, not even a sense of which direction I wanted to go in, and it was divine. That was something I could never do in Manhattan, because after living there all my life, I knew where the maze of streets led. It was no longer an option to get lost inside their labyrinth. In London, though, the possibilities were endless.

I fell in love with it immediately.

Over the next three weeks, that love blossomed. It was not only the sights of the city I adored, it was also the freedom to get to know them at my own pace. If I wanted to watch the sun rise over the River Thames, I could do that, and if I wanted to enjoy a long, lazy breakfast at a local restaurant, I could do that, too. There was no one to answer to beside myself. I tried to start up conversations with people wherever I went, though. Sometimes they would hear my American accent and ask me about my life back home, and sometimes I would take the lead, telling them how fantastic their city was and tossing out a few questions of my own. I wanted to soak up as much knowledge as possible about as many people, as many ways of life, as possible. It was amazing, really, how everybody was so unique, filled with hopes and dreams and goals that were all their own. Even more fascinating to me was the realization that these people would never have crossed my path, nor I theirs, if I had not made the choice to sail overseas. How extraordinary it was, that one decision could sync my life to so many others.

There was the guard at Buckingham Palace, who could not talk to me, of course, but who taught me a lot about patriotism and duty, all without saying a word. There was the elderly woman at the Palladium, who very kindly offered me a ticket to one of the shows being held there when she heard me lamenting that I could not afford to buy one myself, and there was the young boy standing next to me when I stopped to take photographs of the clock tower known as Big Ben. "It was named for Benjamin Franklin, you know," I overheard him telling his mother in the sweetest British accent, and it was all I could do to squelch my laughter. Oh, to be that innocent again.

In a way, though, I was. That was what England did for me.

From the streets of Trafalgar Square to the lush green grounds of Isabella Plantation, which was indeed a beauty to behold, I almost felt like a child again myself, getting to see all the world for the first time. I pondered that as I sat down on a bench in the garden and slipped out my diary from my purse. It seemed like a perfect place to write down my thoughts. I flipped to the next page and was poised to begin, when something caught my eye. Not even fifteen feet away there was a man who looked to be near my age, but instead of sitting on a bench, he was cross-legged on the ground and there was a butterfly perched on his finger. I watched as he talked to it, his voice too soft for me to hear what he was saying. There was something charming about it, this most unlikely of connections they had forged. I sent a smile the man's way as he lifted his arm and the butterfly flew to a nearby pond before settling on the petal of an azalea.

He smiled in return. "Hello," he called.

"Hi." I made room for him on the bench as he walked over to join me. "You must be some kind of butterfly whisperer," I said.

He laughed. "I don't know about that, but I do like them," he said. "I think people could learn a lot from the way they drift through life. They always seem to find somewhere peaceful to rest." He turned to admire the delicate yellow creature for a couple of moments before swiveling back to me and holding out his hand. "I'm Charles, by the way."

"Rose," I said. "It's nice to meet you."

"Likewise." He titled his head to the side. "New York?" he asked. "Philadelphia? Boston? I can tell you are an American, but I can't pinpoint the accent."

"New York."

He grinned. "Ah, guessed it on the first attempt. So what brings you to London?"

"Oh, just doing a bit of sightseeing," I told him. It felt too complicated to go into the whole story with a stranger – even though, I realized, that was precisely what I had done with Henry. Telling him my truths had felt simple. The thought of it made a pang shoot through me. Three weeks later, and I still missed him. I had hoped it would fade with time, that the longer I went without him in my life, the easier it would be not to feel that deep yearning inside my chest. Sometimes that was true, but then there would be a moment like this, when something took my memories and lit them on fire. It happened when I passed by a group of children playing baseball, and when I saw an especially pretty piece of jewelry in a shop window, and always, always, *always* when I came upon a gorgeous display of flowers. The azaleas here in the garden, the lilies in vases at the café where I often ate breakfast, the whole rainbow of varieties at the shop around the corner from my hotel ... I could never look at any of them without thinking of Henry and the way he had asked me about my love for them. For so long, flowers had been my happy place. Now they were a constant reminder of something I wanted to both remember and forget, even though I knew full well that Henry would never be forgettable in my life.

Neither would England.

Even the following week, as I boarded the train that would start my journey to Paris, I knew that London would stay with me forever. I had loved every moment I spent there, even the times when the skies opened up and sheets of rain poured down onto the city below. The sophistication of the place, the history and charm and style, had won a permanent spot in my heart. I was curious to see how Paris would compare. For now, though, I settled comfortably into my seat, my diary in hand as the train pulled out from the station. Since I was officially headed to my next destination, I wanted to take some time to reflect on the first one.

When I attempted to write, though, I could not quite figure out how to find the right words. For as good as I had been about keeping track of every day in the diary, it still felt like there was so much to say, maybe even too much. I averted my gaze from the page and glanced out the window in the hopes of finding inspiration.

Everything was whizzing by quickly. The trees, the houses,

the cars on an adjacent road ... they were all a blur as the train picked up speed. I should not have kept looking at them, because soon it started to do a number on me, making it seem like I was focusing on something that was not there. The lightheadedness crept up on me at first, then crashed down in a powerful tidal wave. I pinched my eyes shut to keep the dizziness at bay, but it did not help. I just felt worse and worse. The irony would have made me shake my head, had I not thought the movement would add to the problem. I had managed to sail all the way across the Atlantic without any motion sickness, but apparently I did not have the same luck on dry ground.

Despite all my efforts to stop it, the off-kilter feeling would not go away.

I felt positively ill.

∾23∾

Grace

There are forty-four Henry Jacksons in the state of New York. Or, at least, there are forty-four Henry Jacksons in New York whose information is obtainable by the click of my mouse. Maybe none of them are the man I'm looking for, but it can't hurt to try, so I print out the list of names and numbers. I don't have time to make calls before work, but hopefully I can squeeze some in throughout the day.

Or not.

The bell hanging on the bookstore's door sings a happy song all morning and into the afternoon. I don't know if people are getting a head start on holiday shopping or if my posts on social media are garnering attention for the book hop that's set to begin the following week, but whatever the case, business is thriving like I haven't seen in awhile. Between helping customers find the books they're looking for, signing them up to reserve a copy of *Jasper Jellybean Jumps for Joy* for the contest, and ringing them up at the register, I barely have a minute to myself until one-thirty.

I pull out my phone to text my sisters. *Best day the store's had in weeks*, I type. *Revolving door of customers, and a few of them registered for the contest. We're up to fifty-three participants now. Maybe things are turning around.*

Josie's response pings back immediately. *That'd be freakin' awesome*, she says.

Abigail chimes in, too. *Fingers crossed*, she writes, *but don't get your hopes up yet.*

I have to laugh.

There it is on the screen, the perfect summation of my sisters and me.

My hopes will always be up, I type. *You know that.*

Then, before the conversation can evolve into anything more – or devolve into anything less – I exit out of the texting screen and switch to the dialing one. It's time to start crossing names off that list. I approach it methodically, beginning at the top and working my way down, introducing myself to the people who answer and explaining that I am looking for a Henry Jackson who sailed on the *SS Harmony* back in 1955. The replies range from polite chitchat about what it must've been like to be on an ocean liner, to prompt dismissals followed by the sound of silence in my ear. But no Henry. I never expected to find him on the first try, but after getting halfway through the list and consistently striking out, I feel like it'd probably be smart to admit that this is a colossal waste of time that I could be spending doing something productive. Books need to be ordered, the kids' section tidied up, and refreshments purchased for this week's author events. I should stop trying to look for a needle in a haystack.

But still, I make one more call anyway, because it just doesn't *feel* like a colossal waste of time.

It feels important.

This time, the phone rings and rings before an answering machine clicks on. "Hello," I say. "My name is Grace Anderson, and I'm trying to get in touch with the Henry Jackson who sailed on the *SS Harmony* in 1955. It left from New York that July. If you have any information, please call anytime. I'd love to talk to you." I leave my number, along with a thank you, and end the call.

I really must get back to work now. In addition to everything else, I still have to draft both of my introductory speeches for the author events. No matter whether my visiting speakers are seasoned pros or first-time presenters, I always like to prepare something to welcome them and their readers to my tiny corner of the literary world. That's where my focus has to be for the rest of the day. The quest to find Henry will have to wait.

And wait, and wait.

Things only get busier as the week goes on, and by the time I'm unlocking the door to The Book Boutique on Black Friday, my mind is on nothing but the insane day ahead. I step into the darkness, just as always, and breathe in the promise held between the pages and inside the shelves. This time is different, though. This morning I'm not alone.

"What are you doing?" Josie asks, as she follows me inside. "Why are we standing in the dark?"

"Yes, why?" Abigail says.

My sisters are here.

There are probably a dozen things they'd rather be doing today, but they're here for me instead. Abigail's carrying the breakfast we picked up on the way, and Josie's balancing a bouquet of balloons in one hand and a cardboard box full of giveaway items – bookmarks, pins, and pens with the store's logo – in the other. I never even had to ask her to help out today. She offered.

"We are standing in the dark," I tell her and Abigail, "because sometimes that's how we can see the best. All the possibilities of this place, they're just waiting to come alive." I flip on the lights and smile at my sisters. I can tell from the way they smile back that they don't particularly get it, what it means to see the store spring to life each morning, but that's okay. They're here, and that's all I can ask for.

Josie holds out the balloons. "Where do you want these?" she asks.

"How about outside?" Abigail suggests, before I can answer. "It's a terrific attention grabber. I know my kids would want to go into any store that had balloons at its door. Maybe it will help to set us apart today."

It's a good idea. On a block filled with restaurants and shops, we can use any advantage we can get to attract the Black Friday crowds. "Sounds perfect," I say. "Thanks. Seriously, thank you both so much for being here today. I appreciate it more than you know."

Josie waves a hand in the air. "No big deal."

But it is.

It is a very big deal. All day long, as I watch my sisters chat with customers, pointing them in the direction of what they're looking for or serving them muffins and tea from the café, I can't believe it is actually happening. That we're here together, all three of us, sharing in the tradition passed on by Gram and Pop-Pop. How many times lately have I imagined them looking down on us, shaking their heads in disappointment over all the tension? Not today. Today I know they're smiling from ear-to-ear, especially when Scott drops by later on with Ben and Macy.

"I like this one, and this one, and this one ... and this one, too," Ben says, wandering through the kids' section and stacking a tower of books into his arms. He carries them over to me. "Aunt Grace, can you read us a story?" He beams up at me with the brightest of eyes. "Then I can read one! I'm learning how in kindergarten."

Macy skips over to join us. "Story time now?" she asks eagerly, her long brown pigtails swinging against her shoulders as she cranes her neck to look up at me. "Pretty please! With lots of cherries on top!"

So that's what we do. Scott offers to man the cash register, and Abigail, Josie, and I scrunch into the bean bag chairs in the children's area. We all take turns reading the books Ben chose, and it's so special, hearing my niece and nephew giggle and gasp from the stories. One is even the same *Pokey Little Puppy* book that Gram used to read to us. I can practically feel my heart burst with joy. This is what our grandparents wanted for us. It's why we must keep going and why we can never *not* keep going, because at the end of the day, this is what it's all about. I think Abigail and Josie understand that a little better now.

Late at night, after the last customer has gone and my sisters and I are sitting by the fireplace, I uncork the bottle of wine I bought to celebrate the occasion. "To a successful day," I say, raising my glass in a toast.

"And to us," Abigail adds. "I'm glad we did this."

"Hear, hear," Josie says.

We clink our glasses together.

They are half full, but tonight, I am more than that.

Tonight, my soul is overflowing.

* * *

I've never liked public speaking. All throughout school, I would dread the days when I had to get up in front of the class and give a presentation. Having everyone's attention on me made it feel like they were just waiting for me to slip up. Give me a paper to write, and I would breeze through with ease. Give me the task of addressing a whole group, and I'd have to take at least half a dozen deep breaths before fumbling my way through it, all the while hoping that I wouldn't humiliate myself too badly.

That's why it always surprises me when I can get up in front of people at the bookstore without finding myself a bundle of nerves. Maybe it's because I've gotten used to it over the years. Maybe it's because I feel so at home here that it's more like talking to neighbors, rather than strangers. Or maybe it's because I'm so excited to share information on whatever it is I'm speaking about that the anxiety fades away. Whatever the case, I'm especially appreciative for it on the launch night for the book hop. The store is brimming with people – everyone who has registered for the contest, along with representatives from area animal shelters and even a couple reporters I convinced to cover the kick-off. It is the most crowded I've ever seen the store. I watch from the side as the people mingle and munch on appetizers.

"Catering this was the right call," Abigail says, from her place next to me.

I smile at her. "Told you so."

Abigail hadn't wanted to spend money on catering the event, but I had insisted. Sometimes it's not about the cash. It's about the cause. And this is a cause I believe in strongly. I'm glad Abigail is here for it. Josie couldn't fly in from California, not after she was just here for Thanksgiving and with another callback scheduled for this week, but she made us promise we'd bring her in via video chat. Abigail gets started on that as I head over to the podium, a copy of my remarks in hand. My nerves might hang in the background here inside the store, but that doesn't mean I can speak off the cuff. I am not a natural at it like my sisters are.

Abigail gives me an encouraging smile as I take my place. Next to her, Jonathan flashes a double thumbs-up. I protested at first, when he told me he was cancelling his evening office hours to come tonight, but now, as I look out at his face, I'm happy he didn't listen. Having him here for this means the world. My mom's here, too, and so is Sofie with her husband and their children, who are playing with Ben and Macy. I watch them for a moment, then let my gaze sweep around the room, taking it all in.

"Good evening," I say, and the quiet murmur of the crowd fades into silence. "Thank you all for joining us tonight, and for supporting The Book Boutique in this newest endeavor. My grandparents opened this store almost twenty-six years ago, and from day one, it has been an honor and a joy for our family to serve you. See, when my Gram and Pop-Pop decided to take a chance on their dream, when they began to set aside money for this place, they had one goal in mind. They wanted to build more than a catalogue of books. They wanted to build a community. I think they did a fantastic job of it, and what a delight it's been for me to experience it firsthand, both as a child who grew up here and as an adult who has the privilege of being one of its owners. My sisters and I are always on the lookout for new ways to expand The Book Boutique's reach," I continue, and out of the corner of my eye, I see Abigail smile again. I know she wasn't expecting to be included in my speech, but I wanted her and Josie to be part of it. It would've been easy for them to dig in their heels and refuse to give me additional time to save the store. Instead, though, they took a chance on me, and I'll be forever grateful.

"Abigail, Josie, and I are proud to bring you tonight's official launch to our book hop," I say. "It's our hope that the books you receive this evening will travel far and wide. Because that is what any book should do. It should get out there, into the hands of readers who will take it even further than its author could have dreamed of. That's the beauty of a story, its ability to mean so many different things to so many different people. As you read *Jasper Jellybean Jumps for Joy* and share it with all your family and friends, I hope you'll take the time to soak in the meaning it has for you, and also for the real life shelter animals who are the inspiration for the story. Maybe this book will convince you to adopt a pet, or to volunteer with one of our terrific area rescues, many of which are represented here tonight. Whatever you take away from the book, though, I think everyone can agree that this is about more than a contest. Even after the March first deadline to send back your books has come and gone, the impact of the story will remain." I smile. "And I am looking forward to hearing about it."

The applause starts even before I finish speaking.

It's humbling and gratifying in a way I can't explain.

So, too, is the response I get to the book hop in the following weeks. Emails arrive from around the city, and posts begin popping up on social media from states as close by as Florida and as far off as New Jersey. Who knows, maybe Josie's fifty-states idea will come to fruition, after all. I hope so. It'd be amazing publicity not only for our store, but also for animal rescue. I already knew a little bit about what an emotional undertaking it is, from the time I've spent volunteering with Jonathan, but now I have a whole new level of respect for it after talking both to the rescue directors and also the author of the Jasper Jellybean book.

"One day," I say to Jonathan, as we sit by the fireplace in his house and toast marshmallows for s'mores, "I'll adopt a pet. Actually, after reading that book, I'm tempted to pick a rabbit. They seem awesome."

"They are." He nods. "They're a lot of work, but totally worth it. I think you'd make a fantastic pet parent," he says. "It's the most rewarding experience. So many of the animals I see at work are either fosters or adoptees, and their families are always talking about how it's changed their lives. It isn't only the animal who ends up being saved, but often the people in some way, too. I think that's why they were so willing – "

I glance at him as he breaks off abruptly. "So willing to ... what?" I ask.

He shakes his head. "Never mind. Hey, do you want another marshmallow?"

"Oh, come on." I raise my eyebrows at him. "I know you're hiding something."

"It's nothing, really," he says. "I just might've pointed some of our clients in the direction of The Book Boutique, that's all."

"What are you talking about?"

He gives an almost shy grin. "You know the flyer you gave me to hang up in the reception area? The one advertising the book hop? Well, I thought it would be good to mention it to the people who brought their pets in, especially the ones who have adopted. Not everybody stops to look at bulletin boards, but they have no choice other than to listen to their vet." He winks. "They were all glad to help. I had a lot of people say they were going to sign up for the contest."

I stare at him. "When did you do this?" I ask.

"The week or so before Thanksgiving, after we talked in the store that night and you opened up to me about your father. I know how much it took for you to do that," he says. "And I wanted to do something in return."

That influx of business in the days leading up to Black Friday

... that was at least partially because of him. The realization nearly brings tears to my eyes. I adore that he did that for me, even after I'd broken our plans. "You're incredible," I tell him, folding myself into his arms. I sit like that for a long while, as we watch the fire and he tells me about the kitten he saved during surgery that day.

And that's when it occurs to me.

Maybe I don't have to solve the Henry mystery anymore. I have called all the people on that list and gotten nowhere, so perhaps this is the time to acknowledge that somewhere inside, I have the power to commit to this wonderful man without knowing how Henry and Rose's story played out. It is certainly something to think about.

Something to wonder about.

Something to dream about.

Until the next week.

I'm in my kitchen early one morning, baking muffins and scones for the bookstore to save some money on ordering them in from our usual supplier, when my cell phone rings. I glance over at it on the counter and don't recognize the number flashing on its screen, but opt to answer anyway. Most of the calls related to The Book Boutique go to the store itself, but all the shelter directors who have partnered with us have my cell number and I don't want to miss the call if it happens to be from one of them. With flour still on my hands and the pot of cherry filling bubbling away on the stove, I grab the phone and cradle it against my ear.

"Hello?" I say.

"Yes, hi, may I speak to Grace Anderson, please?"

"This is Grace."

There's a long pause.

"You called me last month," the man says. His voice is deep and warm, but entirely unknown.

I called him? What is he talking about?

I'd assume he has the wrong number, except he's very clearly looking for me.

And then I figure it out, right before he speaks the words.

"My name is Henry," he says. "Henry Jackson."

∾24∾

Rose

By the time I arrived in France, the dizziness had dissipated. I was exhausted from the long trip, the sort of tired that seemed to siphon all the energy from me, but my head was no longer spinning and my stomach no longer churning. Still, I decided I would give myself the remainder of the day to recoup from the traveling that had taken more out of me than I had predicted. I even let the bellboy at the hotel carry my luggage, something I typically insisted on doing myself. "Thank you," I said to him, as I pressed what I hoped was the appropriate number of francs into his hand.

"Oui, Mademoiselle. My pleasure. Is there anything else I can do?"

"Actually … " I smiled. "I have a question. If you could recommend a place for me to visit here, somewhere I would not know about otherwise, what would it be?" I was determined to ask that of one person in every city I went to, because it had worked beautifully in London. What a terrific way of getting to see the inspiration folded into the very fabric of a place.

The bellboy did not hesitate with his answer. "The Musee de l'Orangerie," he said. "It is one of the finest museums in our city. It's not as well-known as the Louvre, but that is why I like it. You can look at the art without feeling … " He hesitated. "How do you Americans say it … ahh … squashed?" This made me smile again. The man's English was actually quite good, and it sounded charming with his accent.

"Squashed," I echoed. "Yes. Crowded."

He nodded. "Crowded. Oui, that's it. So many people visit the Louvre to see the Mona Lisa, but if you ask me, she's a bit unsettling. That look on her face makes it seem like she knows something about us that we do not yet know about ourselves."

It was an interesting interpretation.

I remembered learning about the painting in high school, its historical significance and even the story of its theft from the Louvre in the early part of the century, but I had never given consideration to the message behind the art. Was that what da Vinci had intended, to reach out to the public and maybe make the public reach inside themselves? It made me think of all my mother's pretty flower arrangements. She mostly gardened for herself, but every now and then she shared her bouquets. There was one time, when I was a teenager, that she had carefully put together a vase of hyacinths and snapdragons to take to a friend who had broken her ankle after a bad fall on the ice. Her friend had gone on and on about how beautiful the flowers were, and had tried to persuade my mother to use her talent for a business venture. Mother had said something about it not being appropriate for her to jump into work, but if she had, I knew the flowers would have served a similar purpose as the Mona Lisa. They would have been such a colorful catalyst.

Flowers could make you evaluate and imagine. They could make you feel.

Perhaps paintings did the same. I had never been much of an art person – it had always felt too stuffy to me, especially when it meant being cooped up inside a shadowy old museum when I could have been out in the fresh air instead, drinking in the sunshine and honeysuckle and birdsong – but now that I was in France, the home of so many of the greats, I was willing to give it a try. In fact, the Orangerie was the first place I visited the following day, once I had a good night's sleep and woke up with the spring back in my step. It was a pretty morning, the sky a robin's egg blue and the smell of freshly baked bread drifting out of the corner cafés. I felt truly happy to be there. How lucky was I, getting to experience so much of what life had to offer, all in the space of a summer? It was beyond remarkable to think that, had my former boss not merged his law practice, I would have been in an office instead, transcribing a call or typing a legal document. My, how things had changed. My, how *I* had changed.

Everything felt different overseas, almost as though it was magnified to the point of being larger than life itself, and I adored it. Why force ourselves into a box when we could break out of it and be free? I saw that sense of liberty and openness in the art I came across that day – Cezanne, Matisse, Renoir, and my favorite, Monet's *Water Lilies*. I stood in front of those canvases for longer than any other, mesmerized by how the brushstrokes transported me into their world, and I realized why, out of so many spellbinding places, the bellhop had suggested this one. There was a wonder to behold inside it.

Everything in Paris seemed to be that way.

I could not get enough of the city. Sometimes I visited the famous landmarks – the Eiffel Tower, Notre Dame, the Arc de Triomphe – but other times I did as I had in London, and set out with no real destination in mind. That was how I came to walk the art-filled streets of Montmartre, and sit along the tree-lined banks of the Seine River, and browse the lovely shops on the Champs-Elysees. It was inside one of those that I met a woman about my age who had her two young children in tow. They looked like baby dolls, these little girls with big eyes and dark curls, and I could not resist the chance to tell their mother how precious they were.

"Merci," she said. "Celine and Elodie, they are the light of my life."

"I can certainly see why," I said, as the girls stared up at me from beneath their long eyelashes.

"Do you have children?" their mother asked.

"Oh, no," I said. "I don't. I'm not married."

The faintest hint of a smile teased her mouth. "So you are an independent woman, as they say. I used to be one of those, too."

"Do you ever miss it?" I asked her.

"I love my family," she said, "and I wouldn't change it, but sometimes, yes, I would give anything for a day to do whatever I wished. People are so quick to settle down that I think we often forget all the joys of being on our own." She bent down to pick up the toy her younger daughter had dropped onto the shop floor. "You are American, oui?"

"Oui," I said.

"And you are here in Paris. I could not simply go to America like you have done here. Enjoy it," she said. "What's next will still come, but that doesn't mean you have to rush it."

It was wonderful advice.

I tried to follow it as I continued to explore France. There was only one problem. For as exciting as it all was, it also sent a twinge of sadness spiraling through my heart, because I still could not help thinking about the memories Henry and I could have made if we were in Paris together. It was such a romantic city. Whenever I saw a couple posing for a photograph by the Eiffel Tower, or sailing up the Seine on a riverboat, or walking down the sidewalk hand-in-hand, my mind went right to Henry as I pictured us doing those very things. It even happened as I sat in a café one day, two weeks after I had arrived in the city. I was trying to decipher the menu so I could avoid accidentally ordering the wrong thing, and all I could think of was a story Henry told me about something similar happening to him during a trip to Spain. It made me smile, even as it felt like the edges of my soul were curling in on themselves.

I tried to compose myself.

It was up to me, after all, to smooth those edges back out again.

I glanced around, searching for a waiter, and used my little English to French dictionary to talk to him in halting French. My cheeks flushed as I struggled to express myself, but my efforts must have worked, because the meal was exactly as I hoped when the waiter brought it over to me.

"Pour vous, Mademoiselle," he said.

"Merci beaucoup."

He gave me a pleasant smile, filled my glass with the wine I had ordered, and disappeared with a little bow. He was so polite, as was most everyone in Paris. No matter where I went, people almost always seemed willing to engage when I struck up a conversation. The street corner artist, who told me that his new baby had inspired his latest creation; the vineyard worker, who explained all about the process of turning grapes into velvety wine; the security guard at one of the museums I visited, who answered my questions about an exhibit ... they were all so friendly, as was the waiter when he returned to check on me midway through my meal. He motioned to it, saying something in French I could not quite figure out, so I took a chance and assumed he was asking how everything tasted.

"Tres bien," I told him.

It *was* delicious ... until I washed it down with a sip of wine. Then, out of nowhere, my stomach felt as though it was pinching together. It was sudden and it was strong, and I had to avert my gaze from the food in front of me because just the mere sight of my ratatouille and baguette was enough to make my body pulsate in protest. What was going on? I had felt fine a minute before. I set down my fork, scanned the café for the bathroom, and took off running. I was marginally aware of people turning to look, and it was mortifying, but I knew I had to hurry.

The tile floor of the bathroom was cool as I sank down onto it. That was soothing in a way, and I tried to concentrate on that instead of how sick I felt. My stomach was twisting itself into knots and the strangest sensation crept up from my neck to my cheeks, making it feel like my entire head was tingling. A half-groan, half-whimper squeezed itself out of my lips, and tears began to well up in my eyes. I could not remember the last time I had felt so ill. This even trumped the motion sickness on the train.

"Mademoiselle?" A voice drifted through the door, soft and concerned. "Are you alright?"

My answer sounded more like a distorted cry.

No, I was not alright.

I was all alone in a foreign country, more than three thousand miles from my family and friends, sitting on the floor of a bathroom with my skirt rumpled around me and my chest on fire from all of the heaving. It was the first time since I had left Manhattan that I actually questioned my decision. Perhaps my parents had been right and it *was* reckless to go gallivanting around Europe on my own. At the moment, there was no denying how much I was craving a familiar face. Instead, the next one I saw was the hostess of the café, who waited for me outside the door and offered me a damp cloth napkin.

"Thank you," I whispered.

She must not have spoken too much English, beyond what she had said before, because she just mimed what she wanted me to do with the napkin, putting her hand to her cheeks and forehead. It was a sweet gesture that made me feel a swell of gratitude, especially when the cool cloth helped to ease my queasiness. It anchored me somehow, and after taking a couple of long breaths, I felt a lot better.

Still, I went right back to my hotel and climbed into bed. I did not know if I had eaten something that did not agree with me or if it was a virus which had turned my insides into a rollercoaster, but I was not taking a chance. I would stay in for the rest of the day, just as I had done whenever I came down with something as a child. When Violet or I got sick, our mother would tuck us into bed with a thermometer and an endless supply of chicken soup. She would check in on us every half hour, and if we were feeling up to it, she would bring in a pile of board games. I missed her now. For all of our disagreements, plus the fact that she never wanted to talk on the rare occasions when I could afford to call home, she was still my mother and I loved her. I knew she loved me, too, and I liked to think she would have kept me on the line if I had phoned home to tell her what happened.

I did not, though.

I just closed my eyes and let myself drift off to sleep.

It was nearly dark by the time I woke up, and I blinked groggily, letting my vision adjust. A quick glance at the clock told me I had been asleep for five hours. I shook my head, stymied. I had never taken such a long nap in my life. Maybe I really *was* ill, even though I felt much better now. Would a sickness really come and go like that, though?

Over the next several days, that is precisely what it continued to do: come and go. Sometimes I felt absolutely fine, a ball of energy that wanted to get outside and bounce around, and other times I felt like I was standing in a tiny canoe in the middle of the river, swaying and wobbling as I tried to keep my balance. It was bewildering and worrisome. Finally, after another spell literally sent me to my knees, right on the bank of the Seine as I was going for a walk and snapping photos, I knew I had to do something about it. I headed back to my hotel room, picked up the phone, and dialed Violet's number.

"Hmm," she said, after I had explained my symptoms. "That *is* odd. Thomas had a bad bout of food poisoning when we were dating, but it was nothing like that. He was dreadfully ill for twenty-four hours straight, but that was the end of it. Perhaps it's just a mild virus that's lingering because you're so active now and not resting?"

"Maybe," I agreed. "It's maddening. Paris is divine, and there's still so much I want to do before it's time to move on, and yet I can't seem to go anywhere without getting sick. Perhaps I should find a doctor here."

"You were fine in England, right?" Violet asked. "And on the ocean liner? There was nothing – "

Her voice dropped off so abruptly, I thought the connection had been lost.

"Violet?" I asked. "Are you there?"

"I ... I'm here," she stammered. "Something occurred to me, that's all."

"What?"

"Well ... I'm sure it is completely ... I wonder if ... do you think there could be ... "

"What?" I said again. "Just tell me."

She exhaled so loudly that it sounded like she was sitting in the room next to me, not all the way across an ocean. "Henry," she finally said. "You told me you two shared a night together on the *SS Harmony*."

"Yes," I said. "We did. Why? What does that have to do with anything?"

Then, suddenly, I understood. In the nanosecond before Violet spoke the words, I knew where her thoughts had traveled.

"Do you think ... " She paused. "Rose, could you be expecting?"

Oh, God.

Oh my God.

The lightheadedness came back at full force, but this time it was more from shock than anything else. A clammy sweat broke out along the nape of my neck, clinging to my hair, and I could feel the color drain from my cheeks. The room was spinning, and I fell into a chair before my legs could give out on me entirely.

I could not be expecting.

I could not be having a baby.

I could not be carrying a piece of Henry's heart inside me.

Except, I knew, I very well could. It would explain why I had been feeling so sick recently. I only knew a little bit about pregnancy – it simply was not something people talked about openly – but it made sense that it would cause a woman to feel ill, having the body work so hard to grow a fragile, tiny life.

I gripped on to the edge of the chair, counting backward in time. It was early September, about eight weeks since my days on the ship. There could have been a different explanation. There could have been many different explanations. Still, sitting there in the hotel, my heart just about beating out of my chest, I knew Violet was right.

"I ... yes ... I could very well be expecting," I whispered.

"Oh, Rose," she said.

For the first time in a long time, possibly ever, she did not know how to comfort me.

I did not know how to comfort myself.

I would have to leave Paris. I would have to cut my trip short and go back to New York, with so many cities still waiting to be explored and so many countries calling my name. I could not, in good conscience, continue on by myself in Europe if I was expecting a baby, not when the only thing I was certain of was the uncertainty. The thought sent tears cascading down my face. I had been excited about this journey, and what a spectacular time I had been having. I did not want it to be over yet. I was not ready for it to be over. There was still so much I had to see, so much I had to do, so much I had to learn.

I did not know what my purpose was yet.

I had not found my meaning.

All the possibilities were still waiting for me. How could I abandon them?

I had never been one to start something I could not finish, but this ... slowly, carefully, I rested a hand on my stomach, trying to imagine the little heart that might be beating inside. It was wild, and mystifying, and completely impossible to comprehend. Perhaps Henry and I had started something together. If so, I had to finish that. I had to protect it.

I had to go home.

Then there was another matter to consider.

"What will you do?" Violet asked. "Are you going to tell Henry?"

∽25∾

Grace

I can't believe it.

It's been more than a month since I left that message on Henry's answering machine, and when I didn't hear back, I just wrote it off as yet another path that led to nowhere. Now, though, standing in my kitchen with the scones' filling sizzling on the stove and *Good Morning America* murmuring on the television, the trail winds right around again. Because this Henry, the one whose voice reminds me of a news anchor, filled with warmth and wisdom ... it's him. I know instantly.

"Hello," I say excitedly. "It's great to hear from you. Thank you very much for calling."

"I'm sorry it's taken me so long," he says. "I was in Virginia, visiting my son and his family for the holidays. I always go before Thanksgiving and stay until the New Year. My son just drove me home to New York yesterday – can't tackle such long distances anymore at my age, I'm afraid – and I heard your message on my machine."

New York.

So he *does* still live there.

I wonder if he ever crosses paths with Rose, then. Does he still think about her, or has he closed that chapter like she seems to have done? Is it odd for him, knowing that they're both going about their lives within the borders of the same state? Or, wait, does he even realize she's still there, too? Maybe he has no idea what shape Rose's life took after it intertwined with his for a moment in time. How do I broach that subject?

I have so many questions. I don't know where to begin.

"Please, no worries," I say, sitting down on one of the stools at my breakfast counter. "I'm just grateful for the chance to talk with you at all."

"Likewise," he says. "Tell me, what is it I can do for you, Ms. Anderson?"

"Actually, I think – or I hope, anyhow – there's something I can do for you."

"Well, consider my curiosity officially piqued," he says.

I smile. I like Henry already. "I'm a bookstore owner down in Georgia," I explain to him. "And I found something I think you may be interested in hearing about. We hold a used book buyback sale twice a year, and inside one of the books we purchased, there was a clipping from the *SS Harmony*, along with a letter you wrote to someone named Rose. I was eventually able to trace the book back to her granddaughter."

"Her granddaughter," he echoes, in a voice much softer than the one I'd heard before. "She has a granddaughter." He gives a sigh that sounds content. "I didn't know that. This is ... it's wonderful. I hope that means she found what she was looking for all along. That's what I've always wanted for her."

And there's my answer: no, he and Rose don't cross paths, and yes, he still thinks about her.

"It sounds like the two of you were very much in love," I say.

"I'd never met a woman like Rose before," he tells me. "I've never met one like her since. There was just something about her that set my world on fire. I still regret it sometimes, the way I let her cut ties," he says, and I find myself gripping tightly to the phone, waiting for him to go on. Listening to Henry is like hearing a story unfold in real time. "It was a chilly day when the *SS Harmony* docked in England," he continues. "I remember it started to rain after Rose and I said our goodbyes ... it was just a drizzle, so light you could barely even see it, but when I turned back around to look at her one more time, I could feel it hit my cheeks. It seemed fitting, like even the universe was crying for us. In a strange way, that was comforting."

"So that was it?" I ask. "You never saw each other again?"

"No," he says. "Which was the exact opposite of what I wanted. I'd hoped, more than anything, that she would say yes and come with me. It broke my heart when she ended things between us. I understood why she had to, and I never would have done anything to stand in the way of what she needed, but ... all these decades later, it still remains my biggest 'what if.' Maybe I should've fought harder for us, instead of letting her slip through my fingers." His voice grows thick, and he clears his throat. "My apologies," he says. "I doubt you were expecting to be subjected to the ramblings of a sentimental old man when you reached out to me."

"I'm glad to listen," I say. "And I was actually hoping to hear about your story. I only wish there were something I could do to help."

In the back of my mind, the spark of an idea starts to flicker.

Maybe there *is* something I can do.

"Have you ever tried to contact Rose?" I ask Henry.

"No," he says. "She went her way and I went mine. I thought of her often while I was in Europe, I wondered where she was and what she was doing, but I always respected her decision. Even after I returned to the States, I stayed true to my word and never tried to locate her. I was tempted to, so I could tell her how much I missed her, but it wouldn't have been fair."

"So you just moved on instead?" I ask.

"As much as a person can move on from something like that," he says. "I threw myself into my work, and that was exciting, creating a jewelry line all my own, but it was also a little bittersweet. It reminded me of a conversation I'd had with Rose. The tagline for the company I founded – there is beauty even inside the broken – is something we talked about at length. It'll always be tangled up in my memories of her. Don't get me wrong," he adds. "It isn't like I have spent decades pining away. I met another woman a couple years later, and we had a terrific life together. Married for forty-five years, three kids, seven grandkids, and twenty great-grandkids. I've led a full and happy life, but I'd be lying if I said Rose didn't cross my mind every so often. I loved my wife and honored our wedding vows until the day she passed, but I think Rose might've been my soulmate."

I don't know what to say.

It is a sad story, a tragic one in its own way, but it is also beautiful.

How lucky Henry is, to have someone he misses so much.

And, it occurs to me, how lucky I am to have someone I'd miss the same way.

Jonathan.

My vision blurs as a swell of tears fills my eyes.

Then I realize ... something smells like it's burning. Oh, no. The filling for the scones.

My pastries are ruined, and I'm going to be late for work, and as the tears spill down my face, I know I'll have to fix the makeup I've already applied. But I don't care. As I listen to Henry talk about Rose, I can appreciate that sometimes our plans simply do not matter. It's like he said: some things, some people, are worth fighting for.

That's exactly what I'm going to do.

The first break I get at work, I dial the phone number Lily gave me when we met in the fall. "Lily, hi," I say, when she answers. "This is Grace Anderson. I'm the one who found the letter inside your grandmother's book."

"Of course," she says. "I remember. Thanks again for returning it. I brought it to my grandmom when I went home to New York for Christmas. You should've seen the look on her face. It was like she'd won the lottery. That book was never supposed to make it into the donation pile. I think she assumed it was lost forever."

"I'm glad she has it back," I say. "I'd like to talk to you about getting something else back to her, as well." I fill her in on my conversation with Henry. "I know she doesn't discuss what happened," I say, "but do you think that'd change if she knew how Henry still feels?"

"I honestly don't know," Lily says. "It's pretty obvious that she never stopped loving him, either, and yet it's like she's built this wall around their time together. She says she wants to protect it, but if you ask me, it's herself she wants to protect. The last thing I want is to bring up painful memories, but hey, maybe this could be a chance to make things better, or to at least give her some closure. I think that's important at this point in her life."

"I feel like it could be important for both of them," I say.

"So what do you have in mind?"

"I'll admit, I'm harboring a fantasy of reuniting them and it being this grand happily-ever-after," I say. "But I also know that might not be the best way to handle it. Maybe a phone call? Or another letter? What do you think she'd be most receptive to?"

"Actually," Lily says, "I think my Great Aunt Violet would be the best person to talk to about this. Her or my mom. Here, let me give you their contact information." She rattles off two numbers, plus an email address for her mother. "Aunt Violet knows my grandmom better than anyone else in the world," she tells me. "And my mom will have a unique take on it because Henry's absence impacted her, too."

"Okay," I say. "I'll get in touch with them. Thanks, Lily."

A group of customers comes in then, so I don't have time to reach out to Ivy and Violet just yet, but all afternoon long, my thoughts keep returning to them. Will they give the go-ahead to turn my idea into something concrete? I hope so. It'd be wonderful to bring Henry and Rose back together. How many times have I read a book about a couple like them, a missed connection or a case of star-crossed lovers who simply fell for each other at the wrong time? It's always satisfying to read about their journey, and to see how their story wraps around itself at the end. Sometimes it ties together neatly, sometimes it leaves its ribbons free to fly, and sometimes it's a combination. That's my very favorite of all. Nothing beats the emotional payoff of seeing the characters find one another again, and yet, there's almost always more to be written and more to be told.

I so badly want it to be that way for Henry and Rose.

Oh, how I hope Ivy and Violet agree.

I try Ivy first, but get her voicemail, so I leave a message explaining who I am and where I got her number, then continue on to Violet. This time, the phone only rings twice before someone answers it.

"Hello?" The voice is soft and sweet.

"Hi," I say. "May I speak to Violet, please?"

"That's me."

A twist of excitement spirals through me. "My name is Grace," I say. "I got your phone number from Lily." I tell her why I'm calling, careful not to leave out any of the details, and Violet listens in a hush.

"Oh, my stars," she says, when I've finished.

"I'm sorry if I'm prying," I say. "But – "

"No, no, dear, it's fine," she tells me. "I have often wondered about Henry. I can't even tell you how many times I considered trying to track him down myself. When Rose came home from France, when I saw how nervous and anxious she was ... when I saw how in love with Henry she still was ... it weighed on me heavily. My sister was brave, tackling it on her own, but sometimes I would find her standing at the window and just staring outside, or sitting on the couch, looking at a magazine which she wasn't really reading ... and I could see the emotion in her eyes. It was difficult for her, trying to find a balance between letting herself be happy and also letting herself be sad. She needed to learn it wasn't just one or the other, and I struggled a lot with that. Our whole lives, we had always been there for each other, but I didn't know how to make it better that time. I thought Henry was history. Maybe, though," she says, and there's a lilt to her voice, "he doesn't have to be any longer."

"Does that mean what I think it means?" I ask.

She laughs lightly. "You sound quite eager to get going with this."

Indeed, I am.

"It's just that they've spent so long without each other," I say. "Why waste another minute? Do you think Rose would be okay with me pursuing this? Because if not, I won't. Her feelings obviously come first."

"I think ... " Violet pauses. "I think she'd tell you that she'd rather live inside the old memories than risk the hurt that could come with making new ones. I know she still blames herself for all that happened between them. My sister carries so much guilt, especially over Henry never knowing their daughter."

Wait ... what? *Their* daughter?

Oh my God. Why didn't I realize it before?

No wonder Lily told me that Henry's absence impacted her mother, too.

"You're saying Henry is Ivy's father?" I ask Violet, just to make absolutely certain.

"Yes," she says. "That's why Rose had to come home early from Europe. She was pregnant."

I am dumbfounded.

I think of my conversation with Henry. All the talk of his family. All the talk of Rose.

He has no idea they share a daughter.

That there is a life in this world who will forever connect theirs.

What was it he called Rose? His biggest 'what if.'

All this time, for six decades, he's been wondering what would have been, what could've been, between them. Also all this time, Rose has likely been reminded of the man she gave up whenever she looks at Ivy. I don't know what prompted her to pick something else over Henry, but whatever it was, I wonder if she, too, is filled with regret. Maybe not the sort that still weighs heavy, a burden unable to lift itself from her shoulders, but the kind that burrows inside, squirreling away a place to hide and get comfortable until something yanks it back to the surface.

How terribly sad that would be.

"She never got married," Violet tells me, "and, therefore, never had any more children. It really devastated her to not be able to give Ivy a sibling, but after Henry, she simply could not find another man who even came close to capturing her heart. I hate that. My sister's had a good life, a fulfilling and happy one, and she'll tell anyone who will listen that she's pleased with where her path led, but I know if she could rewind time that she wouldn't have let Henry go."

"It's never too late," I say quietly. "Maybe we can fix that."

"Yes," Violet says, gentle but firm. "Maybe we can. Maybe we should."

It is the green light I've been waiting for.

And it's also illuminated something else.

Before I can focus on Rose and Henry, there's another person I need to see.

∾ 26 ∾

Rose

*T*he decision all but consumed my mind as I boarded the airplane that would fly me back to New York. My original plan had been to take another ocean liner home, but now that it seemed like time was of the essence, I opted for the fastest alternative, even though it meant spending more money. I decided the extra expense did not much matter at that point, since I would not be using the funds to put down roots overseas. Certainly most people would have viewed my experience in Europe as though I was simply passing through, but for me, London and Paris had been more. They had carved out their own space inside me, or perhaps it was that I had carved out my own space inside them. In any case, they would be a part of me forever, even if I had to leave the seedlings behind before the roots really had a chance to plant themselves in the soil.

I would miss them.

I would miss my travels.

I gazed out the window as the plane lifted up into the air, watching the city grow smaller until it was no more than a pinprick, then leaned back against my seat and shut my eyes. I tried to imagine what Henry's reaction would be if I told him I was expecting. We had talked about a great deal, but the topic of children had never come up. Did he want to have a family? Was he the kind of man to teach his son or daughter to ride a bicycle and read books and play an instrument? He had worked so hard to take care of James after their mother passed away, so I assumed he would have the same inclination toward a child of his own. Still, though, it was hard to envision. Henry was courage and risk, excitement and adventure. He had been my ocean breeze, and I could not picture him settling down yet. Even so, I knew it would be wrong not to fill him in. I would have to figure out some way to contact him.

By the time the plane touched down in New York, I truly thought I had built up enough nerve to tackle whatever was ahead ... and then I saw my sister. She was waiting for me at the airport, and as soon as she opened her arms to embrace me, I nearly crumbled. I had missed her terribly, and now that we were back together, I could finally let out the breath it seemed like I had been holding ever since she first raised the question of me being an expectant mother. "I am so glad to see you," I told her. "It's the only good part about being home."

"Come now," she said, linking her arm through mine. "I am sure there are others. You just have to look for them." She began to list all of the wonderful things about New York in the late summer: the feel of the breeze blowing across the reservoir in Central Park, the sight of the flags standing tall as you eat lunch outside at Rockefeller Center, the sound of Elvis Presley and Nat King Cole records drifting out of opened apartment windows. "It's a lovely time of year," she said. "I hope you can let yourself enjoy it."

That was easier said than done.

I could not go back to my apartment, because my subletters had paid to stay through the end of the month, so Violet insisted I come home with her. "Thomas and I have plenty of room," she said. "I'd love to have you stay. You know what long hours Thomas works. This will give me a chance to have some company. Really, you'll be doing *me* the favor."

"You're the best," I said, as she got my luggage from the baggage claim. "I don't know what I'd do without you."

"Lucky for both of us, you will never have to find out." She waved me away as I tried to take one of the suitcases from her. "You may very well be carrying my niece or nephew," she said. "You have to be careful. You can't lift anything that's heavy. We have to keep the little one safe. It's our job."

We have to keep the little one safe. It's *our* job.

Her words were not lost on me.

Even if Henry wanted nothing to do with me anymore, I would never be alone with this. I would have my sister. The depth of her support filled both my heart and my eyes. I was such a big jumble of emotion. I was disappointed at having to be back in Manhattan before I was ready, but I was also excited at the prospect of experiencing the unique kind of love that came from feeling a life flourish inside me. Whenever I thought about it, something fluttered in my chest ... and yet, I was also afraid of the idea, more intimidated than I had ever been about anything, because I truly did not know the first thing about what it was like to be expecting.

"Let's take it one day at a time," Violet suggested, when I confessed my fears. "You do not have to do anything today, other than get settled in. Then, tomorrow, we can do whatever you want: go for a walk in the park, watch television, eat out at a restaurant and see a picture at the theater ... we can even go to the doctor's office." She glanced over at me, waiting for a reply, but I could not give her one.

I did not know what I wanted, not anymore.

As the next several weeks passed, my confusion only grew.

The doctor confirmed that I was indeed with child, and I imagined what it would be like when a curve began to smile out from my stomach. It was fascinating, intriguing, mesmerizing ... petrifying. It was one thing to have the baby be my little secret, shared only with Violet, but I knew I would not be able to hide it for much longer. Soon enough, my parents would realize that I did not come back from Europe because I was running out of money, as I had told them on the phone the day after my plane landed. Once they figured out the actual reason ... well, that was a confrontation I was hoping to avoid for as long as humanly possible. I could not fathom dealing with that while still processing everything myself and trying to find a cure for the restlessness inside me. It was like I had a constant itch I could not scratch. Sometimes, early in the morning or late at night, as Violet and Thomas were sleeping, I would creep out of my bed and stand by the living room window, looking at the view.

Everything was different now.

It was time to accept that.

It was time to tell Henry.

I was not certain what I hoped would come of it. A reconciliation? A second chance at my first love? Perhaps that ship had sailed, literally and figuratively. Even so, even if being near Henry again only brought me more heartbreak, I knew it was the right thing to do. Henry deserved the chance to know his child, and his child deserved a chance to know him. My own feelings simply needed to be secondary.

I supposed that was what motherhood was: putting your child's interests above your own. For a baby I had never dreamed of, I was still seized by the desire to give him or her all that the world had to offer. Henry was the biggest, and most important, part of that, so I set to work trying to find him. I called every single Henry Jackson in the phone book, but none panned out. One number had been disconnected, another was answered by a woman who said she had just moved in after the previous tenant bought a house, and the rest of them were indeed Henry Jackson, but not the right one. Still, I refused to let that stop me. I wracked my brain, trying to dredge up any details Henry had shared regarding his job. Maybe I could contact him there. The trouble was, he had mentioned a lot about the nature of his work, but never an actual company name or location. It was yet another road that led me nowhere.

"I can only think of one more option," I told Violet. "Henry's brother. If I can find him, perhaps he can lead me in the right direction." Honestly, though, I had no idea if that would be the case. In all our talks, Henry had never been forthcoming about what had happened to James most recently, so I assumed things were still strained between them. I thought it was worth a try, though. I would feel guilty if I did not make every last effort to get in touch ... but as it turned out, James was just as impossible to locate.

"Maybe you should take a break," Violet said one day, after another fruitless attempt resulted in me having what felt like an emotional meltdown on her couch. The tiniest things seemed to set me off at that point. "I know you want to find him," she told me, "but it is also important to take care of yourself. You have a baby depending on you now, after all."

I sighed, leaning my head against hers as she wrapped her arm around my shoulder. "Suppose I can never track him down?" I whispered.

"Your baby will still grow up with all the love in the world," she promised. "He or she will have a wonderful mother, and an aunt who's willing to do anything for you both. You can do it without him if you have to, honey. You're strong enough."

Goodness, I hoped she was right, but how could I not have my doubts? Without Henry, I would have to tackle the challenge of raising a child alone, and also all the scrutiny of people who realized that the baby's father was not in the picture. Being a single mother was unheard of, and I tried not to dwell on it, I tried not to imagine the judgment that was sure to be slung my way, but it weighed heavy on my mind just the same. I could take the surreptitious looks, the disparaging smirks, and all the whispers when people thought I could not hear what they were saying. The thought of my child having to face it, though, broke my heart. I hated that my baby would be labeled by others because of a choice Henry and I had made, and I was fearful that the worst labels of all would come from my own mother and father.

"Maybe this is a mistake," I said to Violet, as we walked up the steps to our parents' townhouse one evening in late October. It had been my idea to have a family dinner so I could break the news, but now that we were actually here, I was tempted to turn around and flee. I was holding the most beautiful bouquet of flowers from the corner stand – chrysanthemums and asters and sunflowers – and yet I felt more like the girl who used to sit on those steps, coloring book in hand, than a woman who carried something much more precious now. "I don't have to do it tonight," I rationalized, as I looked at Violet. "It isn't like I'm having the baby soon. There's still time."

I held my breath as I waited for her answer.

"Yes," she agreed. "There is. The longer this goes on, though, the harder it will become. I think it's like Thomas tells his patients: sometimes it's better to rip off the band-aid, rather than inch it up slowly. It might hurt more in the moment, but in the long run it will actually cause the least amount of pain."

"It's true," Thomas said. He had offered to stay back at their apartment, to let this be a matter just between Violet, me, and our parents, but I had told him not to be silly, that he was a part of the family. In fact, I realized, it made me feel better, having him there with us. I needed all the support I could get, even if he *was* seconding Violet's opinion about sharing my news.

"You're right," I said. "I should get it over with tonight. Thank you for the pep talk ... and, really, thank you both again for everything. You have been so kind to me, and I can't tell you how deeply I appreciate it." I gave them each a fast hug, and then, before I could lose my nerve, I leaned forward and pressed the doorbell. My heartbeat kicked into overdrive as we waited for my parents to open the door, and for the umpteenth time, I rehearsed what I was going to say.

I could do this. I *would* do this.

My father's voice boomed into the chilly air as he swung open the door. "Come in, come in," he said. "Your mother's just finishing up in the kitchen. I think she said something about caramelizing onions."

"Oh, that can be difficult," Violet said, and she launched into a whole description of the process. I tried to listen, but as my father took our coats and led us into the living room, my mind was unable to zero in on anything other than the conversation hanging over my head. I reminded myself that it did not have to determine my own feelings. My parents could be angry. They likely *would* be. That was their right, and I was willing to respect it.

I only hoped they could respect me, too.

"When are you going to tell them?" Violet asked me in a whisper.

"I don't know," I whispered back. "I suppose when the time is right."

As the evening went on, it became clear the timing would never be right. Thomas talked about work at the hospital, and Violet filled our parents in on the recipes she was planning for the second baking contest she was entering. She had won third place in the previous one and was so excited by it that she wanted to try again. I watched as our mother beamed, and listened as our father praised Violet's talent at "turning flour and sugar into gold." I wanted him to be proud of me, too. I wanted them both to be proud of me the way they used to be, before I stopped falling perfectly in line with what they had anticipated for my life. If I thought my parents had been disapproving before, it was about to grow tenfold.

As we all finished our dessert, I set down my spoon and cleared my throat. "I have something to share," I said.

The timing still was not right, but I was going to jump in anyway.

Sometimes that was all you could do, take a leap and hope you somehow landed on your feet ... or at least, that if you did not, if you tripped and stumbled and fell, that you would be strong enough to stand back up. I looked across the table at Violet, who nodded slightly, almost imperceptibly. If I was not strong enough, she would reach out her hand. She would let me lean on her. Knowing that gave me the courage to go on.

"What is it?" my mother asked. "Is everything okay? Please tell me you're not entertaining any new ideas about international travel."

"No," I said. "This is something else, actually!" I hoped that if I pumped enough enthusiasm and excitement into my voice, it would be catching. "You and Father are going to be grandparents! I am expecting."

My mother's hand instantly went to her chest. "You're *what*?" she gasped.

"Expecting," I repeated. "I'm having a baby."

For a minute, I truly thought she was having a heart attack. Her face blanched, and she kept the one hand over her chest while gripping onto the table so tightly with the other that the bones of her knuckles looked like they might pop straight through her skin. She was staring at me, eyes wide, as was my father, but he had not lost the color in his cheeks. It was the exact opposite. He was bright red.

"A baby," he echoed. "You're having a baby."

"When did this ... how could this ... " my mother stuttered. "Are you sure? You do not look like you're with child."

"Perhaps you're mistaken," my father said.

"You can't really tell because I'm wearing a flowy blouse," I said, "but there's no mistake. That's why I had to come home from Paris. It had nothing to do with money. I started to feel sick, like I'd caught a stomach bug that never quite went away, and a doctor confirmed it. I know you must have questions," I added, suddenly wanting to lay all the information on the table. Now that I was doing this, I needed to get everything out in the open. "The baby's father is Henry, a man I met and fell in love with on the *SS Harmony*. He asked me to stay with him after the ship docked, to see where life took us and if we could build something lasting, but

I turned him down. I've missed him ever since," I said, and my voice wobbled a little. "I tried to find him, but I wasn't successful."

"You would be amazed at how well Rose has been handling this," Violet chimed in. "She's been such a champ. The baby is lucky to have her." She was trying to help, but as our parents spun in her direction, I think we both realized at the same time that she may actually have made it worse.

"You knew?" Our mother's voice pitched up about two octaves. Oh, no.

It was one thing to have them be furious and disappointed in me. I did not want Violet to be on the receiving end, not when she had been so unconditionally loving. I opened my mouth to defend her and to explain that I had asked her to keep the secret, but before I could say anything, she spoke up again.

"Yes," she said. "I did know, and I am excited. I hope you can be, too. A baby is a blessing, and Rose and Henry's child will know how much his or her parents loved each other." She looked at me and smiled. "It's also up to us as a family to come together and make sure the baby knows how very wanted – "

"No," our father interrupted.

"Absolutely not," our mother agreed. "This child will never know our family." She narrowed her eyes at me. "You are not," she said, "going to keep this baby."

❧27❧

Grace

*T*he waiting area of Jonathan's veterinary office is empty when I walk inside. There are no dogs barking, no rabbits poking their twitching noses out of their carriers, and no cats meowing in protest of having to be checked by the vet. There is no Jonathan, either, which is what I'd hoped for when I planned my visit for his lunch hour. He likes to go out to eat most of the time, but still, I look around to make sure there's no sign of him.

"Hi, Grace," says Diana, the receptionist who's at the front desk. "You just missed Dr. Miller, I'm afraid. He left ten minutes ago."

"Good." I smile. "I'm actually here to see you, not him." I rest my arms on the counter, leaning forward conspiratorially. "Is there any chance you can give me Jonathan's weekend schedule for the rest of the month? I know he and the other doctors alternate Saturdays. I need to know when he's off."

She gives me a confused look. "You made a special trip for that? Why not just ask him?"

"Because he can't know. I want this to be a surprise."

Now she smiles, too. "You sound like a woman who's up to something," she says.

"I might be."

"Then *I* might be able to help out." She taps at the keyboard of her computer. "Okay," she says. "It looks like he's working this weekend and is off for the next two. He does have that conference in Tallahassee on the twenty-sixth and twenty-seventh, though." She glances up at me. "Any chance I can convince you to tell me what you're planning? You know, since I'm playing an integral role in its timing."

I laugh. "Let's just say I owe Jonathan an answer to something important."

"Hmm," she says. "Cryptic."

"You'll hear about it soon," I tell her. "Promise."

Before anyone can hear about it, though, especially Jonathan, I have a lot to do. As soon as I get home from work that night, I park myself at my desk and begin researching cabins in the mountains. I click on a link for one of them, a traditional looking place with stone pillars, a wrap-around balcony, bird feeders strung outside, and a view that takes my breath away. They're all like that. Cabin after cabin, I'm awed by their beauty. Some are small, situated on the bank of a creek with water trickling over the nearby rocks, and others are luxurious, standing proud on the mountainside with sweeping panoramic views of the valley below. Which one did Jonathan choose? I remember seeing pictures of it, but I can't recall where exactly it was located, or which rental company he'd used to make the reservation.

Maybe it's better that way.

Maybe, instead of duplicating what's already been done, I should try something new.

With a few quick clicks of the mouse, I book a weekend away in a place I hope will set the stage for so many of our tomorrows. Excitement bounces around inside me when the confirmation email arrives in my inbox. Jonathan's spent the past seventeen months challenging everything I thought I knew about life and love, and now it's my chance to return the favor.

But first, I need my sisters' help.

I invite Abigail over for dinner the next night, and as soon as she's slipped off her coat and hung it neatly in the closet, I motion for her to follow me to the sofa. "I have something to tell you before we eat," I say. "Well, something to ask you, really, and Josie, too. I already texted her and said she should expect a call."

Josie is in Las Vegas this week, auditioning for a role in a stage show since the jobs in Los Angeles didn't pan out, but I want her to be a part of this. I still feel terrible about having kept the news of Jonathan's proposal from my sisters for that long and hope this will make up for it somewhat.

"What's going on?" Josie asks, once the video call is connected. "I'm super curious."

"Well," I say, "I have a huge favor to ask. Two weekends from now, I'll be out of town, and I was hoping one of you would be able to take care of The Book Boutique. Mark fractured his arm and has to take time off until it's healed, and Anna's away that weekend for a family reunion, so I won't have any of my usual help at the store. If I have to close, I will, but since we're in the middle of the book hop – "

"Wait," Josie says. "You'll close the store? Okay, who are you and what have you done with my sister?"

Abigail looks at me sideways. "What Josie said."

"I'm the same sister you have always had," I say. "But I'm starting to realize that not every great story is found inside a book. Speaking of which, I have to bring you up to speed on Rose and Henry." I tell them all about my conversations with him and Violet, and they stare at me with nearly identical wide-eyed expressions.

"Holy crap," Josie says. "Henry is Ivy's father?"

"I never even considered that," Abigail says. "I mean, it wasn't exactly common in those days to have a baby out of wedlock." She shakes her head slightly, and the bottom of her brown bob swings back and forth. "How sad is that? Neither of them really got over each other, and Henry's spent the past sixty years never knowing about Ivy. It seems like such a waste."

"It doesn't have to be," I say.

"What do you mean?"

"We could tell him the truth," I say. "What do you think?"

"Hell yes," Josie says.

"Absolutely not," Abigail says. "That's not our place. It's Rose and Henry's business, and no one else's. I know we feel connected to it because we're the ones who found the letter and reached out to Rose's family ... and to Henry, apparently," she adds, raising an eyebrow at me. I knew she'd have a reaction like that to finding out I went ahead with the search even after we'd decided not to, but I am glad I did it. Getting in touch with Henry was important. "This is where I think we need to take a step back, though," Abigail cautions. "If Violet wants to set something up between them, that's one thing. It's not up to us to do it, and it certainly isn't right for us to expose Rose's secret. That would disrespect all of her pain, and emotions, and choices."

She's right. This secret is not ours to reveal.

It is time, instead, to concentrate on my own surprise.

Abigail agrees to fill in for me at the store, no questions asked. Josie, however, fires away. "Are you going somewhere for work?" she asks. "Is this related to the book hop?"

"No," I say. "It has to do with Jonathan, actually." A grin crosses my face just at the mention of his name. "I can't spill the details yet," I tell my sisters, "but be prepared, because as soon as there's news to share, I promise that you two will be the first to know."

"Good." Josie nods. "Exactly as it should be."

Yes. Indeed, it is.

* * *

There is a chill in the air as I walk to my car two Saturdays later, but the sun is shining and, to me at least, the whole world feels like it's golden. This is it. The day is finally here. A smile curls around my mouth as I think about Jonathan. It isn't often that I get to catch him off guard, but as I open the trunk of my car and settle a small suitcase inside, I realize how much I'm enjoying it. Hopefully this will only be the first of many surprises that we have in store for each other over the years. Because that's what I want, I know now. I want so many years with him. I want a lifetime.

It is a beautiful thing, finally figuring out where you belong.

It sends my heart into a little tap dance routine, especially when I knock on Jonathan's door and his sleepy face appears in front of me. His hair is tousled, his eyes bleary. And still, even though it's barely six-thirty in the morning and I'm on his front step with a cup of his favorite coffee in one hand and my keys in the other, he doesn't miss a beat.

"Talk about a great way to wake up," he says. "This sure beats an alarm clock."

"I suppose I *am* a bit less shrill."

When he laughs, it seems to warm the air around us. "And a whole lot more beautiful," he says. "Not that I'm complaining, but what are you doing here?"

"That," I say, "is for me to know and you to find out." I hand him the coffee. "You have half an hour to get dressed and pack a suitcase for a weekend away. Don't worry about breakfast. We can stop on the drive up. Go on," I add, motioning for him to hurry as he stands there, staring at me like I've lost my marbles. "Pretty soon you'll be down to twenty-nine minutes." I smile at the expression on his face. It's nice to do something he didn't expect. Maybe spontaneity is a good thing, after all, and maybe grand gestures don't have to be limited to fairy tales, or romance novels, or heroes who make their heroines swoon.

Maybe we can be our own heroines.

As I drive Jonathan to our destination, that's what I feel like: the heroine of a life that is right on the cusp of opening up in ways I had never let myself consider before. I have spent so long viewing marriage as something that rips people apart instead of pushing them together. But the opposite is true, too. It's funny – I was determined to find out the rest of Rose and Henry's story before I came to a decision about Jonathan's proposal. I suppose I was counting on their happily-ever-after, along with that of my grandparents, to remind me that it *could* happen. That love could conquer all, that it could stand the tests of time, and distance, and whatever else was thrown in its path. Even after I knew that Henry and Rose didn't get their chance at forever, I was still so certain that something in their tale would give me enough faith to take a leap of my own. And it has, but not at all in the way I imagined.

Rose and Henry lost out on a life built from their love. They missed their opportunity.

I don't want that.

I can't let it happen to Jonathan and me.

Rose thought she was making the right decision all those years ago, and maybe she did. Maybe, at that point in her life, she had to discover her own passion before it was possible to link her world with someone else's. I guess I had to do the same. But what I see now is that strength doesn't have to be solitary. Letting another person in doesn't mean I am weak. It means I trust my heart enough to know what's right for it.

Jonathan is right for it, and I can't wait to tell him.

I'm tempted to blurt it out as soon as we reach the cabin, but Jonathan is so excited he hops out of the car the second I pull my key from the ignition. As I watch, he turns his face up to the sun and takes a deep breath, filling his lungs with the air that seems crisper up here in the mountains than it does at home. It is pine needles and lake water, soil and evergreen. The majority of the trees have long since lost their leaves, but the ones that boast a lush jade the whole year through add a pop of color that makes the area look like something out of a postcard.

"I am really sorry we couldn't experience this in the fall," I say, joining Jonathan by the path that leads to the cabin. "It must have been beautiful with the autumn colors. I know this isn't quite the same, but – "

He presses a soft kiss to my mouth. "But nothing," he says. "It's incredible."

And it is. The house is amazing, with its triangular sloped ceilings and huge picture windows and stilted balcony overlooking

Lake Blue Ridge. There's a fireplace in the living room, stunning antique furniture in the bedroom, and shiny granite countertops in the kitchen. Then there's the view. It is truly magnificent, the picture that Mother Nature's painted. As I stand next to Jonathan out on the balcony, the wind ruffling my hair, I can see why he loves it up here. There is a serenity that settles deep into your soul. We're tucked away into the trees like we are the only two people in the entire universe.

"Thank you for doing this," Jonathan says, wrapping an arm around my waist and drawing me to him. "I didn't know what was going on when you showed up at my door this morning, but this ... it's more than I could've imagined."

I shouldn't tell him yet.

I should hold off until one of those moments when the stars seem to align. A hike to the top of the mountain, when the world is a watercolor of blues and greens below us and the sky feels right at our fingertips. A picnic by the fire, with the flames dancing and the smell of burning wood warming us as much as the wine we're sipping with our meal. A walk down to the lake, which acts as a mirror and reflects the trees that tower above it. Any one of those scenarios would be the perfect time to tell Jonathan that I want him to slide that engagement ring onto my finger. That's how I planned it. I had hoped to surprise him with as sweeping a gesture as he made for me up on Stone Mountain in the fall.

But I have waited long enough. I have made *him* wait long enough.

Suddenly, I don't want to do that for even a minute more.

As long as Jonathan and I are together, it's all that matters. *That* is what makes it perfect, and I guess maybe imperfect, too, because that's the best thing about finding your soulmate: each of you has flaws, and quirks, and dents in the armor, but when you're with one another, all of that is swept aside. I think it's like Henry said when we spoke on the phone: there is beauty in the broken. And, I know, there is also beauty in piecing it together.

That's what Jonathan has done for me, and it's why I intertwine my fingers with his, right here on the balcony, with a bird chirping in a nearby tree and a blanket of clouds covering the sunshine up above.

"Three months ago," I say, "you asked me a very important question."

His eyes go wide as he realizes where this is heading. "Yes," he says. "I did." His voice is quiet, but so filled with hope that I could cry. It makes me feel horrible, for having drawn this out, and yet I also feel good about that, because taking those months to be certain of my answer means it's one I truly think will stand firm against any challenge life throws at it.

I am not my mother. Jonathan is not my father.

We are just ... us. I have to believe that's what counts most of all.

"I told you then that I wanted to say yes." My lower lip quivers as I speak. "And every day since, I've wanted to say the same thing, but I wasn't ready yet. Now I am." I squeeze his hand. "The day you proposed, I thought about how safe I feel with you, and even though that's a good thing, it felt like I needed more. I needed someone who could make me throw that safety to the wind, someone who made me want to embrace every plot twist." I smile, even as tears start to fill my eyes. "Know what I have realized?" I ask. "You don't have to make me embrace it, because you *are* my plot twist. You're the one who came into my life and turned it in an entirely new direction. You've shown me it is okay to let myself be loved and to love fiercely in return, even if I don't know what will happen in one year, or ten, or fifty. You make me believe I can take a chance on marriage." The first tears slip out and cascade down my cheeks. "When I was eight years old and my Gram took me into The Book Boutique for the first time since it'd been finished ... that day, it's when I learned that magic can be real. Now you've taught me that all over again."

Jonathan says nothing, he just pulls me to him and kisses

me like I've never been kissed before. Then he reaches into his coat pocket. "I know I told you I put this away in a drawer," he says, "but I have actually been carrying it around with me, praying for a moment just like this. It's a good thing I'm optimistic." He grins, and I do, too, my heart racing a million miles a minute as he gets down on one knee. "Let's try this again," he says. "Grace Anderson, you're the love of my life. Would you do me the honor of being my wife?"

This time, I don't hesitate. "Yes," I say. "That is one adventure I would love to go on with you."

My hand doesn't shake as I hold it out for him to slide on the diamond ring.

It is steady. I am steady.

Just as the engagement ring finds its home around my finger, the most gentle snow starts to fall from the sky. It's delicate and fine, the flakes like the very same pixie dust I imagined when I walked into The Book Boutique on that rainy day almost twenty-six years ago. How fitting that is. Because even though this is like my big scene in a novel, the scene that would normally leave me spellbound as a reader, I know now, as Jonathan lifts me up and twirls me around, that sometimes we have to close the book.

Sometimes real life is even better than a fairy tale.

28

Rose

Perhaps I should have been prepared for a remark such as that. I knew my parents would react poorly to the idea of me having a baby before getting married, especially since Henry was no longer in the picture, and yet I never considered that they would ask me to give my child away. It came as a shock to my system, sitting there and listening to my mother's tirade about all of the reasons why our family could never welcome my baby into its folds. I thought I had steeled myself against every potential response – tears of anguish, admonishments of anger, accusations of reckless imprudence and naiveté – but this was beyond me.

"It is the only way," my mother said brusquely. "You can research adoption agencies."

"I don't think … that is not … I am planning … " No matter how hard I tried, I could not seem to explain myself to her. I closed my eyes, breathed in all the air my lungs could hold, and gradually let it back out before opening my eyes and speaking again. "There is no need for me to research that," I said, and this time my voice stayed firm. "I'm going to keep this baby and be the best mother I can. Just because this is unexpected does not mean it is unwanted. I have never been certain that being a parent was right for me, but this baby has changed everything."

I was proud of myself for standing up to my mother.

Violet was, too. From across the table, she nodded in encouragement.

"Don't do that," our father told her. "You aren't helping your sister by supporting this foolhardy notion. What will happen once the baby is born?" He stared at me unwaveringly, and I half-wished he would just yell or scream, because his calm displeasure was much worse. "How can you afford to give your child the life he or she deserves?" he asked. "You have no job and no husband to provide for you. A baby is expensive. Perhaps you and this Henry fellow needed to think about the possible consequences before you got carried away." He sighed. "Yet, here we are. It would be wise to take your mother's advice."

"We can even get the ball rolling tonight," she said, picking up the napkin on her lap and placing it on the table before pushing her chair back with such force that its legs squeaked against the floor. She walked over to the living room and took out a phone book from the top desk drawer. "I imagine there is someone at the adoption agency who can handle the entire thing," she told me. "I'll make a list of the various agencies and you can choose whichever you like best." She pursed her lips as she sat back down at the table. "The only issue is how we'll hide this until the baby is born. Those loose blouses will only disguise the truth for so long. You'll simply have to keep out of sight. You can stay here with your father and me for the duration."

"No." The answer flew out of my mouth immediately.

"Excuse me?" She arched her eyebrows.

"No," I repeated. "I am thirty-years-old, Mother. I know how to look after myself."

She gestured to my stomach. "Evidently not."

I could feel the heat seep into my cheeks. Let her insinuate that I was an embarrassment all she wanted, but I refused to tolerate her talking about my child like he or she was something that had to be hidden away. "I understand that this is not what you wanted for me," I said softly, "and of course it's certainly not what I had planned on when I left for Europe, but that's what life is: things you can never plan for, not really. I apologize if this does not follow the bright, shiny path you imagined for me ... " I trailed off, and Thomas caught my gaze. He had been quiet until that point, fidgeting with the tablecloth, and the cuff of his sports coat, and anything else within reach, but my sudden silence seemed to worry him.

"You don't have to do this," he told me. "You don't have to defend yourself."

That was exactly right.

It was why I had stopped short, because I did not care for what I was saying. The only thing that I owed my parents an apology for was not telling them the truth sooner. The rest of it, though? No. I wasn't sorry I hadn't followed their predetermined goals or that I wanted to embrace motherhood even if the situation wasn't ideal. If that made me a blight on the family, I would have to learn how to accept it.

"You know what?" I said. "I take that back. I should not have to apologize for being me. No one should. I would love for my child to grow up with our whole family around, and for you to take your grandbaby to Central Park, and down to the river, and even just onto the balcony to see the flowers. That is your decision, though. You can be as big or as small a part of this child's life as you'd like, but know that whatever you choose, I am not contacting an adoption agency. This baby is staying with me, and I will *not* be staying with you."

I sounded confident, bold, and assured.

I felt that way, too, at least in the moment. It was not until later that night, as I was cocooned in the covers, trying to fall asleep, that I started to question everything I had said. Was it selfish of me to keep the baby? My father was right about one thing: I did not currently have the financial means to afford everything a newborn would need, and those costs would only rise as time went on. How was I going to pay for it? I would need a job, but then who would watch the baby? If I opted for the adoption route instead, my child could grow up in a family where he or she wanted for nothing and where there would be a father present each day, rather than someone mentioned in stories about a cruise to Europe that would seem more like fiction than fact. Perhaps it was unfair to insist on being a single mother. I wanted to do right by my baby, even if it meant having to say goodbye.

I sat up in bed and reached for my robe.

There would be no sleep tonight.

I was still living with Violet and Thomas – the couple subletting my apartment had asked for one more month, and quite honestly, it was a perfect excuse to take solace in my sister for a bit longer – and I shuffled out of the guest room and down the hallway. Everything was quiet in the living room, dark and pristine. Through the glass of the window, I could see the city lights twinkling. It reminded me of the fireflies Violet and I used to chase in Central Park when we were children. I wanted to see my own child do that. I wanted to watch him or her grow up. Was that so horrible of me?

My head was swimming with confusion.

My heart was drowning in emotion.

I stood there by the window, just watching, just looking, hoping to find my answers in the lights. That is when I felt it. It was the slightest sensation, like a butterfly fluttering its wings, and I gasped at first, thinking there was something wrong with the baby, before I realized what was happening. It was actually something right. The baby was moving. When Lucy's sister was expecting, she had said it felt like a butterfly, too. I waited to see if it would happen again, and sure enough, it did.

Dozens of tiny goosebumps blanketed my arms.

I had wanted to find answers. Perhaps this was it.

I rested a hand on my stomach and thought, yet again, of Henry. Where was he? Why had I not been able to find him?

I hoped he was alright.

I hoped he was happy.

I hoped for so many things.

I had no idea how long I stood there at the window, or when I sat down on the floor and drifted off to sleep, but the next thing

I knew it was the morning and Violet was at my side, sitting with her legs outstretched and a cup of warm milk in her hand. "Why don't you stay with me even after the Smithsons move out of your apartment?" she suggested, giving me the mug. "At least until the baby is born, and perhaps afterward, too. Let me help you." She touched my wrist. "And please, do not listen to what Mother and Father said. They'll come around."

"I don't know about that."

As I told her about the baby moving, though, there was something I did know: that adoption was not the choice for us. This mama and child would stay together. It would be the biggest mountain I ever had to scale, but I refused to let that stop me. After all, it was the steepest climbs that offered the most breathtaking views.

As the months progressed, autumn chilling into winter's frost, that is precisely what happened. There was the moment the baby's gentle flutters turned into swift kicks, strong enough for Violet to feel when she put her hand on my stomach; the one when I stumbled upon a copy of Anne Morrow Lindbergh's *Gift from the Sea* in the bookstore and was so drawn to its inspiration that I bought it as both a guide and as a treasure chest of sorts to keep Henry's letter safe, because my journal was too difficult to look at anymore; and also the one when I confided in Lucy and Alice that I was expecting and they reacted with delight. I had known they would never judge me, it was not what true friends did, and yet, as they chatted about baby clothes and toys, a swell of relief surged inside me. I would be a single parent, yes, but that did not mean I was on my own.

"Anything we can do, honey," Lucy said. "You just say the word and we'll be glad to help."

"We'll be honorary aunties," Alice added. "That means it's a requirement to spoil the baby."

"What do you think?" Lucy asked. "Girl or boy?"

Violet had asked me that, too, and I supposed I was meant

to have an intuition about it, but I did not. "Honestly," I said, "I don't have the faintest idea. I daydream about it, though, getting to finally meet this little one and see who he or she resembles. I'm hoping there's a lot of Henry in the baby's features."

"You don't think that would make it more difficult?" Alice questioned.

"Do you want a constant reminder of him?" Lucy chimed in. "Wouldn't it be upsetting?"

"I would love it, actually," I said. "That way it will be like a piece of him is still with me." I raised a hand to touch the necklace Henry had given me. I never took it off. One day, when our child was old enough to realize that I wore it every day, we would sit down and I would relay the story of how Mama and Daddy met, how Henry had come into my life and changed it forever. Sometimes I felt so desperately sad that Henry would never know his child, but at least I could make sure that his child would know about him.

I started doing that even before the baby was born. Touched as I was by Violet's sweet offer to stay with her and Thomas, I did not want to impose any longer, so I returned to my apartment once the Smithsons rented a place of their own and moved out. As I sat on the window seat in the living room, watching the sun creep over the buildings in the morning and sink below them in the evening, I would talk to the baby, telling stories about my time on the SS Harmony and overseas. Could he or she hear me? Would speaking out loud now mean that my voice would be familiar in the future? I tried to research it. I tried to research a lot of things, taking books out from the library and reading them each day. I hoped to learn as much as possible before the baby arrived. I also hoped to find a new job, but that proved more difficult than I had anticipated. Nobody seemed to have an interest in hiring a woman who was clearly with child.

I tried and tried and tried, but I failed and failed and failed.

I was at a loss for what to do.

I understood – no mother was going to come home from the hospital and go back to work, and that would only put the employer in the position of having to find a replacement – but it was still so frustrating, because how could I support my child if no one would give me an opportunity? I needed a source of income, and I needed it quickly.

"Perhaps there's something you can do from home," Violet suggested one morning. It was mid-February, about two months before the baby was due, and we were sitting on my sofa after she had accompanied me to a doctor's appointment. "How about sewing or knitting? You have always had such a good eye for design."

"Do you really think so?"

"Of course. Look at that," she said, gesturing to the vase of flowers I had on the coffee table. It was a mix of carnations, statice, and lilies, all of which I had purchased from a flower market over on Sixth Avenue because the corner stand was closed until the springtime. "You arranged them, right?" Violet asked. "You're great at that. It reminds me of our mother." Her eyes lit up. "Actually, wait, what about that? You could start your own floral arranging business. Just because Mother decided not to turn her passion for it into something more doesn't mean you can't. It's something you could do from home, minus the trips to get all the flowers, and I know there would be people who'd love to buy your creations."

It was a good idea. It was a fabulous one, in fact, and the best part was it was something I could continue with, even after the baby was born. I worried continuously about how I would get by, but perhaps this was the answer. As I mulled it over, I thought, also, about that day on the *SS Harmony* when I had gone out to watch the sun paint the sky above and the ocean below. All the possibilities were still endless that day, and I had not known which one to grab onto, but I had been sure of one thing: that wherever I went, whatever I did, I wanted to immerse myself in something which would bring happiness to others.

Maybe this was the way to achieve that.

Flowers had brightened my own life ever since I was a child. They spoke to me when everything else felt too quiet; they silenced me when everything else seemed too loud. I could share that with others by handcrafting these creations that were about much more than petals and stems in a vase. I loved the idea of getting to give people whatever emotion they were yearning for most. Whether it was comfort or celebration, solace or hope, faith or motivation, flowers could do that.

I could do that.

I smiled at Violet. "Sometimes I think you know me better than I know myself," I told her.

She smiled, too. "That's what sisters are for," she said.

Sisters were also for throwing baby showers, and helping to pick out nursery furniture, and, as it became clear that there really was no room for said furniture in my one-bedroom apartment, sisters were also for insisting yet again that no one was ever an imposition if you loved them. "There is not enough room here for you and the baby," she said, as we stood in my apartment with all the boxes of furniture around us. "Please stay with us, if only for a few months, until you feel settled. Then I'll help you find a new apartment."

That time, I could not turn her down, and so that is how my sister also became the one to drive me to the hospital when, in that sweet spot of April as the trees started to burst with color, the baby was ready to make a grand entrance. My heart felt like it was beating right out of my chest as Violet navigated the streets of New York. I was excited, terrified, ecstatic, and nervous ... practically every emotion I could think of, all jumbled together. I had imagined this day so many times, and now that it was happening, I could hardly get a handle on my feelings.

"I wish Henry were here," I said, as Violet and I walked into the elevator at Mount Sinai Hospital and she pushed the button that would take us up to the maternity floor.

"I know," she said, squeezing my hand. "I wish he could be here, too." She kept her right hand wrapped around my left the whole time I filled out paperwork, and as we waited for the nurse, and even while she hugged me goodbye. "I will be right here," she promised. "I'm with you always."

"Always," I repeated, and held her tight.

That is what sisters were for most of all.

I would have given anything for Violet to come back with me, but that was not permitted, and so I was alone when I finally met my baby. "Congratulations," the doctor said. "It's a girl."

My world, it just stopped. It stopped in the best possible way, and then, as I gazed down at the infant who looked like the most beautiful baby doll, with her squinty eyes and button nose and pink heart-shaped lips, it started anew. My whole life began again in that moment. "Welcome, darling," I said, and brushed a delicate kiss to her forehead. I could not get over how dewy her skin was, how marshmallow soft. Was she even real? She was right there nestled into my arms, so she had to be, but my goodness did she seem like a dream. I could not stop looking at her, grazing my finger along the curves of her cheek, the tiny nails on her hands, and the fuzzy tufts of hair on her head. She had my eyes and mouth, and Henry's blonde hair ... and best of all, she also had his dimples. It reminded me of something my grandmother used to say, that when a baby was born with dimples, it meant an angel had kissed its cheeks.

This baby *was* my angel.

How was it possible for a person this small to take up so much room inside of my heart? It was a love just as I had imagined, and still, it was unlike anything I had ever known. I watched, filled with awe, as my baby girl spread her fingers wide. It was as though she was trying to reach out and grab the world.

"I will help you," I promised her. "Whatever you want, my dear heart, Mama will do everything in her power to help you accomplish it." I touched my finger to her tiny ones and they instinctively curled around it, like she somehow knew we were a team. It made me burst with the purest kind of happiness. There was no way to describe it. Some things were beyond words. Some heartbeats in time were simply supposed to be marveled at and memorized.

That's when I knew. I knew what my purpose was, what it had always been meant to be. It was this. Perhaps that journey to Europe had not only been about discovering answers in the museums of Paris and the gardens of London. Maybe it was not even about finding them in the ocean waves. The answers were already inside of me, I realized now. Being a mother and growing my own flower business felt right. It took traveling overseas to make me see what I could have here at home – and to create this new and enchanting home with my daughter.

My daughter.

I was a mother now.

My journey on the *SS Harmony* gave me Henry, and Henry gave me our little girl.

"Ivy," I whispered, cradling her close to me. "That's who you are. Your daddy and I talked about ivies on the ship, and I told him how long it sometimes takes them to bloom. I can't think of a better name for you, because that's what you have done for me ... you showed me how to finally bloom." I loved the name for her, and I thought Henry would, too.

At that moment, though, I wanted to share it with somebody else.

"Excuse me," I said to the nurse. "I know it isn't allowed, but is there any way you could get my sister?"

She smiled. "I'm not supposed to," she said. "Families are only allowed to see the baby through the nursery window. However, if she were to come by when I'm taking my lunch break, there would be no one to stop her."

So that is how it came about, Violet sitting in a chair next to my bed, holding her new niece and singing her the softest lullaby. Seeing my sister cradle my daughter was my blessing, my miracle, my greatest gift of all.

I reached a hand up to my necklace from Henry.

All of this, it was my forget-me-not.

❧29❧

Grace

"*This* calls for a celebration," Jonathan says. His eyes are shining, his cheeks red from the chilly air, or maybe just from the excitement of it all. I rest my hands on them, and his skin is cool beneath mine, but when I kiss him, when I feel his arm encircle me like he could hold me close forever, there is an unmistakable heat. Because he *can* hold me close forever now. It's taken a lot for us to get to this point, and that's definitely worth celebrating, too.

"What do you have in mind?" I murmur.

"Good question," he says. "We could go find a restaurant and order their best bottle of vintage wine. We could go for a walk in the snow and take some pictures to show off your ring." He dips his head down, his mouth so near mine that I can feel his breath on my lips. "Or we could go inside and see if it feels any different, being together as an engaged couple. What do you think?"

"I think," I say, a little contented sigh fluttering from me as he kisses my neck, "that I would love nothing more than to make love to my fiancé."

My fiancé. I can barely believe it.

It actually makes my heart skip a beat. I used to think that was only a phrase writers pulled out when they were describing the power of the love between their characters, a pretty twist of the pen to make the story come alive, but now I know it's real. Standing here in this magnificent place with a man who loves me so much, how could my heart *not* skip a beat? I hope I make his do the same. I certainly intend to try.

But first, there's something I need to do. "Just give me one second," I say. I duck inside to grab my cell phone, then pop back out onto the balcony.

"So you *do* want to go the picture route." Jonathan grins as I snap a photo of my ring.

I crinkle up my nose. "Maybe," I admit. "But it's not only for me. Here," I say, handing over the phone. "Can you get one of both of us? It'll come out better if you do it, since you're taller." I lean close and rest my hand atop his chest, making sure the blue of the diamond is the focal point of the picture. It feels silly and sappy, but also sentimental and sweet. And, after he hands me my phone back and I open the messaging screen to forward along the photos, it also feels special. Really, truly special.

I don't type out a message. It's rare, but in a case like this one, I think a picture really *is* worth a thousand words. I send them off to my sisters, my mother, and Sofie. The replies start pinging back before Jonathan and I even get inside, and it makes both of us laugh, because we can't seem to take even three steps toward the bedroom before my phone lights up yet again.

Oh, sweetheart, I'm so thrilled for you! My mother.

I had a feeling that's what you would decide. Overjoyed for you, my friend! XOXO! Sofie.

Proud of you, little sister. So when do we start planning the wedding? Abigail.

Well, it's about damn time! Congratulations, Grace! Now go consummate it! Josie.

"I knew I liked your sisters," Jonathan quips.

"Wise women," I agree.

I answer them quickly, sending out my love and appreciation for all their excitement, and then I turn off my phone and toss it onto the sofa. There will be time for more photos and messages later. Right now, I just want to be with Jonathan. I want the two of us to be one. As we head upstairs and fall onto the bed, his heart beating above mine as we lose ourselves in each other, everything else in the world fades away.

It is only us, and I adore it.

This must be what a real happily-ever-after feels like.

* * *

The whole weekend is the same. We hike trails that lead down to the lake and up to the summit of the mountains. We cook dinner in the kitchen and eat by the fireplace. We toast marshmallows and drink wine and catch snowflakes on our tongues like a couple of kids. It is, without a doubt, the best weekend I've ever had, and even when I'm back at work Monday morning, I can't stop thinking about it. I catch myself stealing a peek at my ring multiple times, and whenever a customer notices and comments on it, my cheeks flush with a rosy glow. I am happy. How nice it is to let myself feel it. And I won't lie: although we've only been engaged for two days and haven't even talked about a date, let alone set one, I allow myself to daydream a little about what our wedding will be like. I am so looking forward to planning it.

As the winter rolls on, I'm caught up in plans for The Book Boutique, too. We hold a fundraising dinner that Abigail heads up, and begin to toss out ideas for her 'Book it for Books' charity run. Then there's the book hop. The social media posts on it are coming in fast and furious. There are photos of *Jasper Jellybean Jumps for Joy* propped up against a tree in the Everglades, and beneath a beach umbrella in Maui, and even onstage in a Broadway theater, thanks to one of Josie's friends who's in the company for *Wicked*. My favorite shots are the ones with people in them. The twins who stand in front of their kindergarten classroom, holding the book between them. The baby who's staring at the cover like he can read its words. The director of a rabbit rescue, who is sitting on a couch with a bunny next to her and the book in her hand, as though it's story time for her furry friend. Even the author posts a photo. She's been promoting the contest to her readers, and when it comes time for the winners to be announced in March, she flies down from Philadelphia to join us.

"It's a fantastic thing you're doing here," she tells me, as we stand by the door, greeting people as they walk inside. "Raising awareness is key when it comes to shelter animals. There are so many of them that need someone to come along and save them."

"Is that why you wrote the book?" I ask.

"It sure is. I hoped the message would stay with the people who read it, that it'd move them to adopt their next pet." She smiles. "I must thank you," she says, "for selecting it for your book hop. You've helped it get a lot of attention. I am touched by the generosity of you and your sisters." She motions to Abigail, who's checking the screen we have set up to show the social media posts, and to Josie, who's sitting cross-legged on the floor by the side bookshelves with a shaggy dog in her lap. It was her idea to let tonight's event double as an adoption open-house for the area rescues. I loved it instantly, and so did Abigail, even though, as she predicted, her kids are now clamoring for another dog.

"Please, Mommy?" I hear Macy beg.

"Look how cute he is!" Ben adds, and I glance up to see him holding a squirming puppy.

"Think they'll wear Abigail down?" Jonathan asks, as he walks into The Book Boutique and kisses me hello. He and his colleagues are joining us tonight, too. I'm happy for their support of the store, but mostly I'm just happy for Jonathan's support of me. I don't know how I ever could have doubted its permanence.

"Oh yes," I say. "Abigail's a tough cookie, but those kids know how to work her."

"Think it'll be the same for us if we have children someday?"

His question reminds me of the dreams I had on the night he proposed, especially the one with our kids clinging to me after Jonathan and I got divorced, all of us in tears. It had scared me so much then. Now it's nothing more than an image drawn in the sand, only to be erased by an ocean wave. I'm not worried about it happening any longer, which is why I can answer with complete confidence. "Not *if* we have children," I tell him. "But *when*. And yes, of course it'll be the same."

"Wouldn't have it any other way," he says.

I smile up at him. "Neither would I."

It's incredible how life changes when you let yourself change in incredible ways.

As I head over to the podium set up on the side of the store, I can't help thinking about all that's happened since the evening when the book hop launched. Many of the same people filled the store then. They listened to me talk about everything I hoped to achieve, but what they didn't know, and what they still don't, is just how much was riding on its success. Tonight, with good news to share, I am finally ready to tell them.

"I want to thank you all for coming tonight," I say to the crowd, "and, of course, for participating in the book hop. It's gone better than my sisters and I could have dreamed of, and we owe it to you. We began with seventy copies of the book, and over the past three months, they've been spotted in all fifty states, along with Canada and even the Bahamas. I don't know about you, but I think that is pretty impressive."

Here, I have to pause as people clap.

From the front of the crowd, Josie winks and mouths a "Told you so."

I'm glad she was proven right about the book reaching every state.

I just hope Abigail will be proven right, too, when it comes to confiding in our customers.

It's hard for me to speak the words that come next, but as I look at the people standing in front of me – some I have known for decades and others who have been introduced to The Book Boutique only recently – I can feel myself boosted up by them. Old faces or new, they are here because they care. "Maybe you have guessed this already or maybe not," I tell them, "but the store's had a tough time of it lately. Independent bookshops are being forced to close their doors every day. We were worried that'd happen here, and I'll be honest: it still might. The future is far from settled. What I'm so pleased and relieved to tell you, though, is that it won't be happening right now. Thanks to your generosity and support of all our recent endeavors, the store is able to keep itself afloat for at least another several months." I put a hand over my heart. "Please know how truly grateful we are, and how grateful our grandparents would be. They always used to say they had the best customers, and it's true. We couldn't do this without you."

There's another round of applause, this one even louder.

"Alright," I say, once it's quieted down. "Let's move on to the real reason you're here. It's time to announce the winners of the book hop." Josie begins a drumroll, and everybody else joins in as I flip open the cover of the winning book. "With a total of ninety signatures," I say, "congratulations to Bradley Williams and Melina Radcliffe!"

The crowd cheers them on as they make their way up front, and so do I. I've known Bradley for a long time – he used to shop at the store frequently before he moved to Pennsylvania, and I'm glad he happened to stop by when he was here for Thanksgiving to introduce his girlfriend Melina to his family. It turns out he's been very involved in animal rescue himself these days, and so he was glad to buy a book for the contest. I suppose I shouldn't be surprised, then, when he asks me to keep the winner's check and to split it between the bookstore and the shelters represented here this evening. "Y'all can use it more than we can," he says.

"You have such a wonderful store here," Melina adds. "Please let us know if there's anything at all we can do to help out."

That's the theme of the night. The entire remainder of the evening, after the other winners are announced, people come up to me in a steady stream, asking how they can assist. It fills me up with appreciation and love. I was so worried about destroying the joy of the store for people, but it turns out it's the opposite: their lives have been impacted by that joy, and now they're happy to repay the favor.

Abigail *was* right.

"See, you were worried for nothing," she says, after everyone else has gone home and only she, Josie, and I remain. We're sitting on the bean bags in the children's section, in the very spot where Gram and Pop-Pop would gather us around and read to us when we were younger. Maybe it's silly, three grown women choosing bean bags instead of chairs, but I think we all want to feel close to our grandparents tonight.

"Gram and Pop-Pop would be really proud of you," Josie says to me. "For never backing down, even when most people would have. Even when Abigail and I wanted to." She wrinkles her nose. "I owe you an apology about that. I see now how important it is to keep this place alive, and especially how meaningful it is to you. When I'm onstage, with the lights shining and an audience ready to slip into the world of the show, that's what makes me sparkle. Clearly The Book Boutique is what does that for you."

"It's funny," Abigail says. "When you first asked us for those extra months to turn a profit here, I thought it would drag on and we'd end up falling apart. Instead it's been the opposite. Somehow, it brought us together."

"We brought ourselves together," I say.

"Because that's what sisters do," Josie says.

"That's who we are," Abigail adds. She clears her throat. "And sisters should always be honest with each other, too, which is why I have to tell you something. I hope The Book Boutique is able to live on for years and years, but these past four and a half months, and especially tonight, they have shown me that this place is your baby, Grace, not mine. I'll forever treasure all the memories we've made inside these walls ... but my share of this store should belong to you."

What?

She's backing out? Now?

After we're finally headed in the right direction?

"The Book Boutique deserves an owner who's constantly fired up over its success," she explains. "Someone who will fight for it day in and day out. That's you." She reaches for her purse and pulls out a long envelope. I meet her gaze as she passes it to me, and maybe I should be able to figure it out, maybe her words should have registered on multiple levels, but my mouth still falls open when I slide out the paper inside and realize what it is.

A formal document, drawn up by an attorney.

Signing over Abigail's share of The Book Boutique to me at no cost.

I don't know what to say.

I don't know how to react.

All I can do is stare at her. "This is ... Abigail ... it's way too much," I manage.

"No." She smiles. "It's not. I happen to think it's exactly enough."

"She's right," Josie says, and there's something about her voice, something about how it's much softer than normal, that shakes me out of my astonishment and makes me turn to face her. "I'm so stoked that the store is doing better," she tells me. "And I'll always be glad to help out when I'm in town, but ... " A grin snatches control of her face. "I don't know when that'll be for the foreseeable future, because you are officially looking at one of the new actresses in the touring company of *The Lion King*."

"Josie!" I exclaim. "Oh my God, that's amazing!"

"Beyond amazing," Abigail adds excitedly. "What a dream role!"

Josie beams. "Remember that part I auditioned for in Las Vegas?" she asks. "I didn't get it, but the musical director put me in touch with one of his contacts, and I auditioned for this, too. I didn't want to say anything until I knew for sure. Got the official word earlier today, and I wanted you two to be the first to hear about it. Oh, and as an added bonus ... the guy I auditioned with is one of the male leads, and not only is he ridiculously good-looking, but he also asked me out. We've been on a few dates, and I actually really like him." She looks at me. "I figure if you can take a chance on tying the knot, the least I can do is get over myself enough to start dating men who are worthy of my time and commitment."

I lean over to hug her. "I'm so proud of you," I say.

I am proud of all of us.

It takes a lot, to go for your dreams even when they seem so far out of reach. Even when there is no guarantee you'll be able to grab onto them, and even if you do, even if you're lucky enough to be one of those people who turns a dream into reality, that you'll be able to hang on. You need a lot of courage to open yourself up like that, but it's what my sisters and I have done. Abigail has built a family who is her world. Josie has her acting, a career that brings joy and contentment to herself, as well as happiness and entertainment to others. And I have the store, this little slice of hope that our Gram and Pop-Pop created all those years ago ... and, maybe, also a little slice of heaven that they're sharing now. They're here with us tonight. I can feel their never-ending love and support as surely as I can that from my sisters.

Because Abigail isn't the only one turning over The Book Boutique to me.

"I don't have any paperwork," Josie says. "But Abigail's inspired me. I don't know if I can afford to do this, but if I can, I'd like to give you my share, too. This place belongs to you, Grace. It's meant to be yours."

"You really don't have to do that," I tell her.

"I want to," she says.

And in that moment, there's something I want, too.

Something I've been waiting to ask my sisters until I could make it perfect, until I had the time to write letters and print photos and buy picture frames to arrange everything. I had hoped to make it a big deal, but as I look at Abigail and Josie tonight, as I think of what they're giving me, this gift that is so much more than I could ever have imagined, I realize that it doesn't have to be a big deal, after all.

It just has to come from the heart.

"I love you both," I tell them. "We've been through a lot together, and I know we don't always see eye-to-eye, but I admire you, and I respect you, and I'm so truly thankful for you." I smile. "And that's why I want you to be my matron-of-honor and maid-of-honor as I start my life with Jonathan. I can't think of anyone else I'd rather have by my side."

There is lots of squealing, and laughing, and cheering to follow.

There are even a few tears.

And then, once we've all settled into excited chatter over wedding colors and bridesmaid dress styles and event venues, there is something which takes a special night and makes it even better: a text from Lily.

Talked to my mom and Aunt Violet, it says. *We've arranged a meeting between Grandmom and Henry for next week. I seriously cannot wait to see the looks on their faces. Mom, Aunt Violet, and I all agreed – we'd love for you and your sisters to be there to see it, too, if you're up for it.*

Are we up for it?

I look at my sisters.

As Josie would say ... hell yes.

∾30∾

Rose & Grace

I put up quite the argument when my family began to toss around the idea of me moving into a retirement community. The thought of selling my house, the very brownstone I'd signed a contract for on the day Ivy turned six months old, just about squeezed every single emotion from my heart. I loved that brownstone and I always will. It is where my baby took her first steps and spoke her first word, where my tiny flower business blossomed into something greater than I could have imagined, and where I settled into the life I had been meant to lead. Leaving was hard, and even now, nearly a year after moving into the apartment next to Violet's at the retirement community, I still find myself thinking about my former home and hoping that its new owners will always be as content there as I was.

That's not to say I'm not happy here, too. I am. It's a warm and welcoming place, and I've met many excellent people. In a way, it reminds me of my journey overseas back in the fifties. We may not be sailing across the Atlantic or soaking up the light and life of a foreign city, but we get to cross paths with people we never would have known otherwise. Whether I'm joining a book club, taking a painting class, playing canasta with the ladies down the hall, or sitting in the garden with Violet, my days are full and interesting.

Apparently, today promises to be the most interesting yet, at least according to Ivy. She showed up at my door this morning with a glint in her eyes, and insisted I put on my favorite outfit. "I can't tell you why," she said, when I asked. "Could you just humor me?" I could, and I did, selecting a pair of aqua slacks and a blouse that is white with an aqua floral print. I pulled my silvery hair back with two combs, and then, as I do each day, I slipped on Henry's necklace. Ivy beamed when she saw me. She's still beaming, in fact, as she chatters on about what a monumental day it is. I try, again, to find out why, but she only smiles, glances surreptitiously at her watch, and says, "Some things are better left as a surprise."

When my darling Lily walks into the apartment an hour later, I must agree about that: getting to see my granddaughter unexpectedly is the best kind of surprise. "I'm thrilled you're here, honey," I say, hugging her close.

"Me, too," she says. "No better way to spend my spring break from grad school. Kendall really wanted to come up, too, but he couldn't get the time off work. He said he'll call later to hear about it."

"Hear about what?" I ask.

She gives an innocent little shrug that tells me she isn't the surprise Ivy was talking about, after all. "Let's go for a walk in the garden," she says, and though I'm tempted to press her on this, to ask why she and Ivy are being so secretive, I do the opposite and play along. I have seen firsthand how some people's families all but abandon them once they are settled in a place like this, so I opt to be grateful that not only are my girls here, but also that they care enough to arrange for whatever this mysterious surprise is. I know how lucky that makes me.

"So tell me," I say, as Lily leads me out the door and down the stairs, "what's new with you? Are you still enjoying your classes this semester? Any new violin concerts coming up? Maybe we can do that thing where I watch you play through the phone. What's it called again?"

"A video chat," she says.

"Right." I nod a little. "I'll tell you, sometimes all this technology still amazes me. It also makes me feel old, when I think of how much has changed since I was your age."

"You're not old, Grandmom," she says, and we both laugh, because we've had this conversation more times than I can count. Lily is always quick to assure me that I'm only as old – or as young – as I feel, and although sometimes it's hard to agree with that, when I look back on my life and all of the things I've done over the past ninety-one years, mostly I do think there's merit in what she says. I'm not ready to slow down yet. I may be in my golden years now, but that just means the world around me is bright with the possibilities that still remain. As Lily and I step outside, it's obvious that one of those possibilities is about to unfold. There are three women sitting on a bench near the far end of the garden, a brunette, a blonde, and a redhead, and Lily leads me in their direction the minute she sees them.

"Aha," I say. "This was a set-up. You didn't really want to take a walk."

Lily grins. "I think you'll thank me when you find out what's going on." She slows to a stop once we reach the women, and the blonde one stands up to give her a hug. "Grandmom," Lily says, "this is Grace, Abigail, and Josie. They are the sisters who found your book. They wanted to meet you, so we all came up together from Georgia."

Oh, goodness. It takes me a minute to compose myself as I look at the three eager faces.

How do I begin to express my appreciation to them?

When I realized Ivy had accidentally packed that book into the donation box, my heart had sunk. It is one of my most prized possessions, along with the necklace Henry gave me so many years ago, the photograph Thomas snapped of Violet and me with Ivy on the morning we came home from the hospital, and the receipt from the first sale I made after I was lucky enough to open a flower shop of my very own. Losing any one of those things would be brutal, but somehow the book seemed like a particularly strong blow, because the letter and clipping inside were what had started it all. They're the reason my life followed a certain trail ...

or, really, the reason it blazed its own trail. To think that I would have lost my keepsake of that, if not for these women, is enough to make me stretch out my arms and hug each one of them, even though they are total strangers. That is the thing, though: as I sit down on the adjacent bench in the little courtyard area, I don't feel like I'm joining strangers. It's as though I'm joining friends.

As they tell me all about the evening they found the letter, how they had been in the middle of a disagreement over the fate of the bookstore they co-owned together, it seems like I could listen for hours. It's riveting. I am fascinated by their story, especially when Grace tells me how inspired she's been by my own.

"I was holding out hope for you and Henry," she says. "All three of us were. And then after I got to speak with ... " Here, her younger sister, the redhead, pokes her with her elbow. "After I realized you didn't stay together," Grace amends, smoothly but not subtly, "it was a much-needed wake-up call. I hated that you and Henry lost out on your love, and I knew I wouldn't forgive myself if I let the same thing happen with my boyfriend. He's my fiancé now," she adds, and shows me the gorgeous ring on her finger. "We're getting married next spring, and we owe that to you."

"No," I say. "You owe that to yourself. If there's one thing I've learned in this life, it's that we're all responsible for our own decisions. Chance might give us opportunities, but it's up to us what we do with them."

"What about Henry?" she asks me quietly. "Was it the right decision to say goodbye to him?"

"Grace," Abigail whispers loudly. "Stop. It's none of our business."

She's right. It isn't.

It also isn't something I've ever really talked about before.

It's always hurt too deeply.

Even when, as a child, Ivy would ask what happened between her daddy and me, I was hesitant to reveal too much. I loved to tell her stories about our time together on the *SS Harmony*, and I was always sure to explain that he would have adored her, if only he knew he had a daughter, but when I got to the part about leaving Henry behind, it's like the words stuck to the walls of my throat. Going off without him was the right choice for me then, I truly believe that, but it doesn't make it any less painful now. If I had it to do all over, I would have told Henry I needed time – time to figure out who I was, who I wanted to be – but that I would have loved to pick up where we left off once everything else became clearer. I would have asked him to wait for me, just as Grace did with her Jonathan.

That ship has sailed, though, and I won't ever be able to get it back.

I've never wanted to discuss that, but sitting here with these women who are so curious to hear what I have to say, I'm suddenly tired of keeping it locked away. What good is it to have a story if it never gets told? So I do tell them – all about Ivy, and Violet, and the floral business that began in an apartment, flourished enough to let me open a stand, and eventually, when Ivy was eleven, afforded me the chance to open a store. "I no longer run it," I say. "I turned it over to Ivy ten years ago. She inherited a love of flowers from me, just as I did from my mother."

"Hence my name," Lily says. "Mom continued that tradition, and hopefully I will, too, one day."

"I love that," I say. "And I love the life I've led, but I'll always wish that Henry had been a part of it."

Grace's face lights up. "Well, then, you're in luck," she says. "Because as it turns out, my sisters and I aren't the only ones who wanted to see you today." She smiles at something behind me, and I twist around to see what she could possibly be talking about.

Oh, my God.

I swear, my heart stops for a moment.

Ivy is standing there.

So is Violet.

And so is Henry.

I'd recognize him anywhere. His hair is white now, his hands covered in a roadmap of wrinkles, but the warm cocoa brown eyes that twinkle at me from behind a pair of glasses are the same ones that used to set my world on fire. "Rose," he says, and when he smiles, this wide and brilliant smile like there couldn't be any moment better than this one, it instantly awakens those butterflies inside me which have been asleep for so very long.

It's him.

After all this time, it's actually him.

Tears spring to my eyes and my hands go to my heart. I've imagined a moment like this so many times, even after my attempts to find him had failed. When Ivy was a baby, cuddled up on my chest, and when she was a little girl, playing with all her dolls as we had tea party after tea party, and when she was a teenager, earning As in school and going to the prom ... every now and then, I would try to locate Henry again. I'd had no luck, though, and eventually, after Ivy began college, I gave up on the search. Now Henry is here. He's standing in front of me, gripping a cane with one hand and holding a rose in the other.

It's a real rose this time, just like he spoke of all those years ago.

Its color isn't lost on me, either – lavender, to represent love at first sight.

"Henry." My voice is soft, my legs wobbly from the pure emotion of it all as I get up to close the distance between us.

"Rose," he says again, and the sound of my name on his lips couldn't be sweeter. He extends his arm, holding out the rose, and I take it, leaning into his embrace and hoping I never have to let go of him again. I'm not sure how long we stay like that, perhaps a minute or two or five. Right now, time seems inconsequential and immeasurable. All I can think about is how overwhelming it is to feel his arms around me again.

It's like coming home.

"How are you here?" I whisper, raising a hand to his cheek. "How is this happening?"

"Grace," he says. "Also, Ivy, Lily, and Violet. She's the one who called me."

I look at my sister. "You knew?" I ask her. "And you didn't say anything?"

She has tears in her eyes, too, and they glitter in the sunlight. "Ivy, Lily, and I had quite the long talk," she says. "We went back and forth about the best way to proceed after Grace reached out to tell us she'd found Henry. You see, we weren't certain how you'd react if you knew in advance. It's been such a painful subject for so long, and we didn't want you to lose out on this second chance. I hope you aren't angry. We were only trying to help."

Angry?

How could I possibly be angry?

They have given me the most beautiful gift.

"I'm not the slightest bit upset," I say. "You have my everlasting gratitude."

"And mine, as well," Henry adds.

"Come," I say, gesturing to the bench. "Sit down. I want to hear about it all."

Violet and Henry find their places on either side of me, and Lily moves to join Ivy on the third of the benches that create the garden courtyard's little seating area. Then, as I requested, they fill me in on everything. I learn that Grace didn't stop after she'd located Lily and returned the book to her, that although her sisters had backed off on finding Henry, Grace felt compelled to continue on with the search.

"I called every Henry Jackson in New York," she tells me. "It took quite awhile for me to connect with him, but once I did, I was so moved by our conversation. It was obvious how much he still loves you."

"So then Grace called me," Lily explains excitedly. "I told her to get in touch with Mom and Aunt Violet."

"We had a lovely talk," Violet says. "Grace so badly wanted to give you and Henry your happily-ever after."

"I know I was overstepping," Grace tells me. "And I'm sorry, because that isn't something I ever do. It's just ... I can't quite explain it, but I felt like your story wasn't finished yet. Like you and Henry had one more chapter still to write."

She's right.

I look first at Ivy, then at Henry. Although I always knew there was a resemblance, I don't think I realized the extent of it until right now. Ivy is her mother's daughter in so many ways, but she is also her father's. It is far past time that he know about it.

"One more chapter," I say. "That's absolutely right." I take a deep breath and turn to Henry. "I tried so hard to find you," I tell him. "So many times over the years, but especially when I got home from Europe. I called every Henry Jackson in the phone book, and I even tried to track down James in the hope that he'd be able to lead me to you. Nothing worked. I want you to know, though, that you never left my thoughts. You have always been one of the building blocks of my life." Here, my voice cracks, and I have to pause to collect myself. I don't want to get choked up, I just want to tell Henry what he should have known sixty years ago, and yet I can't help it.

"You've always been in my thoughts, too," Henry says. "I may have moved on, but I never really left you behind. And I apologize," he continues, "for dropping off the radar. I stayed in Europe for a year. That wasn't the original plan ... I was supposed to come back to the States after a few weeks ... but I felt lost after we parted ways. I couldn't stand the thought of returning to New York and each of us living separate lives in the same city, so I stayed overseas and threw myself into my work." He winks. "You wouldn't believe how many pieces of jewelry I sold. Disappointment can sometimes be a great motivator."

A twist of sadness uncurls inside me.

"I'm so sorry," I say. "For upsetting you that much."

"No." He shakes his head. "I meant what I said then: you did what you had to, and I understood completely. I still do. And in the end, it was good for me to stay overseas. Spending my days with clients and dealing with all the flawless jewelry collections just made me realize how much I wanted to do something different. So I came back, but not to New York. My apartment was gathering dust, the utilities were off and the phone disconnected – "

"Disconnected?" I stare at him. One of the calls I had made was to a disconnected number. So that *was* him. I just hadn't known it at the time. It was, quite literally, a missed connection. I can't believe it.

"I had everything turned off before I left for Europe," he explains. "Then, after I got back, I left Manhattan and moved home to Maine. James ... he was still having a tough time of it. He had fallen into a bad gambling habit, which is how he'd used all the money I sent to him. He needed help and I needed ... I needed to steady myself. So I quit my job and went back to Portland. I worked with him while he climbed out of the hole he'd dug, and then when everything settled ... here, I'll show you." He reaches into his shirt pocket and pulls out a business card.

"Henry's Gemstones," I read. "Where there is beauty even inside the broken."

Goosebumps tickle my arms.

So very many memories are rushing at me, and I close my eyes, letting myself revel in them. I've always believed people are like sponges, soaking up the moments big and small, good and bad, each one becoming part of us in its own way. I've kept the moments I shared with Henry tucked away for so long, but now, as I feel his hand blanket mine the same way it used to, I let them all come seeping back.

How glorious it feels. How glorious this is.

I open my eyes. "Your own company?" I ask. "Using those imperfect stones?"

"Exactly."

It seems so beautifully fitting. Our time together might not have lasted beyond the *SS Harmony*, but it gave Henry something, just as it did me. Now, sitting here with him by my side again, I get the honor of telling him what else our love brought, what else it created. "There was a reason I worked so hard to find you," I say, and when I look at Ivy, her expression nearly makes me unravel. All that hope ringing her eyes, the excitement of finally getting to know her father ... it breaks me, but in the best way. I flip my hand over so my palm is resting against Henry's. The lines match up. This time, they do connect. "I was pregnant," I say, and immediately, he bursts into a grin.

"Does that mean ... " He gazes at Ivy. "Is she ... "

"Yes," I say. "Ivy is your daughter. I wanted so badly to tell you."

He could choose to be distressed over all the lost years. He could be angry at himself for moving to Portland, or angry with me for walking away in the first place. He could wallow in the sadness of not knowing our daughter until now. He doesn't do any of those things, though. Instead, he simply holds his arms out as Ivy darts over. Watching our girl fold herself into her father's hug is one of the greatest joys of my entire life. It is, also, my proof: that my drop *did* count. Sometimes it feels like a lifetime ago that I boarded the *SS Harmony*, that I let myself be inspired by the ocean and vowed to squeeze everything I could out of the one drop I was given, but right now, at this moment, it seems like just yesterday. Because I know, what I suppose I could *only* know in retrospect, is that no one's drop is really that small, after all, not if we make the most of it.

"It's like you said on the phone, dear," Violet tells Grace. "It's never too late."

Never.

It reminds me of the way my parents eventually came around – not when Ivy was born, but after I invited them to her first birthday party. They showed up at my doorstep, their arms full of gifts and their eyes full of tears, and although it was tricky, navigating the current that had pulled us apart, we managed to do it. It hadn't been too late then.

It's not too late now, either.

"What you've done here, what you've given us," I say, smiling at Grace. "I can't ever thank you enough."

"Not necessary," she says. "Seeing you and Henry together is all the thanks I need."

I want to do something for her, though.

I want to make a difference for her like she has for me.

"You mentioned your bookstore was struggling with finances," I say. "I'd love to help out."

"Oh, goodness, Rose, you don't have to do that," she says.

"It would be my great pleasure," I tell her. "My flower shop has done quite well for itself."

"And my bakery, as well," Violet adds. "Rose is the one who encouraged me to take a chance on starting my own business, as I did with her. We supported each other, and now it would be a delight to support you."

"You just have to promise us one thing," I say.

Grace is so touched, she looks close to tears. "Anything," she says.

"Promise that you'll always be there for each other," I tell her, Abigail, and Josie. "A sister is the best friend you will ever have. Cherish your relationship, and nurture it – when it's on shaky ground, yes, but also when it seems solid. Even the strongest and most vibrant flowers still need sunlight to sustain them. Sisterhood is what we make it, so make yours count."

"Always," Abigail says.

"And forever," Josie adds.

Grace gazes at me as I sit between the man I know that I'll spend the rest of my life with and the twin sister who has been my failsafe. Violet, Henry, Ivy, Lily, and Kendall ... these are my people, and when I look back at Grace, I can see that she realizes how truly lucky she is to have found hers. "It's a promise," she says. "Thank you so, so much."

I know she is talking about more than just the money, and it strikes me, being here with Henry, and my family, and these wonderful women who came so far to see the reunion of two people they had never even met, how right I was all those years ago, when I wanted to sail toward the horizon. I knew the people I met would change my life and that if I only let destiny lead the way, I'd learn how to make some waves of my own.

I have done that.

Grace has done that.

Perhaps now we can even make a splash together.

I smile at her as Henry takes my hand.

"It just goes to show," she says, "that sometimes a happy ending is really only the beginning."

THE END

About the author

Shari Cylinder believes in the importance of dreaming big, working hard, and embracing our own stories. She is a graduate of Arcadia University and lives in the suburbs of Philadelphia, where she spends her time as a writer, transcriptionist, and a member of the Board of Directors for Luv-N-Bunns Rabbit Rescue – and, thanks to her own rabbit, also a makeshift sprinter and gymnast who tries very hard to keep up with a bunny that runs much faster than she does. Sometimes she's even successful.

KRISTEN KIDD PHOTOGRAPHY